I'll Watch the Moon

a novel

Books by Ann Tatlock

A Place Called Morning

A Room of My Own

All the Way Home

I'll Watch the Moon

ANN TATLOCK

I'll Watch the Moon

a novel

BETHANY HOUSE PUBLISHERS
Minneapolis, Minnesota

Published by Bethany House Publishers
11400 Hampshire Avenue South
Bloomington, Minnesota 55438
www.bethanyhouse.com

Bethany House Publishers is a Division of
Baker Book House Company, Grand Rapids, Michigan.

Printed in the United States of America

Library of Congress Cataloging-in-Publication Data

Tatlock, Ann.
    I'll watch the moon / by Ann Tatlock.
        p.   cm.
    ISBN 0-7642-2764-5 (pbk.)
    1. Mothers and daughters—Fiction. 2. Holocaust survivors—Fiction. 3. Belief and doubt—Fiction. 4. Friendship—Fiction. I. Title.
    PS3570.A85I44   2003
    813'.54—dc21

                                                    2003001455

To my dear friends
the Plummers—
Bill, Sona,
Christopher, and Elizabeth
One day, it will all make perfect sense.
Until then, keep faith in the divine mystery.

ANN TATLOCK is a full-time writer. She has an M.A. in communications from Wheaton College and formerly worked as an assistant editor for *Decision* magazine. This is her fourth novel. She makes her home in Roseville, Minnesota, with her husband, Bob, and their daughter, Laura Jane.

PROLOGUE

I want to tell you the story of my mother and a man named Josef. It's a love story, but it's not a romance. I've lived long enough now to know there's a difference and that sometimes the greatest love is between two people whose hearts are someplace else.

I was only a child, nine years old, when the events of this story took place. Much of it I didn't know myself until only recently. Little more than a year ago, as my mother lay dying, she opened to me the book of her life and pointed to pages I'd never seen. Why at long last she took me into her confidence, I didn't ask; I only listened and in the listening came finally to see more clearly the picture of a life that had been, for me, only so many fractured pieces struggling to make a whole.

No story, including this one, is a straight line unraveling smoothly from start to finish. Every story is a tangle of stories within stories within stories, so that a solitary life is part of the web of the world's history, where lives meet and intersect and where individual stories cross at places and times that send the whole design moving off into different directions.

This is my mother's story. This is Josef's story. This is my story. There is no way to unravel the threads. All strands become one.

"Remember Josef," my mother told me shortly before she died. But she didn't need to tell me. How could I forget? Even if those had not been among her final words and her last request of me, I would never forget. To do so would be to forget a part of myself.

I will tell you all, to the best of my ability. I will re-create the story from my own memory, from what my mother told me, and from the notes that she kept of what Josef told her. But you must accept that while I can lay out the events, I can't always give the reason why certain things happened. I only know that they did, as painful as they were, and sometimes, blessedly, as marvelous as they were. But that's the whole point really. Always there remain those questions that no one can answer. But what I cannot yet understand in this, our story, I leave to God, who understands all.

ONE HOT SUMMER DAY

I remember the way the morning-glory vines wove their green web around the pillars of our front porch every summer, casting out their blue blossoms like open hands. My mother's eyes were the same color as those, my favorite flowers, but rather than being joyful and open like the blossoms, my mother's eyes were sad and inward looking, heavy with the things she'd seen. Things I didn't know about but could see reflected there in those two blue mirrors.

It was an oppressively hot afternoon in July 1948 when I sat on the steps of our Selby Avenue house, trying to find some consolation in those blossoms that, being morning flowers, were beginning now to droop and close in the heat. I told myself I wanted to be there, enjoying all that I had waited for through the long Minnesota winter and that my Aunt Dortha had so carefully tended and coaxed into bloom. But it wasn't true. I didn't want to be there. I wanted to be with my brother Dewey, and he and his friends had gone off without me.

Plenty of brothers and sisters don't get along, but Dewey was my best friend. There was no one in the world I wanted to be with more than Dewey. And in spite of the fact that I was a girl four years younger than he, Dewey liked me too. He even told me sometimes I was a pretty good kid sister.

Of course I had other friends, my favorite one being Rosemary Knutson, who lived not far from us over on Portland. But every year her family spent the summer months at their lake cabin, and I never saw her from the time school let out until it started up again in the fall. There were other girls in the neighborhood to play with when Rosemary was gone, and we sought each other out from time to time for hopscotch or hide-and-seek or to hold imaginary tea parties on the lawn. But mostly I tried to shadow my brother and his two best friends, Andy Johanson and Jerry Butterfield.

I wouldn't have described myself as a tomboy, but I rather enjoyed taking part in their boyish escapades. Give me a stick gun, and I could play Cowboys and Indians with the best of them. I wasn't afraid of climbing trees, threading worms onto fishing hooks, catching tadpoles with my bare hands. I thought nothing of swimming in one of the lakes with my clothes on or running barefoot through the sprinklers in the rich people's yards over on Summit Avenue.

One of our favorite ways to pass an afternoon was to traipse down to the city dump and scour for treasures hidden in the piles of St. Paul's refuse. It was there Dewey found a lot of the scraps he used for building telescopes. I liked to collect odds and ends for myself, however dirty or broken— tin boxes, picture frames, empty fountain pens, the occasional piece of costume jewelry. Andy and Jerry hauled away anything that looked like it might belong on a go-cart or that might make a good addition to the fort in Andy's yard. We also rescued old automobile tires that we rolled back to our neighborhood and played with in the streets. After being with the boys I often came home wet, muddy, smelly, and with odd bits of garbage tangled in my hair, but that didn't stop me. Whatever the guys did, I was right behind them.

Dewey and his friends were good sports and didn't complain about my being there, though Andy eventually dubbed me Tagalong Tierney. The name stuck and was shortened to Tag. The guys each had a nickname too, so I wore the name they gave me as a badge of acceptance.

Dewey's nickname was Galileo because he was always studying the night sky, making star charts, building telescopes. He claimed that someday man would reach the moon and that he, Dewey Tierney, would be the very first to set his foot in moon dust. Of course nobody believed him. Not just the part about his being the first man on the moon, but that any man would get to the moon at all. Grown-ups clicked their tongues and said he was a boy who read too many comic books. The kids in school said he was crazy, even Andy and Jerry. "Nobody's ever gonna get that far," they said, though you have to understand that to a couple of untraveled kids like Andy Johanson and Jerry Butterfield, even Fargo, North Dakota, was pretty much beyond the realm of the reachable. But Dewey always had a comeback for the skeptics, be they kids or grown-ups: "Yeah, and they laughed at the Wright brothers too and said they'd never fly." That being a statement of fact, few people bothered to argue with Dewey any further.

Andy Johanson was nicknamed Houdini because he was

forever having his older brother lock him into the coat closet in the front hall of their house. The purpose being that Andy was to work his way out. So far, he had been completely unsuccessful. His mother was beginning to worry about the hours he spent among the woolen jackets and galoshes in that dark cubicle picking at the lock with a twisted bobby pin. Andy, however, swore it would all be worth it when he finally became known as the Greatest Escape Artist on Earth. Personally, I thought Dewey had a better chance of walking on the moon than Andy had of ever getting himself out of that closet.

Jerry Butterfield we called Michelangelo because he was always doodling in class. He had no desire to become an artist, which was probably a good thing, because he had no artistic talent whatsoever. What he wanted to do when he grew up was to drive a streetcar like his dad. And that he could do already—could do it blindfolded, he boasted. So school was a waste of time. Not a single thing he might learn in those hallowed halls would make him a better streetcar driver. And so he doodled away the time until he could finally just grow up and graduate. Doodling was, after all, far more interesting than calculating square roots or reading about the Boxer Rebellion in China.

Anyway, to get back to that particular day in July 1948, Ma had told Dewey and me weeks earlier that we couldn't go swimming anymore that summer. Every year someone went swimming, she said, and spent the rest of his life paying for it. She was right too. There were plenty of ways to get polio during the warm-weather months, but swimming was the most reliable. Every summer when Ma heard that the first case of polio had hit the Twin Cities, our days at the watering hole were over.

I understood Ma's fears; I was afraid myself. Two years earlier the polio epidemic had been so bad that they'd closed all sorts of public places—swimming pools, restaurants, movie theaters. They even shut down the state fair, saying the crowded fairgrounds would be nothing but a breeding ground for the disease that both crippled and killed. A couple of badly aimed sneezes, and the germs would fell a large percentage of Minnesota's population.

When people went out, which most did as little as possible, they wore surgical masks so that everyone would keep his germs to himself. I watched from the front window of our house as pedestrians passed by looking scrubbed and ready for the operating room. In spite of precautions, nearly three thousand people contracted polio in Minnesota alone that summer of 1946, and not a few of them died. Ma was terrified. That was a long, boring summer for Dewey and me, and this one was turning out to be just the same.

Our misery that July was compounded by an unbearable heat wave. Since Independence Day, the soaring temperatures in the Twin Cities of St. Paul and Minneapolis had been at the top of the local news: "Heat Spurs Big Holiday Exodus," "Heat Wave to Hang On," and "Mercury to Go Near 100 Today."

Heat can do far more than leave a person feeling fatigued, irritable, and just plain miserable. It can literally be a killer, and that summer it was. On the seventh of July, a fifty-eight-year-old St. Paul man was found sprawled among the tomatoes and cucumbers in his garden, dead at least an hour before his wife discovered him. The newspaper said he'd had a heart attack, the implication being that it was brought on by the heat. Ma said testily that the man's dying was his own fault. He should have known better than to go out and garden in a heat wave. But Aunt Dortha contended that most everyone was working in their gardens the same as always and the poor man couldn't have known that pulling a few weeds from his tomato patch would kill him.

"Why would you want to blame him," Aunt Dortha asked, "as though he deliberately set out to do himself in?"

"Doing something like that is courting disaster," Ma said sternly. "What could he expect?"

"What could he expect?" Auntie echoed. "How could he have known? The poor fellow—"

"Oh, cry me a river, Dortha. He as good as hung himself."

Aunt Dortha shook her head, obviously perplexed. But I knew Ma. She was afraid, and when she was afraid she got angry. She longed for reason over randomness when it came to the distribution of human tragedies. And so she decided that most disasters were the result of people's recklessness and that if you were careful and played by the rules, life would be more inclined to bypass you as it went about handing out its trials.

Ma thought she knew what would keep Dewey and me alive through the perilous Minnesota summers—and no doubt she very well did—so she laid down certain rules that would harness us to safety. Rule Number One: No swimming for the rest of the season after the first diagnosis of polio was made in the Twin Cities.

Dewey, though, felt certain that his chances of dying of

heatstroke were far greater than his chances of contracting polio, especially after the man was found dead in the tomato patch. My brother decided to take matters into his own hands. On that particular day in mid-July he told me that he and Andy and Jerry were going to the lake for its, as he said, remedial benefits, and it'd be best if I didn't come along.

"But, Dewey!" I protested. "Ma said we're not allowed to go swimming anymore."

"I know, Tag," he said, "but listen, there's hardly any polio this year, and if I don't do something, I'm gonna die of the heat for sure. Just don't tell Ma, all right? I'll be back before she's home from the bakery."

"But, Dewey—"

"Listen, kid, if Ma finds out about me swimming, she'll skin me alive, but if I take you with me and she finds out, not even Aunt Dortha's best prayers would save me then. I'll do something with you tomorrow, all right? I gotta go. The guys are waiting for me."

So I sat on the front porch steps, watching the morning glories fade in the harsh light and trying not to cry because Dewey had left me behind. But I cried anyway, tears of anger and hurt rolling down my cheeks. I wiped them away with the back of my hands, sniffing loudly, sighing heavily, and feeling deliciously sorry for myself when I heard someone gently call my name.

"Nova?"

I looked up quickly. There was Josef, leaning over the porch railing and gazing down at me, his eyes large with concern behind his rimless glasses. "Novelka," he said. "Whatever is the matter?"

I was instantly ashamed that he should see me crying. I inwardly reprimanded myself for not going inside and weeping into my pillow instead of sitting here on the porch for all the world to see.

"I didn't hear you come out, Josef," I said lamely.

He shrugged and held out a hand. "Come," he invited. "Tell me why you are sad."

Rising obediently, I climbed the steps. He put a hand on my bony shoulder and guided me to the porch swing. It squeaked in protest as we sat down side by side.

I wanted to tell my friend what was wrong, for I liked Josef. He was the newest resident in the boardinghouse that Ma and Aunt Dortha ran. He'd been with us for just a few months, but already I saw him as someone who could begin to fill the gap left by my father's death. No one knew I thought of him that way. I was only just beginning to be aware of it myself.

I didn't know much about Josef—no one did, really—except that he was newly arrived from Poland and sponsored by a professor at Macalester College, where he would begin teaching languages in the fall. In the meantime he was doing some private tutoring, meeting with students in their homes two or three times a week. We'd never had a professor rooming with us before, and we wondered why he would choose to live in a boardinghouse. Then again, we wondered about a lot of things when it came to Josef. Where was his family and how had he survived the war and—Ma's most pressing question—why did he wear those same old long-sleeved shirts every day rather than buying himself something new and appropriate for summer? Auntie and Ma and I speculated among ourselves, but we didn't ask any questions of Josef directly. And Josef didn't offer any answers. Not to us, not to our boarders. Like most of our tenants over the years, he contributed his share of pleasantries and newsy comments at the dinner table, but otherwise he stuck to himself.

I guess that's not completely true, because he did spend several hours a week with me teaching me how to play chess. Or rather, I should say, I watched him play chess against himself, as he generally had to make my moves for me. I didn't like games, at least not indoor games that required patience and a head for strategy. My lack of interest made it difficult for me to remember what each chess piece was and how exactly it could be moved. But Ma had been pleased when Josef asked her if he could instruct me in the game. She said it would teach me how to think logically. Dewey stood up for me, arguing that it'd be a waste of time to try to teach a girl to think logically, but Dewey and I were overruled and the lessons began.

At first I was bored, just as I'd feared. We didn't talk much during these chess lessons because Josef had to concentrate. But after a while I actually began to enjoy watching him while he played. Just sitting there, I had plenty of time to study Josef and to wonder about him. I decided that once upon a time he might have been a "looker." That's what Auntie called men she thought handsome, like Joseph Cotten and Gregory Peck. Yes, I could even imagine that Josef had favored Gregory Peck when he was young. There was something about the eyes and jaw that suggested that rugged attractiveness. But now he just looked tired and worn-out and as though he'd been "put through the ringer"—another of Auntie's favorite sayings—

not once but many times over. He was thin and angular and hollow-cheeked. His short, cropped hair was graying, and his whiskers, when he neglected to shave, were decidedly gray. And the scars—so many scars! His hands were all crisscrossed with the remnants of small wounds, and two of the fingers on his right hand looked as though they'd been broken and never set. Even his face was flawed in places by something other than nature. His features seemed a canvas of long-ago nicks and cuts, and the tip of one ear was bumpy and gnarled like a puppy had mistaken it for a favorite slipper. Especially prominent was an elevated scar that nestled against his hairline on the right side of his head. The original wound probably could have used some stitches that it never got. Whatever the case, it was now a nasty pink worm burrowing into his skin and never going away. All in all, Josef gave the appearance of one involved in street brawls all his life, though I knew that couldn't be true. He was far too gentle, and besides, he was a professor, not a common thug. The only explanation I could imagine was that he was prone to accidents and that over in Poland the doctors who treated him had been little more than quacks.

And yet, in spite of my childish emphasis on outer appearance—I liked men to be handsome and women to be beautiful, the way they always were in storybooks—something drew me to Josef. Something on the inside. He always seemed so peaceful as he sat there studying the chessboard, his eyes moving thoughtfully from piece to piece, and I suppose it was that serenity I found so appealing. I felt peaceful just being with him. Every once in a while he'd look up at me and smile, and I'm sure it was during one of our chess lessons that I first started thinking of him as someone who would make a pretty swell father. After all, I couldn't find a single thing I didn't like about Josef. I liked him more every day, and I liked being his little Novelka.

"Now, tell me," he said as we swayed easily together on the porch swing. "Tell me what is causing your tears." Yes, I even liked the way he said that. *What is causing your tears?* It was different from the normal American way of saying, "Why are you crying?" I loved listening to Josef because when he spoke, it was like listening to the song of some far-off place. His sentences were framed with a certain formality, while his words were sweetened with a lilting accent—just a touch of one, like a distant church bell you can hear ringing when the wind is just right. Every time he spoke, I was reminded that he was something different, special, not your run-of-the-mill average Midwestern Joe, however nice those might be.

I shrugged at Josef's question, just so he would repeat himself.

"Come now, tell me, what is causing your tears?"

"Dewey went off and left me," I replied glumly.

"Ah." Josef smiled gently. "I see."

"He and Andy and Jerry were going—" But I'd been sworn to secrecy. That meant I couldn't tell even Josef. "Dewey said I couldn't go!"

"Ah," he said again. He pulled a handkerchief from the pocket of his pants and wiped my tears. Then he held it over my nose and said, "Blow." I complied. "Well, now," he went on, tucking the handkerchief away, "so your brother went off with his friends and left you at home alone."

I nodded. I didn't want to start crying again. "He left me here all by myself and it isn't fair, Josef."

"I'm so sorry, Novelka. I know it hurts to be left out."

He did understand, I was sure, and he wasn't afraid to say so. That's what was so unusual and wonderful about Josef. I don't know what my own father would have said, but Ma would have told me I was silly to cry. "Of course Dewey doesn't want to play with you," she'd have said. "After all, he's a thirteen-year-old boy. Why would he want to spend his time with a little girl? Leave him alone and find your own friends." Ma just didn't understand that Dewey and I really were best friends, most of the time.

"Come," Josef offered, patting his shirt just above the pocket. He put his arm around the back of the swing, and after a moment's hesitation, I leaned against him and rested my head in the hollow of his shoulder. All of a sudden it didn't matter at all that Dewey had gone off without me. All that mattered was that I was here with Josef, and it was almost like—so very close to—being with a father. We were both very warm, and Josef smelled of sweat combined with the lingering scent of an ineffectual aftershave, but I didn't care. I was at perfect peace, resting myself against Josef. I could even feel the word forming itself on my lips: "Pa." What a wonderful word! But, of course, I wouldn't say it aloud. I would only think it, and that for only a moment. Just for one wonderful moment.

I could have stayed there till nightfall, sitting just that way with Josef, waiting for the moon to rise and the stars to come out, and perhaps I would have if Ma hadn't come home early from the bakery where she worked afternoons. She came up the walk carrying her usual bundle of day-old bread and baked goods that Mr. Turnquist gave her at the end of her shift. I usually ran to greet her and to see what she had brought home, but not today. I wanted to stay where I was for as long as I could, tucked beneath the haven of Josef's arm.

But Ma, for some reason, didn't see it the same way I did. She pounded up the porch steps, stood over the two of us, and said in a voice so jarring it made me jump, "Nova, what are you doing?"

She was livid. Something in her crimson face told me I was committing a sin more terrible even than swimming at the height of polio season.

"What is it, Ma?" I cried, genuinely alarmed. I bolted upright from the swing, almost tumbling into Ma as I did. "What's the matter?" But she had already turned her attention from me to Josef.

"Mr. Karski, how dare you!"

Josef too was standing now, his mouth open as he tried to say something. But Ma wouldn't let him speak. "How dare you!" she repeated. "She's just a child. How could you—"

"Ma, what's the matter?"

"I assure you, Mrs. Tierney—"

"I must ask you to pack your things at once. You will have to find other lodging immediately—"

"But, Mrs. Tierney, if you'll allow me to—"

I couldn't believe what was happening. Ma turned and stepped into the house. I followed her. "But why, Ma? What do you mean, he has to pack his things?"

Aunt Dortha dashed out of the kitchen then, her gray bun askew, her apron powdered white with flour. "What's all the commotion, Catherine?" she asked hurriedly. She dabbed at her sweaty temples with one wrist as she spoke. "What's happened?"

"Mr. Karski will be leaving us, Dortha. He'll be leaving at once!" She turned and set her gaze on Josef, who stood in the doorway. His face was a study in disbelief.

"But why? What in the name of the Holy Innocents has he done?" Aunt Dortha looked as aghast and puzzled as Josef. Whenever she called on the Holy Innocents, which was rarely, I knew she felt lost.

"I won't discuss it, Dortha," Ma said. Still clinging to the bundle of baked goods, she marched to the kitchen and slammed the door.

Aunt Dortha turned to Josef and spoke quietly. "You'd better tell me what this is all about, Mr. Karski." She finished her sentence with a sigh, as though she were already worn out by what she might hear.

Josef shook his head, obviously flustered. "I found the child crying," he explained, indicating me with the sweep of a hand. "I tried to comfort her. We sat on the porch swing, only for a moment—"

"Say no more." Aunt Dortha held up her palms like a traffic cop.

If I hoped for an explanation for Ma's behavior—and I did—there was not to be one. Aunt Dortha swung suddenly around and headed for the kitchen.

"But, Auntie," I called after her, "what's going on? Why does Josef have to leave?" I looked from my aunt to Josef and back again before bursting into tears.

Aunt Dortha paused long enough to say, "No bawling,

child. Hear me? Tears won't solve a thing. Now go wash your face and calm yourself and leave the rest to me."

"But—"

"Do as I say. And don't worry. You either, Mr. Karski. Nobody's going anywhere."

Josef and I watched in dumb silence as she strode confidently down the hall and into the kitchen.

SAILING AMONG THE STARS

On summer nights Dewey slept on the screened-in porch at the back of the house because it was cooler there. Also because he liked to lie awake at night and look at the stars. Dewey had big dreams. He was going to be an astronomer, a space traveler, and—like I already said—the first man on the moon. Above his desk in our room he'd tacked a scrap of paper with a handwritten quote by the astronomer Johannes Kepler: "When ships to sail the void between the stars have been invented, there will also be men who come forward to sail those ships." Dewey intended to sail one of those ships. I never doubted Dewey's dreams. My brother could do anything.

The night of the day he went swimming without me, I left my own bed to join Dewey on the rollaway, as I sometimes did when the heat tossed and turned me like meat on a grill. That night I was restless too because I was thinking about Ma and Josef, wondering what he could have possibly done to make her so angry. I wanted them to be friends—more than friends—but if Josef could upset Ma without even doing anything wrong, the chances looked slim of anything good happening between them.

I found Dewey lying with his hands beneath his head, looking out through the screen at the night sky. I quietly slipped onto the rollaway, settled my cheek on the V of my brother's arm, and for a couple of minutes we quietly gazed at the heavens together. My cheek became moist and slippery against Dewey's warm skin, and I wasn't much cooler there than I'd been indoors, but I didn't care. It was nice to be with Dewey.

At length Dewey broke the silence by asking, "You still mad at me, Tag?"

I rolled my head back and forth on his arm to let him know that I wasn't. "Naw," I said. "Not anymore."

I thought he might say he was sorry for leaving me, but instead he remarked, "Just look out there. You know what you're seeing?"

I lifted my eyes once again to the dark canvas of sky, dotted with twinkling lights. "Our galaxy, the Milky Way," I responded dutifully.

Dewey breathed in deeply, let it out. "More than that," he said, the wonder evident in his voice. "You're looking straight out into the past. I ever tell you that, Tag?"

I nodded. "Because the stars are so far away."

"What you see out there," Dewey went on, "isn't the sky the way it looks tonight. That's how it looked thousands, maybe millions, of years ago. The stars are so far away it takes that long for the light to reach us."

"And sometimes," I picked up, as I had heard it so many times before, "when the light reaches us, some of those stars aren't even there anymore. They've gone and burned themselves out."

"That's right, Tag." Dewey sounded satisfied. "The nearest star is twenty-five million million miles away. Alpha Centauri."

"Wow," I said, trying to imagine how far twenty-five million million miles was. It was hard to do when even a mile seemed a pretty good hike. "Think anyone will ever get there?"

"Someday, maybe. Not in our lifetime. Wish I could travel that far, though."

"Me too. But we'll get to the moon, won't we, Dewey?"

"You bet we will. I'm gonna make it that far, at least."

Even now, in his mind he was walking on the moon. I could tell by the way he sounded, by the way he gazed up at that huge lighted rock in the sky. But I didn't really want to talk about the moon and the stars. Not right now anyway. I wanted to talk about Ma and Josef, but at the same time I was afraid to bring it up, to give it words and make the ugly scene real again. Needing to work up my courage, I changed the subject by asking, "Where'd you go today, Dewey?"

"Swimming, you mean?" When I nodded, he sighed, a reluctant Galileo returning to earth. "We went over to Cedar Lake," he said.

"How'd you get to Minneapolis?"

"The Butterfield line."

"Oh yeah." Mr. Butterfield, Jerry's father, was a motorman on the Selby-Lake line that ran from St. Paul into

Minneapolis. Sometimes he'd let the boys hop a ride for free. "You have fun?"

Dewey shrugged, and my head lifted slightly with the movement of his shoulders. "It was all right, I guess. But Clara Duncan was there with her brother and some of their friends having a picnic. I said five words to her, and you should have heard her brother giving me the business. The way he was carrying on and all, you'd have thought I was trying to drag her into the bushes or something instead of just asking her how she was doing."

I thought a moment, puzzling it out. "Why would you want to drag anybody into the bushes?"

"I wouldn't. That's the whole point. At least not Clara Duncan. I mean, she's a nice girl and all, and I was just trying to be friendly and say hi, seeing as how I know her from school. But then her brother comes around with his fur all up, like he has to protect her or something. He said if we didn't shove off I'd be eating a knuckle sandwich, so Andy and Jerry and I had to find someplace else to swim. We found a different beach, but it wasn't near as good as where we were to begin with."

"That's too bad, Dewey."

"Yeah, well, I think he was just showing off because that new girl, Eleanor, was with them. You know the one I mean? Clara and she have been best friends practically since the first day Eleanor showed up at school."

I'd seen Eleanor once. She was pretty. Maybe that's why Dewey had spoken to Clara. "You sweet on her, Dewey?"

"On who?"

"Eleanor?"

"Naw. I don't even know her." But the way he said it, kind of wistfully, made me think he was sweet on her, even if he didn't know her.

Something strange had been happening to Dewey since his thirteenth birthday a few months before. Suddenly the medicine cabinet in the bathroom was crowded with a variety of shaving creams, colognes, razors, deodorants, talcum powders, and hair tonics—the likes of which I'd never seen before, there being no other males in the family. He had an Old Spice shaving mug that seemed to sit on the shelf just for decoration and a bottle of something called Barbasol, which advertised itself as a sanitary beard softener for modern shaving. Dewey didn't have any beard to soften, at least none that I could see. But he did have plenty of thick hair on his head, and for that he had accumulated bottles of Vitalis, Vaseline Hair Tonic, and Wildroot Cream-Oil. I couldn't fathom what was going on until Ma told me Dewey's childhood was behind him now, and he was preparing to step into manhood. Manhood! It was going to be one very long step getting from where he was to where he wanted to be if he didn't allow himself a few years for the trip. Ma didn't seem to mind at all that Dewey spent so much of his earnings from his grocery store job on a host of obviously unnecessary items. Ma said when I turned thirteen, I'd probably start thinking about womanly things, and I said over my dead body. No one was going to rush me into being a grown-up. No sir. I was going to enjoy every minute of my childhood, thank you all the same.

I didn't like to think about Dewey growing up. I wanted him to stay in the place of childhood with me. But there were certain things I couldn't stop, and one was time. The best I could do was try very hard to keep Dewey as my best friend, come what may.

"So I guess it wasn't so much fun, huh?" I was secretly hoping I hadn't missed much by not being invited.

Dewey shrugged again. "Then on top of everything else we didn't even stay that long because Andy said he wasn't feeling so good."

"What was the matter with him?"

"I don't know. He had a headache or something, so we just swam and horsed around awhile, and then we got dressed and hopped the streetcar back home. Say, Tag, you won't tell Ma I went swimming, will you?"

" 'Course not. I'd never tell."

"You're a good kid, Tag. I'm going to name my machine after you, you know. The Nova Machine. Perfect, isn't it?"

"Yeah." I felt happy and proud.

The Nova Machine was another of Dewey's dreams. He wanted to build a machine that could capture the music of the spheres. He told me about how the ancient Greeks believed the stars and planets made a beautiful sound as they moved through the heavens, but it couldn't be heard by the human ear. So Dewey wanted to capture and record the music in a special machine that would play it back for the world to hear. He said it would be more beautiful than anything we'd ever heard before.

My brother got his love for the heavens from Ma, who introduced him to a telescope before he was three. Pa had given Ma a telescope as a wedding gift, and Dewey said it was probably the one good thing Pa ever did for her. For a decade Ma and Dewey had been gazing at the night sky together, setting up the telescope in the backyard and viewing the constellations the way other people go to the movies for entertainment. Dewey built his own telescopes from cardboard cylinders and the lenses of magnifying glasses. He even made tripods from the legs of castoff tables he found at the dump. Ma encouraged him and sometimes helped him in his efforts. Of course, none of his telescopes were quite as good as the store-bought models, but they sure did fill him with a sense of pride.

Sometimes, to get away from the city lights, Ma and Dewey rode the streetcar twenty-five miles out to Excelsior, where they could view the stars shining over the vast expanse of Lake Minnetonka. They sometimes got so caught up in stargazing they'd lose track of time and wouldn't think about returning home until the last of the streetcars had stopped running for the night. Fortunately we had a distant cousin in Excelsior who let Ma and Dewey stay the night with her whenever they missed the last ride home.

I was named, of course, out of my mother's love for the stars. I don't know what my father thought of my being named Nova. Most likely he didn't have an opinion; as I later learned, he had other, more pressing relationships on his mind when Ma was expecting me. But that was part of a different life, and right now I was more concerned with the pa I hoped to have than with the pa I had lost.

"Dewey?"

"Yeah?"

"Ma tried to throw Josef out of the house today." My heart thumped just saying the words.

"Yeah?" He sounded interested. "What for?"

"I don't know. She came home from the bakery, and Josef and I were sitting on the porch swing talking, and Ma just got mad as a wet hen and said he had to pack his bags and leave."

Dewey thought a moment. "But she didn't say why?"

"No. But you'da thought he murdered someone the way Ma was carrying on."

"So what happened? He's not leaving, is he? I mean, he was here for supper and all."

"Yeah, I guess he's staying. Auntie and Ma spent a long time alone in the kitchen, and I could hear pots banging and cabinet doors slamming shut, but I couldn't make out anything they said. And then Ma and Auntie came out, and Auntie told Josef it had all been a mistake and he could stay if he wanted to."

"Oh yeah? So what he'd say?"

"He said if his being here was only going to cause a problem then he'd better go, but Auntie said, no, no, no, they wanted him to stay, and she gave a look over to Ma that could have stopped a bull dead in its tracks. So Ma said, 'It's all right, Mr. Karski, you can stay,' and that was it."

"Wow, Tag, that's kind of strange. I don't know what got Ma's dander up this time. Could have been anything. Want me to talk to her about it?"

"Naw, don't do that. She'll just get mad again. I think there's just no understanding grown-ups sometimes."

"Yeah, you got that right, Tag."

"I'm just glad Josef's staying."

"Well, I'm glad you're glad, then."

After a moment I asked, "You know why I'm glad, Dewey?"

Dewey sniffed a little. "I guess I don't."

"Well, I'm sort of hoping Josef will be our new pa someday."

Dewey was quiet then. He must have been thinking the idea over. Finally he said, "I thought you wanted old Tom Diehl to be our pa."

Thomas Diehl was our neighbor across the street. Everyone knew he would marry Ma in a minute, everyone except Ma, I guess. She never seemed to notice him, even when he was seated right at our own table every Sunday afternoon for dinner. But ever since Mr. Diehl returned from fighting the Germans in Europe and discovered himself to be divorced—Auntie said his marriage was a casualty of war—I'd been hoping Ma would marry him and make us a regular family.

"I did," I said, responding to Dewey's remark. "I mean, I still do. But I don't know. Now I like Josef too."

My brother belched out a huge laugh at that. "Well, don't spend too much time trying to choose between them, Tag. It's not up to you, is it? It's up to Ma, and I don't think she wants to marry again, not after Pa and all that."

"Why? What's the matter with Pa?"

"Nothing's the matter with him—or *was* the matter with him. But I don't know; it's hard for a little kid to understand."

"I'd understand if you'd explain it to me, Dewey."

Dewey shrugged. "I'm not sure I understand it all myself, and I don't spend much time thinking about it anyway. I don't care if we never have another pa."

"You don't?" My surprise was genuine. I thought he'd

welcome another man in the house. He was surrounded by me, Ma, and Aunt Dortha, who, by the way, wasn't really our aunt but one of Ma's distant cousins several times removed. But that was it. We three females were his whole family. Dewey didn't have anyone to do father-son things with, like whittle and fish and talk baseball scores or maybe even say a curse word without having to apologize. But then, maybe that was part of growing up. You didn't think you needed a father anymore.

"Why should I?" he asked. "Everything's fine the way it is."

"But everyone else has a pa."

"No, they don't."

"Yes, they do."

"Well, look at the Newberry twins. They don't have a pa. He got killed in the war. Remember?"

"Oh yeah. But still, most kids have a pa, or would have if it hadn't been for the war. It's just not natural not having one."

Dewey shrugged again. "Can't have everything, Tag."

I frowned at his reply. "I don't want everything. I just want a pa."

"Well, it probably isn't going to be Josef. At least I hope not."

"Why do you say that!"

"I don't know. He gives me the creeps, kinda. It's like he's hiding something or knows something the rest of us don't know, and he's looking down his nose at us for not knowing."

"He's not like that, Dewey! He's nice."

"Well, whatever you want to think, Tag. Makes no difference to me."

"I think you're saying that just because he's smart, and he's a teacher at a college, and he's not like the other people around here who don't have any reason to stick their noses up in the air anyway."

"I don't know." Dewey shifted his arm under the weight of my head. "Maybe. But like I say, it doesn't matter. It's up to Ma, and she'll never marry again anyway. So what are you going to do?"

His question, offered with a shrug, was the period at the end of his argument. He didn't expect an answer, but I gave him one anyway. "I'm gonna wish on a falling star. That's what I'm gonna do."

Dewey turned his head and smiled at me. After a moment he said, "All right, Tag. If it means that much to you, I'll wish for a pa too."

"Thanks, Dewey." I moved my face a little closer to his. Sometimes having a big brother like Dewey was almost as good as having a father.

We both watched the night sky then, waiting for a falling star. And then and there I decided I'd wish on every falling star, every first star, every and any star that would listen to me until I had a pa and my family was complete. And until that time, I'd thank my lucky stars that at least I had Dewey.

"Dewey?" I asked.

"Yeah?"

"When you go to the moon, will you take me with you?"

"Sure, kid." He nodded. His hair tickled my forehead. "When I go to the moon, you can come too."

PA

3

I was always on the lookout for a father, I guess because not only did I not have one, but no one ever talked about the one I once did have. Not even Ma. Maybe especially Ma.

My father died when I was four, and it was not so much a death as a disappearing act in which all traces of his life were wiped out, obliterated, paved over with a blacktop of conspiratorial silence. In fact, he was dead for a year before I even knew he was dead because no one bothered to tell me.

No one, that is, until Aunt Dortha decided I should at long last be let in on the secret. I don't know whether she decided it was my right to know or whether she just grew tired of my watching at the window for a father who was never going to come. Either way, she sat me down one day and told me my pa wouldn't be catching any train to St. Paul because he'd long ago died and was buried over where we used to live in Chippewa Falls, Wisconsin. She broke the news gently, of course, but that didn't ease the shock of it.

"If Pa were dead, Ma would have told me!" I argued.

"When your father died," she explained patiently, "it was just as though he'd never lived, as far as your mother was concerned. No use telling you about the death of someone who'd never lived."

That was probably the first time it struck me that the ways of grown-ups were beyond comprehension. Pa never lived? Of course he'd lived! I remembered him! I didn't have a whole lot of memories, but enough to know that the man with the mustache was no phantom of my imagination.

So I didn't quite believe Aunt Dortha at first when she told me Pa was dead. I was only five years old, but that was old enough to know that when someone dies, a funeral follows, sprinkled with friendly condolences, neighborly casseroles, and at least a smattering of widow's tears. There had been none of these a year ago when Pa had supposedly died. There *had* been an abrupt uprooting and shifting of our lives from Wisconsin to Minnesota, but that didn't mean my pa was six feet under. When we moved into Auntie's boardinghouse on Selby Avenue in St. Paul, I naturally began waiting for Pa to join us, which I assumed Ma was doing too.

Even though I was skeptical of Aunt Dortha's revelation, I was still afraid to ask Ma or Dewey to confirm the news of Pa's death—just in case. For a time I kept my solitary vigil at the window, kneeling there on Auntie's lumpy old divan, my elbows on the sill, waiting for Pa to walk on over from Union Station. As I waited, I remembered again and again the day Ma, Dewey, and I left Chippewa Falls. I slowly and carefully played it over in my mind, looking for clues.

"Where are we going, Ma?" We stood on the station platform waiting to catch the early train west. The platform was dusty and hot and filled with strangers, and all I wanted was to be back in the familiar rooms of my home.

"St. Paul. And don't ask me again, Nova."

"But why, Ma?"

Silence.

"Where will we live?"

"With Aunt Dortha. It's all arranged."

"But will we ever come back here?"

"No."

"But when will Pa be coming to Aunt Dortha's?"

I'd never seen Ma looking the way she looked that morning, and I don't think she ever looked quite that way again. It was as though sadness had made its home on her face and was determined to settle there for good.

When Ma didn't answer, I looked to Dewey. But he only turned away, shrugging. Later, when Ma was asleep on the train, Dewey told me Pa would be coming when he could, but I shouldn't expect him for a long, long time.

"But when, Dewey?"

"I don't know. Someday. When he's ready."

And so I kept watching for him even after we'd been in St. Paul for a year. Even after Aunt Dortha told me he was dead. I sat at the window and waited until Dewey himself came and told me I had to stop waiting. He said he knew what Aunt Dortha had told me and that it was true.

I didn't respond for a long time. I didn't even move. I just kept watching two little girls playing hopscotch on the sidewalk halfway down the block. Maybe, I thought, if I didn't look at my brother, I could pretend he wasn't there, that he hadn't said what he'd just said. Maybe if I just kept looking down the street as I had done a thousand times and for a thousand hours, I would finally see Pa coming from the station, a suitcase in his hand, a smile on his face.

At length I mumbled, "Are you sure, Dewey?"

"Yeah, I'm sure."

"Why didn't you tell me before?"

"Ma said I couldn't talk about it. But Aunt Dortha said you needed to know."

"Does Ma know you told me?"

"Yeah, she knows."

"But how did he die?"

"In a fire." He shrugged as he said it, as though it were commonplace, as though most everyone's pa died in a fire sooner or later. "Sorry, Nova," he murmured solemnly. And I remember trying to smile at him, because I knew he really was sorry that he'd had to tell me the truth. But my lips quivered, and the tears in my eyes spilled over, and Dewey, in his awkward way, put his little boy hand on my shoulder. He was, after all, only nine years old.

After that I pretended Pa was a war hero, that he'd been killed fighting the Germans like the father of the Newberry twins. I even told friends and acquaintances alike that he'd been shot down while flying a mission over Germany, his plane falling from the sky in a blaze of golden glory. His body was never recovered, I explained. It was gone, burned to ashes before it ever reached the ground. And that's why we didn't have a grave to visit or a marker with his name on it.

It wasn't that I was trying to lie when I told this made-up account of my father's death. I just needed somehow to fill in the gap. I needed something to explain the mystery of my father's disappearance.

Not until I was grown and very nearly old myself did I come to learn the truth about my father's death. It was when Ma herself was dying that she told me some of the stories I had never heard before. As I mentioned earlier, Ma's life was largely a closed book to me. She was by nature a reticent person, reluctant to speak of herself, and she remained so almost right up to the end. What made her open up to me shortly before she died, I can't say for certain, though she may have simply decided she possessed a gift that should be passed along rather than carried to the grave. I, for one anyway, ultimately saw her collective stories, the portrait of her life, as a gift.

The truth about my father, I learned, is that he was never even near the war. The closest he got to the conflict was to act as head of the draft board in Chippewa Falls, deciding who went and who didn't. The only uniform he wore was that of the civil servant, sounding the alarm in case of an air-raid drill and walking the streets afterward to make sure everyone had their black-out shades drawn. Pa was also a lead figure in the occasional victory parades that encouraged folks to invest in war bonds. One of the few memories I have of my father is of him waving at the crowds from the backseat of a banner-streamed convertible as it slowly made its way from one street to the next in our small Wisconsin town.

Ma said that while Pa had never suffered any health problems at all before Pearl Harbor, he had been deemed 4-F at the outset of the war, unfit to serve due to the sudden and ill-timed onset of asthma. While he bemoaned—to all who would listen—his inability to defend his country personally, he was proud to do his bit by sending other men over. It may be of little surprise, perhaps, that the son of the doctor who diagnosed Pa's ailment was also kept Stateside during the war. Pa declared the young man 4-F, though he was hale enough to become athletic director at a private boys' school shortly after V-J Day.

My father was a handsome man, and charming, and people said he was aptly named. Royal Tierney, while something less than a king, was a man of some prominence in Chippewa Falls. A successful businessman, a church deacon, a political activist, and even a bit of a philanthropist, Royal Tierney was a man well known and well respected in his hometown.

And that's probably why my father's death produced such a scandal. For his body wasn't lost in a blaze of glory over Germany but was found in the arms of a Mrs. Forrest Brown, who also died of smoke inhalation when the Eau Claire apartment building where she lived went up in flames. The incident made front-page headlines in both Eau Claire and Chippewa Falls and had the phone lines humming for weeks between the two cities as reporters tried to dig up new tidbits to feed a hungry readership.

I don't know what happened to Mr. Forrest Brown. But Mrs. Royal Tierney caught the early morning train west on the same day her husband was buried. The funeral itself was probably well attended by the city's curious and perhaps even by a few genuine mourners, but the wife and children of the deceased weren't there. We were moving over the rails toward St. Paul and a new life, mother and children alike wondering each in our own way how on earth it had all so suddenly come to this and what in the world would be waiting for us at the other end.

OUR NEIGHBOR MR. DIEHL

Not long after I accepted the fact of my father's death, Thomas Diehl came home from the war. He was our neighbor across the street, but because he'd been shipped out to Europe before we moved to St. Paul, we'd never met him. We did know his wife, however. Vivian Diehl was a flighty, nervous young woman, who sometimes came over to seek solace from Aunt Dortha. She couldn't stand being alone one more minute, she'd wail, and when was this crazy war going to end so all of the soldiers could come home and everyone could go back to living like people were meant to live? Aunt Dortha would pat her hand and offer her a cup of tea and tell her she must be patient and leave it all up to Providence, as he would give us the victory in due time. But I don't think Mrs. Diehl took Aunt Dortha's advice, because she disappeared unexpectedly sometime before V-E Day and wasn't there to greet Mr. Diehl when he finally did come home.

When a taxi dropped him off and Thomas Diehl walked

up the sidewalk to his house for the first time in years, it was with a bit of shrapnel permanently embedded in his skull, a purple heart pinned to his chest, and a legally signed and dated decree that he was now divorced. It seems his wife had left him for someone older, wealthier, and perhaps most important, here on the home front. Mr. Diehl and his wife had had no children. I don't believe he ever saw her again.

Dewey and I got to know Mr. Diehl largely because he bought a Muntz television set sometime in late 1946. It was the first television on the block, and when word got around that he had it, all the kids of the neighborhood started knocking on his door and asking to see it. Ma warned us not to bother him too much, and for me she tacked on the extra restriction of never, ever going to Mr. Diehl's house without Dewey. I asked her why, but she only gave me the answer she'd give when she didn't really have a reason: "Because I said so." At any rate Mr. Diehl didn't act like we kids were a bother; in fact, he was friendly and seemed actually to appreciate our company. Sometimes he even made popcorn or root-beer floats for us to enjoy while we sat cross-legged on the floor in front of the television's tiny screen. It didn't take long for me to start falling in love with Mr. Diehl and wishing he were my pa.

Thomas Diehl was definitely a "looker," though I believe I would have liked him even if he weren't. He was tall and slender, with an oval face of perfectly proportioned features. Nothing was too big or too small—eyes, nose, mouth, ears, all seemed of uniform size so that the result was a well-crafted visage, pleasant to look at. He was rather dark complected, with thick wavy hair combed back from his forehead and deep brown eyes as gentle as the eyes of a fawn. His smile was quick and easy, revealing flawless white teeth and opening a fan of laugh lines at the corner of each eye.

He didn't have any visible scars the way Josef did, but he harbored a slight bump on the side of his head that he let me feel on occasion, guiding my fingers to a spot just beyond his right temple. He said the bump was a little souvenir from the Germans. "But what *is* it?" I asked the first time he let me touch it.

"Just a bit of shrapnel," he remarked cheerfully, as though he were pointing out a freckle or a birthmark or some other benign flaw of nature.

"What's shrapnel?"

"Oh, it's the metal that comes flying out when a shell explodes."

My thoughts went to the ocean, where I imagined conch shells and oyster shells exploding into small bits all along the shore. "But why do they explode?"

"Well, because the enemy is trying to kill you! Throwing a shell at you is a pretty good way to do it."

"But how did they get all those shells?" I pictured German children scouring sandy beaches and collecting shells the way we Americans collected scrap metal and rubber and even milkweed pods during all the endless war drives. But how much more fun it would have been to collect shells!

"They made them, of course," explained my new friend, "in their ammunition factories."

"But why didn't they just collect them on the shore?"

When he finished laughing, he said, "No, dear, not *that*

kind of shell. Well, never mind. Whatever it was, it didn't kill me, and that's what matters."

Yes, that was what mattered, that he came home from the war alive. But then I wondered what kind of homecoming it had been, returning to an empty house the way he did. For other soldiers there had been open arms, hugs and kisses, tears of joy, laughing children. There had been nothing like that for Thomas Diehl, not even a dog to wag its tail. Not that I knew about anyway. Not here in this house across from ours on Selby Avenue.

I wanted to tell him I was sorry, but of course I didn't. I couldn't. Aunt Dortha had warned me never to mention "that dreadful Mrs. Diehl—not to me, not to anyone, and certainly not to *Mis*ter Diehl." She had looked heavenward then and clicked her tongue, a sign of stern disapproval on her part. "It's a sin," she added, "what she did to that poor man. Why he ever married her in the first place, I'll never know."

Thomas Diehl must have been sad, I thought, because some terrible things had happened to him. Yet I couldn't help but notice that his eyes didn't hold the same kind of look my mother's did. The sorrow I'd seen on Ma's face the day we left Chippewa Falls had pooled into those two blue orbs after a while, settling there the way rainwater settles into the lowest parts of a field. But Mr. Diehl's eyes were bright and clear, as though nothing at all in the world bothered him.

Maybe he hid his sadness better. I don't know. But I do know that he went on living, picking up easily where he had left off before the war. He returned to his appliance store on University Avenue, inherited from his father half a dozen years earlier. Established by the elder Diehl in 1924, the store's longtime slogan, "You get the best deal at Diehl's," was painted in a patriotic tangle of red, white, and blue on the huge plate-glass window facing University.

Mr. Diehl's brother-in-law, a man named Philip Townsend, had kept the place up and running during the years Mr. Diehl was in Europe. He had in fact done very well, and the store had prospered under his care. Not only was Mr. Townsend regarded as a competent and honest businessman, but he was something of a draw for the neighborhood boys, who liked to go in and ask him to take off his leg. It was that wooden leg that had kept him out of the war. He'd lost the lower half of his right limb in a childhood scuffle with a train. Rather than being offended by the hordes of curious children, Mr. Townsend seemed to enjoy entertaining them by unstrapping his prosthesis and passing it around. I'd witnessed the act a few times myself, having tagged along with my brother and his friends on a lazy summer afternoon. It wasn't my favorite pastime, being a bit squeamish about removable body parts, but I oohed and aahed with the rest of them. What I didn't realize was that Mr. Townsend considered even this a viable means of drumming up business. I later did my duty at home by reminding Aunt Dortha that the next time she needed the toaster fixed, she should take it to Mr. Townsend at Diehl's. He could do anything, I repeated, even remove his leg and put it back on. Yes, I was a dependable cog in Mr. Townsend's marketing machine, but so were a lot of other kids.

I've since come to realize that Diehl's Appliance Store might not have survived without Mr. Townsend. While both Mr. Diehl and his brother-in-law could fix any appliance that needed fixing, it was Mr. Townsend who had the head for business, who kept the accounts, ordered from suppliers, arranged for advertising, and thought up the gimmicks—"$25 to the customer who guesses the correct number of screws in this glass jar!"—to attract new business. Thomas Diehl's head was elsewhere. "In the clouds," Auntie might have said, though I wouldn't quite put it that way myself.

It seems Mr. Diehl was actually an artist at heart, who had inherited the family business by default rather than by choice. He was a man who loved beauty in all its forms, and yet—out of a sense of filial duty as well as the simple need for money—he was up to his elbows in toasters, irons, and electric razors. His was the quandary of all sons who want to please their fathers and all artists who have to make a living—how to make beauty and poetry out of something as prosaic as iron plating and electrical plugs. Poetry and painting and gardening were his real passions, and he spent most of his spare time engaged in one or the other of these. His garden was one of the finest in the neighborhood, and people came from all over St. Paul to see it each spring. Ma was the lucky recipient of many bouquets of flowers grown and nurtured by Mr. Diehl's own hand, though I suppose it would be more accurate to say that the enjoyment fell to Aunt Dortha. Auntie was the one who always exclaimed over the latest arrangement, putting the flowers in water and setting them on the dining room table, while Ma scarcely took note of either the flowers or their bearer.

I don't know that he wrote poetry, but I know he read it by the volume. My best friend Rosemary Knutson's aunt Myrtle was head librarian at the downtown library, and she reported to Rosemary's mother that Mr. Diehl checked out more books of poetry than any other library patron. Myrtle Knutson understandably judged people by the books they read. She wasn't fond of people who dabbled in D. H. Lawrence or James Joyce, and she had no regard whatsoever for the readers of Camus, Sartre, or any of the other existentialists. But Thomas Diehl, now, he was right at the top of Myrtle Knutson's admiration list. She said he had checked out *Sonnets From the Portuguese* eleven times, and divorced or not, any man who read Elizabeth Barrett Browning's love sonnets that many times was a good fellow as far as she was concerned.

Myrtle Knutson was a spinster, and I think she kind of had a thing for Thomas Diehl. Thankfully, though, she was far too old and not nearly pretty enough for a man like him. Ma was a few years older than Mr. Diehl too, but she looked younger, and at any rate she was beautiful. I wasn't the only one who thought so. Aunt Dortha told Ma many times that a pretty young woman like herself ought to marry again and it was nothing less than a shame that she didn't. When she was in a good mood, Ma just gave a little laugh and waved her hand at the idea. When she was in a bad mood, well, only once did I stick around long enough to catch the drift of what Ma thought of Aunt Dortha's suggestion of marriage. It wasn't something I wanted to hear very many times, because it tended to put a damper on my hopes of having a father.

I think Aunt Dortha wanted to see Ma marry Mr. Diehl nearly as much as I did. He had a standing invitation for Sunday dinner at our table, and Auntie sometimes invited him over during the week as well. Occasionally Ma complained to Aunt Dortha, saying our neighbor was showing up at meals far too often and that we were, after all, running a business and not a soup kitchen. Why, we could hardly afford to keep the tenants fed as it was! But Auntie said that wasn't the case at all. There was adequate money in the kitty and plenty of food in the larder, and anyway it was our Christian duty to look after any neighbor in need of a home-cooked meal once in a while.

Aunt Dortha went right on inviting Thomas Diehl over for dinner, I think to give Ma the chance to figure out that the two of them might make a good pair. He was, after all, available, dependable, a good Christian man, and taken with Ma. What more could she ask?

Ma just wasn't getting it, though. As I said already, Ma wanted nothing to do with Mr. Diehl, as far as I could tell. But I wasn't about to abandon my dreams of a father. When Ma had known Mr. Diehl for two years and still scarcely offered him a how-do-you-do when he showed up at our door, that's when I more or less gave up on our neighbor and started thinking the professor from Poland might make a pretty good pa.

SUNDAYS ON SELBY

On Sunday mornings Aunt Dortha rose before dawn to start the noon meal, which was always formal and abundant in food. She came downstairs from her second-floor room wearing her bathrobe and slippers, her face pale and creased with sleep, her uncombed hair pulled back into a loose knot. She sailed in quick, determined steps across the kitchen, slippers swishing against the linoleum, heels kicking up the hem of her robe. She paused first at the sink to draw water for coffee, scooped grounds into the filter basket of the electric percolator, and flipped the switch to On. As the water began to gurgle and churn, Auntie began vigorously to wash vegetables, peel potatoes, mix up biscuit dough, roll out piecrust.

Because my bedroom was next to the kitchen, it was Aunt Dortha's puttering that woke me up every morning. Most days I'd get up to help, being an early riser anyway, but on Sundays I'd lie a little longer in bed, drifting in and out of my dreams and listening to Auntie at work. Dewey, who shared the room with me when it was too cold to sleep on the porch, complained about the clanging of pots and pans and what he referred to as "Aunt Dortha's spiritual revival meetings." But I rather enjoyed listening to Auntie singing her hymns. Her voice was untrained but strong, and she had a range of several octaves. She moved within that range like a spring colt, bounding energetically toward a note and only occasionally stumbling. She sang every day, but on Sundays Auntie had a musical routine she followed. She'd start with "O for a Thousand Tongues to Sing"—Dewey would moan and crawl deeper under the covers—and end with the "Doxology," working her way through the stack of songs in her mind like she was a jukebox dropping records onto a turntable.

After an hour or so, Auntie would slip back upstairs to dress for church. Then I'd hear Ma stirring in the living room. The apartment Ma and Dewey and I lived in had once belonged to Aunt Dortha and her husband, Marvin Severson. Uncle Marvin died about a year before my own pa died, and when Auntie invited us to live with her, she gave us the first-floor apartment and moved up to a room on the second floor. Our apartment had only the living room, a bathroom, and the one bedroom furnished with the twin beds Aunt Dortha and Uncle Marvin used to occupy, which were now mine and Dewey's. Ma slept in the living room on a hideaway bed that folded up into a couch during the day. She would get up to take Auntie's place in the kitchen, where she'd spend the rest of the morning preparing the Sunday dinner while Auntie and I attended services.

Dewey had gone to church with us until only recently but stopped the practice on his thirteenth birthday. This was the result of a compromise Ma made with Aunt Dortha shortly after we arrived in St. Paul. Our first Sunday morning at the boardinghouse, Auntie was horrified to find the three of us still in bed even as the bells of the nearby St. Paul's Cathedral were calling the righteous to worship.

"We won't be going to church anymore, Aunt Dortha," Ma announced after Auntie shook her awake. I woke up too, as sometime in the night I'd crawled onto the hideaway bed with Ma.

Auntie's jaw fell, her face turned deathly pale, and I almost thought I saw hellfire burning in her startled eyes. A lifelong member of the Methodist church, Auntie was a religious person who was forever talking about Providence as if God was our next-door neighbor. Ma's Sunday morning declaration must have struck her as an announcement of doom—*our* doom.

"And why not?" she cried.

"I don't have any use for it," Ma explained mildly. She turned over then as though to go back to sleep.

"But, Catherine! You've always gone to church."

It was true. We *had* always gone to church. Pa was a deacon and a lay reader and one of those men who pass the offering plates up and down the aisles. I remembered the way he smiled kindly at all the ladies as he went from row to row, while all the other men looked like they were sucking lemon drops. I was always proud of Pa, the way he was so friendly with everyone and drew a flock of admirers around him wherever we went.

Ma opened her eyes reluctantly and peered up at Aunt Dortha. "I have a new life now, Dortha. Everything's changed.

I'll have lunch ready for the tenants by the time you get back."

Auntie's mouth snapped shut and her jaw tightened, and I watched as a tiny muscle jumped and bobbed about in her cheek. She wanted to say something, but she knew when she'd been dismissed. She went to church without us that morning and for several weeks afterward, until she finally decided to try once again to confront Ma.

"Even if *you* won't go, at *least* let me take the children," she pleaded. "Then, when they're old enough, they can make up their own minds about whether or not to go. It's only right, Catherine."

Ma generally didn't like Aunt Dortha making decisions about Dewey and me. Auntie's being a childless widow posed something of a threat to Ma, it seemed. Even before we left Chippewa Falls, Ma had worried that the older woman's long defunct maternal instincts would suddenly revive at the sight of Dewey and me and she'd want to go about the business of raising us. Ma said she wasn't going to compete with anyone when it came to raising her own kids. While we were on the train coming over from Chippewa Falls, the one thing Ma said in the midst of her silent misery was, "Now, once we settle in with Aunt Dortha, you must remember that I am still your mother. Aunt Dortha is a fine person, but you don't need two mothers. I have the final say in anything concerning the two of you, understood?"

So I figured Ma would put her foot down and say that Dewey and I were going to be heathens the same as she was. But to my surprise, after some thought Ma agreed to let Auntie take us to church. She did balk, though, when Auntie suggested we could stop going once we'd reached the age of twenty-one. Ma argued that we'd be perfectly capable of making up our minds well before then, probably even by the age of twelve. For a while the two women tossed out numbers like a couple of farmers haggling over the price of chickens, but Auntie could get Ma to go no higher than thirteen.

Defeated, Auntie gave in and said she'd do the best she could with the little time she had. When this particular compromise was struck, I was four years old and Dewey was eight. That meant Auntie had five years with Dewey, nine with me, to try to persuade us to walk the straight and narrow.

When Dewey announced on his thirteenth birthday that he wouldn't be going to church anymore, he was greeted with mixed reactions. Aunt Dortha wept unashamedly. I was disappointed because Dewey would no longer be there to play tic-tac-toe with me on the church bulletin during the sermon. Ma said solemnly that she respected Dewey's decision and would abide by it, but I'm sure she was secretly pleased.

Dewey tried to comfort Auntie by saying, "Don't worry, Aunt Dortha. It's not like I don't believe in God or anything. I mean, I do. It's just that, well, I think I know everything I need to know about him. And besides, church is boring."

Auntie blew her nose and tried to smile, but I don't believe she felt much better. Thinking I could help, I patted her hand and added, "Anyway, I'm still going to church with you, Auntie." To which she replied, "You certainly are!"

I hadn't yet decided what I would do when I reached thirteen, but I was leaning toward going. I didn't care for the church services, but Sunday school class was fun. Our teacher told us interesting stories from the Bible, and we always had a snack of vanilla wafers toward the end of the hour. Some of my friends from school were in the class, and together we'd chitchat over the cookies and juice and quietly make fun of the boys with their neat bow ties and their polished shoes and their hair all slicked down with Vaseline.

Thomas Diehl went to the same church Auntie and I went to, so after the service he'd meet us outside and walk us home. In the winter, he'd give us a lift both ways in his Ford Coupe. By the time the three of us arrived at the boarding-house, Ma had the meal ready and the dining room table set with Auntie's best china and flatware. She had also added a leaf to the table to make room for Dewey and me. Normally, the two of us ate in the kitchen, which we preferred. We could talk about kid stuff and interrupt each other without saying "Excuse me." We could reach all the way across the table for something without saying "Please pass the salt" or "Please pass the potatoes." We didn't care if the other one burped or talked with their mouth full or put their elbows on the table. It was so much easier to eat without manners. But when the Sunday noon meal rolled around, we reluctantly joined the grown-ups at the dining room table, where the use of manners was forced upon us.

The faces around the table were a changeable scene, though by the summer of 1948 all of our boarders, except for Josef, had been with us for more than a year. Henry Udahl, at four years, had been with us the longest. He went to a Pres-byterian church, which made him, Auntie said, a Calvinist, someone who believed in predestination. Auntie explained that meant the future was set and no one could change it. Ma added that that was why Mr. Udahl never complained when we raised the price of room and board. Whenever anything happened, no matter what it was—the rent was increased, Mrs. Harringay had triplets, Clyde Munson fell off the porch in a drunken stupor—Henry Udahl remarked, " 'Twas meant to be."

Dewey called him "the Mole" because he lived in a room in the basement and because he looked a bit like a mole too. He had a tiny face and tiny brown eyes and a tiny mouth that could flash a surprisingly large smile if someone at the table cracked a joke. He must have been pushing seventy, but he still worked as a janitor at the public high school. He was a widower, and his only child, a son, had disappeared into the heart of Texas many years ago. Mr. Udahl received an occasional postcard letting him know Henry Jr. was still alive and thinking of him. There was never a return address. The postcards, a small collection of cowboys, sagebrush, and armadillos, were taped carefully to the wall in Mr. Udahl's room. He didn't say much at the dinner table, but he occasionally spoke wistfully about his son. It was obvious he missed "the boy," and I had the feeling he wondered why this one remaining member of his family was predestined to become a wanderer.

The Baptist church was represented at our table by a Miss Betty Singletary. In addition to being a Baptist, she was a spinster. And she was everything you might picture a Baptist spinster to be—plain, proper, and prudish. At least that's how Ma put it. Auntie claimed that wasn't so at all, saying Miss Singletary was really quite personable once you got to know her and had even ventured a joke or two when Auntie had shared a cup of tea with her. It seems Miss Singletary had confided to Aunt Dortha that she was in search of a husband. Not wanting to be limited by the selection of men offered in her own small hometown of Worthington, Minnesota, she came to St. Paul in 1939 believing the place to be a haven of eligible bachelors. She had been unpleasantly surprised to discover that the pickings weren't so plentiful—especially during the war years—but nevertheless, she persevered in her search. Her strategy included going from job to job, from one residence to another, in an ongoing attempt at finding Mr. Right somewhere around the corner. She presently worked as a secretary in a lawyer's office, though she didn't know how long this particular job would last before she quit, nor did she know how long she'd be living in our house on Selby Avenue. "Don't be offended," she told Aunt Dortha, "when I have to give you notice. It's just that, well, I have to keep moving. One can't become stagnant and still expect change, you know." She accentuated her remark with a philosophical nod. "And anyway," she added, "God helps those who help themselves." Auntie told her not to worry. She wouldn't be offended when Miss Singletary moved on; in fact, she would send her off with all good wishes for success.

And then there were the flamboyant Lassiter sisters. I don't know whether Lassiter was their real name or a stage name, but they both used it despite the fact they'd been married five times between them. They had been vaudeville performers since childhood, so they may have stuck with Lassiter from the get-go so as never to have to change the billing, which was probably a whole lot easier in the long run than changing their name every time they got married. Around the house we called them Miss Eva and Miss Ida so they both wouldn't answer if we said "Miss Lassiter."

Two of the Lassiter sisters' former husbands were dead, two were now married to somebody else, and one was rumored to be hiding in Mexico City to avoid apprehension by the FBI. Both Miss Eva and Miss Ida had been divorced at least once, and for that reason they were confirmed Episcopalians. They had been raised Catholic but had switched their allegiance to the Episcopal church sometime around the First World War. As they explained it, in the Episcopal faith the priests could marry and the parishioners could divorce, and all the while everyone stayed within the good graces of the church. "It's more in keeping with our view of the Man Upstairs," Eva said while Ida nodded her agreement.

The sisters were in their sixties now and retired from the stage, but they still tended to dress like flappers, in drop-waist dresses of bright and busy patterns, pumps with straps and stockings with seams, long strings of pearls tied in a knot between their breasts, and yes, occasionally one or the other of them showed up wearing a feather boa. Auntie didn't particularly care for the Lassiter sisters, saying they didn't have enough sense to let themselves grow old gracefully. She claimed she could hardly even see the sisters' real faces beneath the layers of makeup they wore. "Old ladies should never try to make themselves look young," Auntie argued. While I had no opinion on that as yet and so couldn't say whether I agreed with her, I admired Auntie for abiding by her own rule.

The Lassiter sisters had lived in the one spacious room on the third floor of our house for over two years. I think Auntie might have evicted them solely on the grounds that they weren't suitable company for children—Dewey and me—but Ma rather liked them and fought to let them stay, saying they were cheap entertainment and good for a laugh, and "heaven knows some of us need a good laugh once in a while." Besides, Ma reasoned, if we let them go, we might end up with two more like Clyde Munson.

Clyde Munson was our resident atheist, and while Ma didn't object to his lack of religious beliefs, she was put off by his habit of showing up at the Sunday meal with a hangover. She also complained about his being stupid and generally offensive. No doubt most people, even Auntie, would have had to agree with Ma to some extent. At least there were times when Clyde said things that seemed to prove Ma right. Case in point was when Mahatma Gandhi was assassinated and everyone was all abuzz about it. Clyde's contribution to the conversation was, "Who's Mahatma Gandhi?" But at least that was just an innocent question and not downright rude and annoying like the lousy things he said about the Jews some months later when the grown-ups were talking about Israel becoming a state. Henry Udahl told him to put a clamp on it or he could leave the table, and Clyde Munson said Henry Udahl couldn't make him leave the table, and Aunt Dortha said maybe not, but it was *her* table and *she* could make him leave, so he put a clamp on it. After that, Ma told Auntie that Clyde Munson really ought to go.

Surprisingly it was Auntie who argued for him to stay. "As long as he's here," Auntie remarked, "we can show him the goodness of Providence and hope he'll come around."

"Well, now, Dortha, you could say the same for the Lassiters, but you'd have them out on the street in no time flat if I didn't stand up for them."

"Oh no!" Aunt Dortha let go a little laugh. "I don't care for the way those two have lived their lives, but I wouldn't send them out homeless, the poor dears. And you're right, I suppose there's hope for them too."

"Well, whatever the state of their souls," Ma said, "at least the ladies don't come to the table hung over. If we got rid of Clyde, we'd have his room rented again by evening. You know that, the housing shortage being what it is. Why, not a day goes by without someone inquiring about a room."

"I'm well aware of that, dear. I've been in this business a lot longer than you have. And believe me, Catherine, Clyde is hardly the worst I've seen. At least he pays his rent on time, and he shovels the snow and does a dozen other chores around here without my even having to ask. He's really not a bad fellow when he's not under the influence."

Though Ma and Auntie repeatedly argued about it, Clyde Munson stayed. He was a hangdog young man who worked on the assembly line over at the Ford plant. He'd spent the war in uniform but had sat behind a desk on the home front for the duration. He'd been a clerk who had typed up reports in spite of the fact that he couldn't type and he couldn't spell and half the time he was staring at the typewriter in an alcoholic stupor. With the help of Alcoholics Anonymous, though, he seemed now to confine his drinking to Saturday nights, and he bragged that he'd never once put a car together while he was loaded. He had a girlfriend he was planning to marry as soon as he'd saved up enough money. His girl, Charlotte Beacon, was still living on her parents' farm down near

Owatonna, next to the farm Clyde himself had grown up on. He called her once a week on the telephone in the hall, and the whole house stopped to listen to his frenzied promises to tie the knot as soon as he had his nest egg saved up. Ma said the nest egg was being cracked open every Saturday night to buy another bottle of Jim Beam, and judging from what Clyde Munson looked like on Sunday mornings, I've no doubt that was true.

And then there was Josef, who attended the huge St. Paul's Cathedral downtown. Aunt Dortha told me he was Catholic, just like most of the people in Poland who weren't otherwise Gypsy or Jew. She added discreetly that we should regard him as a true fellow believer, in spite of the fact that Catholics held to some practices otherwise rejected by the rest of us at the time of the Protestant Reformation. "When I dust his room," she explained, "I always notice that the bookmark in his Bible has been moved from one place to another. That means he's been reading it. Besides, with Josef, there's something about him. You can just tell he's a man whose faith means something."

Josef's was the room directly across the hall from Auntie's upstairs and just above the bedroom I shared with Dewey. He was generally an early riser, and every Sunday morning at seven o'clock sharp I heard the squeaking of bedsprings and the patter of footsteps overhead, and I knew Josef was getting up for eight o'clock Mass. He'd shave and shower and dress, then eat a hurried breakfast of toast and coffee that Ma set out for him. By seven-forty he'd step out to catch the streetcar that would take him down the hill to the cathedral. Rain, shine, or snow, he never missed that early-morning Eucharist.

Though we all went off in various directions to worship, afterward we'd convene back at the boardinghouse, the eleven of us seated around the dining room table in an odd sort of ecumenical gathering that was our Sunday dinner on Selby.

MISTAKEN IDENTITY

A couple days after Dewey went swimming and Ma tried to evict Josef, we were all seated around the dining room table, our plates piled high with pot roast, mashed potatoes, gravy, and peas. Eva Lassiter, accustomed to the spotlight and continually longing to get back into its glow, was repeating a funny story she'd heard on Eddie Cantor's radio show. It was a Sunday dinner like every other Sunday dinner, with Aunt Dortha presiding primly over the meal, Clyde Munson rubbing at the pain in his temples, and Miss Eva chattering theatrically while the rest of us listened with varying degrees of attention. Dewey and I were anxious to finish eating and to be excused. We were going to meet Jerry Butterfield after lunch and then head on over to the city dump to rummage for treasure. We'd wanted Andy to come along too, but when Dewey called his house, his mother said he was sick with the flu.

Just as I was spearing the last of the peas on my plate with my fork, something happened. As though about a thousand volts of electricity hit him, Clyde Munson broke out of his morning-after stupor, jumped halfway up from his chair and, reaching across the table, grabbed Josef's arm just as Josef stuck his hand out for the saltshaker. Clyde pulled so hard he lifted Josef right up out of his chair. The two men's thighs rocked the table, sending peas and gravy over Auntie's clean tablecloth. Everyone gasped, and then the whole room fell silent. Clyde Munson gripped Josef's wrist in a white-knuckled clasp and studied it, his brow a tangle of puzzlement, his face a canvas of questions. And then, as though he finally understood, he raised his gaze to Josef's face, and the two men locked eyes. Josef didn't try to pull his arm away even when Clyde's eyes closed up into two narrow slits of contempt. "So that's it," he hissed quietly. "You're a Jew."

For a long moment we were all shocked into dumb silence. No one moved or spoke, not even the two men facing off across the table, their arms a fleshy arc suspended over the pot roast. A hundred thoughts added themselves up in my mind and spat out one conclusion: Josef couldn't be a Jew. He went to Mass. He was Catholic. What in the world was Clyde Munson carrying on about?

As though to answer, the younger man's free hand flew up to point at Josef's left wrist. "See?" he cried out to no one in particular. "See here? This means he's a Jew."

Before Josef pulled his arm from Clyde Munson's grip, I saw briefly what was bothering Clyde. Tattooed onto Josef's skin was a series of numbers—black, evil-looking marks across his wrist.

I had only a glimpse, because Josef pulled his arm to his

side then and, with the opposite hand, tugged at his sleeve to hide the tattoo. Startlingly composed, he settled himself back in his chair. Slowly, silently, he picked up the saltshaker he'd been reaching for, sprinkled a few grains over a mound of potatoes, replaced the shaker on the table, and picked up his fork. Then, almost as an afterthought, he said, "I am not a Jew, Mr. Munson. But if I were?" His words posed a quiet and deliberate challenge.

His accuser leaned over the table as though ready to pounce again. My eyes darted back and forth between the two men. I didn't want to miss a single thing. Nothing like this had ever happened on any other Sunday in my whole life. It was the completely unexpected breaking into our tedious but comfortable routine. My heart raced as I waited to see what would happen next.

Clyde's whole face twisted up into an angry red ball as he accepted the challenge. "Yeah?" he muttered. "I heard about it—I heard about all this stuff from the fellows down at the plant. I know what that tattoo means. If you're no Jew, why were you in one of those camps where they slaughtered them like pigs?"

Aunt Dortha gasped. All the color drained from Ma's face. I watched Dewey chew his lower lip in anticipation.

To my surprise, Ma collected herself enough to speak. "Sit down, Mr. Munson," she said firmly, finding courage, I assumed, in her dislike for Clyde Munson. "I'm sure that is Mr. Karski's own business. He doesn't owe you an explanation."

Clyde Munson glanced at Ma, then sat reluctantly, his bloodshot eyes still half-closed windows of disgust. Josef looked at Ma, then back to Clyde. Everyone looked at Josef.

He took a couple of bites of the salted potatoes before laying down his fork. He owed no one an explanation, just as Ma had said. But certainly we all wanted one. Nobody dared to begin a new conversation. We wanted to leave the opportunity open for the present train of discussion to move forward. We were all waiting, hoping that Josef would say something in his own defense, something that would ease our curiosity. When he spoke, his words were measured and quietly controlled. "You are right, Mr. Munson. I was in one of the camps where they slaughtered the Jews."

A shiver seemed to make its way around the table in spite of the heat. The room was so quiet I could hear the blood pumping in my ears.

"But you see," Josef continued, "those camps were not for the Jews only. You are mistaken if that is what you believe." He sounded like a schoolteacher correcting an errant pupil. "Hitler would have destroyed every single person in my country—Jewish or not—had he been able."

Another prolonged hush fell over the room. No one seemed even to breathe. I thought I might suffocate if someone didn't say something, anything, in response to Josef's confession. And then, finally, words broke in, puncturing a hole in the tense atmosphere through which I could finally get some air.

"You were in Auschwitz, Mr. Karski." Thomas Diehl spoke gently, as though offering an apology or a word of consolation. He was sitting next to Clyde Munson, across the table from Josef.

Josef nodded slightly to acknowledge Mr. Diehl's comment. "Yes. That was the only camp where the prisoners were tattooed. You know of the camps, Mr. Diehl?"

"A little. Were you still there at liberation?"

"No." Josef picked up his spoon and stirred some sugar into his iced tea. The ice cubes had long disappeared. "I was transferred to Dachau near the end of the war. It was there I was liberated."

He looked up from his glass, his eyes meeting Mr. Diehl's. Josef smiled slightly. Thomas Diehl did not. Thomas Diehl said, "I was with the U.S. Seventh Army." He seemed to expect a response from Josef. When he got none, he repeated, "The U.S. Seventh Army. Dachau, April 1945."

Understanding flooded Josef's face. In the next moment he pushed his chair back, stood, extended his hand over the table where moments before Clyde Munson had shanghaied his arm. "Then, sir," Josef said to Thomas Diehl, "I should like to shake your hand."

Mr. Diehl stood too and took the outstretched hand in his own. It was the climactic act of a play I wasn't following very well, but I knew something significant had happened. Later Auntie would explain to me that Mr. Diehl was among the group of American soldiers who liberated the prisoners at the German camp of Dachau. And so for months now a former soldier and a former prisoner had been eating together at our dining room table, not realizing they shared this part of recent history.

Now they knew. Each clasped the other's hand firmly, seemingly reluctant to let go. At length the two men nodded to each other and sat down again. I had the feeling they'd said something the rest of us couldn't hear.

I thought the interruption to our meal might be over now, but Clyde Munson wasn't satisfied. "So how is it you were in the camp, Mr. Karski?" He spat out Josef's name like it was a bit of overcooked meat.

"I think that's quite enough, Clyde," Auntie started, but Josef interrupted her with a wave of his hand.

"It is all right, Mrs. Severson. I will answer his question." He paused long enough to adjust the rimless glasses that tended to slide down the bridge of his nose. "I was arrested by the Gestapo for my involvement with the Polish Under-ground. I suppose I was one of the lucky ones, Mr. Munson. Many arrested by the Nazis were executed immediately. I ended up in Auschwitz instead."

"So why are you here? Why didn't you stay in Poland with your family after the war?"

"Really, Clyde!" Aunt Dortha dabbed at her face with her napkin before setting the linen down beside her plate. She looked sternly at Clyde, her blue eyes flashing disapproval. I thought she might be reconsidering her position on allowing Clyde Munson to board with us.

Josef's face registered only mild indifference, or so it seemed to me when he turned his gaze to Clyde. "You see, Mr. Munson, I came to your country after the war because I have no family left in Poland. They were all murdered by the Nazis. Not one survived."

The way he said it—so calmly, so matter-of-factly—left me feeling disoriented, like I wasn't quite sure where I was. Josef might have been mentioning the weather—"I hear we are in for a thunderstorm tonight"—not speaking of some-thing so horrible as the death of one's whole family. But there it was. Josef had given Clyde his answer, and now it was up to us, the hearers, to make some sort of sense out of it. I was just beginning to chip away at the words' whitewashed coating, trying to get at the meaning underneath, when I was interrupted by Ma's quiet remark. "Dewey, Nova, you may be excused."

"But, Ma," Dewey complained, "we haven't had dessert yet." I knew it wasn't dessert he wanted. He wanted to hear everything that was going to be said, just as I did.

But Ma thought we had heard enough. "You can have dessert later, in the kitchen. Now go."

Dewey and I gave each other a glance of disappointment, but we gave in. Dewey asked, "Then can we go over to Jerry's now?"

"Yes. Go ahead."

I eyed Josef curiously as I rose from the table. He looked the same but different somehow, like a sculpture I was finally viewing from the side rather than the front. Now I could see what was hidden behind his back. Dense shadows, tiresome loads that he had to carry around on his shoulders. They were not Josef, but they clung to him, a weight of horrors that no one else at the table had ever carried. They made him different, different from us, and different from the Josef I had sat with at the chessboard, the man I'd been wondering about for months.

As I stood to leave, Josef smiled at me, but I dropped my eyes shyly. It wasn't Josef I was afraid of; it was his past, all those terrible things. It would take me a while to get used to this new Josef.

"I just can't believe it," I blurted to Dewey as we trekked

over steamy sidewalks toward Jerry's house.

"Can't believe what?"

"That Josef's whole family was killed."

Dewey squinted against the sun. He shrugged. "That's what he said. Why would he make it up?"

"I don't think he was making it up, but—it's just so awful! It's too terrible to believe!"

Dewey nodded his agreement. "But I guess that happens in a war."

"Poor Josef," I whispered.

"Yeah, well, don't let him hear you saying that."

"But I just can't believe it, Dewey," I repeated. "What if I lost you and Ma? I don't know what I'd do!"

Dewey shrugged again. "That's not gonna happen."

"How do you know?"

He jumped up and grabbed at the branch of a red maple that hung over the sidewalk. He pulled off a leaf and twirled it between his forefinger and thumb. "It's just not," he said.

It didn't seem like a satisfactory answer, but I knew I wasn't going to get more. My mind went back to Josef and the incident at the table. "Now I know why he always wears long sleeves," I mumbled thoughtfully, more to myself than to Dewey. I tried to imagine Josef getting that tattoo in the camp where they slaughtered the Jews. I couldn't imagine it, not the numbers being burned into his skin, not the camp itself, not the wholesale slaughter of people as if they were pigs. I didn't want to imagine it.

"You still want him for a pa?" Dewey asked.

I thought a while. "I think he needs us, Dewey."

"Needs us? I doubt it. And he probably doesn't even want

us either—another family, I mean."

"Why wouldn't he?"

"Because then he's got something else to lose."

I ground my teeth together in thought. "I lost a pa, and I still want another one," I argued. "Maybe he had a daughter once and now he wants another."

Dewey let the leaf fall to the ground. "I wouldn't count on it, Tag."

"Well, maybe I could ask him—just about a daughter. Just see if he used to have a daughter—"

He interrupted me by shaking his head. "Listen, Tag, if your whole family was wiped out, would you want people asking you a bunch of questions about it?" When I didn't answer, he went on, "Don't start trying to play matchmaker with him and Ma, like you think you can make a happy ending out of everything. Just leave Josef alone, all right? The nicest thing you can do for him is just don't say anything."

"All right," I agreed. "I won't say anything."

But I knew I wouldn't stop dreaming either. Surely Josef had a big hole in his heart, probably even bigger than the hole that was in mine. We needed each other. What other ending to the story could there possibly be except that one day he would be my pa and I would be his daughter?

MRS. TIERNEY MEETS MR. KARSKI

The next morning I was helping Aunt Dortha make scrambled eggs and toast for our boarders when Ma called me into the parlor. She'd been setting the table in the dining room only a moment before but apparently decided abruptly that the parlor needed a bit of housekeeping before people started coming down for breakfast. I found her dusting the upright piano with a feather duster.

"Nova," she said, letting the feathers hover momentarily just above middle C. She didn't turn to look at me but kept her eyes on the piano. "Run upstairs and knock on Mr. Karski's door and see if he's awake."

For a moment I couldn't speak. I felt fear inflating my heart like a balloon. Finally I mumbled, "Why, Ma?" Surely she wasn't about to throw him out again.

"Just do as I say, Nova. If he's up, please tell him I'd like to speak with him for a moment."

She knew he was up. The only boarders who ever missed breakfast on occasion were the Lassiter sisters, as they didn't have to hurry off to jobs the way Clyde Munson, Henry Udahl, and Miss Singletary did. Josef always put in an appearance at the breakfast table, whether or not he had a tutoring session scheduled for the morning.

"Okay, Ma."

She looked at me then and offered a brief, timid smile that made her look pretty and young and shy as a schoolgirl. I should have obeyed right away and headed upstairs, but sometimes I was drawn to my mother's face the way an art lover is drawn to a beautiful painting. She looked literally as pretty as a picture standing there in the morning sunlight, and it made me both proud and envious at once but mostly just glad she was my mother. The light shone on her soft blond hair and sparkled in the blue pools of her eyes, which for a moment didn't look so sad because they looked more extraordinary than anything. Her features were fine, her skin creamy and perfect, and her body was lithe as the dancers I'd seen in the movies. To me, she was a princess in a blue cotton housedress and flat shoes just waiting for a fairy godmother to come and work her magic. How I wished that mythical do-gooder would show up soon and give us all a prince.

"Go on now, Nova," Ma prodded gently.

"Okay, Ma," I repeated reluctantly. "I'll be right back."

"Just send him down and then go back to the kitchen, all right?"

"Sure, Ma." Then, "Ma?"

"Yes, Nova?"

"You sure look pretty today."

A pause, then a smile, bigger than the last. "Thank you, sweetheart." She took off the apron she'd been wearing, touched her hair, and indicated with her eyes that I was to do as I'd been told.

Going upstairs was, for me, not an everyday occasion. At times I would visit with Aunt Dortha in her bedroom. I'd take her a glass of milk or a cup of tea, and she'd brush and braid my hair and tell me stories from her childhood. But other than that I had no reason to visit the second floor where our tenants lived. In five years I'd been to the third floor only once, and that was when Eva Lassiter called on me to button about a thousand buttons up the back of her dress one afternoon when her sister Ida wasn't home to do it for her.

The only time I had ever ventured to one of the boarders' rooms on my own was a few weeks back when Josef didn't show up for my chess lesson. Before that, he had never so much as been late for a lesson. One thing about Josef, he was so punctual you could set your watch by him. So I thought it odd when ten, then twenty, then thirty minutes went by and Josef didn't show up. I worried that he might be sick. He had hinted to me a couple of times that his heart wasn't what it should be, and I could just imagine him sprawled across his bed with his hand on his chest and who-knew-what happening to his heart inside. So I scurried up the stairs and knocked on his door, but Josef didn't answer. I could hear music coming from the room. It might have been a radio, but it sounded more like a record scratching away under the needle of Josef's old record player. He'd recently bought the player secondhand from Thomas Diehl, but where he got the records, I didn't know. I didn't recognize the music either. It sounded foreign and like something only grown-ups would listen to. I almost turned to go, but I couldn't shake the thought that something was wrong and that maybe Josef was dying. I couldn't just walk away and let him die. I'd never forgive myself.

I reached for the doorknob. Opening the door of a boarder's bedroom was strictly forbidden. Auntie and Ma had repeated that rule often enough. So reaching for that doorknob went against everything that had been hammered into my brain, and I felt as though I were a burglar breaking into a stranger's house. But what choice did I have? Auntie and Ma would understand why I did it when they realized I had saved Josef's life.

I pushed open the door. Not all the way but enough to peek into the room, enough to see that Josef was not sprawled across the bed but sitting in a chair by the window with his face in his hands. He had taken off his glasses and laid them on the windowsill, and now his two large, scarred hands covered his face completely. The record went round and round on the player behind him. The arm of the player was close to the center of the disk, and I knew in another moment the music would stop and Josef would turn to lift the needle and settle the arm back on the rest. I didn't want him to see me standing in the doorway. I started to close the door, but before I did, I noticed that Josef's shoulders shook slightly, his head lifted and fell into his hands almost imperceptibly. It took me a moment to realize he was weeping.

Never before had I seen a grown man cry. I didn't even know grown men *could* cry. But they could, because Josef was crying now, and I thought something awful must have happened, though I couldn't imagine what.

A half hour later he came downstairs and found me sitting at the chessboard.

"I'm sorry, Novelka," he said mildly. "Have you been waiting here all this time?"

"Yes," I lied, not knowing what else to say.

His face was apologetic, his voice kind. "You must forgive an old man his faulty memory. I promise not to keep you waiting again. Now, shall we begin?"

He didn't look like he'd been crying. There were no tell-tale signs—no blotchy skin, no red-veined eyes. I wondered whether I'd been mistaken. Maybe he had only been listening to the music, had forgotten the time, just as he said. Maybe he'd only been resting his head in his hands, rubbing his eyes in fatigue. I wondered, but of course I didn't ask. I had opened his door without permission. Questions would only be evidence of my own wrongdoing.

Now as I headed to Josef's room again, I paused halfway up the stairs. Suddenly I knew that Josef *had* been crying, and now I also knew why. He had told everyone yesterday during Sunday dinner.

The door to his bedroom opened as soon as I knocked. Josef greeted me with a puzzled look as he fiddled with a cuff link, pushing it through the two little holes at the end of his sleeve. "Well, good morning, Novelka," he said pleasantly, "and what brings you to my door?"

I swallowed hard. I didn't like being a messenger of doom. "Ma wants to see you," I reported. "She's in the parlor."

"Oh?" He adjusted his glasses and tugged at his sleeves, pulling the cuffs down past the knobby bones of his wrists.

"She doesn't look mad," I whispered, trying to assure myself as much as Josef.

Josef offered me a lopsided smile. "Please tell Mrs. Tierney I will be down in a moment."

Reluctantly I tore my gaze from his and went back downstairs to deliver his message to Ma.

"Thank you, Nova," she said. She laid the feather duster on top of the piano. "People will start showing up for breakfast any minute now, so run along and see if Auntie needs any more help."

I wanted to ask Ma why she wanted to talk to Josef. Even though she didn't seem angry, maybe she was going to ask him *nicely* to leave. I just couldn't imagine what else it would be.

"Please let him stay, Ma," I mumbled, but the words came out so quietly I could scarcely hear them myself.

"What's that, Nova?" She had clasped her hands in front of her, waist high. Her fingers were clenched so tightly her knuckles were white. I recognized in that instant that she was as nervous as I was. "What did you say?" she asked again.

I shook my head. "Nothing, Ma." When she was afraid, she easily became angry, and I didn't want to make her angry. Not right now, with Josef on his way to see her.

"Go on, then. I'll be there in a minute."

A door opened and closed upstairs, and I knew it was Josef on his way down. With one last pleading look at Ma, I dashed to the kitchen.

"Auntie!" I cried breathlessly. "Auntie, why is Ma talking to Josef?"

"Goodness, child," she said, turning toward me from the stove. "You look as if you've seen a ghost."

"I think Ma's telling Josef to leave again!"

Aunt Dortha shook her head and chuckled. "Nonsense," she replied as she transferred a small mountain of scrambled eggs from the skillet to a platter. "What makes you say that?"

"She's talking to him—in private! In the parlor! Right this minute!"

"Well, she may be talking to him in private, but she isn't asking him to leave."

"But how do you know, Auntie?"

"Because this is still my establishment, and I'm the one who decides who stays and who goes. She can't send anyone off without my permission."

"You won't let Josef leave, will you?"

"Of course not. Why should I?"

"Well . . ." I paused and accepted the butter knife Aunt Dortha handed me. I spent a few minutes absently spreading butter over the toast, allowing myself time to calm down. Finally I asked again, "Well, why do you think Ma wants to talk to him?"

Auntie sighed, as though wearied by the question. "I'm sure I don't know, child," she replied. "But I do know one thing, it's none of our business. I'll finish the toast, and you be a good girl and get those eggs on the table. Mr. Udahl is already seated, and you know he's cranky until he gets something in his stomach."

I picked up the platter of eggs and, with my shoulder, pushed open the swinging door to the dining room. To my surprise, Josef was already there, chatting amiably with old Henry Udahl. When he saw me, he smiled but continued uninterrupted in his comments to Mr. Udahl. Miss Singletary came and sat down, then the Lassiter sisters arrived, and finally Clyde Munson was there, and it was just like any other morning, with Aunt Dortha coming from the kitchen with a tray of grapefruit halves in little white bowls and Ma arriving with the tray of toast and a pot of coffee. I studied Ma a moment, but her eyes were steady and her face unreadable, offering not a clue as to the drama that had taken place in the parlor.

After setting the eggs on the table, I went back into the kitchen to pour myself my usual breakfast of Post Toasties with banana slices drowned in whole milk. Ten minutes later I was reading the back of the cereal box when Dewey stumbled in from the porch wearing only a pair of checkered pajama bottoms. His hair was disheveled, his brow was furrowed, and he gave no hint that he so much as saw me as he padded barefoot across the linoleum floor to the pantry. Silently he poured himself a bowl of Kellogg's Krumbles, then joined me at the table. He yawned loudly, stretched, rubbed his eyes, scratched his bare chest. I could have done it with him. He did the same thing every morning. He took a couple bites of cereal, chewing slowly, thoughtfully. Those two bites seemed to give him the energy he needed to start in on his morning complaints. He liked to say how even a deaf man couldn't sleep with all the noise in the house: Aunt Dortha singing holy-roller songs while she scrambled the eggs, and the Lassiter sisters laughing like a couple of crazy hyenas every time their grapefruit halves spit juice across the table, and Miss Singletary sipping her coffee so loudly it sounded like mud being sucked down a clogged drainpipe. "If you want to live in a normal family, Tag," he'd finish up, "you should wish we lived in a regular house and not in this boardinghouse with a bunch of loony birds."

Some things I could count on. Some things were completely predictable, like Dewey in the morning. Others were a huge mystery, like Ma most of the time.

———————

"You wanted to see me, Mrs. Tierney?"

Josef found Ma waiting for him by the front window. She turned at the sound of his voice when he entered the room. She had already decided she wouldn't mince words. She'd plunge right in. Otherwise she would lose the courage she had spent all night gathering. "I owe you an apology, Mr. Karski. I had no right, and of course no reason, to get so angry with you on Friday afternoon. I hope you will accept my apology."

"I see," Josef said guardedly. He appeared not quite certain what to make of Ma's about-face. "Of course, I—"

"I didn't know, you see. I mean, about your family and the war and what happened." Ma felt she was stumbling badly, but she tried to carry on. "I had no idea as to what had happened to you during the war—" She stopped suddenly, silenced by the look on Josef's face.

"Would it have made any difference, Mrs. Tierney, if you had known?" he asked. His voice was strained but not angry. "Please don't apologize because you feel sorry for me."

"Oh no!" Ma was sincerely alarmed. "Don't misunderstand, Mr. Karski. No, I was wrong . . . on Friday when I came home . . . I was wrong to think—" The words were in her throat—she could feel them, but she couldn't get them out. Instead, she squeezed her fingers together until they ached. When she told me the details of that morning years later, she said the pain of squeezing her hands together like that had kept her from crying.

She tried again, saying, "I was wrong to think . . ." But she couldn't get past those words to explain what she had thought. For a moment she agonized over what she should say, how she should go on from there. At two, three, four o'clock in the morning it had all made sense, but now that she was face to face with Josef, her carefully chosen words deserted her; her pretty little speech was in a shambles.

Josef saw her dilemma. Not only did he see, but he understood. Quietly, very gently, he said, "Mrs. Tierney, you were only concerned about your daughter."

Ma nodded and let out a sigh. She felt as though she had been holding her breath for years. "Yes, I was concerned for Nova."

"Please let me assure you that you have nothing to fear from me."

"Of course, yes. You are fond of Nova, and she of you. It was foolish of me. It's just that . . ."

Josef took a small step toward her. His gaze became more intent, as though he wanted to make sure she heard what he had to say. "You too have your story, Mrs. Tierney. Things that I would not presume to know."

She had never before noticed the scar on his forehead, she told me later, or the way his rimless glasses sat halfway down his nose, or the deep lines that fanned out from the corners of his eyes. "It was as though I'd never even seen him at all before," she marveled. "And then, suddenly, I did."

But she didn't say that to Josef. What she said to him that

morning was, "Thank you for your kindness, Mr. Karski."

He made no reply in return. Instead, he smiled and bowed. That was it. Just smiled and gave the tiniest bow from the waist, like he was a butler or a footman or maybe even the Prince welcoming Cinderella to the ball, before moving away and sitting down to Aunt Dortha's scrambled eggs and toast.

DEWEY FOR PRESIDENT

The upcoming presidential election provided our boarders with grist for the conversational mill at breakfast that Monday morning. Ours was not a particularly educated group except for Josef, but still it wasn't unusual to hear them talking politics and world events. In fact, most conversations at our dining room table, rather than being of a personal nature, revolved around newspaper headlines and radio commentaries.

Auntie was a cheerful moderator of these mealtime dialogues, but Ma was never very impressed with the verbal exchanges of our boarders, her own contributions being mainly sighs and yawns. She complained secretly to Auntie that only five blocks away on Summit Avenue one could find the palatial residence of the late railroad magnate James J. Hill, the former home of F. Scott Fitzgerald, the manor house that Sinclair Lewis escaped to when he tired of Sauk Centre, the gated and guarded governor's mansion, and a whole host of magnificent homes belonging to Minnesota's wealthiest luminaries, while our own house on Selby Avenue seemed to attract only the dimmest lights in the St. Paul population. Aunt Dortha argued that if you opened a boardinghouse expecting to entertain the likes of governors, railroad magnates, and famous novelists, you were setting yourself up to be bitterly disappointed.

"Houses like ours are for the common folk," Auntie said, "and there's nothing wrong with that."

"Nothing," Ma agreed, "except that our boarders are so harebrained, they don't have the slightest idea what they're talking about half the time."

"Well, that means the other half of the time they *do* know what they're talking about, which is a better percentage than we have any right to expect."

Besides, Auntie added, when Josef Karski and Thomas Diehl were both at the table, statements were made and sentiments expressed that were undoubtedly always worth listening to.

Dewey and I were able to hear from the kitchen what was said in the next room, especially when the swinging door was propped open, as it often was during the summer. In my opinion, the boarders all sounded smart enough except for Clyde Munson, who had to have a lot of things explained to him, and Ida Lassiter, who had an irritating way of cackling about things. For instance, whenever someone mentioned the Berlin Airlift that had begun earlier in the summer, Miss Ida would throw her head back and laugh, "Here we go again, talking about Operation Vittles," as if it was the funniest thing in the world. Dewey and I didn't know the Berlin Airlift really had been code-named Operation Vittles. We thought Ida Lassiter had just made that up. It sounded like something she'd come up with anyway.

Every morning and evening Dewey and I listened and tried to make sense of it all while the grown-ups talked about the airlift into Berlin, the Russian threat, communism, Stalin, the Iron Curtain. We were confused about some things, like what was happening in Berlin. We knew the United States and Russia had been allies in the fight against Germany during the war, but now the United States was flying food into Germany, trying to save the West Berliners from the evil grip of the Russians, who had suddenly become nothing more than dirty Red Commies. How had such a change of allegiance come about, and how could your allies suddenly become your enemies, while your enemies were suddenly people worth saving?

Now that Russia was on our list of bad guys, the grown-ups in the dining room had a lot of animated conversations about the whole world coming to an end if the Reds figured out how to make what they called the "Big One." Henry Udahl said one bad day in the Kremlin, and we'd all be blown to kingdom come, and even quiet Miss Singletary ventured to say that if it came to that, she hoped the United States bombed Russia first so that all the Commie pigs were wiped out before the rest of us.

I didn't like to ask certain questions of Ma because I was afraid she'd think I was as harebrained as the boarders. So with all the talk of atomic war, I asked Dewey one evening, "Do you think the Russians will really bomb us?"

" 'Course not," he answered confidently. "Why would they?"

"All of them"—I nodded toward the dining room—"think they're gonna do it."

"Aw, don't listen to them. Grown-ups just like to worry about things. If they're not worried, they're not happy."

I thought about that for a moment. Dewey was happily eating a ham sandwich and looking as though he didn't have a care in the world, which he probably didn't, in spite of the predictions of complete annihilation coming from the next room.

"Are you sure, Dewey?"

"Sure I'm sure."

"Well, how come at school we're always having to dive under the desks like the Russians are going to be coming any minute?"

Dewey rolled his eyes. "Think about it, Tag," he lectured. "Grown-ups. They want us to be as scared as they are."

"How come?" After all, I thought adults were supposed to shield us from the bad stuff and comfort us when we accidentally saw something awful.

"Guess they think it's good for us. Keeps us on our toes or something."

"So you're not worried at all, Dewey?"

"Nope." He wiped a dab of mustard off his chin with the back of his hand.

I was still a bit worried myself about the Russians and their bombs but not on that particular Monday morning when the grown-ups were discussing the upcoming presidential election. That morning I was worried about a Truman victory, with Dewey left behind in the dust. I really didn't know anything about the election except that the candidates were President Truman and some governor from somewhere named Thomas Dewey. What each man stood for I hadn't a clue. Nor did I care. I was for Dewey, for obvious reasons, and I asked my brother if he thought Thomas Dewey would win the election.

"How should I know?" He lifted his shoulders in an unconcerned shrug. "If they got any say in the matter"—he glanced toward the next room—"it sounds like Truman's going to win."

Dewey was right. If a straw vote were held in our dining room that morning, Truman would win hands down. Clyde Munson said he was sticking with the President because he had once been a farmer, just like Clyde and Clyde's father and grandfather. The Lassiter sisters wanted to see Truman back in the White House because he could play the piano like nobody's business, and his daughter was a pretty good singer too, no matter what anyone said. Henry Udahl was of the opinion that whoever was meant to be in the White House would be there, but personally he liked Truman because the man from Missouri had had the derring-do to drop those atomic bombs on the Japanese and get us out of the war. Miss Singletary said she didn't much like him for that very reason—"There must have been a nicer way. After all, we defeated the Germans without killing so many of them at once"—but she did appreciate the fact that Truman had been raised a Baptist. She wasn't certain of Thomas Dewey's religious persuasion, but if she found out he was something other than Baptist, she'd probably have to give her vote to Truman.

Aunt Dortha announced that she would accept as president whomever Providence ordained, but she rather hoped Providence was inclined to be in favor of Truman. I thought her statement had a Calvinistic bent to it, but I never would have told her that, her being Methodist and all.

Ma, I knew, was for Truman because I'd already asked her if we could put a Dewey sign in our yard. Since late June signs had sprung up all over town: "The Country Needs Dewey" and "America Wants Dewey." Every time I saw one, I felt ready to burst with pride.

Ma didn't share my enthusiasm for putting up a sign. "Certainly not," she replied, mumbling around a clothespin in her mouth. She was hanging laundry out to dry on the line in the backyard. She took the pin out of her mouth and jabbed it onto the shoulder of one of Dewey's shirts. "You don't think anyone in this neighborhood is going to support the Republican candidate, do you?"

"Why not?"

"The Republicans don't care about the little fellow, people like us."

"We're little fellows, Ma? We're the same size as anyone else."

Ma's lips formed a taut, pale line. She squinted against the sun. "Never mind, Nova," she sighed. "But I'm not voting for Dewey. I'm voting for Truman."

"But why, Ma?"

"Because if anyone can keep us out of a war with Russia, Truman can."

"But Dewey says there's not going to be a war with Russia."

Ma looked puzzled. "Governor Dewey?"

"No. *Our* Dewey."

To my surprise, Ma laughed. "What does Dewey know? He's a thirteen-year-old boy!"

"He's old enough to decide not to go to church! He must be old enough to know about Russia too."

Ma shook her head and went back to pinning up clothes.

"So we can't put a Dewey sign up in the yard?"

"The answer is no, Nova."

Each word was the bang of a gavel, and Ma's verdict left me feeling flat. I stared at this traitor, my own mother, for a few minutes, trying to figure her out. How could she possibly not be for Dewey?

The only person who gave me any hope of a Dewey victory that morning was Josef. As he sipped his coffee and listened to Aunt Dortha say she hoped Providence was in favor of Truman, Josef commented that it might indeed take a miracle to get Truman back into the White House, as the press was predicting a landslide victory for Dewey. I hoped Josef and the press were right.

Now as I finished up my Post Toasties and Dewey poured his second bowl of Corn Flakes, I looked at my brother. "Well," I said, "no matter what anyone else says, I'm for Dewey."

Dewey met my gaze and smiled. "Say, it's supposed to be a clear night tonight," he said. "You wanna get out the telescope and look at the stars with me?"

"You bet!" I cried.

How I loved it when my brother showed me the stars.

———

I suppose Dewey and I peered through the telescope at the night sky together hundreds of times during our childhood, so now, looking back on those days from a distance of half a century, much of that stargazing becomes one large blur of twinkling light.

But that night I remember, that night of July 19, 1948. Not because of the moon or the constellations or the planets made large by our telescope, but because of something else.

The sky was open and cloudless, with the stars scattered across it like marbles cast from a giant hand. The air was sweetened by an even-tempered breeze and full of the pulsating lullabies of crickets and katydids. Ma called all that rhythmic chirping the heartbeat of the night. She said it was the music that the stars danced to.

It was already past my bedtime, but Ma let me stay up late on nights like this. Though she wasn't with us, she had allowed us to use her telescope, the big one Pa gave her as a wedding gift. It had a collapsible tripod that Dewey adjusted to match my height rather than his. That meant he had to bend over pretty far to look through the eyepiece himself, but he didn't seem to mind.

While Dewey fiddled with the telescope, I stood there with my head thrown back, gazing up at the mesmerizing panorama of lights. Compared with Ma and Dewey, I knew very little about the arrangement of the universe, but I did know that nothing in the world made me feel more secure than looking up at the night sky. As long as the moon was in its place and the stars were burning and the planets were moving through their spheres, I could believe that no matter what was happening on the face of this one lone planet and in my one small life, everything was all right.

Dewey straightened up and took a step back from the telescope. "Okay, I got Ursa Minor, the Little Dipper. Wanna see?"

I nodded and bent over the eyepiece. I had seen Ursa Minor a hundred times before, but I could see it a hundred thousand times again and not grow tired of it.

"Now, if you look at the last star on the handle—see it?—that's Polaris," Dewey explained. "That's the North Star or the pole star, either one, because it's almost exactly above the North Pole. You ought to remember this, Tag, because it's important. If you're facing Polaris, you're looking due north. Got that?"

I drew back from the eyepiece far enough to nod obediently without knocking the telescope.

"Because if you ever get lost, you can look up at the sky and find Polaris," Dewey went on, "and that way you'll know you're facing north. If you can read the stars, you can find your way anywhere. That's how the sailors do it, you know. Or at least they did in the old days before radar and all that stuff."

I looked at that twinkling light and hoped I could find it again on my own if I was ever lost without Dewey. Remembering something he once said, I repeated, "It's like there's a huge map in the sky, and we just have to know how to read it."

"That's right, Tag."

I straightened up. Dewey was gazing at the moon.

"One of these days," he said, "I'm going to look through that new two-hundred-inch telescope they got out at Mount

Palomar in California. It's so big you have to sit in a cage just to get up high enough to look through it. Right now people are seeing stars that no one's ever seen before."

"I sure would like to look through it too," I agreed.

Dewey nodded, though I wasn't sure he had heard what I said. He was walking on the moon, I could tell. Sometimes he took me with him, and we imagined what it would be like up there where the atmosphere was so thin a person could practically fly. We imagined ourselves soaring over the barren craters and hills, in and out of shadows, all the way to the dark side of the moon and back. We wondered how Earth would look from such a distance, and if we sat and watched for a day and a night, could we see the world revolving and the continents waking and sleeping and the tides waxing and waning? We believed we could, and even though he had an astronomy book that said it seemed quite certain that humans would never visit the moon except in their imaginations, Dewey said the book was wrong, that a man would step on the moon one day and look back toward Earth and know that he had done the impossible.

"Dewey?"

"Yeah, Tag?"

"You on the moon?"

"I was just thinking."

"What about?"

"Something Ma told me."

"What's that?"

Dewey paused a moment, pursed his lips. I knew he was trying to figure out how to put whatever it was into simple terms so he could explain it to me. "Well, there's these two guys," he began, "a couple of scientists, and they've come up with this theory about this huge fireball, see?"

"A fireball?"

"Yeah, a huge cosmic fireball."

"So?"

"Well." Dewey shifted from one foot to the other. He looked at me, then back up at the sky. "According to their calculations, the universe was really, really hot when it was young, and they think there was this really gigantic glow of radiation that we should still be able to see today if we just had the right equipment to see it."

"Yeah?"

"Well, if we could see this cosmic fireball radiation, that would prove that the universe began in an explosion."

Dewey fell quiet then. Finally I said, "So?"

"Well, see, it would change everything. I mean, most scientists now believe the universe had no beginning. That's the Steady State theory; that's what they call it. The universe has just always sort of been here, and it'll always be here. So most scientists think these two guys—the cosmic fireball guys—are just plain crazy."

"Well, what do you think?"

Dewey shrugged. "I wish we could see some of that radiation so we could know for sure."

"You think it makes a difference?"

"Yeah. I mean, if the universe had a beginning, then we ought to know that and not just go on believing something that isn't true. We ought to know what the facts are, see? There've been other guys who've predicted an exploding universe, and we know for sure that the galaxies are moving away from each other at a super-high speed. There's Hubble's Law, you know, the law of the expanding universe. The farther away a galaxy is, the faster it moves, and that means the universe is expanding."

I was trying hard to follow Dewey, to understand what he was getting at. But I found myself confused. "Do you want there to be a beginning to the universe?"

He shrugged again. "I just want to know what happened, whatever it was."

"Don't you think God created the universe like the Bible says?"

Dewey didn't answer for a long time. Finally he said, "The Bible isn't proof enough for scientists, Tag. The universe will tell us its own story if we can just figure out how to listen."

"But if we find out there was a beginning, maybe it's the same beginning the Bible talks about when it says 'In the beginning God created the heavens and the earth.'"

"Could be, Tag." Dewey nodded. "But right now we just don't know. There are so many things we don't know today that people are going to know someday."

"Like what the music of the spheres sounds like?"

Dewey smiled. "That's right. But don't worry about that. Someday we'll know, when I get the Nova Machine built. You and I will be the first people ever to hear the music of the spheres."

"We'll be famous, Dewey," I said, my voice quiet with awe.

"Yup."

"Maybe even rich."

Dewey took a deep and pensive breath, then let it out.

"Naw, not from the Nova Machine."

"But how come, Dewey?"

He shrugged. "I don't know," he said, "but the music of the spheres isn't mine to sell, you know? I mean, it's not like I'm making the music. If I charged people for listening to the Nova Machine, it'd be like, well, like stealing from God, I guess."

Dewey bent over the telescope, moved it, focused it.

"So you're just going to let people listen for free?" I asked.

"Sure."

I frowned momentarily. I would have liked to have the money, since Ma was always saying we didn't have enough. But Dewey was right. We couldn't sell what wasn't ours in the first place. "Yeah, you're right, Dewey," I conceded. "We should let people listen for free."

Dewey didn't respond. He went on looking through the telescope. After a moment he straightened up again and sighed.

"What's the matter?" I asked.

"Nothing," he replied. "I just don't feel so good."

"But what's the matter?" I repeated.

"I don't know. I just feel tired all of a sudden. Think I'll go to bed. Do you mind?"

"Naw, I don't mind." But I did. I wanted to stay outside longer, just to be with Dewey. But I wouldn't say so. "Do you think you should tell Ma?"

"What for?"

"Maybe you're getting sick."

"Naw. I'm just tuckered, like I said."

"Okay, Dewey."

He folded up the telescope and hoisted it up under his arm. He hadn't taken half a dozen steps toward the house when his knees buckled and he was suddenly kneeling on the ground. I was alarmed, but Dewey only laughed a little, said he was more tired even than he'd thought, and pulled himself up again. He did let me take the telescope from him—even though it was heavy and he usually didn't let me carry it—and we walked to the back porch where he fell into bed, clothes and all.

And that was what made that night different from all the previous nights we'd looked at the stars. Funny how seemingly small the event might be that divides your life into before and after.

THE CRIPPLER

Dewey seemed fine the next day and even the day after that. At least he didn't complain, and when I asked him if he was all right, he said he was just tired from the heat. But on Thursday when he woke up with a headache and muscle aches, Aunt Dortha diagnosed him with the flu, and Ma told him to take it easy and stay in bed. Ma gave him aspirin and orange juice and tried to get him to eat something, but he could only manage a little bit of broth and some soda crackers. I volunteered to read to him, but he said the sound of people's voices hurt his head and if it was all the same to me, he'd just lie quietly on the porch, maybe sleep if he could.

I tried to read the expressions on Ma's and Auntie's faces, to take my cue from them as to how worried I should be. Under normal circumstances, Auntie didn't look worried about anything, and Ma looked worried about everything, and that was how they appeared that morning. I told myself that when Auntie began to look worried and Ma was beside herself, then there'd be reason for concern.

Auntie did her usual puttering around the kitchen, glancing out the window of the kitchen door from time to time to where Dewey lay. She went about her hymn singing as she baked and washed dishes, pausing only during the occasional glance, then picking up the thread of the song again.

"Stay away from Dewey," she cautioned me casually on my own hundredth trip to the window. "Last thing we need is the two of you down with the flu at the same time."

Ma spent the morning catching up on some mending and ironing; then just before she left for her afternoon job at the bakery, she kissed my forehead and said, "Let Aunt Dortha look after Dewey, all right? I don't want you catching whatever he has."

I reluctantly agreed to keep my distance from Dewey, then went about the task of moping around the kitchen. Auntie's face remained a steady barometer, an indicator of normalcy. Still, each time I went to the window to check on Dewey, I felt the same thing: a growing swarm of butterflies rising up from the pit of my stomach, their wings beating madly against my rib cage. I looked from Dewey to Auntie and back again and didn't know what to think or feel.

At length Auntie decided she was tired of my being underfoot. "Make yourself useful," she suggested. "Find something to do. It's early, but you can set the table for supper if you don't have anything else to do."

I shook my head. "Chess lesson at three o'clock today, remember?"

"Oh yes. So kind of Mr. Karski, volunteering his time like

that to teach you how to play chess. Is it making any more sense to you?"

"No. I can't keep all the pieces straight."

"I never could either. But"—she smiled, shrugged—"it can't hurt for you to keep at it. You might learn to like it."

"I doubt it. But I like being with Josef."

"You mean Mr. Karski, don't you?"

"He said I could call him Josef."

"But that doesn't mean you should."

"Why not?"

"It shows more respect to call him by his surname."

"But every time I do, he says to call him Josef."

"Oh." Aunt Dortha was rolling out a piecrust, the rolling pin gripped firmly in her two plump and flour-dusted hands. When she finished, she arranged the dough into a pie pan and started pressing down the edges with a fork. "Well, it's three o'clock now. You best not be late."

I wouldn't be late. I had only to walk from the kitchen to the parlor where I would meet Josef at the chessboard. I cast one more glance at Dewey before leaving the kitchen. He was sleeping a restless sleep, and even through the window I could see the pain that had settled like gauze over his pale face.

"Dewey's sick," I told Josef a few minutes later after he had seated himself in a chair across the chessboard from me.

"I'm sorry to hear that." Josef looked up from the board and adjusted his glasses on the bridge of his nose. "What seems to be the matter?"

"He has the flu."

"Ah." Josef nodded. "Not uncommon this time of year. You mustn't worry. Shall we begin?" He reached across the board and moved one of my pieces for me.

"I'm not worried," I countered.

Josef knew I was lying. He lifted an eyebrow, smiled slightly. "Your brother is lucky to have a sister who cares for him as you do."

I shrugged nonchalantly but felt secretly pleased by Josef's comment. "Well, don't you—" I began. Then abruptly I shut my mouth, cutting off the words in midsentence. I had been about to ask him if he didn't have a sister who cared for him too when I remembered that his entire family was gone, and if he had ever had a sister, she was no longer around to care about him or even to know what had become of him after the war.

"Don't I what, Novelka?" Josef asked quietly. His eyes were on the board. He moved one of his own pieces, a black pawn.

"I mean, do you think Dewey will be better soon?"

"Of course," he assured me. "A day, maybe two, and he'll be just fine. You'll see. Now, tell me what you think your next move should be."

I wanted to take Josef's words to heart, to assume that by Saturday Dewey would be up and about again, back to his old self. But I couldn't shake the feeling that something was terribly wrong. After twenty minutes of bad guesses and even worse moves on my part, Josef patiently suggested that we call it a day, maybe sit on the porch with a cold drink or listen to the radio together instead. "Your mind's not on the game today, Novelka. Or should I say, it is even less on the game today than usual?" He was smiling when he said it, but I could see that he was worried because I was worried.

I poured us both a glass of lemonade, and we sat on the porch swing, where we could watch the afternoon begin to wind down. The morning glories were hanging their heads, blue faces turned away from the sun. The air was full of moisture, an unbreathable humidity, a stagnant pool of invisible water suspended cruelly above the thirsty grass. The street was a dark river of searing asphalt stretched out between the houses, little waves of heat rippling over its surface. In the distant sky rain clouds hovered, taunting, promising relief that wouldn't come.

"Have you ever been scared, Josef?" I asked.

He took a long drink of his lemonade before answering. "Oh yes, Novelka. I have been afraid many times. Terribly afraid."

I remembered then the horrors that were clinging to him, those horrors I had glimpsed on Sunday but that I didn't fully know or understand. But I understood this: He had lived through a war. He had been in one of those death camps. Of course he had been afraid.

"Do you still get afraid sometimes? I mean, even now?"

Josef nodded slightly. "Yes. Sometimes still I am afraid." He gave a knowing smile. "Even here in America we are not completely without fear, are we?"

A corner of my mouth drew back as my mind formed a question. "What do you do? I mean, when you're so scared you don't know what to do?"

Josef looked out over the street. His eyebrows sank beneath the tops of his rimless glasses as he frowned. "What are you so afraid of, little one?" he asked gently.

I sighed, shaking my head. "I don't know, Josef," I

answered truthfully. "Sometimes I don't know what it is, and sometimes I think I'm just pretty much afraid of everything. I feel like my stomach is all filled up with fear, and I feel like running as fast and as far as I can, but I know I can never run fast enough or far enough to get away from whatever it is that's making me scared."

Josef nodded, looking pained. "I have felt that way myself, Novelka."

"But then what do you do?"

"I pray for strength."

The words were simple, straightforward. Josef pushed against the floor with one foot and the swing moved back and forth, cradling us.

"And then you're not afraid anymore?"

"No," he replied. "Then I am still afraid. But then I know that God knows I'm afraid, and that is what makes the difference."

The street shimmered and rolled; a car sailed by, sleeveless arms dangling out of open windows; and a woman's faraway voice reached us through the watery air, calling a child home.

———————

I prayed that night to tell God I was afraid. Before I fell asleep, I told him I was afraid that Dewey might be sick with something really bad. I was afraid that I'd grow up without a father. I was afraid Ma would always be sad.

When I finished, I was still afraid. Worse, I wasn't sure my prayer had made any difference.

Hours later I was convinced that it hadn't.

It was shortly after midnight that we were awakened by

the screams. At first they were simply part of the night thoughts of my mind, a sound breaking into a dream image. But I quickly became aware, as I edged up toward consciousness, that it was all very real and that someone was screaming. In the next instant Ma was rushing past my bed on her way to the back porch.

Fully awake, I sat up in bed. I knew who was screaming now—I recognized the voice. It was Dewey. Stumbling out of bed, I hurried toward the back of the house, stopping short on the threshold between the kitchen and the porch. In the dim moonlight I could see Ma kneeling by the bed, her hand on Dewey's forehead. Dewey's eyes were closed, his face knotted in pain, his knees drawn up almost to his chest.

"What is it, Ma?" I cried. I had to shout to be heard over Dewey's screams.

Before Ma could answer, Aunt Dortha rushed into the kitchen. She turned on the overhead porch light, then pushed me gently out of the doorway so she could get by. "Don't come any closer, Nova," Auntie warned as she joined Ma at the bedside. "Get back inside." She waved an arm at me while studying Dewey.

"But what is it, Auntie?"

"I don't know. Get inside."

I took one step backward into the kitchen.

"He's burning with fever," I heard Ma say, her voice low, anxious.

Ma lifted her hand from Dewey's brow and Auntie's hand replaced it. After a moment Auntie said, "Well over a hundred, I'm afraid."

By now Josef, Miss Singletary, and Clyde Munson had

gathered in the kitchen. Josef lifted his hand to my hair, a small warm crown of comfort. "What is it, Novelka?" he asked softly.

"Dewey's dying." I hadn't meant to say that. The words just came out.

And they made Ma furious. "Be quiet, Nova!" she scolded. "Nobody's dying."

"Best call Dr. Vinson," Aunt Dortha suggested calmly. "See if he can come."

"You call him, please, Dortha," Ma said. "I don't want to leave Dewey."

Aunt Dortha rose, and Josef and I made room for her to pass through the doorway into the kitchen. I tried to catch her eye, but she wouldn't look at me.

"Tell the doctor he's burning up with fever," Ma called out, "and that the muscles in his legs are . . ."

She didn't finish. She put her head down on the bed, her face buried in the sheet. I wanted to go to her, took one step toward her, but Josef held me back. "You must stay away, child," he said.

Behind us Clyde Munson cursed. "We'll all be coming down with it now," he spat out. "Just wait. Every single one of us—"

"Please be quiet, Mr. Munson," Josef interjected. "You're scaring the child."

"The boy will be all right," Miss Singletary offered. "Flu's going around."

"Yeah," Clyde Munson muttered, "flu and the crippler both. What this boy's got sure ain't like no flu I ever seen."

Aunt Dortha came back from the phone in the hallway.

"Dr. Vinson is sending out an ambulance."

"An ambulance?" Ma looked up from the bed in alarm. Her mottled face glistened as her tears reflected the porch's pale light. "What does he think it is?"

Auntie glanced nervously at the rest of us before replying. "He wouldn't say." Her words were vague, filmy. She wasn't used to telling an untruth. "But he thinks it's best for Dewey to be seen at the hospital."

A hush fell over the whole house. Even Dewey quieted. There is no such thing as reading other people's minds, but I have no doubt at all as to what every last one of us was thinking. The doctor knew very well what was wrong with Dewey. So did we. Even Clyde Munson could diagnose this one. It was the crippler.

QUARANTINED

Before that night the only time an ambulance had come to our house was when an elderly boarder, Hugo Osborne, collapsed from a heart attack while playing Chopin on the piano. That time it was kind of exciting, what with all the grown-ups running around and the neighbors rushing over and the stretcher bearers bursting in through the front door to scoop Hugo up from the piano bench and carry him away.

But this time, when the ambulance came for Dewey, it wasn't exciting at all. It felt to me like the end of the world. Total annihilation without a single atomic bomb. The silent invasion of one tiny unseen germ and everything was over. That's what it felt like.

Hugo Osborne never came back. He died before he even reached the hospital. So when Dewey was lifted onto the stretcher, I was almost certain I'd never see him again. I watched in horror from the kitchen, forgotten momentarily by Ma and Auntie, though I knew Josef's hand was on my shoulder. I could feel the gentle weight of it, but I was aware of it only fleetingly, like a thought that passes by and disappears. As Dewey was carried out through the hall, I followed, ignoring Josef, being ignored myself by the ones intent on rushing Dewey to the hospital. Outside on the sidewalk a small crowd had gathered—our boarders, a few neighbors who had been awakened and had come out to see the show. Thomas Diehl was there, his Ford Coupe parked in front of the house, engine idling. Aunt Dortha had called him and asked him to accompany Ma to the hospital.

I pushed through the crowd to see my brother's face one last time. His eyes were closed, but when I said his name, he opened them. Never before had it registered with me that he had blue eyes just like Ma's. They'd never looked like Ma's eyes until that very moment when, under the streetlamp, they shone with a terrible sadness and an even more terrible fear. I lifted a hand toward him, but the two burly stretcher bearers hoisted Dewey into the back of the ambulance, jumped in themselves, helped Ma in, and then slammed the door shut. The ambulance sped off, light flashing, siren wailing, with Thomas Diehl following close behind.

We stood there then, the rest of us, a motley crowd of nightgowns, T-shirts, hair rollers, hastily thrown-on robes and pants, listening to the siren growing smaller. When I couldn't hear its wailing at all anymore, I looked up at the sky and wondered why the stars were twinkling so fiercely tonight, almost breaking apart like firecrackers, until I realized their splintered light was because of the tears in my eyes.

Then finally after a few mumbled words we scattered like lost sheep, the neighbors back to their houses, the boarders back to their rooms. Auntie, though, sat down in the chair next to the telephone table in the hall to await word of what was happening. She said she wasn't moving an inch until she heard from the hospital or from Ma.

Suddenly she saw me again, remembered I was there. "Go on to bed, Nova," she said gently.

"I can't, Auntie."

"But—"

"It's all right." Josef was there, his hand on my shoulder again. "Come, Novelka," he said, "let me tell you a story about when I was a little boy in Poland."

I didn't think it strange at all that he should choose this moment to tell me a story. I went with him willingly as he led me by the hand into the parlor. We settled on the couch, me with my head on a pillow in his lap, he with his hand on my hair, stroking gently. "Many years ago," he began, "when I was a child . . ."

I shut my eyes, taking in the warmth and comfort of his hand, his voice. If I had a pa, I thought, this is what he'd be doing right now—telling me a story to keep out the thoughts about Dewey.

I don't remember what Josef said, not one word of it. I'm not even sure I heard what he said while he was saying it. It wasn't the story I needed but the sound of his voice and the warmth of his hand, and before long I was drifting, floating in a quiet place, sheltered in a dreamless sleep.

The next thing I remember is the ringing of the telephone and waking up with a start. Josef woke up too, lifting his head from the back of the couch with a small throaty cough. He'd fallen asleep sitting up, my head still in his lap.

The first dim light of morning filled the room, and outside birds sang their rising-up song. The only harsh sound was the ringing of the telephone, but it rang only twice before Aunt Dortha's voice, heavy with sleep, came from the hall. "Yes? Hello? Catherine, is that you?" She must have fallen asleep with her head on the table while waiting for the call.

In another moment she was standing before Josef and me in the parlor, looking down at us with a gaze both of tenderness and despair. With one hand she pinched absently at the tie strings of her cotton robe; with her other hand she pushed back a few strands of gray hair from her round, tortured face. "They did a spinal tap," she said quietly. "Dewey has polio."

We had expected nothing else, but it was a slap in the face just the same. How we hope, oh, how we hope—until we know.

Without waiting for us to respond, Aunt Dortha went upstairs and moments later came back down wearing a housedress, pale blue with a pattern of lavender flowers. She went barefoot out to the backyard and started a fire in the ash can. Then she stripped Dewey's bed and burned the sheets, the pillowcase, the pillow, even some of Dewey's dirty clothes that she found under the bed. She dragged the mattress out to the grass, where she doused it with bleach, hosed it down, and left it to dry in the sun. Then, with a handful of rags and another bottle of bleach, she washed the frame of Dewey's bed from head to foot. When she was finished with that, she went upstairs, bathed, and changed her clothes again. Finally she descended to the kitchen, where she put on a pot of coffee and started making breakfast for the boarders. She didn't sing. I never saw the pale blue dress with the lavender flowers again.

I'm pretty sure it too went up in smoke.

Aunt Dortha announced at the breakfast table that morning that Dewey had been diagnosed with polio. The initial response of our boarders was silence, as though the very word polio had a way of erasing all other words.

When at length someone spoke, it was Ida Lassiter, who fingered her imitation pearl necklace and whispered, "That poor child." Then she and her sister both made the sign of the cross over themselves in small, swift movements, a talisman against the disease.

Auntie continued, "If any of you feel you need to give notice, I understand."

Clyde Munson actually laughed out loud. "No offense, Mrs. S, but just where do you think we can go to get away from it? Summers like this, there's nowhere far enough to outrun polio."

"Just how bad is it, Mrs. Severson?" Miss Singletary stirred sugar into her coffee, trying but failing to appear nonchalant.

"We don't know yet," Auntie explained.

"Some cases are real mild," Henry Udahl offered. "When I was a kid, a cousin of mine got over it just like that." He snapped his fingers. "We were back to playing baseball in less than a week. He died last year at eighty-one."

"Yes, well . . ." Aunt Dortha, who had been standing, took her seat at the head of the table. "Biscuits?" She passed the basket of freshly baked biscuits to Henry Udahl on her right.

Josef, who had been listening quietly, cleared his throat and said, "We will hold out every hope for the best, Mrs. Severson."

Aunt Dortha smiled faintly and nodded her appreciation. "Thank you, Mr. Karski. God willing, Dewey will be home soon."

———

Ma was at the hospital all that day. Josef left in the late morning for a couple of tutoring sessions, so I spent the hours trailing Auntie, taking comfort in her familiarity. It was a long day, made longer by the relentless heat and humidity. I found myself pushing against a heaviness both inside and out.

Thomas Diehl finally brought Ma home early in the evening, said a few words to Aunt Dortha, then discreetly slipped away. As soon as he was gone, Ma collapsed in a chair at the kitchen table, laid her head on her arms, and cried. Auntie pulled up a chair beside her and put an arm around her shoulders. "There," she soothed, "calm yourself, Catherine, and tell me what the doctor said."

I stood by the table, my hands clenched, waiting for Ma to speak. I had said hello to her when she came in with Mr. Diehl, but she didn't seem to hear or even see me. It was as though I disappeared for Ma the moment the ambulance came, and I hadn't yet reappeared.

A long minute passed before she raised her head and took in a series of deep breaths, trying to collect herself enough to talk. Auntie waited patiently, patting Ma's shoulder all the while. Ma dug a handkerchief out of the pocket of her skirt and wiped her face. It must have been Mr. Diehl's handkerchief, because it was a man's. It looked as though it had already caught a thousand tears just in that one day.

"He's been put in quarantine," she said finally, sounding angry and frustrated. "I won't be allowed to see him for two weeks. I can look at him through the window in the door, but that's all. He's completely alone, Dortha—" Another sob cut her off, and she buried her face in the handkerchief.

"He's a strong boy, Catherine," Auntie said. "He'll be all right. Of course he's been put into quarantine—that's to be expected. Everyone is once they're diagnosed with polio."

"I don't know how I'll get through the next two weeks not being able to see him."

"We will get through them with the Lord's help."

Ma drew in a breath. "Don't speak to me of the Lord, Dortha—"

"Now, Catherine—"

"I don't want to hear it. Not right now."

Auntie looked hurt, but she gave Ma's shoulder another reassuring pat. "Do they have any idea how bad it is?"

Ma shook her head. "Not yet. We just have to wait and see, they said."

"We mustn't assume the worst, my dear. Many people have had polio and have been just fine."

"While others have died," Ma snapped.

Aunt Dortha dropped her eyes, as she did whenever her compassion came up against Ma's anger.

"Oh, Dortha," Ma said, sounding suddenly contrite. "I know you're just trying to help. It's just that . . . I'm so afraid."

"Of course you are, dear. We're all afraid. But we must

hope for the best until we know otherwise. There is no other way to get through it."

Ma nodded. "Yes," she said with a sigh. "Yes, I know you're right. But, Dewey's friends . . ." Her voice trailed off.

"What about his friends?"

"Two of them are there . . . at the hospital . . . with polio. It turns out Andy didn't have the flu at all. It was polio, and he's been in the hospital for a couple of days now. And then Jerry was admitted just yesterday."

"Oh dear." Auntie raised her fingers to her lips.

"I ran into Millie Butterfield today," Ma went on. "Jerry's in quarantine too, of course, and she can't visit him, but she was at the hospital just to be near him. You know what she told me?"

Auntie, wide-eyed, shook her head.

"Jerry told her the boys had gone swimming together last week at Cedar Lake."

"Oh no!"

I gasped along with Auntie and felt myself go weak. The cat was out of the bag.

"Yes, and Andy already wasn't feeling well. It could be that Dewey picked up the virus from Andy, just from swimming with him. I'm so angry with Dewey—I told him not to go swimming, and he did it anyway."

Ma was red-faced and white-knuckled as she squeezed her hands together on the top of the table. She still didn't look at me, didn't return my gaze. Auntie walked past me to the window and looked out. She too seemed to forget I was there. After a moment she turned to Ma and asked, "How are they? Andy and Jerry, I mean."

"Jerry's not so bad, but Andy was having such a hard time breathing, he was put into an iron lung today."

An iron lung! Our teacher had shown us a picture of an iron lung she'd found in a magazine. She'd cut it out and passed it around the room with the warning that this was what could happen if we weren't careful. When the picture reached my desk, I'd glanced at it through the peephole of one half-opened eye, then quickly passed it on. I didn't want to see it. I didn't want to acknowledge that such things existed. It was the ultimate horror, the very worst thing on earth. Even that one swift glance seared the iron lung's image on my brain: a huge silver cylinder with knobs and dials and a human head sticking out one end. In this instance, a little child. A child up to his neck in that metal cocoon, unable to move, more dead than alive, maybe never coming out.

Now that child's face was replaced with a familiar one, that of Andy Johanson, the first of Dewey's friends ever to call me Tag.

A wave of fear hit me and nearly knocked me over. What if the same thing happened to Dewey?

"You'd have thought Alice Johanson would keep Andy home if he wasn't feeling well," Aunt Dortha was saying.

I thought of the afternoon that Josef found me crying on the steps of the front porch, the afternoon that Dewey went swimming with Andy Johanson and Jerry Butterfield. Suddenly I didn't want to hear any more of what Ma and Auntie might have to say. I tiptoed out of the kitchen and went back to my bed to lie down.

The room I shared with Dewey was crowded with the trappings of my brother's life: astronomy books that Ma had given him, his homemade telescopes in various stages of construction, model replicas of the solar system made out of plaster of paris and tin foil. Mobiles of suns, moons, and planets dangled from the ceiling, and the walls were papered with hand-drawn maps of the stars. He also had a few possessions unrelated to his first love: a Saints pennant and other baseball memorabilia, a collection of Superman and Captain Marvel comic books, a college fraternity paperweight that had once belonged to Pa.

There wasn't much of me in the room other than a sampling of Early Reader and Nancy Drew books, my box of treasures from the city dump, my Cracker Jack prize collection that I kept in a lady's size seven red patent-leather slingback—found without its mate in the alley behind our house. The room was mostly Dewey, and I liked it that way. I wasn't like other girls who wanted their own feminine room, with frilly curtains and pink wallpaper. I liked being on the inside of my brother's world. When Ma said on Dewey's last birthday that he'd have to move into his own room up on the second floor before too long, I felt sad about it. It seemed one more bit of evidence that Dewey was outgrowing me.

I was lying on my bed, staring up at Dewey's mobiles with my hands under my head when Ma found me. There was still a slice of daylight left before evening arrived, and it was as yet several hours before my bedtime.

"What are you doing?" Ma asked, sounding alarmed. She came to the bed and put a hand on my forehead.

"Nothing, Ma," I answered. I sat up, happy she could see

me again. "I was just thinking, I guess."

"Do you feel sick?"

"No." I shook my head.

"You don't feel feverish."

"I'm all right, Ma. Really."

"Then why are you lying around?"

I didn't know what she expected me to do, but at the moment I'd do anything to please her. "Do you need help in the kitchen?"

"No." She sighed. "No, it's all right. You can rest if you want. I know the heat is wearing."

She started to leave the room, but I called her back. "Ma?"

"Yes, Nova?"

"Don't worry, Ma. I won't get polio."

"That's right, you won't," she snapped. "You won't have the opportunity to get polio, because I won't have you playing with the neighborhood kids for a while. Not until the danger has passed."

I calculated the meaning behind that statement and didn't like what I came up with. "I can't play with anyone until school starts?"

Ma hesitated. She knew such solitude was a lot to expect from a kid. She chewed her lip in thought. "We'll find things for you to do," she offered. "There's plenty for you to do around here that'll keep you busy."

I started to protest. What was there to do around the house that would keep me busy? The summer suddenly stretched out ahead of me, one vast empty playing field, no

one to play with, nothing to do. The boredom seemed tanta-
mount to torture.

But Ma had made up her mind, and there was no use
arguing. I stifled the urge to complain and asked instead,
"When will we know for sure that the polio's gone?"

"First frost. There usually aren't any new cases after first
frost."

"But I'll be back in school before first frost."

"Yes, unless so many kids come down with it they close
the schools."

I hoped it wouldn't get that bad. I couldn't survive until
first frost without seeing any of my friends.

"Do many people have it right now, Ma?"

"Well, it's not as bad as some years, certainly not as bad
as in '46, but heaven knows there's enough cases right now to
keep the hospitals busy. And it's only bound to get worse
before summer ends."

I had a thousand questions I wanted to ask: "Is Dewey
going to be all right? What if he has to go in a lung? What if
he ends up a cripple?" and a thousand things I wanted to say:
"I'm scared, Ma," but I knew it would be best not to speak at
all. Because any one of those thousand things might only
deepen the sadness in my mother's eyes and darken the shadows of worry on her face. Even if I told her I loved her, she
would know in the end that it was only because Dewey was
sick and all of life was wrong. Because if Dewey were well and
here at home, we'd all be doing chores or listening to the radio
or going our separate ways through all the small and routine
details of our lives. We wouldn't be saying that we loved each
other. We wouldn't be saying that at all if Dewey were well.

"I think I'll read awhile," I said at last.

"All right, Nova. Call me when you're ready to go to sleep so I can say good night."

I fell asleep reading. Sometime in the night I awoke, not fully, but enough to know that Ma was there, her weight on one side of my bed, her hand on my forehead. And then she slipped away, once more assured that I didn't have a fever.

———————

Over the next few days, Dewey didn't get any better, but he didn't get worse either. I found myself worrying less and figuring that once he was out of quarantine, he'd be allowed to come home. I actually started planning his homecoming. Aunt Dortha let me put clean sheets on his bed on the porch, and I lined up all his razors and hair tonics in the medicine cabinet in the bathroom. I checked to see if we had all the ingredients for German chocolate cake, because that was his favorite and he'd want some once he got out of the hospital. I'd bake it myself on the day of his homecoming and have it waiting for him on the dining room table when he came through the front door.

But a phone call early one morning interrupted my plans. Aunt Dortha and I were in the kitchen preparing breakfast when Ma picked up the extension in the hall. She was on for less than a minute. When she came to the kitchen, her face was as pale as the bread dough Aunt Dortha was just putting into the oven.

"Catherine?" Auntie asked.

"Andy Johanson has died."

Those were the only four words she could manage before she collapsed on the floor.

THE DAY THEY BURIED HOUDINI

The day they buried Andy Johanson, I just kept telling myself that even if he really had been Houdini, he was now in a box he would never get out of. Not even the World's Greatest Escape Artist could finagle his way out of the grave. There were no tricks, no sleights of hand, no keys conveniently hidden between gum and cheek that would unlock the lid of the coffin. I had to keep telling myself that because I was having a hard time believing I'd never see Andy again.

Ma and Aunt Dortha went to Andy's funeral, though Auntie advised Ma not to go. She said it would be too hard on Ma, that she was in no state to see Dewey's best friend laid to rest. But Ma argued that it would be unthinkable not to show up at the funeral. After all, Ma and Alice Johanson had volunteered on several school committees together over the past few years and had grown somewhat fond of each other. How could Ma not show her support at a time like this?

While Ma sat at her vanity table putting on her makeup, I came up quietly behind her. She could see me in the mirror. She paused, a tube of lipstick halfway to her lips.

"You can't go, you know," she said quietly.

I pressed my lips together to keep from crying, but it didn't work. Ma put down the lipstick, pulled a tissue from the box on the vanity, and handed it to me. I took it and wiped my eyes and blew my nose.

"I'm so sorry, Nova," Ma continued, "but there will be lots of people there. You know I don't want you in crowds until autumn sets in."

"I know, Ma," I whispered. "It's just that . . ."

I couldn't finish. Ma spoke the words for me. "You wanted to say good-bye."

I nodded. Ma seemed always to know what I was going to say even before I said it. Somehow, that comforted me.

"I promise to say good-bye for you." She gave me a small, strained smile, took my hand, and squeezed it. I squeezed back, holding on for dear life.

"He named me Tag."

"I know, sweetheart."

"Does Dewey know that Andy's. . . ?" I couldn't say the word. It was too final.

"Yes, he knows. He knew before I did."

"Do you think he's all right?"

Ma looked pensive. "I've been asking the nurses about that, and they tell me he won't talk about Andy."

"Maybe he thinks if he doesn't talk about it, Andy won't really be . . . you know . . . gone."

Ma cupped my face in her hands and kissed my forehead,

a planting of maternal comfort on my brow. She was, you see, actually a loving and gentle woman. It's just that she was lost, hidden way deep down inside somewhere, in a place of no light, the bottom of an ocean of too many hard years. And yet there were moments when she rose to the surface, breaking through the sadness and the anger like a diver coming up through murky waters. When I glimpsed her then, in those moments, I knew that this was the real Catherine Tierney, the good and kind woman, my mother, and someone I wouldn't see very often because she had to work so very hard to find her way out of that dark inward place.

"When do you think you'll be home, Ma?" I asked.

"I don't know for sure," she said. She turned back to the mirror and applied the lipstick. "Midafternoon, I suppose." She moved her eyes from her reflection to mine, lifted her brows. "You'll be all right alone?"

I nodded. "Josef will be here."

"Yes. We've asked him to answer the phone while we're gone. If it rings, you let him answer it, you hear?" She paused and drew in a deep breath. She seemed to be trying to gather her thoughts. "I'm not expecting any calls but, well, just in case there's any word about Dewey."

"All right," I said.

Dewey had been transferred the previous day from St. Paul's Anchor Hospital to Minneapolis General. Affiliated with the University of Minnesota, General Hospital was an old gray-stone and yellow-brick building in the heart of downtown Minneapolis. Ma had agreed to the transfer, while at the same time feeling a bit unnerved by it. She wondered what it meant for Dewey. One nurse tried to brush off Ma's concerns by saying that the hospitals were receiving so many polio patients, they were playing a sort of musical chairs game to try to make room for them all. But one of Dewey's doctors told Ma that General was better equipped to handle a higher number of the more severe polio cases. By the doctor's accounting, Dewey's transfer hardly sounded like a game to Ma, and she was bracing herself—almost uncannily, as it turned out—for bad news.

Ma applied a little more powder, another dab of rouge. "Well," she said, sighing heavily, "I guess I'm as ready as I'll ever be."

I stationed myself at the front window in the parlor and watched as Ma and Auntie left to catch the streetcar to the funeral. I decided I would stay right there on the divan until they got back. I had a lot of thinking to do.

I had to convince myself that Andy Johanson was dead, and it wasn't going to be easy. The last time I'd seen him, not very long ago, he'd been in perfect health—pink-cheeked and energetic. He could run faster than either Dewey or Jerry, swim farther than almost any other kid, and jump effortlessly onto the tail of Mr. Butterfield's moving streetcar, even when the other kids had to leap twice or even three times to make it. He was unstoppable. Or he had been until polio stopped him.

I wondered how he had caught it, or maybe more accurately, how it had caught him. Had it been hanging around the Grandview Theater when Andy went to a matinee? Had it been lying in wait in the kitchen of Mickey's Diner when Andy ate there with his dad? However polio got him, it hadn't happened the day they went swimming at Cedar Lake, though that may have been when it got Dewey. But Dewey said Andy was already sick by then, already showing signs of it, though at first they thought it was the flu.

When he got worse, Andy's parents kept him in bed for days, trying to nurse him back to health with mustard packs and chicken soup. By the time his father carried him out to the car and drove him to Anchor Hospital, he was scarcely able to breathe. Almost as soon as he was diagnosed, he went into the lung. And almost as soon as he went into the lung, he caught a cold. It started out as just the sniffles, something you would otherwise hardly even notice. Just a bit of a runny nose that turned into a cold that turned into pneumonia and soon got so bad that not even the respirator could keep his lungs pumping the air in and out of him. That's what Ma learned from Alice Johanson when Ma called to offer her condolences.

She also learned that Mrs. Johanson blamed herself. She said she should have listened to her own common sense and taken Andy to a doctor much sooner. She just kept thinking—hoping—it was flu and that he'd get over it with rest and home remedies.

Ma speculated to Aunt Dortha that the Johansons' finances probably had something to do with it. She thought they probably didn't take Andy to the doctor because they were having too much trouble paying their bills as it was. Mr. Johanson had been out of work all those months last winter with his back injury, and the family had gone into debt. Now he was working again, but it was going to take a while to get back to where they were before Mr. Johanson's accident.

Ma knew about the Johansons' money situation only because Andy told Dewey and Dewey told Ma. Dewey added that when he went to Andy's house, Mrs. Johanson was more often than not lying on the couch with a headache brought on by worry. "She has a sick headache," was how Andy put it, "because we don't have enough money to pay the bills. Dad tells her to get up and just keep taking care of us kids and let him worry about the money, but she says she can't help worrying, and she can't get up either, not when the sick headaches come."

So she'd lie there worrying about losing the house and going hungry and having to appeal for help to her brother in Albuquerque or maybe her brother-in-law in Sausalito. But even if her brother or brother-in-law would take in a family of five and feed them, how would the Johansons get from St. Paul to Albuquerque or Sausalito when they didn't even have the bus fare to get as far west as the border with South Dakota?

She worried a lot about these things, but she needn't have worried. They didn't happen. What did happen instead was that Andy caught polio. He went out somewhere and caught polio and then caught a cold that turned into pneumonia, and now Andy Johanson was dead.

There was a time when I sat at the same window I was sitting at now waiting for my dead father to arrive from Wisconsin. If I had learned anything, it was that dead people don't come back. Not my father. Not Andy Johanson.

Still, I couldn't bring myself to believe it. How I wanted Andy Johanson to be not Houdini but Lazarus, the man who unwrapped his own shroud and walked out of the tomb after three days of hobnobbing with human bones.

It didn't help that Eva Lassiter chose just that moment to sit down at the piano and sing "I'll Be Seeing You." She didn't seem to notice me kneeling on the divan by the open window, my elbows propped up on the sill, the tip of my nose kissing the screen. She just came walking into the parlor as she did almost every morning to play the piano and sing for an hour or so. She was wearing one of her drop-waist paisley print dresses and a pair of spike-heeled sandals that revealed the fiery red polish on her toenails. Her fingers were likewise capped in red, and every one of them, save for the thumbs, was dressed to the hilt in gold and gemstones. Rhinestones were her favorite, she said, though she also owned a sapphire ring that had belonged to her second husband's first wife, a jade ring that her first husband, in the Merchant Marine, had brought back from the Orient, and a turquoise ring that was a gift from an Indian she'd met when she and Ida were playing vaudeville in Arizona back in 1922.

I turned from the window, slumped down on the divan, and watched her for a moment. Her profile, with the dark mascara-thickened eyelash, the circle of rouge on her cheek, the vibrant red on her lips, was sadly unflattering. All the makeup in the world couldn't hide the sagging jowls, the hanging bag of flesh beneath her chin, the iron-rod tendons protruding from her neck. Her arms were white and flaccid, and her muscles quivered from shoulder to elbow as she ran her fingers over the keys. But her voice wasn't bad. In fact, she was a very good singer, and she could even hit some notes that, on a day like this when the windows were open, could send a whole flock of birds on the telephone lines into a fluttery flight of alarm.

Generally speaking, I enjoyed listening to her sing. But not today. Not at the very moment that Andy Johanson was being put into the ground. When she started in on "Danny Boy," it nearly broke me up, but when she moved on to "It's Only a Paper Moon" and "You Are My Lucky Star," I burst out crying. I couldn't think about the moon and the stars without thinking of Dewey.

She couldn't hear me weeping over her own singing, and by the time she finished with a chorus of "Boogie Woogie Bugle Boy," I had dried my eyes with the front of my shirt and more or less pulled myself together.

Just then she turned to me abruptly and, fingering the knot of her pearl necklace, said, "You know what I'm going to do, Nova?"

I was startled by her words and by the fact that she knew I was there. I shook my head and said, "No, Miss Eva. What?"

Her eyes brightened as she threw up her hands. "I'm going to teach you to play the piano!"

"You are?" Not particularly interested in learning to play, I didn't know how to respond. Ma had never suggested I learn, and I was rather relieved to have avoided thus far what so many of my peers were forced to undergo—the dreaded piano lessons.

"Yes, child, of course! Why didn't I think of it days ago?" Eva Lassiter was visibly excited by her idea. "You need something to do until your brother comes home."

I caught my breath. What had she said? In the slow crush of days since Dewey had entered the hospital, no one had suggested to me so positively that he would be coming home. But here was Eva Lassiter, throwing out the suggestion as though it was a given. *"You need something to do until your brother comes home."* Just like that!

Suddenly I liked Eva Lassiter more than I ever had.

"All right," I said. "I think I might like to learn—"

Before I could finish, though, something happened that I was quickly beginning to dread. The telephone rang.

————

Ma didn't cry when Josef told her the hospital called to say Dewey had been put into an iron lung. She just stood there in the front hall like she was one of Michelangelo's sculptures on display in a museum in Rome. Though even a face carved out of stone undoubtedly held more warmth and expression than Ma's face at that moment.

It was almost two o'clock when she and Aunt Dortha returned from the funeral, looking flushed and wilted from the heat. They were pulling off their hats and gloves as they walked in through the front door, and that's where Josef met them, saying, "Mrs. Tierney, there's been word from the hospital."

She hadn't even pulled off her second glove when Josef told her about the call. She stood there frozen in the steamy afternoon heat, one glove on and the other one off, crushing her hat in clawlike hands, the black hat with the little fishnet veil that she kept for occasions like funerals. I remember thinking that the hat would be ruined if she didn't stop squeezing it so hard.

No one moved or spoke, until it seemed that the house

might come crashing in on us under the unbearable weight of the silence. I thought Ma would want to know all that the hospital had said about Dewey, but she said nothing at all, not one word.

At long last Josef spoke again. "His breathing was becoming increasingly difficult. They felt they had no other recourse but to put him into the respirator. I'm sorry, Mrs. Tierney."

Aunt Dortha took a few steps forward, laying her hat and gloves on the telephone table. She turned to Josef. "Did they say how long they expect him to be in it?"

Josef shook his head. "No, Mrs. Severson, they couldn't say for certain. But they did say he was cooperative, that he wanted to be put in the machine and that he found it to be a great relief. They said he is doing well now."

"Doing well?" Ma's words startled me, startled us all. She said them again, only louder this time, and the eyes she turned on Josef were wild with anger. "Doing well?" And then she laughed, and it was a laugh that came from a bitter place, welling up from somewhere inside and escaping her throat like a curse thrown over the world. "How can they say he's doing well when they've put him into an iron lung? Don't you know what that means?"

She directed her question at Josef, and she took one step toward him, openly challenging him for an answer. "Don't you know what that means?" she repeated.

Josef raised a hand, a white flag of surrender. "Mrs. Tierney, I—"

"Catherine," Aunt Dortha interrupted, "Mr. Karski is only telling you what the hospital—"

"It means he can't breathe!" Ma shrieked. "It means if he

weren't in that lung, he'd be dead! Dead!"

I took a few steps backward into the parlor.

"Mrs. Tierney—"

"Catherine," Aunt Dortha said firmly, stepping toward Ma, reaching out for her hand. Ma pulled away. "You must calm down, Catherine. We'll call the hospital. We'll go there, if you want, and find out exactly what's going on. Going into an iron lung isn't a death sentence. People come out of them, you know. People do survive and come out of them."

The hall was quiet again. Josef took a breath. "Mrs. Tierney," he said gently, "they cannot say, of course, how long he will be in the lung, but their assumption is that it will only be temporary. That is what they told me."

"Of course," Aunt Dortha said, trying to sound optimistic. "Of course it's only temporary. As I said, people come out of these iron lungs and go on to lead productive lives. We'll pray for just that same outcome for Dewey."

By the time Auntie finished, Ma was stone again. She turned blue marble eyes on Auntie's face. There was nothing in those eyes now, not anger, not bitterness, not sadness. Nothing at all. The emptiness of her eyes was chilling.

She spoke so quietly it was almost a whisper. "Thirty years ago I prayed. Have you forgotten, Dortha?"

Auntie held out her hand again and took Ma's arm, a pleading grip. "Oh, Catherine," she sighed. "You mustn't—"

"As soon as I change my clothes," Ma interrupted, "I'm going to the hospital. I need to see"—she shut her eyes, raised a hand to her head, opened her eyes again—"I need to be near my son." She turned and entered our apartment, quietly shutting the door behind her.

I was left to wonder what had happened thirty years ago and what it had to do with Dewey and the iron lung and our lives on Selby Avenue in 1948.

SPANISH FLU

I had a lot of time to wonder about it because I wouldn't know for years what had happened in 1918. At least not what had happened to Ma, though somewhere along the way—in school, most likely—I did learn about the more significant world events of that year. Specifically, I learned that 1918 brought the end of the Great War, which was pretty big news for the United States, of course. What I didn't learn—in school or otherwise—was that that year marked another major event as well. Beginning in the autumn of 1918, Spanish flu swept the globe in a vast epidemic, wiping out more people even than those who had died in the war.

Historians call it the forgotten pandemic. Who, after all, would want to remember a modern-day plague, this deceptive intruder that tiptoed in with a sneeze and a cough only to drown millions of men, women, and children in the bloody fluid of their own lungs? Once it was over, all mention of influenza was dropped from conversation, shoved to the untapped places of the mind, and consequently not passed along to the next generation the way the stories of our victory in the war were passed along. Certainly Ma never talked about it. It had changed her life completely, wreaking far more havoc in her family than the war, but she never once mentioned it to me until she started telling her tales just before she died.

Catherine Tierney was born in 1913 in Mankato, Minnesota, the first child of Frederick and Marianne Skoglund. Her father was a carpenter by trade, a rogue at heart, and something of a disappointment to his own father, who, at the time of Catherine's birth, was a well-respected and longtime banker there in Mankato. It wasn't that Frederick Jr. was such a rascal. He wasn't really. He was simply full of wanderlust, restless when he wasn't moving. When he married Marianne Renwick in 1911, everyone said it couldn't last—not the way Freddie came and went, traveling here and there on a whim and no one ever quite sure where he was.

But time showed the rumormongers wrong. The marriage did last, was quite happy, and was the one thing that could and did make a settled man out of Frederick Skoglund Jr. He worked for a time at a sawmill before starting his own business, and he moved his wife and infant daughter out of his parents' home and into a small but respectable house in the same neighborhood.

Catherine remembered her father as the man with the unshakeable smile. Frederick Skoglund would go to work smiling, and he'd come home smiling, and if he was momentarily not smiling because he was busy reading the newspaper or shaving or tying a tie, still his face seemed poised on the edge of mirth, his muscles just aching to break into a grin. He was a kind man who loved his wife and daughter and did his best by them.

Catherine described her mother as a woman of grace and equanimity. A rock of serenity, Marianne Skoglund allowed very little to upset her. Burnt pudding, a cracked teacup, her husband's occasional announcement that business was slow and money was tight—all left her equally unruffled. She went about her tasks of homemaking and mothering as though they were the most delightful tasks in the world.

From Catherine's perspective, hers was an idyllic childhood, filled with the security of her parents' love and the simple pleasures of a house filled with sunlight and pretty things, a table set with floral china and good food, a bedroom that was a haven to her and her dolls and her beloved cat Maisie.

But it was a childhood that didn't last long. Instead, it was all too short, cut off as it was by the Great War, left terrifyingly insecure on the day her father stepped out and enlisted.

Frederick Skoglund put on a uniform, said good-bye and, smiling still, went off to defend democracy. Marianne said she was proud of him and of course he had to go. It was his duty. And she sounded very brave when she said it, though she was crying all the while. It was the first time Catherine ever saw her mother cry.

For Catherine, life changed completely in one swift moment, and she found herself feeling unbearably lost. Papa, who had always been there, was gone, and Mama, who had never cried, was crying, and even the house that she'd always called home wasn't their house anymore. Papa had thought it best to rent it out while he was gone, so Catherine and Mama went back to live in the big old house with Grandfather and Grandmother Skoglund.

"We will pray," Mama told her. "We'll pray every day, without exception, that your papa will come home to us safely and we'll be a family again." And they did. Every day. Morning and evening they asked God to bring Papa home from battle so they could all be together, just like before.

Whenever a letter from Papa arrived, Mama and Grandfather and Grandmother and Catherine all gathered in the parlor to read it. Grandfather slit open the envelope carefully with his silver letter opener, then settled his pince-nez on the end of his nose, and squinting slightly at the flimsy square of paper, he'd begin to read in his gruff, monotonous voice.

Papa always said he was fine, that he missed and loved everyone, and "Don't worry, Mother, I am keeping my head down and saying my prayers." He never said where he was, but he tried to give what news he could of the war, though he had to be vague and even cryptic, and sometimes when he got a little too talkative, thick black lines tied a gag around his sentences, courtesy of the government censor.

He never failed to include a special message for Catherine that left her feeling warm and as though Papa wasn't so far away after all: "I love you, my darling girl. Be good for Mother while I'm away," or "I think of you all the time, dearest Catherine, and send you a kiss and my love."

As the days passed, life settled into a comfortable routine, and Catherine's initial fears grew to a more manageable size. She heard about doughboys and Huns and mustard gas and

General John Pershing and faraway places like Belgium and France, but it all meant little to her. There was too much on the home front to hold her attention—Liberty bond parades, Red Cross canteens, and everywhere boys playacting in the streets, pretending to be Eddie Rickenbacker, flying ace, pride of the American Army Air Service! And then too holidays still came and went, and children still had birthday parties, and people still went to the movies and laughed at the bumbling antics of the Keystone Kops and the endearing stupidity of the Little Tramp.

And then there was Aunt Lizzie the suffragette, a person of some interest to Catherine, a dependable distraction in a time of war. Papa's older sister, she was a large beefy woman who marched though the streets with a sash across her bosom and a sign in her hands demanding the vote for women. She'd been arrested several times and hauled off to jail, but that left her undeterred in her fight for the cause. Aunt Lizzie's husband was opposed to the idea of women voters, a fact that caused some friction in their marriage. So whenever it came time for Aunt Lizzie to host the meeting for her fellow suffragettes, she invited them all to Grandfather and Grandmother's house. For Catherine, it was like having a party every time the women came, with the shouting, the whooping, the singing, and the general gaiety among the suffragettes. Even Grandmother and Mama attended the meetings, though they were more reserved than most and never ever wore a sash across their bosoms or marched in the streets.

In January of 1918, when Papa had been gone for half a year, a wondrous thing happened. A baby arrived in the house! Catherine was sent off to Aunt Lizzie's one morning, and when she arrived home in the evening, there she was, a baby sister, pink, perfect, adorable.

"Her name is Amanda," Mama said, smiling. She looked up at Catherine with shining eyes and added, "God is good."

Oh yes! God was good! Never had she expected something like this. A baby sister! How grand it would be when Papa came home and all four of them were together living as a family again in their own little home.

Winter passed, then spring, then summer came. Mama and Catherine were playing with baby Amanda one warm afternoon when a young delivery boy from Western Union rang the doorbell. Grandfather answered the door, grimly accepted the telegram, tipped the boy, and sent him on his way.

"What does it say?" Grandmother demanded. She had an arm around Mama, who was holding Amanda. Grandmother seemed angry with Grandfather because the telegram had arrived. "Tell us what it says, Frederick. Don't keep us waiting."

Grandfather opened the telegram slowly and read the message in silence. Mama swayed slightly as though she might fall, but Grandmother's strong arm held her up. Grandfather looked up, took off his pince-nez, and let it rest against the stiff, starched whiteness of his shirt. "He's been wounded." Mama's knees almost buckled; her face turned upward. Grandmother sighed audibly, a balloon losing air. "He's in a hospital in France," Grandfather continued crisply.

"Thank God, he's alive," Grandmother whispered.

Catherine threw her arms around her mother's waist. Papa was wounded but alive!

"Then he'll be coming home, won't he?" Mama asked.

"I don't know," Grandfather said. He glanced once more at the telegram before folding it up. "It's possible they'll send him back—"

"Oh no, they couldn't! Not if he's been wounded."

Grandmother led Mama down the hall toward the kitchen, saying, "We'll find out more in time. For now, let's just be glad he's out of harm's way for a while."

In time they did find out. His wounds were such that he couldn't go back into battle. He'd be coming home! He wrote to his wife and daughters, "I'm fine, my darlings. I shall be home soon, and we'll all be together, all four of us."

Oh yes, God was good.

"Papa's coming home," Catherine told her baby sister, and the child cooed and smiled just as though she understood. Catherine showed Amanda their father's photograph and told her stories about him so the baby would know who Papa was when he came home from the war. She could just see it now—what a day! Papa coming up the walk in his uniform, smiling like he'd never smiled before, opening his arms as Catherine came running to meet him! What a day it would be.

Mama talked about moving home again and putting up new curtains and planting a vegetable garden in the spring. Catherine was sure all would be just as it had been before Papa left, only better because now Amanda was with them.

While Mama and Catherine were planning and dreaming, something was happening in faraway Boston. On September seventh, at Camp Devens, a soldier of Company B, Forty-second Infantry, went on sick call with a cough, sore throat, fever, headache. Something like common flu, the doctors said, only worse. The next day a dozen men of the same company showed up at the hospital with the same symptoms.

By September twenty-third more than twelve thousand men were ill at Camp Devens. By the end of October, the number rose to seventeen thousand. And by then nearly eight hundred of them had died.

They were calling it the Spanish influenza. It exploded across the East Coast, then the West Coast, and then it traveled inward and merged in the Midwest. It showed up in Minnesota during the last days of September, just as autumn was settling in.

The Bureau of Health warned that anyone exposed to the Spanish influenza would come down with the illness within two days. Stay home, they admonished. Stay home! And if you must leave the house, do not cough, do not sneeze, do not spit! And wear a mask. Don't go anywhere without wearing a mask.

Everywhere, people walked the streets with gauze wrapped around their faces. Mummies paraded about the town. Eyes flashed fear, but what could be done? People had to go to work, had to go to the market for food, had to make their way home again. People had to at least do this much, though many places—theaters, restaurants, schools, pool halls, even churches—closed their doors during the epidemic. Cities everywhere—all over the state, all over the country—shut down like ghost towns. Only the hospitals were bustling, their wards and hallways crowded, overflowing with the ill, the feverish, the delirious. Overflowing with the dead. So many dead the morgues and the gravediggers couldn't keep up with them all. So many dead there weren't enough coffins to hold them all. So many dead the bodies of those who never even made it to the hospital were left in homes for days on end until the bereaved went out and dug the graves for the dead themselves.

And oddly, eerily, out on the sidewalks, in backyards, in echoing alleyways little girls jumped rope, chanting, "I had a little bird / And its name was Enza. / I opened the window / And in-flew-Enza." While they jumped and chanted, their mothers died and their fathers died, their brothers and sisters died, and half the town lay on their death beds, yet still the girls went on chanting about a bird named Enza.

For Catherine, confined to the house, watching the world through small square panes of glass, it started as a dull ache behind the eyes. So small as to be almost imperceptible. So dull as not to be worthy of any attention at all at first. She went on stroking Maisie's fur and teasing the cat with a piece of yarn. She had seen all the worried looks passed between Mama and Grandmother, heard all the whispered words:

" . . . wife and son both, and they were all the family poor Mr. Grady had. . . ."

" . . . and the hospital so full, the sick are lined up side by side in the halls. . . ."

" . . . calling for volunteers . . ."

" . . . and yet how could we, of course, knowing we might bring it home. . . ."

"It's everywhere, everywhere. France too, of course, and I can't help but think of Freddie there in the hospital among all the sick. . . ."

"We can pray. That's all we can do. . . ."

" . . . and yet how many more? How many more before this is all over?"

Catherine hadn't been exposed, of course. Since the first warnings of flu had hit the newspapers, Catherine hadn't been allowed out of the house. Not even to play alone in the yard. She couldn't come down with this Spanish influenza. And yet the ache grew a little bit worse, and her eyes began to burn. She was tired—yes, that was all. She would just lie down and close her eyes, and everything would be all right.

Mama came and laid a cool hand on her forehead, and Catherine thought, "Funny, her hand is so cool, but her eyes are bright, like fire." She couldn't guess that it was horror burning in her mother's eyes. What was there to be afraid of, after all? Catherine hadn't been where people were coughing or sneezing or spitting. She hadn't been around anyone at all except Mama and Grandmother and Grandfather and baby Amanda. She was simply tired. She wanted to sleep.

She slept, a restless sleep. It may have been minutes or hours. It may have been days. She had no way to know. Time no longer flowed but existed only in fragments. Faces appeared in those fractured spaces, one at a time, hovering over her. Mama, Grandmother, a gray-haired woman wearing a gauze mask, a bespectacled man who held her wrist and pried her eyelids apart with his doughy fingers. When he spoke, his words came out only as a dull buzzing noise, not as words at all. Who was this man standing over her droning like a bee, this old woman who came wrapped up like a mummy with only her piercing black eyes blinking above the gauze? Who were they, and why had they invaded these passing tableaus that had become her life?

Then there were the strange, vacillating seasons of hot and cold. One moment she was so cold she was shivering, and in the next so hot she felt a fire licking her bones. The cold was bearable. She just had to roll herself up in a ball, her arms hugging her legs, until the shivering passed. It was the heat that gave her no relief. Whenever the fire came, a lake appeared in the distance, a lake that rippled as a breeze blew across its back, and she knew if she could just reach the lake she'd be all right. She could step into the cool water, sink into it, submerge herself in it, and let the cold put out the fire in her bones. If she could only reach the water. But hands held her back. No, not hands but vines, growing up out of the earth like leafy snakes and twining themselves around her arms, her legs, even her skull, squeezing so tightly that every muscle, every joint ached. She strained against them, turning this way and that, pulling against the savage vines, but they were too strong. They would never let her go, never let her reach the lake. They would hold her until she was completely consumed by the fire, a martyr tied to the stake.

Grandmother's face hovered above her, frowning, etched with lines of concern. Grandmother came and went . . . but where was Mama? There was the mummy in her shroud of gauze . . . but where was Mama? The man with the spectacles who buzzed like a bee and, from some bottomless canyon in her brain, children chanting, "I had a little bird. . . ." But where was Mama? If only she could reach the water, that cool, shivering lake . . . Mama . . . "And its name was Enza, / I opened the window . . ." Mama, where are you? "And in-flew-Enza. . . ." Mama!

Once she thought she saw her father's face, but Catherine knew she had to be dreaming. Papa was in France, in a hospital in France. She shut her eyes, and when she opened them again, there was no one there. She turned on her side toward the pale light in the window. Was it morning or evening? She didn't know. Wondering, she fell again into a deep sleep.

When she awoke, the window was radiant with sunlight, a full afternoon light that sliced through the window in sharp, slanted rays. She lay there thinking, wondering, feeling something that only at length she came to recognize as nothing. It was the absence of pain. The fire no longer crawled through her bones. The vines were no longer wrapped around her limbs. She had escaped the darkness and the fire and the cold and had returned to her room in Grandfather and Grandmother's house.

"Catherine."

She turned toward the voice. For a moment she thought the face gazing intently upon her own was only another fragment out of chronological sync, a fever image surfacing from another time, because it was her father's face there above her bed.

It couldn't be Papa. It couldn't be. This man was old and tired, his face webbed with furrows that shouldn't be there. His eyes were sad, and worse, there was no smile, not even a hint of a smile around his lips.

"Papa?" She raised her small hand to touch his face, as though to see if the image were solid, made of flesh.

"Yes, darling." He took her hand, pressing her palm against his cheek.

Catherine gazed up at him in amazement. It *was* Papa. He was alive! He was home!

"Papa!" She tried to sit up. She wanted to throw her arms around his neck, but she couldn't find the strength to do more than lift her head, and that only for a moment.

"You rest," he ordered quietly. He kissed her hand, laid it gently on the bed. "You rest now."

"But, Papa, where's Mama?"

He touched her forehead, pushing the hair back from her face. "You rest."

He rose to go.

"But, Papa—"

A finger to his lips, he left the room. Catherine didn't understand, but still—Papa was home! Of course he was tired. He'd been fighting in the war. He'd been wounded in battle. He'd spent weeks in a hospital in France. Of course he was tired. But things would get better. Everything would be all right now that Papa was home. God had answered her prayers. God was good.

————————

It might have been the next day—time was still elusive—that she ventured from her bed to go next door to her mother's room. Never had she felt so weak, every step a reaching into the reserves of her strength just to put one leg in front of the other. By the time she reached the door of her mother's bedroom, she was exhausted. She had to lean up against the doorframe for a moment to catch her breath. Across the room, in the large canopied bed, she saw her mother's face upon the pillow. Mama was sleeping.

Catherine smiled briefly. "Mama?" It was a whisper, all she could manage. Her mother didn't hear her. She would have to go closer to wake her up.

One deep breath and she moved forward. She had almost reached the bed when she stopped. Baby Amanda lay at her mother's side in the crook of one arm. Mama's other arm rested across her own rib cage, and her hand rested over Amanda's heart, as if Mama was soothing the infant, comforting her before sleep. But Amanda was still. Too still. Mama was still. The quilt that partially covered them didn't rise and fall. No eyelid fluttered, no muscle twitched in sleep. Their skin was the color of white ash with splotches of brownish purple.

"Mama?" It was still a whisper.

Catherine studied the figures on the bed, trying frantically to understand. What were they doing, Mama and Amanda? Why were they lying there like this? When were they going to get up? Because they would be getting up again, wouldn't they? Surely they would wake up just as she herself had come back from that fractured place and opened her eyes to see the light in the window.

"There are so many dead," Grandmother had said, *"that there's no place to put them any longer. They are lying in their homes for days, waiting for the undertaker. . . ."*

"Mama!" she screamed, and she felt herself falling, but before she could reach the floor, strong arms caught her up and carried her away from her mother's side.

———

God had brought Papa home safely, but Mama and

Amanda would never rise to greet him. They would never even know he'd made it back, and that made everything wrong! This wasn't how Catherine had pictured her father's homecoming at all. This wasn't what Catherine had prayed for. It was a cruel joke or a dreadful twist of fate or maybe a nightmare come true, but it wasn't the answer a child expected from a merciful God.

She had never feared for her mother and herself all the while the war was raging, not even for a moment. They'd been safe at home, after all. They'd been watching the Liberty bond parades and going to Charlie Chaplin movies and cheering on the suffragettes, never suspecting their safe routine could be toppled by something like flu. It was Papa who had been in harm's way. It was Papa who might have been killed any minute, caught in a barrage of enemy fire. Papa was the one who had to stay alive so the family could be together again.

"The irony of it," Grandfather muttered. He spat out the words like he was spitting at the feet of someone who had cursed him.

Catherine didn't know what Grandfather meant by irony. She only knew that Papa was alive, and Mama and Amanda were dead, and in spite of her prayers and hopes, their family would be forever broken.

Papa tore apart a wardrobe and fashioned it into a coffin. Then he slung a shovel over his shoulder and walked to the cemetery to dig a grave. About noon the next day a horse-drawn wagon stopped at Grandfather's house and took the coffin away. If there was a funeral, Catherine heard nothing about it.

———

Only days later she was stunned to see people dancing in the streets. All the whistles and sirens in the town were let loose; fire engines screamed down the avenues while the firemen tossed confetti from atop the pumpers. People rang cowbells, waved flags, danced, sang, cheered.

"What is it, Grandma?" Catherine asked.

"The war is over," Grandmother answered. She closed the latches on Catherine's suitcase.

Catherine was holding her cat, stroking its fur. "Are you sure Maisie can't come with me?" she asked.

"I'm sorry, child," Grandmother said. "But don't worry. I'll take good care of her. I promise."

Hours later, people were still celebrating at the station as Catherine stood waiting for the train with Papa. A bitter wind blew across the open platform, chilling Catherine to the bone. She held on tightly to her father's hand while nestling against his coat for warmth. She thought she must be the only one to notice the cold. Everyone else was too busy waving flags, laughing, whooping, slapping each other on the back. A tipsy reveler reached for Papa's hand to shake it, tripped as he did and fell, very nearly dragging Papa down onto the platform with him. Papa pulled his hand away, frowning, disgusted.

The carnival atmosphere made a strange stage of the station platform, and the scenery was all wrong for a little girl whose script called for her to say good-bye. Catherine Skoglund had a ticket for the afternoon train to Chippewa Falls, Wisconsin. That was where Mama's sister, Susannah Biddle, lived with her husband, Haddon Biddle, and their four sons. After a long telephone conversation, Papa and Aunt Susannah had decided it was best for Catherine to live with the Biddles.

When the train pulled into the station, stopping in a great hiss of steam, Catherine knew instinctively that she would never see Papa and Grandmother and Grandfather again. She knew she was leaving Mankato forever. And she was right.

THE PICKUP TRUCK

Toward the end of the first week of August, Dewey was let out of quarantine. By that time, of course, when Ma finally got to see him, he was just a head sticking out of that huge awful cylinder known as an iron lung. I don't know what happened during that meeting, what was said between mother and son when they saw each other. Neither one ever told me. But I think it just about killed Ma to see Dewey like that. When she got home, she didn't even look like a person any longer. She looked more like a ghostly apparition, a doomed soul stuck between heaven and earth, forever forbidden to rest in peace.

Ma gave up her job at the bakery to spend the afternoons at the hospital instead. It meant a loss of income for our family, but I don't think she debated for as much as a minute how her time could best be spent. "Whenever you want to come back," Mr. Turnquist assured her, "your job will be waiting for you." Mr. Turnquist, the owner of the bakery, had a son who'd come down with polio when the big epidemic hit in 1946, so he knew what Ma was facing. "Tommy—he got better!" the baker exclaimed, waving his arms as though he were performing a magic trick. "To look at him today, you'd never know he was one sick kid a couple of years ago."

Ma tried to take comfort from the fact that Tommy Turnquist came through his bout with polio without any apparent lasting effects. But then, Tommy Turnquist hadn't had to spend time in an iron lung. He hadn't even been in the hospital for very long. Ma tried to be encouraged, but there wasn't any use comparing Tommy and Dewey, apples and oranges.

Aunt Dortha still needed Ma's help running the house in the morning, but by two o'clock each afternoon Ma was on the streetcar headed for the hospital. She might take the Selby-Lake line into Minneapolis and change at Chicago Avenue, or she might walk nine blocks up Lexington to catch the direct line into downtown. In the extreme heat or brutal cold of Minnesota, either route could be equally unpleasant. But all that would eventually change, thanks to our neighbor Mr. Thomas Diehl.

Mr. Diehl had been coming over every night since Dewey went into the hospital. He generally showed up with fresh-cut flowers from his garden, and I assumed his intentions were to talk with Ma. But Ma, of course, wouldn't talk with him because she said she wasn't up to talking with anybody. He came over anyway and sat at the kitchen table with Aunt Dortha, who gave him the latest news on Dewey while they downed tall glasses of iced tea.

Shortly after Dewey was moved to Minneapolis General,

Mr. Diehl didn't show up for several nights running. Ma didn't bother to inquire about his sudden absence. She may not have even noticed he was gone. But on the third night that he didn't cross the street to our house with a bunch of phlox, columbine, or larkspur in his hand, I asked Aunt Dortha what had happened to him.

"He's gone to his uncle's funeral over in Sioux Falls," Auntie explained. "He should be home in a day or two."

He had gone by train to South Dakota, but he returned home a few days later behind the wheel of a car. No, that's not quite true. He came back to St. Paul driving the ugliest pickup truck ever to roll down Selby Avenue. Its hubcaps were missing, its brick-red paint was freckled with rust, and its rear bumper—what was left of it—was tied on with chicken wire and rope. It didn't sound right either. Instead of a smooth, humming motor sound, it seemed to growl and moan and scream all at the same time. When it appeared on our street like some animated metal creature in a horror flick, all the neighborhood kids, including me, ran out to get a look at it.

Thomas Diehl pulled up in front of his house, cut the engine—the silence was jarring—got out of the truck, and patted its flaking hood. "Well, boys and girls," he said to the gathering crowd, "what do you think?" He actually looked kind of proud.

"What is it, Mr. Diehl?" shrieked Hannah Lou Houlihan.

Her older brother Harry answered. "It's a pickup truck, stupid. Don't you know nothing?" He sounded disgusted, but he was generally disgusted where Hannah Lou was concerned.

"It's a 1937 Chevrolet pickup, to be exact," Thomas

Diehl stated emphatically. "Belonged to my uncle Luther before he died. Now she's mine. Isn't she something?"

Harry Houlihan looked at the truck doubtfully. "She's something, all right."

By now at least a dozen kids were circling the vehicle, their eyes reflecting a morbid curiosity, their faces pinched as though they smelled something bad. No one appeared certain they wanted to touch it. I heard Sally Winter whisper to Mary Jane Prescott, "I bet that thing's got a million cooties."

"But what are you gonna do with it, Mr. Diehl?" It was Hannah Lou again, and she was still shrieking.

"I'm going to fix her up." He patted the hood once more, with definite pride this time. "Another week or two, you won't recognize her." I didn't like the way he kept referring to the old rattletrap as a "she," but I didn't say anything.

"Whadd'ya need a jalopy like this for?" Harry asked skeptically. "You got a car already."

Just then one of the boys, Billy Lundeen—he wasn't afraid of anything—jumped up on the running board on the driver's side, stuck his hand in through the open window, and honked the horn. ARR-ROO-GAA! "Hey!" he cried. "Sounds like a Tin Lizzy!" He laughed and honked the horn again, and the truck must have suddenly appeared friendly after all, because instantly all the kids wanted to honk the horn while plying Mr. Diehl with a dozen questions at once.

"Will you take us for a ride in the back, Mr. Diehl?"

"Will you teach me to drive it, Mr. Diehl?"

"Will you pull us from behind when the roads are icy?"

"You think it can do fifty?"

"Can we jump outa the back?"

"Can I work the gearshift while you're doing the clutch, Mr. Diehl?"

The old jalopy's new owner patted the air with both hands, palms down. "All right, all right. Listen, kids," he said, "I might take you for a ride or two, but soon as I get it fixed up, I'm giving it away."

"Aww!"

"Giving it away!"

"Who to, Mr. Diehl?"

"You can't do that!"

"Who'd want it anyway?"

Yes, who'd want it anyway? Thomas Diehl didn't answer any of our questions, but he let us all take a turn sitting behind the wheel. The hot leather seat was cracked in places so that the stuffing beneath showed through, the glass covering the speedometer and the odometer was shattered, and the inside of the cab smelled like must, mold, and what I can only describe as a thousand pounds of sweat that Thomas Diehl's uncle must have shed in there over the years. Who in the world would want to ride around in a smelly old truck like this?

Certainly Ma didn't. She didn't even have to say so. I could see it clearly on her face the next evening when Mr. Diehl came over and presented her with the key. She stared at that key for the longest time, speechless. Mr. Diehl was grinning so hard I think he must have thought she was overcome with emotion or gratitude, but I knew it was nothing like that. When she finally mustered up the strength or maybe the civility to ask him what the key was to, she was hoping he wouldn't say it was to the truck he'd brought home from

South Dakota, but he said it anyway.

"Belonged to my uncle Luther, but he passed away," Mr. Diehl explained. "Aunt Miriam says she has no use for it now, so she gave it to me. But I want to give it to you, Mrs. Tierney. As soon as I get it all fixed up, that is. Maybe I should have waited till then to tell you, but I wanted you to know it's coming."

He was still smiling. Ma wasn't. She was speechless again. Aunt Dortha chose this moment to join them at the front door. "Evening, Thomas," she said, wiping her hands on her apron. "Won't you come in? Plenty of fresh iced tea in the refrigerator. Lemonade too, if you prefer."

"Can't stay, but thanks, Dortha," he said. "Thought I'd start sanding down the truck this evening. I'd like to get it ready soon as possible for Mrs. Tierney."

Now Mr. Diehl and Aunt Dortha both were smiling. Ma wasn't. "But for what, Mr. Diehl?" Ma asked, sounding flustered. I was watching from the parlor, and at that moment I crossed my fingers behind my back in hopes Ma wouldn't get mad. I still hadn't dropped Thomas Diehl completely from my short list of potential fathers. "What on earth would I need a truck for?"

"To visit Dewey, of course." He said it as though it should have been obvious in the first place.

"To visit Dewey?" Ma repeated.

"Why, yes. He's been moved to Minneapolis, hasn't he?"

"But I take the streetcar—"

"Yes, but you see, with your own vehicle you can come and go as you please, set your own schedule. No more waiting for the streetcar."

"But I've never minded—"

"Especially in the winter, when it's cold—"

"But we don't know whether Dewey will be in the hospital that long—"

"And it should be cheaper too," Mr. Diehl went on, plowing ahead in spite of Ma's reluctance. I admired his tenacity. "You'll have to pay for gas, of course, but as I figure it, that should add up to less than the fare to—"

"But, Mr. Diehl!" Ma fairly shouted his name. "I don't know how to drive!"

Thomas Diehl remained unruffled. "That's no problem, Mrs. Tierney. I can teach you. There's really nothing to it." He rolled up on the balls of his feet and back down again, like a businessman closing a deal.

"I don't think—"

"It's a splendid gift, Tom," Aunt Dortha interrupted. "Of course this will make it so much easier for Catherine to get back and forth to the hospital every day."

"But, Dortha, in *that* thing?" Ma pointed toward the street. Parked along the curb was the pickup truck in question, that ugly metal monster, that city dump on wheels.

"That's what I was figuring, Dortha," Mr. Diehl admitted easily. "The streetcars aren't as dependable as they used to be, ever since they started talking about phasing them out, you know—"

"No, and you're right about the winter, Tom," Auntie interjected. "It's such a terribly cold wait for one of the cars to arrive. Had a tenant once, a Mr. Setterquist—he got frostbite waiting for a trolley that was stuck in the snow. Cost him three toes, if I remember."

"He wouldn't be the only one that happened to," Mr. Diehl remarked happily. He was unquestionably glad to have Aunt Dortha on his side. "I can teach Mrs. Tierney to drive in no time. It'll take a little getting used to, but she'll catch on to the gears pretty fast."

"Like I say, there's plenty of iced tea. Won't you come in?" Aunt Dortha swung an arm invitingly toward the kitchen.

The sanding job notwithstanding, Thomas Diehl obliged this time around and followed Aunt Dortha down the front hall. Ma remained motionless by the door, staring alternately at the key in her hand and the truck in the street. Finally the argument about seeing Dewey more easily must have won her over, because she slipped the key into the pocket of her dress. I uncrossed my fingers and let out my breath.

We had ourselves a truck.

LESSONS

_14_

"What's the matter, Josef?"

He sat at the kitchen table, his head hung, his hands wrapped around a sweaty glass of something cold to drink. When I spoke, he looked up swiftly. "Oh, Novelka." A smile flickered, disappeared. "Nothing is the matter. I am simply drinking some water."

"But you don't look so good."

Everyone was eyeing everyone else suspiciously these days, looking for signs of polio. I didn't think I'd be guilty of it, but polio was the first thought that came to mind when I found Josef looking flushed and breathless, his long-sleeved shirt damp with sweat.

"I walked too far in this heat, I'm afraid. It didn't seem so bad when I started out but—" He waved a hand. "I have to remember my heart. . . ." His words trailed off. He took a long drink of the water.

"Where'd you go?"

"To the cathedral." St. Paul's was a straight shot down Selby Avenue, a steamy two-mile trek across shadeless sidewalks at the height of summer.

"Why didn't you catch the streetcar?" I asked.

"I did on the way down. But I decided to walk back. The day looked so beautiful when I stepped outside."

"You go to Mass?"

"No, only to say a prayer for your brother."

Our eyes met. I smiled. It made me feel better knowing Josef was praying for Dewey. "Thanks, Josef," I said.

He nodded, drank some more water. "I prayed for your mother as well."

"Ma?" I asked. Josef answered with another nod. "What for? On account of she's out learning to drive with Mr. Diehl?"

Ma was even at that moment out for her first driving lesson, with Aunt Dortha along for support. The truck wasn't fixed up as yet, but Mr. Diehl said the sooner they got started on the lessons, the sooner Ma would be driving herself back and forth to the hospital.

Even though Ma had voluntarily pocketed the key, it took her some time to work up the courage to use it. Aunt Dortha spent three days prevailing upon Ma the importance of accepting this gift, which surely had come straight from the Almighty. "Really, Dortha," Ma quipped, "I was unaware that God himself lives right across the street." But it seems it took an act of the Almighty, or at least a failure on the part of the streetcar lines, to get Ma behind the wheel of that Chevy pickup. The streetcar that usually carried Ma over to Minneapolis broke down, and Ma had to stand for thirty minutes with the thermometer at ninety, waiting for a replacement car to be sent out from the trolley barn. She said the lady standing next to her at the stop fainted dead away in the heat. Said Ma, "She was just standing there telling me she was going out to buy a cut of veal for supper, and next thing I know she's facedown in the street with her nose spurting blood all over the asphalt." I think Ma pictured herself sprawled there in the street with a crowd of gawkers circling overhead, and that was what finally got her courage up to learn to drive.

Josef's eyebrows lifted. "Ah yes, the driving lesson. I almost forgot about that. No, I prayed for your mother this morning because she is so afraid. She cannot live with such fear."

I gazed at Josef for a moment. "She's afraid Dewey's going to die like Andy did, isn't she?" When Josef didn't respond, I added, "What do you think, Josef? Is he going to die?"

Josef leaned back in the chair. It creaked beneath his weight. "I cannot answer that, Novelka. Only God himself knows that."

I didn't like his answer very much. I asked grown-ups like Josef and Auntie if Dewey was going to die only so they could tell me that he wasn't. Auntie was reassuring, saying she was sure Dewey would eventually be fine. But Josef wasn't doing his part.

"I don't think God will let Dewey die, Josef. He can't let Dewey die." My words were as firm as I could make them, a challenge, daring Josef to contradict me.

Josef slid his glasses up his nose, looked at me with expressionless eyes through the lenses. Quietly, he said, "God will do what's right."

For me there was only one right thing. If Dewey died, that would be terribly wrong.

And yet Josef's family—all of them—had been wiped out in the war. When that happened, was God doing the right thing? Wasn't that terribly wrong?

"Josef?"

"Yes, Novelka?"

"Does God always do what's right? Or do some things just happen anyway, even though they're not really right or good?"

Josef sighed, tried to smile, looked as though he were about to answer, but before he could say anything the front door burst open, and Ma stepped heavily down the front hall, followed by Aunt Dortha. Ma flew into the kitchen in an uncharacteristic burst of energy, opened the pantry door, took an apron off the hook, and tied it around her waist. "Well, Nova, I'm glad you're here to help," she said. "We must get lunch under way."

I studied Ma quizzically. She didn't look like herself. She looked happy!

And Aunt Dortha, come to think of it, didn't look like herself either. She looked terrified! Instead of putting on her own apron and stepping up to the stove, Auntie dropped into a chair at the table and fanned herself rapidly with a folded newspaper. Her great chest heaved with every strained intake of air. Her cheeks shone scarlet, her eyes were unnaturally wide, and two great streams of sweat rolled down the sides of her face. I'd have taken her for someone who'd just escaped a purse-snatcher and was fleeing on her overburdened lace-up Enna Jetticks through the streets of St. Paul if I hadn't known she'd simply been out for a ride with Ma and Mr. Diehl.

"How was the driving lesson, Mrs. Tierney?" Josef asked.

Ma paused in her task of pulling pots and pans out of the cupboards. "It went very well, thank you, Mr. Karski," she said confidently. "It's really much easier than I ever imagined."

"I knew you'd do well, Mrs. Tierney."

"But you almost hit—"

Aunt Dortha was interrupted when a pot landed heavily on the stove. "I told you a dozen times, Dortha. I didn't even come close to hitting Mr. Springer. It just looked like it from where you were. If you'd been behind the wheel, you would have seen it all from a different angle."

"I could see quite well from the truck bed, thank you, and I still say if he hadn't jumped when he did—"

"Nonsense, Dortha. Even Mr. Diehl said there was plenty of room."

"But you were going too fast—"

"Ha! Thirty miles an hour was all. Maybe twenty-nine."

"But you were going around a curve—"

"Mr. Diehl said I handled the truck just fine. He said he's never seen anyone learn to drive so quickly."

"Yes, well, perhaps he's never taught anyone else how to drive. . . ."

"Why don't you stop fussing and give me a hand, Dortha. Otherwise we'll be late getting lunch on the table. You too, Nova. Set the table for me, will you?"

And then Ma did something that wasn't like her at all. She started to hum. She took some potatoes out of the refrigerator, grabbed a paring knife, and started to hum as she dropped the peelings into the sink.

I looked at Josef, my eyebrows raised, and thought he must have prayed some powerful prayer. Auntie, the generally unflappable one, was a little worse for the experience, but as for Ma—"Shazam!"—she was suddenly Captain Marvel, ready to fly on the wings of a 1937 Chevrolet pickup truck.

There was no question, though, that Ma was still afraid. Not of the truck—that was her unexpected ticket to freedom—but of what was happening to Dewey. In the short time he had been sick, Ma had grown thinner than ever, and her eyes were a deeper shade of sad. She obviously didn't sleep well for worry. I could tell by her nocturnal visits to my room to lay her hand across my forehead. At least once a night I'd find myself pulled up from a dream, not completely, but enough to know she was there, her cool hand on my face checking for fever.

For the two weeks he was in quarantine, she had wanted nothing more than to be able to visit her son. Now that she could see Dewey again, she was finding the visits a strain. To see him so sick, reduced to such helplessness—that was enough to tax any mother's strength. But she also found herself fumbling, searching for words, anything to fill in all the vast stretches of time. Dewey, who had once been an easy conversationalist, now didn't seem to have anything to say. But after all, what is there to say when you can't even move and your life has suddenly been squeezed into a stifling routine of eating, sleeping, and using a bedpan? Yet Ma didn't want to leave him there alone. She wanted desperately to be with him. So at times they were simply silent, Ma's hand resting on Dewey's brow while Dewey pretended to sleep.

"What he needs is diversion," suggested Aunt Dortha. "Something to keep him occupied, to get his mind off his problems. He may be in a respirator, but his mind doesn't have to be there."

"Well, what do you suggest I do?" Ma asked.

"What interests him? What does he like?"

After that Ma went to the hospital with armloads of books on astronomy. She spent a great deal of time just reading to Dewey and holding up the books so he could see the pictures. They talked about the times they took the trolley out to Excelsior and tried to recount the constellations they had seen on their various trips. They discussed things like the cosmic fireball and Hubble's Law and the new two-hundred-inch telescope at the Palomar Observatory and how exactly Dewey might design the Nova Machine to capture the music of the spheres. Ma told Auntie that Dewey did seem to perk up for a time whenever they talked about these things.

Ma and Dewey also worked crossword puzzles together, and sometimes it became a group activity for all the patients on the ward. There were generally about ten polios there, some in lungs, others in beds, and even at times one or two in rocking beds. Ma said the rocking beds made her dizzy just to look at, the way they moved back and forth head to toe like a vertical cradle. The purpose of the bed was to keep the patient's diaphragm moving up and down, pushing air in and out of the lungs. The patients who used them had graduated from respirators, but they still weren't able to breathe on their own. Anyway, Ma took in crossword puzzle magazines, and anyone who wanted to join in, could. She said she sometimes had half a dozen words thrown at her at once, and the guys would get so wound up trying to outshout one another that the whole ward broke up into laughter. Even Ma. She said it was good to laugh. It kept her from crying.

She also read Dewey the cards and letters he got from well-wishers. Once Mr. Randall, who managed the grocery store where Dewey worked until he got sick, sent him a card signed by all the employees and a can of sausages that he knew Dewey favored. The kids in his former Sunday school class sent him a pocket-sized red-letter edition of the New Testament in which they'd signed all their names. They also sent a crumb cake that the teacher, Mrs. Farmington, had baked herself. His seventh-grade teacher, Miss Northcutt, sent him a book by Jules Verne, *From the Earth to the Moon*. Dewey had already read the book probably half a dozen times, but now he had a copy of his own. Inside on the cover page Miss Northcutt wrote, "Hold fast to your dreams, Dewey." Ma was grateful to Miss Northcutt for that and even forgave her for the time she gave Dewey a D in penmanship. Dewey might have felt the same. I don't know. He didn't say.

Ma taped any cards to the rim of the lung where Dewey could see them and left them there a few days before replacing them with new ones. Dewey said he was glad to have something to look at other than his own face in the mirror. This mirror was attached to the lung so Dewey could see what was going on in the room behind him, but he couldn't glance into it without seeing his own face, and he told Ma it was a face he didn't much care to see anymore. It didn't look anything like the old Dewey. It was too thin, and the eyes were too big, and it was always framed by a pillow. Ma didn't know how to respond. Dewey *was* thin and pale and sickly looking, not at all the Dewey we had known at the beginning of the summer. But Ma finally told him not to worry, because he wouldn't look like that forever. Dewey said that was right, he wasn't going to look like that forever. He was going to look even worse when he was an old man still lying there with his head propped up on a pillow.

Ma had to hold back her tears when she said, "You can't grow old in that thing if you expect to walk on the moon, Dewey."

She hoped her comment would give Dewey some encouragement, but Dewey didn't say anything. He just lay there as if that was where he belonged and there was no such thing as the moon.

"That's only to be expected," Aunt Dortha assured Ma later. "Of course he feels down. Who wouldn't, being stuck in an old respirator like that? One day he was feeling fine and the next the whole bottom fell out of his world. Our job is to keep him as upbeat as possible, though heaven knows we can't expect it to be easy." Auntie visited Dewey too, only not as often as Ma. Maybe once or twice a week, when she could take time away from the house.

I told Ma what would really cheer Dewey up would be a visit from me, but I had barely got the words out of my mouth when she said, "Absolutely not, don't even think about it. That hospital is the last place I'd let you go." Since Ma didn't want me to go anywhere, the hospital was really only on the same list as everywhere else.

When Ma suggested that I write to Dewey, I couldn't believe I hadn't thought of that myself. Of course I should write to Dewey! Now that Ma could visit him, she could take the letters to him for me. Not only might it be good for him, but it would give me one more thing to do to help ease the boredom of my days.

Not that there was terribly much to write about during this summer of solitude. I wasn't allowed to play with other children, though I did sneak outside on occasion, like when Mr. Diehl brought the truck back from South Dakota. Other than that, I was left to occupy myself with things like going through my treasure box or working on my scrapbook of magazine pictures. If I wanted to be with someone, I had to make myself an appendage of one of the grown-ups for a while. I became Auntie's right hand when it came to the care packages of baked goods she made for Dewey and the other patients at the hospital. She let me stir up the ingredients and lick the bowl afterward, and I helped her pack the goodies in little boxes that Ma carried with her on the streetcar. With Ma, I tended to get underfoot during the few hours she was home in the morning, though I tried to make myself useful by helping with laundry and other chores just to be with her and have something to do. I also developed a sudden desperate interest in Miss Singletary's stamp collection, just so she might spend an evening with me pointing out the little squares of colored paper she had so carefully preserved in a variety of scrapbooks.

Josef was still giving me chess lessons, of course, and added to that, I was now taking piano lessons under the tutelage of Miss Eva Lassiter. Sort of, anyway. After the first lesson, Miss Ida decided to join us, saying she would teach me how to sing at the same time. It didn't take long for my lessons to turn into small-scale vaudeville productions. Miss Eva hammered out the tunes on the keys while Miss Ida sang and danced her way around the parlor on her pencil-thin legs, her arms waving like a couple of tree branches in a violent storm. The sisters even re-created some of the hundreds of skits they'd performed on dingy stages around the country. One minute Eva would be listening to my attempt at a scale and the next Ida would throw out a joke, and all at once Eva would jump up, and the sisters would go through a whole comedy routine, tossing shtick back and forth like hot potatoes, slapping their knees and whirling around the room with their elbows linked. At such times they completely forgot I was there. The first few times this happened, I sat on the piano bench and watched them dumbfounded until I realized their antics were getting me out of the piano lesson and I might as well just enjoy the show.

And so I chipped away at the hours of my solitude, waiting for school to start again, waiting for first frost, waiting for Dewey to come home, and sometimes simply waiting for anything to happen at all.

I'LL WATCH THE MOON

Dear Dewey,

Ma said I shuld write you and she would bring you the letter and I don't know why I did not think of it before myself. That was stupid. You can't believe how much I wish you were home, Dewey. This is the wurst summer of my whole entire life. I can't even play with anyone else becose Ma's afraid I'll get sick from them. I am so bored and lonely by myself and I miss you.

I hope you are doing alright there. What is it like to be in a hospitol? I hope the docters and nurses are nice to you. I wish I could visit you but Ma says no.

Josef is still teaching me how to play chess and now Miss Eva and Miss Ida think their teaching me to play the piano and sing but mostly they just sing and dance and stuff by themselfs and don't even know if I'm there or not. But it is funny and anyway I am not so bored when they do that.

I am making a scrapbook out of pretty pictures I cut out of magazenes that Auntie gives me. Auntie gave me the scrapbook too, it is an old photo album with black pages. She helps me make the paste out of mostly flour and water but Auntie also puts in alum and a few drops of oil of cloves and it makes a good paste. I will show you the scrapbook when you come home. It is fun and anyway it is something to do. Sometimes I lissen to the radio too. And Josef and I like to look in the newspaper to read about the Olympic Games. Did you remember they are having them in London this month?

Ma is learning how to drive on account of Mr. Thomas Diehl is giving her a pickup truck that was his uncel Luthers but he died. She is doing good. On her first lesson she allmost ran over Mr. Springer and I wish she did becose he is such a mean old goat. I can't wait til you see the truck. It is ugly but I think you'll like it.

Do you like the care pakages? Auntie lets me help her make them.

Well, I will say goodbye for now. I will write you again soon. Please come home soon Dewey because I miss you and I love you.

Your loving sister,
Nova Tierney

Dear Tag,

It was swell to get your letter. I'm glad you wrote. A nice lady named Miss Evans is writing this for me because of course I can't write it for myself. But I'm telling her what to say, and she's writing it down. She is a volunteer here at the hospital. She will probably read your letters to me too from now on because when Ma read your letter to me she started blubbering all over the place. She said it was because the letter was so sweet, but I think it was because you are such a terrible speller. She held up your letter and showed me, then started crying.

It is pretty boring here too. Probably even more boring than at home. All I can do is lie here. Sometimes the nurses plug a radio in and let us listen to some music or a ballgame. And yes, some of the volunteers read to us about the Olympic Games too. Some of the other polios—that's what we call ourselves—are pretty swell, and we talk and tell jokes and play Twenty Questions, stuff like that. We all like the care packages, so keep on sending them. Tell Aunt Dortha to make some more brownies but next time leave out the nuts.

The food here isn't so good. I miss Ma's and Aunt Dortha's cooking. You are lucky to still be at home where you can get a decent meal.

Some of the guys that come onto the ward are real creeps. There was this one pretty old guy, maybe about thirty years old, and he said he was a nightclub singer and was glad his own lungs were still working and he didn't have to be in an iron lung. He thought he was a big deal, and he kept singing all these stupid love songs like he thought the rest of us wanted to hear them even though no one did. Finally people started asking him to shut up, but he must have thought they were kidding because he just went on singing like he thought he was Bing Crosby or something. It just about drove me nuts. I think he would have got himself beat up pretty bad if anyone in the ward could have walked over to his bed to hit him. He's lucky none of us could walk. He finally got transferred somewhere else. I think it was because the nurses took pity on us. They didn't like him either.

But after he left, the sound of all the iron lungs on the ward seemed louder than before. It's kind of a pump-hiss-gush sound, and it goes on and on day and night, and as long as you hear it, you can never forget where you are. The first day after the creep left I almost wished he would come back, just so I couldn't hear the lungs.

I always thought that if you were paralyzed you couldn't feel anything, but with polio, even though you can't move, you can still feel everything. And everything hurts because my muscles are real tight and sore. But they put a lot of hot packs on me, and they really feel good. They start to loosen up the muscles, but then the physical therapist comes and stretches my legs and arms all over the place, and everything hurts all over again but even worse. Sometimes they have to give me codeine for the pain, it hurts so bad.

Tomorrow they will start to take me out of the lung for about one minute at a time to get me used to being out of it. I can't wait. After that it will be two minutes and three minutes and so on until I can just stay out of it for good.

I lie here all the time looking up at the ceiling. I can't remember the last time I saw the moon. I guess that night we were out in the yard with the telescope. Sometimes, especially at night, I wish I could invent some special glasses so I could see right through the ceiling to the moon and the stars.

I will stop talking now before Miss Evans gets writer's cramp.

Love,
Dewey

———

Dear Dewey,

    Don't worry, I'll watch the moon for you until you come home. As soon as it got dark last nite I went out in the backyard and looked up. There was the moon, almost full, and all nice and shiny. I will try to watch it every nite til you come home, even if I have to go out in rain or snow. I have to go to bed now but I will write some more tomorrow.

Your loving sister,
Nova Tierney

BREATH

It has been said that something beautiful—a mountain range, a painting, a song—can take your breath away, but don't believe it. Things like that don't really steal your breath, not the way polio did before the Salk vaccine. Polio at its worst, if you contracted the bulbar type, paralyzed the muscles of the chest that normally pulled air into your lungs. Once those muscles became paralyzed, your lungs lay dormant underneath, and your breath was gone, stolen away. That's when they'd put you in an iron lung so it could breathe for you. From fifteen to thirty times a minute a pump on the lung would withdraw all the air from the tank, creating a vacuum in which your chest would rise, and that's when you'd inhale. Then, conversely, the tank would fill up with air, the pressure would push down on your chest, and you would exhale.

That's how Dewey breathed. Without the iron lung he would have been dead. And that was the really awful thing—

181

how close to death he was. No iron lung, no Dewey. It was a simple and terrifying equation.

Most people got out of the lung eventually, though a few never did. Those who got out had to be weaned off the respirator slowly. Muscles once paralyzed had to get used to working again. To begin the weaning process the patient wasn't necessarily taken out of the iron lung. At first the tank might simply be turned off for a minute, then two minutes, then three. This too was Dewey's experience.

The first time a therapist came in and flipped the switch on Dewey's respirator, he said he thought he would die. He'd been anxious to start the process of getting out of the lung, but when he was actually forced to try to breathe on his own, he panicked. He discovered what it was not just to be afraid but to become fear itself, because the panic is so large there isn't room enough inside for anything else. He explained it all to me in one of his letters.

> I felt like I was choking. The room started filling up with black spots, and I couldn't even get enough air to scream. I wanted to scream and beg the therapist, Miss Snyder, to turn the lung back on, but I couldn't. I couldn't do anything but hope she'd turn it back on before I died, because that was what I was doing. I hate the lung more than anything I've ever hated in my life. I hate lying in it and not being able to do anything for myself, not even move. But when Miss Snyder turned the lung back on and the pressure inside made my chest work and I could finally breathe again, I was just so glad, Tag, so glad for the lung because it's keeping me alive.
>
> One of the things that scares me most right now is

what would happen if the electricity ever goes out. Will they get to me in time? They'd have to hand-pump all the respirators here on the ward to get us through the power outage, and maybe there wouldn't be enough people to come and pump all the lungs. Well, I'm not going to think about that. I'm just going to think about getting out of here and sitting up like a regular person and breathing on my own again.

Sometimes I'd stop in the middle of whatever I was doing and hold my breath. If I was eating a bowl of Post Toasties or sitting in the bathtub or looking up at the moon, all of a sudden I'd decide to see what it was like to stop breathing, to exhale without inhaling. To exhale and simply stop as though my lungs no longer worked. I don't know that I ever made it through even a whole minute without giving up, because as soon as I began to grow dizzy and my heart started pumping against my chest, I'd draw in a breath of air almost involuntarily, and I'd hold it a moment while the feeling of my lungs expanding flooded me with relief. I couldn't help but cry for Dewey then, knowing he couldn't take breathing for granted the way I did. I prayed for him, that he'd get out of the lung and start breathing on his own again.

But then there was the question, as Ma kept pointing out to Auntie, of how far back toward normal he would come. All the way? Halfway? What would be the ongoing effects of polio in his life, if any?

Ma came home from the hospital with assurances from various doctors that, yes, most people do recover from polio. "Eighty-five percent," one doctor vowed. "The number of polio cases that end up completely cured is about eighty-five percent." And yes, a full recovery was possible even for someone who has spent time in a lung.

But Ma didn't feel very reassured, especially when she tried to get Dewey into the Sister Kenny Institute and they wouldn't take him. The Sister Kenny Institute was right there in Minneapolis, and it was famous for its success with polio victims. But they didn't take respirator cases, at least not in 1948. By 1949 they would, but that didn't help Dewey in 1948.

Whoever Ma talked with at the Institute told her they didn't take patients in iron lungs because their recovery rate wasn't as good. But during epidemics like this, Ma was informed, Kenny therapists were dispatched to work at area hospitals, including Minneapolis General where Dewey was. So he was being well taken care of even if he couldn't get into Sister Kenny where miracles seemed to happen.

Ma supposed she was meant to feel good about Dewey's care after that, but the fact that he couldn't get into Sister Kenny ate away at her. She spent her time pondering recovery rates, statistics, and variables the way a mathematician might work an ornery numerical problem. She seemed to want to figure out exactly where Dewey fell on the scale of recuperation so that there would be no surprises, either good or bad. "If Dewey can't get into Sister Kenny," she said, "his chances for recovery are less than average. If eighty-five percent of polios recover, then fifteen percent are permanently crippled. Of the fifteen percent left crippled, a certain portion never walk again, while another portion need a portable chest respirator to breathe."

"Land's sake, Catherine," Auntie scolded one morning, "you're going to wear yourself out trying to see into the future. God doesn't give us any crystal balls, you know. We have to trust him for what comes."

"Oh, Dortha," Ma sighed heavily. "You can spare me your sermons. I just want to have some idea of what we're facing."

"Most people with polio get better," Auntie replied firmly. "And if you need numbers, think of the eighty-five percent the doctor mentioned. The odds are in our favor."

"Yes, but think of the fifteen percent. You've seen them, Dortha. People with their legs all shriveled up, their arms useless. People in wheelchairs—"

"Catherine, dear." Aunt Dortha shook her head impatiently, though her voice was gentle. "Why do you always dwell on the worst possibility? I hope you don't talk like this in front of Dewey."

"Of course not. I don't want him to think about anything other than getting better."

"Then why do *you* think any differently?"

Another heavy sigh. "It's just—well, I can't help but worry. It's just so hard—all the not knowing. That's the very worst of it all, not knowing what this will mean for Dewey."

"You have to try to believe he'll be all right," Auntie countered. "The dark thoughts will eat away your hope. Above all else at a time like this, you have to have hope."

Ma didn't say anything after that. She must have known I was listening, because I was right in the next room setting the table for breakfast while they spoke. The swinging door between the rooms was propped open with a cast-iron doorstop shaped like a cat. When the talk in the kitchen stopped,

I looked up from the forks and knives in my hand to find Ma standing in the doorway gazing at me. I looked at her quizzically.

"Do you have a letter for me to take to Dewey today, Nova?" she asked.

I shook my head. "But I was going to write one this morning," I explained.

Ma nodded. "That's good. He likes to hear from you."

"I know, Ma."

She smiled at me then, and because she smiled I wanted to prolong the moment, though she had already turned to go.

"I found some pictures of the Milky Way," I said quickly, calling her back, "in one of the magazines Mr. Diehl gave me. I put them in my scrapbook yesterday. I want to tell Dewey about them."

"He'll like that," Ma said.

"I'm going to show Dewey my scrapbook when he comes home," I offered. I thought it might give her some hope. That's what Auntie said we needed.

"Yes," Ma said, nodding almost imperceptibly. "When he comes home." And then she went back to her work in the kitchen.

"Polio Epidemic" was the simple headline to a photo layout in *Life* magazine. It was early afternoon on a hot and drowsy day, and once again I was looking for pictures to paste into my scrapbook. *Life*'s August thirtieth issue had just arrived in the mail, and none of the grown-ups had had time to read it yet. But Auntie, knowing I needed something to occupy my time, told me to go ahead and cut it up anyway. "Just leave the cover story intact," she said. "I always like to read the cover story."

Sitting cross-legged on the parlor floor, I was slowly, almost absentmindedly, turning the pages when I came across the photo layout of the polio victims. Just the word "polio" was enough to knock me out of my lethargic state. I jerked awake, laid down my scissors, and began to read. "Once again summer spawned poliomyelitis epidemics all through the U.S.," one photo caption said. "The mysterious crippling disease has so far hit forty-seven of the states, leaving only Rhode Island untouched."

So it was everywhere! It was even now reaching fingers into nearly every state in the country! It was probably reaching around the world as well, but that was too big for me to think about. Most of the time I didn't even think about the havoc polio was wreaking in the state of Minnesota, nor even in the Twin Cities. All I could think about was Dewey. All that mattered to me was what polio was doing to my own brother.

Yet here was a photo of dozens of other polios, young boys and girls in a ward of a North Carolina hospital. They lay there atop the white sheets of the metal-framed beds, naked save for the uniform loincloths they wore in place of underpants. Beneath the photo was the caption: "Stretched out in a row at Greensboro Hospital, young polio sufferers are treated with rolls under knees, boards against which to brace feet." Throughout the ward, at this bed and that bed, nurses gazed helplessly down at the children.

On the next page a three-year-old girl, Mary Ruth, was lying on a bed in a convalescent hospital, a crayon pinched between her toes. She was slowly, painstakingly, learning to write with her foot. The implication was that she would never again write with her hands.

On the next page were photos from a hospital in Guilford County, North Carolina, where "parents watched their children take their first steps on crutches, or learn how to get along without the use of arms. Some just watched their child lie on his bed and waited to see whether or not he would be crippled for the rest of his life." Oh, the faces of those parents. The hollow eyes, the downturned mouths, the worried brows.

Bad enough that, but there was worse to come. The picture that disturbed me most was on the last page of the photo spread. A four-year-old boy, both legs in braces, sat on a bridge soliciting money from passersby. He terrified me, this little boy with the slicked-down hair and the smiling face. He terrified me because the cumbersome leather and metal braces he wore from hip to heel made him look more like a factory-styled machine than a real live person. It was as though the whole of his humanness had been swallowed up by the effects of the illness, and he'd never set foot into real life again. Because who could live—I mean, really just live a normal life?—when you were shackled with those metal bones, those leather muscles, those braces that weighed almost more than you did and which, after all, could never replace your real flesh and blood?

I didn't want Dewey to end up like that. I didn't want Dewey to end up a cripple.

I almost slammed shut the magazine then and there. But I didn't, because something else about the photo caught my eye. The child on the bridge was collecting money for the

March of Dimes, the organization created to find a cure for polio.

Officially known as the National Foundation for Infantile Paralysis, it had been the brainchild of President Franklin Roosevelt, who everyone knew was crippled by polio even though no one was willing to talk about it. Few photos were ever taken of the president in his wheelchair, and none were ever printed in the papers. Years later, after Roosevelt was dead, historians would admit that nobody wanted a crippled president. Best to ignore the wheelchair, prop him up at the podium with his leg braces locked, and let him give his speech, all the while pretending he had walked to the podium himself and would just as easily walk away from it. He hadn't walked in decades, but nobody was going to say the emperor wasn't wearing any clothes. And so a cripple was voted into the White House four times over, because everyone in America was willing to pretend he wasn't crippled.

Even though he himself wasn't officially considered a victim of the disease, Franklin Roosevelt and his advisor Basil O'Connor started the National Foundation for Infantile Paralysis in 1937 to raise money for polio research. The following year the effort was nicknamed the March of Dimes by comedian Eddie Cantor who, along with a host of other celebrities through the years, asked Americans to send their dimes to the White House to help find a cure for polio.

The March of Dimes. Of course! How many times had I sat in a movie theater with Ma or Auntie or Dewey, only to have the picture stopped halfway through so the March of Dimes collection canisters could be passed up and down the aisles? How I hated the interruptions! They always seemed to come at the most critical juncture of the show. Just when the Indians were about to attack the circle of covered wagons or just when the hero was about to pledge everlasting love to the heroine, all of a sudden the houselights came up and the ushers came forward with canisters in hand, and we had to step abruptly out of our fantasy world to think about something as dreadful as polio. Nevertheless, Auntie, for one, always dropped a dime in the can, reaching inside her bag for the coin she'd slipped in there just before leaving for the theater. Ma gave sometimes if she was in the mood. I generally pouted until the canisters had been collected and the picture started again.

After the war "porch-light campaigns" were started, which I thought an altogether better idea than breaking into the movies. You were supposed to turn on your porch light at seven o'clock at night if you wanted to alert a campaign solicitor to come to the door. As a reminder, just before the hour, church bells rang out, and fire stations blew their horns. That's when Auntie would go and turn on the light if she hadn't already.

"Why are you always so quick to give our money away?" Ma sometimes complained.

"Because people need our help," Auntie replied, her jaw firmly set. "And anyway, I'm also thinking of us. God forbid we should need such help ourselves someday, but it just may be so."

And so it was. Dewey had polio, and the March of Dimes was paying for all of his hospital bills. More than that, the money was going to help find a vaccine against polio and perhaps a cure for it.

Suddenly I knew what I could do to help Dewey. I could give to the March of Dimes! The only problem was that of how to get the money so I could give it away. I had no money myself, no piggy bank to raid, not even a few pennies stashed away somewhere. Ma and Auntie, I supposed, had no extra money to give me either. Ma was always commenting to Auntie about how we had to be much more careful now since she wasn't working at the bakery. And I certainly couldn't go from door to door collecting dimes, because Ma wouldn't let me, lest I come home with polio instead of money.

The only thing I could do, I decided, was to pray. Auntie always said God would give you what you asked for as long as you weren't asking for something selfish. As far as I could see, asking for dimes wouldn't be selfish because the money wasn't for me. God knew I needed the dimes to help Dewey get better.

Right then I jumped up from the floor of the parlor and kneeled on the divan by the window. Not beside it, but on it, with my elbows on the windowsill, my hands folded and tucked beneath my chin. This was the spot where I'd spent so many hours watching for Pa to come down the street. It seemed the place to go when I wanted something, when I was looking for something. And now I was willing to wait for dimes with the same patience and hope with which I had waited for Pa.

I had already spent a lot of time praying for Dewey. But the prayers seemed kind of murky and indefinite. "Please make Dewey better, God, and bring him back home." I'd said it a thousand times, and so far I hadn't seen any evidence that God had heard. Dewey had only gotten worse, not better, and he seemed a very long way from coming home.

To pray for a dime was much more specific. I could easily measure the results and see if God was listening. Either he would give me a dime or he wouldn't. It was that simple.

I squeezed my eyes shut tight and clasped my hands together so firmly my fingers ached. God had to know I meant business. "Please, God, please," I whispered. "Please give me a dime. It's not for me. It's for Dewey." Over and over I asked for a dime, hesitant to stop, assuming the longer I prayed, the greater the likelihood that God would answer.

"What are you doing, Novelka?"

Startled, I turned to see Josef standing on the threshold between the front hall and the parlor. "I'm praying for a dime," I explained eagerly. "For the March of Dimes. You know, so Dewey can get better."

"Ah." Josef nodded. "Then I won't disturb you."

He turned, and when he did I saw that Ma was beyond him, standing in front of the mirror that hung over the telephone table. She was adjusting her hat before leaving to catch the streetcar to the hospital.

"You might put your time to better use by helping Aunt Dortha with the lunch dishes," she said. She drew on a pair of white gloves, then smoothed her skirt with the palms of her hands. "I'll be home at the usual time," she continued. She picked up her purse from the table and snapped it shut. "I'll expect you to be a good girl for Auntie while I'm gone."

"Please give my greetings to young Dewey for me, Mrs. Tierney," Josef said.

"Thank you, Mr. Karski. I will."

As Ma exited the front door, Josef climbed up the stairs to

his room. I stayed where I was, still kneeling on the faded old divan and watching Ma as she made her way down the street to the trolley stop at the corner. She didn't think God was going to answer my prayer. I felt angry with her for doubting, but at the same time, determined to show her wrong.

DIMES

When Ma told me the start of school might be delayed because of the polio epidemic, I didn't want to believe it. She read me the piece in the paper about the school board weighing the pros and cons of starting classes as late as October, and I suddenly felt more miserable than I'd felt all summer. The added weeks of isolation would be almost more than I could bear. I longed to be back in school surrounded by other kids, with something to do other than paste pictures in my scrapbook, watch Josef play chess, and listen to the Lassiter sisters revisit vaudeville.

But as it turned out, after repeated discussions with area-wide hospitals, school officials announced that classes would begin as planned, the Wednesday after Labor Day. And so, when the day arrived, mothers sent children off to school with some trepidation, warnings to take the usual precautions against contagious disease, and prayers for an unusually early first frost.

After saying a hurried good-bye to Ma and Auntie, I ran into the September morning, my face exploding with grins. How beautiful the world looked as I skipped through the streets, moving toward people again, leaving behind my unhappy state of reverse quarantine. I was free!

Not exactly the thoughts of most children going back to school at the end of summer vacation, but those were my feelings on the morning I entered fourth grade. I made my way through the crowded halls of the elementary school—oh, glorious crowds!—and fell into the arms of my best friend, Rosemary Knutson, when I found her in our classroom. She was a bit surprised but gave me a hug and a satisfying squeal in return.

We were welcomed back to school by our teacher, Miss Connor, a white-haired wisp of a woman who must have had forty years of public schoolteaching under her belt. I liked her at once, mostly because I was in the mood to like everyone. We were given crisp new textbooks and instructed to fashion covers for them out of paper bags as soon as we got home. I wrote my name inside each book with one of my brand-new, freshly sharpened number two pencils. How I loved those yellow pencils fresh from the store—long and sleek with untarnished erasers, miles yet from the stubs they would be worn down to. Those, and the tablets of spanking clean writing paper, their pages unsoiled by lead or ink. I fancied they smelled as yet of the paper mills that had churned them out. Nothing gave me the sense of a fresh start like those pencils and writing tablets. I was ready for the challenges of fourth grade. I was ready for the delicious routine of learning.

My friend Rosemary didn't share my enthusiasm. But

then, she couldn't understand the confinement I had endured. She had summered at her family's lake cabin as usual, surrounded by her brothers and sisters and any number of other kids vacationing there. Polio hadn't reached Otter Tail Lake, and so the Knutsons were free to fish and swim and listen to the loons calling across the water without having to worry about doctors' reports and iron lungs.

I didn't want to be envious of Rosemary, but when she said to me, "Jiminy cricket, the summer went by too fast," I knew I was sunk. I knew her vacation had gone by too fast because she had actually had fun. "I can't believe we're already back in school," she complained.

It was recess, that half hour or so after lunch when kids are supposed to run off their energy and teachers are supposed to recuperate from the morning before the start of afternoon classes. But it was too hot to be active, so Rosemary and I were sitting in the school yard in a dubious strip of shade provided by the west wall of the gymnasium. The ground was dry and dusty from the long summer heat, and the tufts of grass struggling up through the dirt were just this side of dead. With a spit-moistened thumb, Rosemary methodically rubbed the dust off of one of her new Red Goose shoes.

"I don't know," I said. "I'm kind of glad to be back."

Rosemary shot me a look that questioned my sincerity if not my sanity. "It's hotter than blazes here. I wish I was back at the lake."

"Yeah," I offered reluctantly, "I bet you had a swell time of it there." I watched her thumb working the dark circle of spit-shiny leather. On top of her summer at the lake, I envied her those new shoes. I had to make do with last year's pair until Ma could afford to buy me new ones. No matter that these were beginning to feel a tad bit tight.

"You bet we did!" my friend exclaimed. Her blond curls bounced as she nodded. "Howie taught me how to dive off the dock and right through the hole of an inner tube. It was swell all right! We went swimming every day and fishing and caught a bunch and we ate 'em too. Mom fried 'em up, and were they ever good. And now that Howie's sixteen, Mom and Dad let him take the rest of us out in the rowboat without any grown-ups, and boy, can you ever have a whole bunch more fun without any grown-ups around. You don't have to watch what you say or be polite or anything, and if you want to go exploring somewhere you never been before, you can go without anybody telling you to be careful. You shoulda been there, Nova."

If only I had been. If only I'd been there instead of here in the city surrounded by grown-ups, with no other kids at all.

"Think your mom might let you come with us next year?" Rosemary asked.

"I don't know." I shrugged. "Maybe."

"Well, I already asked my mom, and she said you could come because they're not going to notice one more kid when they already got six kids around. She said if your mom said it was all right, then you can come."

"Really?" My eyes widened with excitement.

"Sure. Only you have to not mind using an outhouse and taking a bath in the lake instead of using a bathtub. Oh yeah, and you can't have your own bed neither. You'd have to share one with me and Ginny."

"I don't mind."

"Then ask your mom if you can go, all right? If you start asking her now, you'll have the whole school year to try to get her to say yes."

I nodded eagerly, excited by the prospect of actually having a good time. I saw myself diving through the middle of an inner tube, curving into the cool waters of the lake, down into the lazy green silence and up again, bursting up out of the water to see the approval on . . . no, not Howie's face, but Dewey's. Dewey! I wanted to go to the lake, of course, but what good would it do to be there without Dewey? Suddenly I couldn't bear the thought of leaving my brother for a whole summer. No, if I had to choose between staying home with Dewey or going without him, I knew without a moment's hesitation I'd stay at home.

Rosemary seemed to read my thoughts. "Of course Dewey can probably come too, at least for part of the time, if he's better and all."

"Oh, he'll be better by then," I responded quickly. "That's a whole year off."

"Yeah." Rosemary frowned and squinted, whether because of the sun in her eyes or because she was thinking about Dewey in an iron lung, I couldn't be sure. "Yeah, he'll be better by then," she echoed, but she sounded less than certain. She licked her thumb again and started in on the other shoe. She was always fussy about her footwear, especially when her shoes were new.

I didn't know what to say after that, but before I could say anything at all, Rosemary suddenly looked up at me and remarked, "I can't hardly believe about Andy Johanson, can you? I mean, when Daddy came up from the city that weekend and told us Andy was dead, everyone thought he was making it up. No one but Mom believed him. She started bawling right away and saying what a nice boy he was and poor Mrs. Johanson and all that."

I didn't like the way our talk of Dewey had led to the mention of Andy Johanson, as though the two boys were inevitably linked. Though I suppose they were and Rosemary couldn't help but to make the connection. I said quietly, "Andy *was* a nice boy," but I don't think Rosemary heard.

"The rest of us didn't believe it," she went on, "until Daddy pointed to Andy's name in the newspaper where they list all the dead people. We still didn't *want* to believe it, but I mean, why would they put it in the newspaper if it wasn't true? So we finally decided it must be true. But, you know, when I saw him talking to Howie the last day of school, I never thought I'd never see him again. It's really scary that someone can be there one minute, and then you go away, and when you come back he's not there anymore."

I nodded my agreement but decided to steer our talk away from the depressing topic of Andy Johanson. "Jerry Butterfield's doing really good," I said. "He's not even in the hospital anymore. He's in some sort of place where he's learning how to do everything he did before. His mom told my mom they're hoping he'll be back in school starting January."

Rosemary frowned again, as though trying to find her way onto this new track of conversation. Finally she said, "Oh, that's good." But then she said, "Funny how Jerry's getting better and Andy went and died. . . ." Her words trailed off and our eyes met. A look of understanding blossomed on her face. She gazed at me sheepishly and said, "I'm real sorry Dewey got sick and all."

"Yeah, thanks, Rosie. Me too."

"I'd hate it if Howie got sick like that and ended up in one of those lungs. Jiminy!" She hugged herself and shivered. "Gives me the creeps just to think about it." A summer at the lake, new shoes, and a brother who wasn't in a lung. Rosemary had everything. No, that wasn't quite true. I had something she didn't have, and I was anxious to tell her about it.

"Well, Dewey's not going to be in the lung forever, you know."

"Well, how long do you think before he can get out?"

"I don't know, but listen." I leaned closer to my friend. "Guess what? You won't believe it. I've been praying for dimes, and God's given me four so far."

I sat back, waiting for her response. Surely she would regard me with wide-eyed wonder and ask me to tell her the whole story.

Instead, she put a hand on her hip the way I'd seen her mother do a thousand times. "Nova Tierney, what are you talking about?" Her voice even sounded like her mother's, with the same disbelieving tone.

"I've been praying for dimes," I explained slowly, "you know, for the March of Dimes. So they can find a way to make Dewey better. The first time I prayed, well, the next morning, the first dime showed up! I could hardly believe it myself, Rosie, but it's true. And there's been three more since then."

Rosemary narrowed her eyes and looked at me quizzically, as though she suddenly didn't know who I was. "Jiminy cricket," she sniffed, invoking her favorite expression. "You don't really believe God is dropping dimes from heaven, do you?"

"How can I not believe it, Rosie? I prayed for dimes, and there they are! How else can you explain it?"

"I don't know, Nova, but a whole bunch of people live in that house of yours. I mean, someone's got a hole in his pocket, and he's dropping dimes or something. You should see the loot I dig out of the sofa at home—nickels and stuff that fall out of Daddy's pocket when he sits on the couch and reads the paper."

"No, no, no!" I shook my head firmly. "It's not like that at all. They always show up at the same place—on the windowsill in the parlor. How could they fall out of somebody's pocket and end up on the windowsill?"

My friend stared at me for what seemed an interminably long time. "Well, I don't know, Nova. Somebody's leaving them there, then."

"But why would somebody do that?"

"To make you think God's doing it."

That's exactly what Ma had said.

The morning after my first prayer for dimes, I'd stopped by the parlor window as soon as I woke up. I was going to pray morning and night, I decided, so that God would know beyond doubt that I was in earnest. Kneeling on the divan, I was just about to fold my hands and lean my elbows on the sill when I was caught off guard by the little silver object lying there amid the dust and paint chips. For a long moment I couldn't even move, I was so amazed. Was there really a dime there on the windowsill? Slowly I lowered my hand and touched the object tentatively with my index finger. It was solid! It was real! I'd prayed for a dime, and God had left one on the windowsill!

"Ma!" I screamed. I scooped up the dime and ran to the kitchen where Ma and Aunt Dortha were preparing breakfast. "Ma, look!"

Ma wiped her hands on her apron and met me in the middle of the kitchen. "Goodness, Nova," she said. "What is it?"

"A dime! A dime, Ma!"

Ma glanced at it and shrugged. "So you've found a dime. What? Are you hoping to go out and buy some candy?"

"No, Ma! Remember? Yesterday I prayed for a dime, and this morning this was on the windowsill!" I jumped up and down in my excitement, forgetting that Henry Udahl was asleep in the room below. "God gave me a dime!"

"Oh, Nova." Ma sighed, shook her head. "I hate to disappoint you, but it must have been Josef. After all, you told him you were praying for dimes."

I stopped jumping. I couldn't believe it. Ma was determined to sabotage my miracle. "It wasn't Josef," I said firmly. "It was God. God left it there."

"Well, you can just ask Josef when he comes down to breakfast. He may not want to admit it, but he won't lie about it either."

"I don't have to ask Josef, Ma. I know he didn't leave it there."

Ma had gone back to cutting out biscuits at the kitchen counter. She spoke to me over her shoulder. "It must have been Josef, Nova. He shouldn't have done it, playing on a little girl's hopes like that, but I suppose he was just trying to be nice."

I would have to appeal, I decided, to someone better acquainted with God's mysterious ways. "Auntie," I wailed, "what do you think? It could have been God, couldn't it?"

Auntie turned from the stove where she was stirring a pot of oatmeal. Her face was shiny with sweat, a dew-laced tomato. "You say you prayed for a dime?" she asked.

"Yup."

"And there was one on the windowsill this morning?"

"Yes, Auntie."

"Well . . ." She put the lid on the pot and turned from the stove. "Of course it's possible for God to have left it there. It's hard to understand the ways of Providence—"

"Oh, don't start talking about Providence, Dortha," Ma interrupted. "You know as well as I do that God doesn't go around leaving dimes on windowsills."

"I know no such thing, Catherine."

My heart leapt, but Ma laughed. "And anyway," Ma added, "if God were going to give you a dime, Nova, you'd think he'd leave a nice new shiny one. Look at that tarnished old thing. It's been circulating for years, and the last place it was before it landed on the sill was in Josef's pocket."

"That's not true, Ma!"

"Catherine, now don't upset the child."

"But, Dortha, such nonsense . . ." Ma stopped fiddling with the biscuit dough long enough to give me that pitying look grown-ups resort to when their children just can't seem to understand something. "The next thing you know, Nova, you'll be believing in the tooth fairy again."

I did ask Josef about the dime, sort of, though not directly, and not that morning, but after the second dime appeared a couple days later. We were sitting on the porch swing together one evening that last week of August. We were talking about school—about my entering the fourth grade and his starting a new teaching career in America—when I thought the time had come for me to ask him about the dimes. "Josef won't lie about it," Ma had said, and I knew she was right. If he told me he was leaving the dimes, I'd be disappointed, but at least I'd know the truth.

"Josef?" My breath caught in my chest.

"Yes, Novelka?"

"Did you know that God has been leaving me dimes? For the March of Dimes, I mean."

"Ah yes. Your mother mentioned something about that to me."

"Oh? Ma doesn't believe it. I mean, she doesn't believe the dimes are from God. She thinks someone's leaving them on the windowsill."

"Does she?"

"Yeah. But God can do anything, can't he? That's what Aunt Dortha always says. She says God can do anything he wants to do, because, after all, he's the one who created everything in the first place."

"Yes." Josef nodded slightly. "Yes, he did."

"But, well, it *could* be God, couldn't it, leaving the dimes on the windowsill?"

Josef looked thoughtful a moment. Then he said, "What do you think, Novelka? Do you think God is leaving the dimes on the windowsill?"

I didn't even have to think about it. "Yeah, I do, Josef. I think God is giving me the dimes so I can help Dewey get better."

"Then, child"—Josef patted my hand—"if you believe the money is a gift from God, don't let anyone tell you otherwise."

After he said that, I studied his face a few minutes to see if there was anything there that might give him away—a twinkle in the eyes, a little patronizing smile—but there was nothing. If he had been leaving the dimes, he would have told me. It had to be God. There was no other explanation.

"You're wrong, Rosie," I told my friend now as we sat on the hard, parched ground of the school yard. "I know what I know, and I know it's God."

"Well," she said, "let me see the dimes, then."

"I can't."

"Why not?"

"I dropped them in the can at Shoemaker's on my way here this morning." Like many businesses, Shoemaker's had a March of Dimes canister prominently displayed beside the cash register on the store's counter. I passed the store on my way to school, so I figured it would be a good place to drop any dimes I found on the windowsill. Otis Shoemaker—who, oddly enough, owned a shoe repair business—had had polio himself as a child, which was why he made sure to put a canister out on his counter every summer. "Someday," he predicted, "there's going to be a vaccine, something to keep you kids from getting the polio. You wait and see." I told him I hoped he was right.

To Rosemary, I said, "But anyway, what difference would

it make if you saw the money? You'd still say someone had dropped the dimes by accident or left them on purpose."

Rosemary shaded her eyes a moment and looked out over the yard. We had only a few moments left before the bell called us back inside. "I don't know, Nova," she said quietly, not turning to look at me. "It just seems kind of creepy or something."

"Creepy?"

"Well, you know, freaky. I never heard of God doing anything like that before."

I sighed. "Rosie, you're my best friend. You gotta believe me."

She finally met my gaze and dropped her hand from her eyes. "All right, Nova. If it'll make you feel better, I'll believe you."

But I knew that she, like Ma, really didn't believe me at all.

TAKE ME WITH YOU

Dear Tag,

Thanks for all your swell letters, and I'm sorry I haven't written you in a while. It isn't that I don't think about you, but sometimes it is just hard to do anything. Maybe you know what I mean. Sometimes I get really down and it isn't helped by the little kids who come on the ward and start crying for their mothers. And boy oh boy there's been a lot of them here lately. It seems like there's always some little kid crying night and day, and after a while I think I'm going to go crazy, not because of the crying but because I can't do anything about it. I feel real sorry for the little kids who don't know what's happening to them. For most of them it's the first time they've ever been away from home, and here they end up sick in a scary place like this, and I think it must be worse than their worst nightmare. The nurses are nice to them, but they don't want a nurse, they want their own mothers. No little kid deserves to have something bad like that happen, and just thinking about it makes me mad. Sometimes I'd like to put my hands over my ears to block out the crying, but I can't do that because I can't do anything but lie here, and then I get even madder.

I'm glad you're happy to be back in school. When I had Miss Connor for fourth grade, I thought she was nice but kind of stupid. Do you remember me telling you about the time Jerry and I crawled out of the room during an air-raid drill when we were supposed to be hiding under our desks? We snuck out of school and played hooky the rest of the day, and of course we thought Miss Connor would tell our folks and then they'd really give us the business when we got home. But neither of us got in trouble, and the next day the other kids told us that after the air-raid drill was over Miss Connor just went on teaching and didn't even notice Jerry and me weren't there anymore. We got away with a whole bunch of stuff in her class after that. I guess it was because Miss Connor was about a hundred years old and nearsighted and maybe even a little bit deaf. But I'm not telling you this so you'll act up in her class. I know you won't because you never make trouble the way I used to.

They have teachers that come around to the ward here to tutor the kids like me who should be in school but aren't. It isn't like really being in school, though, and the lessons only last about an hour a day and not all day like if I were really in ninth grade like I'm supposed to be. I don't know how I'll ever catch up with my class after this. I feel like everyone else is moving ahead and I'm standing still, like I'm stuck in the mud or something. I'm really scared about getting behind. I've always worked really hard, and I'm not bragging or anything, but you know how my teachers have always said I'm at the top of my class. I have to be, Tag. I have to study real hard if I'm going to be an astronomer. Now I wonder what's going to happen. You know, Jerry's been transferred over to that rehab center, and he's already walking around, and that means even he's leaving me behind.

I was afraid if I wrote you I'd start saying depressing things and sound like I was feeling sorry for myself, and that's what I've gone and done. I don't mean to sound that way. I promise I will try to do better next time.

Tell Rosemary to tell Luke and Howie I said hi. I'm glad they had a swell time at the lake.

Love,
Dewey

———————

Dear Dewey,

I want to tell you something I've been afraid to tell you becose I was afraid you wuldn't belief me. But its true. This is it—God has been giving me dimes to put in the March of Dimes canistur so they can find a way to make you better. I started praying for dimes last month and ever sinse then I have been finding dimes on the windowsill. I know it is hard to belief and Ma doesn't belief me and nether does Rosie, but Josef does and I think Auntie does too. You sounded sad in your letter so I finely decided to tell you. God wuldn't give me dimes if he didn't think you were going to get better, wuld he? I will keep praying and all the dimes I get I will put in the canistur right away so you can get better and come home. Even if you do get behind in school, Dewey, don't worry. You are so smart you will catch up again in no time.

I like Miss Connor a lot but sometimes when we are working at our desks she falls asleep. She is still sitting up like she is reading the book on her desk but we know she is asleep becose her eyes are closed and sometimes she even snores a little bit. Everyone laughs then and I laugh too and that wakes her up and she gets mad. She acts like she is mad at us but I think really she is mad at herself and embaresed for falling asleep. I feel a little sorry for her and when she falls asleep like that I try to be extra nice to her. Ma says Miss Connor will soon be put out to pasture, whatever that means.

You know Josef started teaching classes over at Macalester College and he says he likes it very much. He said he didn't know how much he missed being in a classroom. He is not giving me chess lessons anymore and that is just as well. I will never learn how to play that game if I try for as long as I live. Ma is doing good at her driving lessons. Mr. Diehl always looks very happy when he comes over for one of Ma's lessons. He brings a lot of flowers from his garden. He says it will be under a pile of snow all too soon.

Miss Singletary had a date last night with a man she met when she was playing bingo at some church. His name is Martin Popp and when he came to pick her up his shoe caught on a nail on the front step and he tripped and fell and landed on the porch. Well, Clyde Munson was just going out the front door right at the same time and when he saw Mr. Popp on the porch he started laughing so hard I thought he would fall over himself and die right there. But next thing I know Mr. Popp jumped up and punched Clyde Munson in the nose and blood was spurting everywhere and old Clyde got mad and started swinging back and poor Miss Singletary ran out and started screaming and then Auntie ran out and said she'd call the police if they didn't break it up. By that time Mr. Popp had a bloody nose too and his hair was all messed up and boy did he look funny. Miss Singletary was crying but after she blew her nose a few times and Mr. Popp got his nose to stop bleeding they went ahead and went to the picture show anyway. Now Miss Singletary won't speak to Clyde Munson anymore but I don't think she ever did before anyway.

I go out every nite to look at the moon. Last nite was cloudy and I am always sad when I can't see the moon for you. But I know it is up there and it will come back so I keep going out.

I have to do my home work now. We are starting to learn long devision in math.

> Your loving sister,
> Nova Tierney

Dear Tag,

I think it's swell about the dimes and I believe you. Really I do. And I'm glad you decided to tell me because it did make me feel better. Don't worry about Ma not believing you. You know she gets bothered about religion. Don't tell her I said so. I stopped going to church too but only because it's so boring and not because I don't believe in God.

Boy oh boy I wish I could have been there to see the fight on the porch. I hope I don't miss too much stuff like that. Poor Miss Singletary, she finally gets a date and look what happens. She doesn't have very good luck.

It's good of you to be nice to old Miss Connor. I hope she can help you learn to spell. Please don't try to ever enter a spelling bee, because you would never make it past the first round.

Before I forget, would you tell Aunt Dortha that Byron—he's one of the guys on the ward here—wants to know if she can hold the raisins in the next batch of oatmeal cookies she sends? I like the raisins myself, but maybe she can make a few without. Thanks.

Right now the fellows have the radio tuned to a ball-game. I don't know who's playing. That reminds me, Mr. Butterfield had said he'd take Jerry and me to Lexington Park sometime this summer to see the Saints play. Boy, I sure would love to see them out there against the Millers. But I don't guess I'm going to make it this year.

I wish I could go to the movies. I heard *Key Largo* was good, that new one with Humphrey Bogart. I wish I could have seen it. I know you always fall asleep when you watch Bogart, but I bet you would have stayed awake for this one. Well, we'll never know, will we, since Ma won't let you go to the movies till winter's here, and I won't be getting out of here until way after that.

I am trying to stay busy so I don't have time to get down about things. When no one's around like Ma or the therapists or Miss Evans who writes these letters for me, I spend a lot of time going over the names of the stars and the constellations, things like that. I sure hope I can look at them all through the telescope again soon. That's the worst thing, not seeing the stars or the moon. But I guess I already told you that. Sometimes I'm lying here and my arms and legs feel so heavy, it's like they're made of stone, and on top of that they're aching to beat the band too. But then I shut my eyes and pretend I'm floating around on the moon. If I'm lucky, sometimes for two or three minutes I can concentrate so hard it's like I really am on the moon. Those are the best minutes of the day.

I hope you will keep writing me even though you are busy with school. If I were home I could help you with long division, because math has always been one of my best subjects.

Love,
Dewey

Dear Dewey,

Last nite I was looking at the moon like I always do every nite and I got to wondering, when you go to the moon for real some day will you still take me with you?

Your loving sister,
Nova Tierney

Dear Tag,

Don't worry. I'm not going anywhere without you.

Love,
Dewey

IN THE SMALL HOURS
OF THE MORNING

Josef and I sat on the porch swing enjoying the sweet evening air. September was always the very best time of the year to be outdoors, a thin slice of days between summer's crushing heat and winter's brutal cold. It was the month that Minnesota decided to be gentle, to caress with a cool touch, a kindly hand wearing the jewels of early autumn. The air was a tangle of pleasant sounds—children laughing, radios playing, insects humming, a train whistle blowing. Sitting there with Josef, I felt myself in the midst of an almost perfect moment. And it might have been completely perfect if only Dewey were home.

"You know, Josef," I said, "I dropped another dime off at Shoemaker's on my way to school this morning."

We swung in silence for several long seconds until Josef responded by saying, "And?" He seemed to know there was more to the story. He was right.

"Well, Mr. Shoemaker said to me, 'Hey, kid, where you getting all these dimes?' And I didn't know how to answer at first, but I finally decided I might as well tell him the truth, even if he laughed. So I said, 'God's giving them to me so I can give them to the March of Dimes.' Well, he didn't laugh, but he looked kind of surprised and said, 'Really?' And I said, 'Yeah. I started praying for dimes and that's when they started just showing up.' And he said, 'No kidding, huh?' And I said, 'It's all right if you don't believe me, Mr. Shoemaker.' And I was about to leave when he said, 'I didn't say I didn't believe you, kid. But, holy Toledo, Nova,' he said, 'as long as you're in the praying business, why don't you pray for a million bucks?'" I looked up at Josef then to see if there was any reaction. There wasn't, so I continued. "I didn't know whether he was kidding or not, but he still wasn't laughing. I sure didn't know what to say, Josef, so I finally just said the March of Dimes doesn't want a million bucks, they just want dimes. And that's when Mr. Shoemaker laughed."

All the while I spoke, Josef gazed out over the street, squinting in thought. I went on. "I didn't say so to Mr. Shoemaker, but it just seems wrong to pray for a million dollars. It seems like too much. I mean, how could you expect God to just up and give you a *million dollars*?"

Josef lifted an arm and laid it to rest on the back of the swing, his long fingers touching my shoulder. I loved it when we sat this way. It felt wonderfully right, exactly how fathers and daughters were supposed to sit. We knew Ma didn't care anymore if Josef and I sat together on the swing. Sometimes we were there in the evenings when she came home from the hospital, and she'd smile at us and stop to talk for a minute before going in the house to help Auntie with the evening chores. I considered this change in Ma a step in the right direction, with the final step, of course, landing Ma and Josef at the altar.

Josef cleared his throat. "I understand what you're saying, Novelka. It doesn't seem right to ask for so much money. It seems a selfish prayer. Because what man, if he got a million dollars, would give it all away to help somebody else?"

After thinking about that, I concluded that not even I would give away the entire million dollars. Most of it, maybe. Much of it, certainly, to the March of Dimes. To help Dewey. But I'd no doubt hold a little back for myself, thinking it wouldn't be missed. A couple hundred dollars, maybe a thousand. No, I was glad I wasn't tempted to ask for a million bucks. It was far easier to give away a dime.

"Besides," Josef continued, "I think Providence prefers small blessings to large miracles."

I should have asked Josef what he meant, but I was too busy chuckling. Josef looked at me sideways. "And what is funny, Novelka?" he asked with a grin.

"Nothing, really," I replied. "It's just that Aunt Dortha is always talking about Providence, and it makes Ma crazy. 'Don't start talking to me about Providence.'" My voice squeaked in the attempt at mimicry. "Maybe Auntie should just say God like everybody else, and then Ma wouldn't get so mad."

"Ah." Josef smiled again. "I'm not so sure. Your mother would probably get angry no matter what name your aunt used for God."

I shrugged. "Well, I wonder why Auntie always says Providence anyway? I mean, who else goes around calling God Providence? Not even the pastor at our church goes around talking all high and mighty like that. He just calls God *God* like everybody else."

"Perhaps, Novelka, that is the way your aunt sees God. To her, the most important thing about God is that he is providential, and so perhaps that is why she chooses to refer to him in that way."

"Maybe." I shrugged again. Josef's hand rode up and down with my shoulder. "But whenever she says Providence, all I can think about is Providence being the capital of Rhode Island, the way we learned in geography last year. It doesn't make me think about God at all."

"Maybe it would if you knew what providence meant. Did anyone ever tell you?"

I thought a moment, shook my head. "I don't think so."

"Well, you see, it comes from the Latin word *provideo*. The prefix *pro* means 'before,' and *video* means 'I see.' So *provideo* means to see something beforehand."

I let that sink in. "So God is Providence because he can see what's going to happen even before it happens."

"Yes." Josef nodded. "That's right, Novelka."

"Oh."

Dusk had fallen, and the morning-glory vines on the porch railings nodded and swayed in the breeze. Suddenly the air was almost chilly, whispering of first frost. How anxious Ma was for first frost! Sometimes she stood at the window as though she were watching for it, that advancing army of cold that would drive out the polio virus for another year. She said she wouldn't stop worrying about my going to school until after the frost settled in. I was beginning to hope it'd come early so she'd stop worrying so much.

"Josef?"

"Yes, child?"

"Do you think God knew Dewey would get polio?"

He hesitated only briefly. "Yes, Novelka. I believe he knew."

"Well, why didn't he keep Dewey from going swimming at the lake, or wherever it was he got it?"

"Ah," Josef said again. He sighed deeply. "That, my dear, is a question for the theologians. But even they, in all their wisdom, most likely cannot answer it."

I frowned. "You mean, no one can answer it?"

"No one but God."

A trolley rumbled up the street, and I turned my gaze toward it. The porch shivered as it passed by, its wheels rolling heavily over the tracks. Even as the trolley turned onto Lexington and disappeared, I kept looking at the street, thinking. I didn't like feeling left out of anything, even God's secrets. "But, Josef?"

"Yes, Novelka?"

"If you were God, say . . . well, wouldn't you have done something to keep Dewey from getting polio?"

This time he waited such a long time before answering, I almost thought he wasn't going to answer at all. Finally he patted my shoulder and said, "You are your mother's daughter."

I looked up, startled. "What do you mean?"

"She too is full of such questions."

"She *is*?" I tried to imagine Ma talking with Josef just as I was now, but my imagination couldn't reach that far. "You mean Ma talks to you about stuff?"

"Yes, sometimes."

"She asks you *questions*?"

Josef shrugged noncommittally.

"What *kind* of questions?"

Josef took a deep breath, let it out. "Well, she wonders about God and about the war."

God and the war? I stared at my friend wide-eyed in disbelief. Ma had no interest in God, and she had no business asking Josef about the war.

"She asked you about the *war*?"

Josef's expression said he wasn't following me. "Yes, she has asked about the war."

I fidgeted and turned away from him. I felt suddenly too embarrassed to look at him. "I'm sorry she did that, Josef," I said quietly.

"Why would you be sorry, Novelka?"

"Well, because Dewey said not to ask you about the war."

"Did he?"

"He said you wouldn't want to talk about what happened to your family and all."

"Ah. He is a sensitive young man, but I do not mind talking with your mother about the war."

I lifted one eye to look at him. "What did you tell her?" Did he tell her he had a daughter? That was what I really wanted to know.

"I told her many things."

"Like what?"

Josef smiled. "You are young, Novelka. Perhaps one day,

when she chooses, your mother will tell you."

Disappointment flooded me, and the feeling that once again I was shut out from secret places. If Josef answered Ma's questions about the war, why couldn't he answer mine? Just because I was young? What could it hurt for him to tell me whether or not he had had a daughter? I felt the question banging its head against the roof of my mouth, and yet, in the end, I couldn't bring myself to let it out. I would have to bide my time and hope that someday Ma would tell me everything she knew about Josef's past.

Many years later, she did.

———————

They'd been meeting for several weeks, Ma and Josef, in the early hours of the morning. Well, somehow that makes it sound like something other than what it was. Perhaps I shouldn't say that they met but rather that they ran into each other, always in the kitchen, almost always long before dawn. Not one of their meetings was planned. At least that's how Ma put it when she told me the story years later just before she died. She said the meetings were the result of two sleepless people stumbling across each other in the wee hours. Every few nights one would find the other drinking coffee, eating leftovers, or simply sitting at the kitchen table, deep in thought, while the rest of the world slept.

The first time it happened was in late July, not long after Dewey went into the hospital. Ma hadn't slept more than a few hours at a time since they'd taken Dewey away, and the more she tossed and turned, the more fearful she became. Finally, on this particular night, she decided to go into the kitchen to make a pot of coffee. Perhaps she could gather her thoughts, calm herself, if she simply got up and did something.

She threw on a light cotton robe over her gown and treaded quietly through my room, stopping briefly to lay her hand across my forehead as I slept. When she was satisfied that I wasn't feverish, she moved on to the kitchen, flipped on the light, and very nearly died of fright to see a figure seated at the table.

"Mrs. Tierney!" Josef sputtered, just as surprised by the sudden light as Ma was by his unexpected presence. He dropped his spoon and jumped up from the table. "Mrs. Tierney," he said again, "I am very sorry to have startled you."

Ma lifted a hand to her chest and felt the pounding of her heart beneath. "Scared me half to death is more like it," she said. "I . . . I just wasn't expecting anyone."

"Nor was I. I am very sorry, Mrs. Tierney," Josef repeated.

When Ma's initial fright had passed, she realized she was standing there in her nightclothes, which to her was almost as good as no clothes at all. She wasn't even wearing slippers on her feet. Her hair, loose from its combs, fell around her shoulders in thick blond strands. Outside of Dewey, Auntie, and me, she never let anyone see her like this. She almost turned and fled, but before she could take a step away from the kitchen, Josef Karski gestured toward a bowl on the table. "I was hungry. Mrs. Severson said if I were ever hungry I should come to the kitchen and help myself." Looking sheepish, he dropped his eyes and moistened his lips with his tongue. "I found some stew from last night's meal. . . ."

His words trailed off as Ma eyed the bowl. Her embarrassment over her appearance melted away, replaced by an odd compassion for this man who had come to the kitchen in the middle of the night looking for something to eat. "Of course, Mr. Karski," she replied gently. "You mustn't worry. If you're hungry, of course you should eat. But were you able to heat it up?"

"Heat it?" Josef looked startled, as though the thought of heating food was a novelty.

"Well, you don't want to eat it cold."

Josef looked at the stew in the bowl. "It is delicious, Mrs. Tierney, just as it is."

He remained standing. He was wearing a pair of slacks without a belt and a sleeveless undershirt. Gone were the long sleeves that hid the tattoo on his inner forearm. Ma turned her eyes away but not before she saw it. She remembered then. Auschwitz, where a bowl of cold stew became ambrosia.

"It's better warmed up. Here, let me heat it for you."

She reached for the bowl, and Josef, complying, lifted it from the table and handed it to her.

She spooned it into a saucepan and lighted the gas stove with a match. "I thought I'd make myself some coffee," she went on. "Would you like some?"

"Thank you, yes. That would be nice." Finally Josef sat again and folded his hands on the tabletop while Ma worked at the stove.

"It's almost two o'clock," he said.

Ma paused and looked up at the clock on the wall. "Yes." She sighed as she scooped coffee into the basket of the electric percolator.

"You were not able to sleep?" he asked.

Ma shook her head, stirred the stew in the pot.

"You are worried about Dewey." It was a statement, not a question.

A moment later Ma spooned the stew back into the bowl and set it down in front of Josef. "Yes." She pulled out a chair facing him and sat down. "I haven't slept well since he got sick. And you? You were simply hungry?"

Josef offered a wan smile. "I haven't slept well since . . . well, not in quite some time, I'm afraid." He lifted the spoon and began to eat.

Ma rose again, nervously, and pulled two cups and saucers down from the cupboard. She settled the cups into the craters noisily, then stopped and gazed out the window over the sink. There was nothing out there beyond the back porch except darkness. But in the light from the kitchen she could see the bed where Dewey slept before he became sick. She knew she shouldn't ask, but she had to know. She had to know. "How do you bear it, Mr. Karski?" The words were little more than a tortured whisper.

She didn't turn, but she could feel Josef's gaze upon her back. "Bear what, Mrs. Tierney?" he asked gently.

"All of it. The war. The loss of your family. If Dewey dies, I won't be able to bear it."

"You will, Mrs. Tierney. I do not think Dewey will die, but if he does, you will bear the sorrow because you will have no choice. But God will help you—"

"God?" Ma swung around. She gave a little laugh that was really a cry. "God will help me, Mr. Karski?" She shut her eyes. She could feel the anger, the familiar hot lava churning upward, rising to the surface. She opened her eyes. Josef gazed at her without expression. "You should curse him, Mr. Karski," she said. "You should curse him for doing nothing while the Nazis—" She raised a hand to her mouth, knowing she had to stop. Josef was the innocent. She had no right to hurt him.

Josef laid down his spoon and slowly, purposefully, resettled his glasses on his nose, pinching both shafts just beyond the end pieces. "Curse him?" he echoed. The eyes behind the lenses were full of questions but full too of understanding. When he spoke, his voice was quiet, kindly. "And if I curse him, Mrs. Tierney? What then? If I turn away from him, what do I turn toward?" Josef paused, shook his head slowly. "No. Better to keep one's face toward heaven, even if you are angry with God, than to turn away and find nothing at all."

When he finished, he kept his eyes locked on Ma's, as though to challenge her. For a long, uncomfortable moment, Ma didn't know what to do. But she was saved when the corners of Josef's mouth curved into a small crescent smile and he said, "I believe the coffee is ready, Mrs. Tierney."

Flustered, she turned from him to the coffeepot. Her hands trembled as she poured the coffee into the cups, but with her back to Josef she knew he couldn't see. She took a certain small comfort in that. Taking another deep breath, she asked, "Cream and sugar?"

"Just black, thank you," Josef replied.

She placed the two cups on the table and settled again into a chair. She took the lid off the sugar bowl at the center of the table and dropped two cubes of sugar into her cup. Stirring the coffee gave her a moment to think. She wanted to ask him something, but she wasn't sure what. Her mind was filled with so many questions she couldn't grab hold of one long enough even to know what it was. Finally she let one tumble out on its own, and to her surprise, it was this: "Why are you here, Mr. Karski?"

Josef cocked his head and looked uncertain. "I have a sponsor at the college, and the school had need of a linguistics instructor—"

"No." Ma shook her head. "I mean, *here*. In this house. How did you end up coming here to this place from Poland?"

Josef shrugged, sipped his coffee. "It is a long story, Mrs. Tierney."

"Will you tell me?"

Settling the cup back on the saucer, he said, "You mean, tell you about the war?"

"Yes."

Josef dropped his gaze. He sat quietly for a long moment. Through the open windows came the persistent chirping of crickets, a nocturnal clock ticking off the seconds. Finally Ma said, "I'm sorry, Mr. Karski. I shouldn't have asked. Of course you don't want to speak of it."

"It isn't that I don't want to speak of it," he said, looking up. "I can speak a dozen languages and can read several more, but still, none of them contain the words for me to tell you what happened in the war."

Ma wanted to touch his hand, to comfort him. She almost did but stopped herself and let her hand rest on the table instead. "I'm truly sorry, Mr. Karski," she said gently.

"No." Josef shook his head. "I shall tell you. I will try, at least, if you are certain you want to hear."

Ma closed her eyes a moment, opened them. "Yes," she said. "I do want to know your story."

Josef drained his coffee cup and pushed it aside, along with the empty bowl. He leaned forward and folded his hands on the table. He didn't look at Ma but off toward the far wall of the kitchen, as if the words he needed were blooming there amid the wisteria vines on the wallpaper.

At length he began. "In 1939, at the time of the German invasion, I was living in Warsaw with my wife and children. . . ."

JOSEF IN THE POLISH UNDERGROUND

Until September 1, 1939, Josef Karski lived in an apartment in a pleasant section of Warsaw, not far from the University of Warsaw. He had been an integral part of the university almost from the time it was established in 1918, first as a student and later as a well-respected professor of linguistics. It was there that he met his wife, Helena Woda, in 1922, when she was studying biology. Helena might very well have become an academician herself had she not found herself married and expecting a child within a year of meeting Josef. When their daughter, Zosia, was born in 1923, Helena—not unwillingly—put aside thoughts of higher education and never looked back. Four years later their second child, a boy named Stefan, was born.

Josef was undoubtedly what every man wanted to be. He was lucky in love, adored by his children, satisfied in his work. Life was good for Josef Karski—or as good as life can be in a country accustomed to upheaval and prone to conquest.

Poland had had trouble with its neighbors for centuries. In the eighteenth century alone, in the span of some twenty-five years, Poland was divided up three times by Russia, Prussia, and Austria. With its borders and its infrastructure ever fluctuating, uncertainty and instability were the only constants. Through it all the Poles yearned for a strong and independent homeland, but they could never quite wiggle their way out from under the conquering thumb of their neighbors.

Josef and Helena, born in 1899 and 1900 respectively, had come of age under Russian rule. Twice in the nineteenth century, the Poles tried to drive the Russians out of Warsaw but failed. They would not succeed until the conclusion of the Great War in 1918. The cost was great, Poland being the chief battleground for the war. Josef, like many Poles, was drafted into the German army to fight against the Russians, and like many Poles, he fought against relatives and friends who had been drafted by the Russian army to fight against the Germans. He spent nearly a year in the trenches until he was released by the Allied victory. At that time Poland proclaimed itself—yet again—an independent republic.

The Poles worked to rebuild their country, though too often they found themselves working against each other. Endless clashes between the population's minority groups and the government's many political parties made it a difficult task to achieve any permanent stability. By 1939 Poland was as yet attempting to strengthen itself as a democratic country.

Even so, Josef and his family were enjoying the present moment and making plans for the future. Zosia was sixteen by then, a bright, pretty girl who flocked with her school friends, flirted with the boys, and, as yet unable to distinguish between the two, dreamed of romance and marriage. Her schoolbooks were filled with hearts drawn around her name and the name of her latest true love, the latter as changeable as the Polish government: Jan, Tomasz, Leon, Wladyslaw, Konrad. Zosia lamented to her mother that it would be impossible, when the time came, to choose just one person for life. Helena laughed and assured her that when the time came, it wouldn't be difficult at all. "Your papa will let you know who is good enough," she said.

Stefan, at twelve, was a studious child with a precocious interest in physics and chemistry. Zosia called him "The Bore" because he rarely socialized the way other children did. He had little interest in games, parties, sports, adventure. Instead, he preferred to spend his time reading the science textbooks his mother had saved from her one year of college. He would, of course, go on to the university. Neither he nor his parents doubted that. Then afterward he would carve out for himself a distinguished career in the sciences.

And so it might have been if not for a man named Adolf Hitler. Stefan might have become a scientist, Zosia might have known marriage and motherhood, and Josef might have gone on teaching at the university and living out his life with Helena if the German chancellor hadn't decided he wanted to expand the house of Germany. What he wanted was more room. *Lebensraum* it was called. Living space. A larger area for the Germans to stretch out, put up their feet, enjoy the good life. So Adolf Hitler studied his maps and decided that the land directly to the east of Germany was a good prospect for increasing his country's total square footage. Unfortunately this coveted space was occupied momentarily by somewhere in the neighborhood of twenty-five million *Untermenschen*. Subhumans. The Poles.

This will never do, thought Hitler. *We must get rid of the Untermenschen to make way for the* Herrenvolk, *the Master Race.*

And so on August 22, 1939, Hitler authorized the killing "without pity or mercy all men, women, and children of Polish descent or language. Only in this way can we obtain the living space we need."

The killing began on the morning of September 1, 1939. As the last night of August passed and the first morning of September dawned, the German armies crossed the vulnerable Polish border and started in on a systematic slaughtering of civilians. The Germans came on foot and in tanks, rolling out a path of destruction, crushing everything in the way. They came in the air, the Luftwaffe dropping its incendiary bombs without discretion—on apartment buildings, on hospitals, on open streets, on peasants toiling in the fields. On September seventeenth, Poland's neighbor on the opposite side saw a golden opportunity to regain what they had lost, and the Poles found themselves in battle once again with their age-old enemy, Russia. The Poles fought valiantly, but village after village and town after town was destroyed by the waves of Germans rolling in from the west and Russians rolling in from the east. By September twenty-second, Poland was sliced in two by a military demarcation line that separated the German territory from the Russian. It would remain a divided country until June 1941, when the German army drove the Russians out of Poland and the entire country fell into the hands of the Nazis.

Warsaw, one of the cities hardest hit in the earliest days of the war, fell on September 28, 1939. A casualty of the relentless bombing by the German Luftwaffe, Warsaw literally collapsed into a pile of rubble. What had once been a great metropolis, a center of culture and learning, disappeared almost as though it had never been.

But that was only the beginning. Once Poland was conquered and subdued, the Nazis began a quieter but equally horrifying campaign of genocide by execution, forced labor, and starvation. It lasted for six years. By the time Hitler's campaign ended, it had claimed the lives of six million, twenty-eight thousand Poles. With the extermination of nearly a quarter of its population during the Second World War, Poland had the highest ratio of losses to population of any country in Europe.

Josef and his family survived the destruction of Warsaw by escaping to their country home, a one-time farmhouse outside the city, which had been in Helena's family for close to a century. It had been for them a weekend retreat, until the war, when it became their salvation. Their apartment in the city was leveled; none of its contents were salvageable.

While the invading Nazis ransacked many homes in Poland, confiscating some for their own use, the country house somehow escaped notice. Nothing was missing when the Karskis arrived except for the caretakers, a man named Avram and his wife, Lea. They had lived in a little cottage there on the grounds not far from the main house. Josef and his family found the little cottage empty, with dirty dishes still on the table and an open Torah on the floor of the bedroom. The caretakers had fled the very place that the Karskis had come to for refuge.

Josef urged his older sister Tonia and his younger brother Tadeusz to come to the country with their families. There would be room for them all to live in the country house, he said, and while the whole of Poland was under siege, their chances were better in the country than in the city. He would have invited Helena's parents to join them there, as well, if the elder couple hadn't moved to Lwow the previous year to live with Helena's brother. Now they were caught in the Russian-occupied provinces and were too far away to take advantage of the country house.

After the first week of the siege on Warsaw, Tadeusz showed up at the country house with his wife and infant son. But Tonia's husband refused to leave the city. "On principle," he said. "I won't let the Nazis drive me from my home." Before Warsaw fell, Tonia, her husband, Henryk, and their three children were numbered among the forty thousand citizens killed in the bombardment. They were buried in the rubble of their apartment house for weeks until word reached Josef and Tadeusz that they were dead.

"Well, Henryk got what he wanted, then," Tadeusz said bitterly. "He will never leave his home again. And neither shall our sister and her children." He cursed the Nazis, but he cursed Henryk too and called him a fool.

"Tadeusz, brother," Josef said, "we must do everything we can to keep our families alive. Germany would crush us, every last one, but we mustn't let them."

Tadeusz cursed again and spat on the ground. "I would kill them all with my bare hands, given half a chance." A butcher's apprentice, his hands were used to blood.

Josef offered a small pained smile. "Brother," he said, "you are young"—for he was only twenty-two, far younger than Josef—"and the young are impetuous. But we can't afford to be, not if we are to save our families and help save our country."

"But our army is defeated. What can we do?"

"I don't know yet, but we will find a way."

The Polish army was already defeated, the Polish people were being slaughtered, Polish society was being dismantled by the Nazis, brick by brick. Schools and universities were closed. Churches and seminaries and monasteries shut down. Businesses were destroyed, newspapers forbidden. The country's arts and scholarly treasures were ransacked and either destroyed or sent to Germany.

Death was everywhere. Men, women, and children were pulled from homes, rounded up on the streets, tormented, tortured, executed. Mass graves abounded. Intellectuals throughout Poland—doctors, businessmen, teachers, priests, landowners, artists, even university students—were targeted for concentration camps or execution. Only weeks into the war several of the University of Warsaw's leading professors were already imprisoned or dead. Those not yet detained by the Gestapo were warned that they might be arrested at any moment.

Not surprisingly, most Poles found themselves without jobs to return to after the country was taken over by the

Germans and the Russians. What to do then with all these unemployed men and women? For those in the German-occupied territory, the Nazis had an idea. Because so many Germans had suddenly become soldiers, why not bring in the Poles to take over the civilian jobs they'd left behind?

And so in late October 1939, the Germans introduced labor duty for unemployed Poles between the ages of eighteen and sixty. This, it was to be understood, was not at all like the forced labor imposed upon the Polish Jews. Registering for labor duty was strictly voluntary, a chance for non–Jewish Poles to be usefully employed.

The Poles were less enthusiastic about this plan than were the Germans. In fact, only a piddling number of Poles volunteered to be sent to Germany. It wasn't long before Gestapo agents began rounding up people by force—sometimes entire villages or the whole of a city district—and sending them into Germany to fulfill the Nazi quotas for laborers.

"Will we register?" Helena asked her husband.

"We will not," Josef stated firmly. "We will not help Germany win its war against Poland."

"How will we live, then?"

Josef gazed quietly at his wife, at his brother Tadeusz, at his sister-in-law Rachel. "When I was last in the city," he said, for he went into Warsaw periodically to buy food and other items for the family, "I was approached by an acquaintance of mine from the university. He invited me into what was left of his home, where he served me biscuits and tea. He told me of the work he is doing now." Josef dropped his eyes a moment before continuing. "He holds an important position in the Polish underground."

Helena drew in her breath. Rachel shook her head slowly. Tadeusz looked delighted.

"The underground, Josef?" Tadeusz asked. "And this friend of yours, he asked you to join?"

Josef nodded. Before he could continue, Helena asked, "To do what? To fight the Nazis? To take part in secret bombings and sabotage?"

Josef touched his wife's shoulder briefly, comfortingly. "To fight the Nazis, yes, my dear. But not with weapons. With words. You see, all across Poland there are already being printed hundreds, maybe thousands, of underground newspapers. Some are military, some political. Some are for the intelligentsia, others for the working class. But they are all for the cause of Poland. There is a great need in the secret press for linguists, people who can listen to radio broadcasts from other countries—from England and America and other Allied nations—and translate what is being said over the airwaves so that the messages reach the citizens of Poland."

Josef paused a moment and looked around the table, taking in the intense faces of his listeners. "The underground will provide me with all the necessary papers. I will be given a new name, a new history, a new occupation. What these will be, I don't yet know. How often my identity will change, that I don't know either. But with the papers provided by the underground, I should be able to travel freely throughout Warsaw—throughout Poland, if necessary. For my work I will receive a small stipend on which to live. It won't be much, but we will find other ways to get by."

"Is there a place for me in the underground?" Tadeusz asked eagerly.

"I should think so," Josef said, nodding. "I will ask."

"Tell them—I am no linguist like you, Josef, but tell them this: I am brave and not afraid of dynamite. And I can find my way around like a bat in the dark! And"—the young man leaned back in his chair, smiling mischievously—"tell them I have had much practice with a butcher knife."

Josef returned his brother's smile sadly and said, "I'm sure you will be of great use to the resistance."

"But it is all so dangerous!" Rachel cried, lifting her delicate hands to her face.

Tadeusz looked at his pretty young wife. In that moment his excitement subsided, and his eyes clouded over with pity. Didn't she know there was no such thing as safety for any of them anymore? That if they were Polish, as they all were, there was nowhere to turn from the danger? And that if they were Jewish, as Rachel was, there was yet far more to fear?

Even while the Jewish ghetto was being organized in Warsaw, Josef and Tadeusz erected a secret room in the attic of the country house for Rachel and her little son, Emil. There they could go to hide at a moment's notice should Nazi soldiers be seen on the roads or in the fields around the house.

Rachel's immediate family no longer lived in Poland. Her father, a Zionist, had emigrated to Palestine in 1938, taking his wife and younger children with him. Rachel, the eldest daughter, had elected to marry Tadeusz and remain in Warsaw, much to her parents' sorrow. Now that the Nazis had come, Rachel took some comfort in knowing her family was safe elsewhere.

But the members of her extended family—uncles, aunts, cousins, her maternal grandparents—all were herded into the Warsaw ghetto after it was established in 1940. Once the Jews had entered the ghetto, they could not leave again. At least not on their own. They would not leave until they were divided up and loaded onto cattle cars headed to unknown places across Poland and throughout Germany—lambs to the slaughter, though certainly no one among the Jews could imagine the fate that awaited them at the end of the line.

Eventually the German government decreed that any Poles caught hiding Jews would receive the death penalty. But that was only one more threat in a life filled with threats. If one were a person of culture and learning, he would be imprisoned and executed. If one ridiculed a Nazi officer, he would be put up against a wall and shot. If one were simply walking down the street minding his own business, he could be rounded up, dragged out of the city, and murdered by the side of the road. What was the value of a Polish life during the German occupation? The Poles were only flies to be swatted, insects to be crushed in the palm of the Nazi hand.

Josef began his work for the Polish underground, hiding in secret places and listening to secret radio broadcasts. He sent his translations, via underground courier, to whatever basement, cellar, or barn the press happened to be headquartered in at the moment. If caught, he knew he would most likely be immediately executed. At best he would be sent to prison for an indefinite amount of time. From there, who knew what might happen? Too many members of the underground had simply disappeared.

Tadeusz became a courier, traveling across German-

241

occupied territories to take messages to the Polish Government in Exile in London. He was ordered to commit suicide if caught by the Gestapo so as not to give away secrets under torture. When he wasn't traveling, he took part in the sabotage-diversionary actions conducted by the resistance. He helped to destroy railroad cars, set transports on fire, blow up bridges, disrupt electrical power in Warsaw, burn military warehouses.

Helena, Rachel, and the children, though out of the action, were undoubtedly in no less danger at the country house where they went about the task of living while trying not be noticed. Mostly they stayed indoors, though during the warmer months Helena, Zosia, and Stefan worked a small garden behind the house, where they grew beans, radishes, cucumbers, and tomatoes. Helena had traded a pair of gold-plated candlesticks for the seeds. She developed a bartering system of sorts with several neighboring farms, trading household items and later, vegetables for milk and eggs and an occasional chicken.

Tadeusz discovered a way to bring in food as well. In spite of the severe rationing imposed by the Germans, almost anything could be had on the black market—meat, fish, butter, bread, coffee, wine. As one foreign correspondent reported, "For those who know their way around and have money, no food restrictions exist in Warsaw." Tadeusz Karski learned his way around quickly, trading valuables for food for his family. He collected everything in the country house that might work as currency on the black market—jewelry, silverware, coins— and hid it behind a wall in the cellar. He withdrew from this savings account slowly, hoping that it would last out the war.

The cellar became their sanctuary too, a place to go after dark when they couldn't risk having lights on in the house. The best times were when the men were home and they were all together and they carried to the cellar their candles and any number of books Mr. Woda had kept at the country house. They'd sit on crates there in the dank underground room, and while little Emil fell asleep on his mother's lap, Josef read aloud long passages of poetry and prose.

One poem quickly became the family's favorite, Aleksander Fredro's "Our Fatherland." A tribute to Poland, it had been written more than a hundred years earlier. Surely, somehow, Fredro had foreseen the coming of the Nazis, the juggernaut called Germany, and one small family's need for courage and hope.

The country where naught can the race ever spoil,
The country that for its faith, language and soil
Stands ready its breast, heart and hand to lay bare
To the sword of the foeman, to wrong everywhere. . . .

That, so long as life lasts, will not cease from the fight,
So long as it breathes will strive on for the right:
One man, with one sword, ever firmly will stand:
That's Poland, our Poland, our fatherland!

As Josef breathed out the last words, the candles caught his breath and flickered, casting shadows on the walls. Such were their nights together, a small bit of light in a dark place, a whisper of words, a hushed and lovely refuge from the turmoil. All of them sat transfixed while Josef read, their minds dancing with the poetic rhythms of the works not just of Fredro but of other great Polish artists as well—Adam Asnyk,

Marja Konopnicka, Henryk Sienkiewicz, Antoni Lange.

For hours the little group was one, sharing a common vision, letting the words carry them to another place and time, where one's living wasn't all chained around with the relentless fear of dying. Without ever leaving the cellar, they ventured to places where courage and hope and sometimes even joy waited like roses waiting to be plucked, and at times the little group forgot themselves and laughed. Those were the very best moments, when they sat in the cellar and laughed in the flickering candlelight while a war raged over their heads and the whole world fell to ruins.

Even Helena said so once to Josef after they had left the cellar and settled into their bed for the night. "These have been some of our best moments, Josef." She sighed heavily in the dark, a sigh of satisfaction and of wonder. "Even with the war, these are some of our best moments—you and me and the children."

Josef smiled and kissed his wife. "Yes, my dearest," he said. And while she slept, Josef lay awake, searing the moments in his mind, saving them against the day that he might need them.

It was an oddly normal routine, the life the family sculpted for themselves out of the ugly raw materials of war. The men went off to work with the underground; the women stayed home and cooked and kept the house. Zosia spent her time helping the women, and Stefan read his way through all of his grandfather Woda's books in an attempt to keep up with his studies.

It went on this way for days and weeks and months and

might have gone on this way right up to the end of the war, except that one night the routine was abruptly interrupted when Josef walked out the door of the country house and into a Gestapo trap.

JOSEF IN THE CAMPS

Ashes fall like snow here, Josef thought. He looked up at a grim gray sky, at the whirling flakes drifting to earth. *Ashes fall like snow all over the camp.*

Three months had passed since his arrest. Three months of beatings and interrogation by the Gestapo at Pawiak, a prison in Warsaw. "Give us names," they said. "We want to know who you report to, who is working with you. Give us names and it will go well for you."

He refused to speak. They beat him, starved him, threatened him with death, thinking that if they kept at him relentlessly, he would finally break. There were moments when Josef wished they would stop talking about killing him and mercifully carry through. One bullet, a fraction of a second, and the pain would be over.

But they were not merciful. To the interrogation room and to his cell, back and forth they dragged him, all hours of the night and day. Beating upon beating upon beating until there were so many layers of pain there was no relief, not even in sleep. In the place of semiconsciousness he managed to drift into from time to time, pain was there to greet him so that even in his dreams, he was all wrapped up in suffering.

The only salve for his wounds was the thought of his wife and children and the few letters that reached him from home. Shortly after Josef's arrest, Tadeusz learned of his brother's whereabouts through underground contacts. The families of prisoners were allowed to write and to send an occasional care package. The letters from Helena and the children were a tenuous lifeline for Josef, keeping him from sinking so far into the pain he could never come out again. With the little strength he could muster, Josef wrote to his wife and told her not to forget the joy that had been theirs.

Whether by luck or whim or fate, he didn't know, but eventually the Gestapo gave up on him. Rather than being taken to the wall in the prison yard for execution, as had been the fate of so many in the underground, he was placed with a group of prisoners awaiting transport to Oswiecim. The Germans didn't call the place Oswiecim, though. They had their own name for it—Auschwitz.

At least I am not in Germany, Josef thought. *At least I am still in my homeland of Poland.*

But it was small consolation in this place that little resembled Poland, this place of barracks and barbed wire, where people arrived only to disappear and black snow fell even in July.

———

What was this place, Josef wondered, where trains came

day and night, spilling out their load of depleted human cargo? What was this place where, with the slightest movement of a finger, one man condemned a thousand to the ovens, a thousand more to slow death by labor and starvation?

At first most of the prisoners were Polish intellectuals like Josef. But after a little while, that began to change. Soon all kinds of people arrived from all over Europe, whole families coming from places like Hungary, Belgium, Yugoslavia, Norway, Italy. Some were Aryan like Josef. Others, mostly Russians, were prisoners of war. But ultimately, most of the arrivals to Auschwitz were Jews. It was a mass involuntary migration of European Jewry, with the majority of the Jews not knowing where they were going. They thought they were being relocated to temporary living quarters for the duration of the war. But as soon as the train came to a halt at the platform, they began to understand otherwise. The doors of the cattle cars were flung open by SS soldiers wielding machine guns and screaming, "*Raus, raus!* Out, out!" From inside the cars the Jews peered out, frightened, bewildered, wild-eyed as hunted animals. Weakened by days without food, they hurried out the doors on stone feet, dragging with them the sick and the dying. On the platform they were greeted by the cudgel blows of the SS and the barking and snapping of the camp's German shepherds. In the midst of this swirling, crushing confusion, men were lined up on one side, women on the other. And then came the selection.

To the left went the elderly, the sick, mothers with little children. These were immediately and conveniently disposed of. Stripped and shorn of their clothing and hair, as well as their few possessions, which now belonged to the Third

Reich, they were herded into a shower room, bathed there in the steamy mists of Zyklon-B, and finally dried in the fiery furnaces of the crematorium.

To the right went the young, the healthy, the strong. They were stripped and shorn as well, then registered and tattooed with a prisoner number, given ill-fitting and inadequate clothing, quarantined, and finally put to work. But this was only a reprieve. They were worked to death or until they were so weak and sick that in the next selection the finger pointed them toward the showers, the gas, the ovens. In the end, all was death. The very air the prisoners breathed was filled with the ashes of the dead.

Selections were commonplace, held every few days. Time and again, Josef survived. He was allowed to live, allowed to work, as long as he was useful for the purposes of the Reich.

For the first year or so Josef was assigned to a work crew doing road repair and other maintenance jobs. When an SS guard discovered Josef's fluency in languages—most importantly, in German—Josef was reassigned to the central office of the camp, where he became a block clerk. The camp was a polyglot community, and the Nazis needed help in keeping all the prisoners' records straight. So Josef exchanged a shovel for a pencil, and he no longer suffered the long marches to the work sites outside of the camp. Because he worked beside the Nazis, he was given better food and allowed better hygiene. It was a position of privilege, and Josef knew his chances of survival were better than for most of the prisoners now arriving at Auschwitz.

From early morning until evening Josef and the other clerks kept the files on the inmates, dutifully recording transfers, illnesses, deaths; making work assignments; preparing the daily roll call; maintaining an accurate prisoner count. Also, secretly, they took advantage of their position to help the other prisoners as they could. They changed around work assignments, crossed certain names off transfer lists, got hospitalized prisoners sent back to work rather than to the ovens, and occasionally—though very rarely—bungled the daily count to allow a prisoner or two to escape. In this way they saved a few lives, prolonged others, gave a taste of hope to many.

Still, Josef carried the guilt of knowing that his work, though involuntary, was aiding the Third Reich. Josef, keeper of the names, was haunted day and night by the names of the dead. Part of his work assignment was the daily recording of the prisoners who had died. Some of these names belonged to people he knew, people he had met in the camp, people he had known in Warsaw before the war. Bad enough the long lists of names, hundreds of them, yet greater still was the number of the nameless dead. These were the people who had not been registered as prisoners. Their names had not been written in the books. They were the ones who had gone straight from the train to the ovens. Who were they? Josef wondered. Who were the hundreds of thousands that arrived in the cattle cars and escaped only through the chimneys, rising up over the camp in a gray smoke? Who were all these people that perished day after day, morning till night?

He couldn't know, but the trains kept on coming, endlessly. And Josef kept on writing down the names and the work assignments of the prisoners, giving a semblance of order, a patina of tidiness, to this well-oiled vehicle of genocide.

Josef was putting together a work list when he recognized the name of a prisoner who had arrived only recently from the Warsaw ghetto. His name was Eliezer, and he was the cousin of Josef's sister-in-law, Rachel. That evening, a cold and harsh midwinter night, Josef sought him out.

"Elie?"

"Who are you?"

"I am Josef Karski, Rachel's brother-in-law."

The barrack in which they met was drowned in a permanent twilight. When the men spoke, their breath hung suspended in the air, their words shrouded in a cold fog.

Eliezer sat up on his bunk and swung his feet over the side to the floor. Josef started as the young man's face caught the dim light of the electric bulb. He was little more than twenty years old, but he looked much older. His face was pale and gaunt, his hair streaked with gray, and a number of his teeth were missing, including both front teeth. From beatings, Josef knew. Eliezer, ill at ease and distrustful, gazed at Josef for a long moment. Josef wondered whether he himself had changed so much the young man wouldn't recognize him. But at length Eliezer's face relaxed, and he said, "Yes, I remember. Tadeusz is your brother."

"Yes. Do you have news of my family?" While some of the non–Jewish prisoners were allowed packages from family, Josef had had no word from his wife since he arrived at the camp.

The young man hesitated a moment before saying, "It was difficult to receive news in the ghetto."

"Yes, but do you know something?" Josef pressed. "Anything? Please, you must tell me."

Eliezer cast his eyes to the side. His jaw tightened. "Your brother is dead, Josef."

Josef lifted his chin, dropped it again, a single nod of acknowledgment. "And the others?"

"Alive. At least they were alive a month ago."

"All of them?"

"Yes, Rachel and the boy, and your wife and children."

Josef took in the news like air filling hungry lungs. They were alive. "And Tadeusz?" He had to know. "What happened?"

"He and two others were caught by the SS while trying to blow up a train. They were executed immediately."

Again the simple nod. Tadeusz had died fighting. If death had to come, this was how he would have wanted it. "And Rachel knows?"

"Yes. Josef, it was Stefan who brought us the news. He is working with the resistance to smuggle food to the Jews in the ghetto."

Josef drew back, alarmed at the thought of his young son in the resistance. "But he is only a child!"

"No, Josef," Elie said sadly. "Not anymore."

The two men fell silent. In one corner of the barrack someone was chanting and praying the Kaddish, the prayer for the dead.

"Day and night he prays for the dead," Eliezer whispered bitterly. "I wish he would stop before he drives us all crazy."

Josef shook his head slowly and replied, "Let him pray, Elie. If he prays day and night for the rest of his life, he still cannot say enough prayers for all who have died."

Eliezer lifted his eyes and settled his gaze on Josef. "And how long is a lifetime in Auschwitz, Josef?"

How long was a lifetime in Auschwitz? How long would Eliezer live? Months? Days? Hours? Here in the camp, life expectancy was no longer thought of in terms of years. Josef knew. Josef was keeper of the names.

"Your family, Elie. They were on the transport with you?"

"Of course." The young man's voice was oddly flat. "My sister Talka, she was taken to the women's camp. The rest . . ." He lifted a hand to indicate smoke rising up out of a chimney.

Josef laid a hand on Eliezer's shoulder. "I will bring you some food tomorrow, Elie," he whispered. "There is an underground working even here in the camp. I will bring you what food I can."

"Thank you, Josef."

The two men shook hands. By the time Josef returned to the barrack the next night, Eliezer was dead. He had been beaten to death by a Kapo, a fellow prisoner, for failing to show up at evening roll call on time.

––––––––––

For four years this was Josef's life. It was sheer dumb luck, he sometimes thought, that he survived in a place where hundreds of other lives were wiped out every day. *If I did not know German,* he told himself, *I would be dead by now.* But even as a clerk, life was not assured. He might come down with typhus or dysentery or fever or any of the dozens of diseases that made their way around the camp. He might anger an SS guard and be shot in the same instant. He might be beaten to death by a Kapo or a block elder, one of those prisoner-leaders who loved to wield their power over—or vent their fury on—the other prisoners. He might simply be caught in a hail of bullets from a guard tower while on his way to the latrine in the morning. Even the best of situations for a prisoner in an extermination camp holds no guarantees at all.

Josef watched the tediously slow, elongated changing of the seasons as the ashes of Auschwitz mingled with the summer sun, the spring rain, the winter snows. He moved through the misery and monotony of the endless roll calls as the hundreds of sick, starving, emaciated prisoners stood five deep while the guards counted and counted again. He suffered the gnawing hunger of never having enough to eat. He carried the burden of guilt for his participation in camp life, watching the prisoners march off day after day to bone-wearying work around the camp or in nearby factories, knowing he himself had assigned many to their tasks. He shivered each time he heard the whistle of the train, the arrival of another transport at the railway platform at Birkenau.

For Josef, as for all the prisoners, time was not divided by weeks or days or even hours. Time was divided by minutes. One could think in terms of only the smallest of increments, forgetting what happened yesterday, not daring to think of tomorrow, but narrowing the eyes of the mind to look only upon an interminable Now. Prisoners anchored their hopes to the thought that they could survive this one minute, just this one more minute. Each day from waking till sleeping was a careful treading through this one moment in the hopes of arriving alive in the next.

Josef knew there was more to surviving than keeping the

body alive. It wasn't unusual for a prisoner to step into the next moment while leaving his very self behind. His body moved forward, but it was hollow. There was no longer anything there behind the eyes. When he walked through the camp, the other prisoners dropped their gaze, not wanting to look. There was a name for people like this. They were the *muselmenn*. The walking dead.

It was important, Josef knew, to keep walking and to stay alive both.

Through every minute of every day of every year, Josef clung to the memory of his wife, Helena, and his children, Zosia and Stefan. Wherever he was, whatever he was doing— drinking what passed for a morning cup of coffee, standing immobile during roll call, recording the names and the numbers of the dead and the dying—he felt their presence. If, for a moment, the memory began to fade, he quickly called it back, reliving the days in Warsaw when they were together, when war was a distant fear, when they dreamed of a future. Now all that remained was his love for them, but he believed it was enough to keep him alive until the end of the war, until he could find them again.

Rumors of liberation sprang up and died, sprang up and died again, until at last, in January 1945, the prisoners could hear the distant guns of the advancing Soviet army. Russian soldiers, it was said, were heading toward Cracow and Auschwitz while pushing across the crumbling German Reich toward Berlin.

The Nazis, terrified in the face of imminent defeat, hastily began to withdraw from the camps across Poland—but not without the prisoners. From Auschwitz alone, fifty-eight thousand men and women were rounded up and forced on a death march toward Germany. Only the very sick were left behind, many of them murdered before the evacuation. Some were spared only because there wasn't enough time to kill them all. When the Russians entered Auschwitz on January twenty-seventh, they found some eight thousand prisoners still alive.

Josef was not among them. One of the stronger prisoners, he had left the camp days earlier. He was one among the masses swarming across the frozen landscape of Poland, bent against the cold, against the relentlessly falling snow, willing numb feet to keep walking. Flanked by the SS guards who waved their machine guns and yelled and cursed and ordered the weary wanderers to move faster, faster, the masses surged through frigid days and nights, heading no-one-knew-where. Many died or were murdered along the way, left behind where they fell, a grim testimony to the stronghold of cruelty right up to the very last days of the war.

The masses broke apart, often climbing onto cattle cars that carried them to various camps throughout Germany. Josef found himself first in a camp outside Stuttgart and then, weeks later, in another camp called Dachau. When the snow began to melt and the winter let go and gave way to spring, Josef witnessed the last changing of the seasons in a Nazi concentration camp. At the end of April, Dachau was liberated by the U.S. Seventh Army. The American soldiers came with food and medicine. The war was over. Nazi Germany was defeated. Josef's first thought upon seeing the American soldiers was, "I'm alive, and I'm almost home."

Along with the other prisoners, Josef was transferred to a camp for displaced persons on the outskirts of Monachium. He was still surrounded by barbed wire, but he was free. And unlike most of the Jewish victims of the Nazis, he still had a family and a home to return to.

As soon as he was able, he made his way back to Poland, to the country house outside of Warsaw. He had been afraid many times during the war, but never had he been consumed by such a fear as the one that bound him as he walked the road leading up to the house. Would they be there, his wife, his children, the ones for whom he had survived? Would they come running to greet him? Would they recognize him?

Weeds had overgrown the yard, making it a tangled patch of green. Almost every window in the house was broken. Jagged bits of glass made pointed teeth along the sills and around the frames. The front door hung open on its hinges.

Josef climbed the porch steps. He walked into the front hall. He almost called out Helena's name, but in that same moment he realized that no one would answer. They were not here. He had found his way home, and the house was empty.

ENDINGS AND BEGINNINGS

Josef didn't tell his whole story to Ma the first night they came across each other in the kitchen. She said he revealed it piecemeal over a number of nights, reluctant, it seemed, to tell her the whole overwhelming tale at once. Every time Josef told her a little bit more, Ma went back to our apartment and, sitting at the small rolltop desk in the living room, scribbled down all that she could remember of what she had just heard. "I sometimes stayed awake till dawn, just trying to remember everything, trying to get it all written down," she confessed years later. "I'm not really sure why, except that I knew it was something I should never forget. At the same time I was afraid if I fell asleep without writing it down, I'd wake up unable to believe I'd really heard such a story. It was all so horrible I was sure I'd wake up and think I'd dreamed it."

It was hard for Josef, Ma said, to separate the words from the emotions inside him. It was hard for him to bring up the words without dragging up the feelings as well. He had to pause often, taking long moments to collect himself before going on. But he cried only once, according to Ma's memory, and that was when he told her about how he came home and found the house empty.

"They had been murdered by the Gestapo," Josef whispered, his eyes beginning to gleam in the dull kitchen light. "Even the child, Emil."

"How did you find out what happened?" Ma asked gently.

"A neighbor—the man with whom we traded vegetables for milk. Vitzek was on his way to our house when he saw them, three men in the dreaded uniforms of the Secret State Police. They had two German shepherds with them, on leashes. Vitzek hid in the bushes, too terrified even to run. He watched as the men broke their way into the house, smashing windows, kicking open the doors front and back. He heard the Gestapo yelling, the dogs barking, and then he heard screams in the house, and in a moment the Gestapo dragged my family out to the yard, near the garden. Vitzek listened as the men spoke angrily in German. He couldn't understand all of it, but he understood a little. He thought they said something about the Polish resistance. My wife, my children said they knew nothing. But, of course, what did it matter whether or not my son Stefan was with the resistance? Rachel and Emil were Jews. My family was hiding Jews in the house, the very worst offense. An offense punishable by death. The Gestapo forced them, women and children both, to kneel there in the grass. Rachel held little Emil to her breast. Vitzek said they were very brave, they did not cry out. He saw Helena cross herself and lift her face toward the sky. Then the Gestapo shot them, one by one, in the back of the head."

The tears slipped out from beneath Josef's rimless glasses as he spoke. "They left them there," he went on, "lying in the grass beside the garden. The next day Vitzek returned with his brother and buried them."

At first Ma was numb with disbelief. How, she wondered, could a person accept so huge a loss? It seemed beyond anything that a mere human being could take in and still go on living. Yet she didn't doubt the truth of what Josef had told her. Here he was, a Polish man with a tattooed wrist and a dozen scars, sitting at her kitchen table thousands of miles from where his life began. What would bring him here alone except such a horror as this? Why would he leave his homeland except that nothing was left for which to stay?

It was only the second time in her life she had seen a man cry. The first was when her father found her beside her dead mother's bed. Frederick Skoglund had cried as he took Catherine in his arms and carried her back to her room. She knew her father was heartsick, and she might have comforted him, but in that moment she couldn't think of anything other than her own grief.

This time, though, when Josef cried, Ma said it was the first time in weeks that she didn't think of herself and Dewey. She said it might have been the first time in years that she completely forgot about her own life. She was surprised to find that she was weeping and even more surprised to realize that the reason for her tears had nothing at all to do with herself. She was crying for Josef Karski, for all that he had suffered.

Many years later when she was dying, Ma directed me to a certain drawer in that rolltop desk where she kept her notes in a stationery box tied with ribbon. With tired and trembling fingers, she opened the box and spread the pages of Josef's story across the covers of the bed where she lay.

"This is what he told me," she said. "It's all here."

She smiled then and shut her eyes, as though to sleep under the blanket of Josef's words. And she did sleep, but not before she told me one more thing. What Ma said was this: She didn't think she really started to live until she was thirty-five years old. She said she was lucky she didn't find out any later in life that a person can use up her entire allotment of years without ever living at all. Something like being a *muselmann* was how she put it. Except that you're not dead because your surroundings have destroyed you from the outside but because you've done such a good job of strangling yourself on the inside. I asked her what she meant, and she said she couldn't explain exactly, except to say that the night she cried for Josef was the beginning of everything, and all that had happened to her before that night started to become small and insignificant, like a shoreline disappearing as you watch from the deck of a moving ship.

AUTUMN

Sometime in early October, Ma asked Josef to tutor Dewey in French and algebra. Josef agreed, and the two afternoons a week that he didn't have classes at the college, he and Ma caught the streetcar together to the hospital. Ma didn't yet have her driver's license, though Mr. Diehl was certain she'd be ready to get it soon. At any rate, I wasn't home from school in time to see Ma and Josef leave, but I did like to watch the two of them walking back from the trolley stop later. That sight was the fuel for all sorts of youthful dreams.

I remember those days as a happy time, in spite of Dewey's lingering illness. Dimes continued to appear on the windowsill, and because of those dimes, I had every hope my brother would get better. I was convinced the money was being dropped directly from heaven, delivered to Selby Avenue on the wings of divine couriers. As an experiment, I sneaked out of bed a couple of times and set up a lookout post there on the divan by the parlor window. I wanted to stay awake—and tried—but figured that even if I fell asleep, which I did, no mortal being could put a dime on the sill without waking me up. The first time I did this I awoke in the morning to find an empty sill, but the second time a dime materialized in the night. Surely only an angel could have come around so quietly! I knew Ma would be skeptical, but my excitement drove me on to tell her.

"So you think an angel left it on the windowsill because you didn't wake up?" Ma asked.

"Yes, Ma, of course!" I cried happily. "If someone had leaned over me to leave it there, I would have known."

Ma shook her head. "I hate to tell you this, Nova, but an entire marching band could parade by your bed and you still wouldn't wake up."

This wasn't true, of course. I often knew when Ma laid her hand on my forehead during the night. If a gentle touch could wake me, surely I wouldn't sleep through an entire marching band. I almost said as much to Ma but decided against it in the end, as I knew nothing I said would convince her that the dimes were a miracle.

So I ignored her comment and once again sought out the opinion of others. "Manna from heaven," Aunt Dortha announced.

"*Jehovah-jireh,*" Josef said. "That's Hebrew for 'God provides.' "

Even Rosemary started to believe me when she prayed for a dime one morning and found not a dime but a quarter in the road on her way home from school that afternoon. She didn't use it for the March of Dimes, though. As soon as she found the quarter, she made a beeline for the drugstore and bought herself a banana-nut sundae. Since then she'd prayed for more money but hadn't found any. I told her it was probably because she'd spent the quarter on herself and didn't give it away to help somebody else. She agreed that was probably true and congratulated me on having the willpower to drop the dimes without exception into the canister at Shoemaker's. I felt kind of proud of myself, but I generously told Rosemary it would have been easier for her to give up the quarter if one of her brothers was in an iron lung.

Autumn arrived in a ripple of colors, and when the leaves began to fall, Clyde Munson offered to help me rake the yard and burn the leaves out back in the ash can. I happily accepted his offer. Dewey and I had done the job the year before, and I thought I'd be expected to tackle the chore by myself this time around. It wasn't the immensity of the task that scared me, it was the loneliness of doing it without Dewey. But on two or three Saturday mornings, Clyde met me with rake in hand, and while we worked, he told me stories that made my belly ache, I laughed so hard. I gained a whole new respect for Clyde, as did Ma, who could only shake her head in wonder and say, "I guess that goes to show there's a little bit of good in everyone." Clyde even made it up with Martin Popp, who was still coming around to court Miss Singletary. The two men actually became pretty good friends, though Miss Singletary still didn't say much to Clyde.

Yes, I can honestly say I was happy that autumn. I was happy after the long summer to be back in school with Rosemary and my other friends. I was happy every time I dropped a dime into the can at Shoemaker's and heard it clink against the other coins on the bottom. I was happy in my belief that

Dewey would be home by Christmas.

We did receive some news in October that most people would consider unfortunate, though, and that was word of the Reverend Haddon Biddle's death. I didn't know the old fellow from Adam, so the only thing I felt about his dying was curiosity over Ma's reaction to it. When the telegram arrived telling us that Uncle Haddon had succumbed to a massive brain hemorrhage, Ma looked up with a smile and said, "It's about time we had some good news around here."

I could only assume that Ma didn't much care for her uncle Haddon. I had to assume a lot about Ma because, at that time, I knew so little about her. The story of her life before I entered it was sketchy at best—a few brushstrokes to let me know her mother and sister had died, her father had given her away, her aunt and uncle had raised her. It was far from enough for me to hang a completed picture on.

I often wondered about my mother's past, about the parents she had lost, the aunt and uncle she had lived with. I wondered exactly what was hidden in her early years that made my mother the woman she was. But Ma wasn't the type to invite questions, and so we left a lot unsaid, though I did ask her once where her father was. She said she didn't know; he could be anywhere, if he was even still alive. He was a drifter, she had said, a wanderer. "Shouldn't we try to find him?" I asked. After all, he was her pa. He was our family. "No," she said. She didn't want to find him, even if she could. As far as she was concerned, he was dead.

I never met the Biddles, in spite of the fact that before Pa's death we all lived in the same small town of Chippewa Falls, Wisconsin. Actually, it may be more accurate to say the Biddles and I were never properly introduced, as it's most likely I did meet them several times over. I think now they must have been the strangers Ma and I ran into on occasion, those people who made Ma angry without so much as saying a word. Just by appearing on a street corner, at a trolley stop, in the same aisle of the A&P, they could render Ma speechless with fury, a magician's trick that never failed. Once or twice I heard one of them call out Ma's name, but instead of responding, Ma just turned away, crimson-cheeked and tight-lipped. I couldn't understand it because she was generally polite to people, always saying "Good morning" and "Good afternoon" and "How do you do?" But she wasn't polite to these people. Not once. And that's why I eventually decided they must have been members of the Biddle clan.

So word of Haddon Biddle's death left Ma rejoicing. And Ma's rejoicing left Aunt Dortha mortified.

"I can understand your feelings about your uncle, Catherine," Auntie said, "but I think you should telegram your poor aunt right away and tell her how sorry you are. We'll make arrangements for you to go to the funeral."

"Oh, I'll send Susannah a note, Dortha," Ma assured her. "And I'll even try to be nice. But if she thinks I'm going to Chippewa Falls for the old man's funeral, she's got another think coming."

"Oh, Catherine! Won't you go simply for Susannah's sake?"

"Wild horses couldn't drag me there to mourn over that man's grave," Ma retorted. "I'd sooner dance on his tombstone than mourn for him, Dortha, so at least I can spare Susannah that."

"I think you're making a mistake, Catherine." Auntie shook her head. "You ought to put in an appearance at that funeral, whether you cared for the man or not. Propriety calls for it."

Ma laughed. "Oh, Dortha," she said, "if I went to that funeral and pretended to mourn, I'd be as much of a hypocrite as our dear departed Haddon Biddle. Two wrongs don't make a right, as you've been known to say."

I didn't understand it, but I'll admit I was kind of glad Ma had one more thing to be happy about, on top of her driving lessons and the coming of autumn, which meant first frost wasn't far behind. She was about as happy that fall as I'd ever seen her, which wasn't exactly happy, of course, mostly because of Dewey's still being in the lung, but she did seem less sad, which was a step in the right direction. I didn't know what had happened or what was happening to her, but I was hoping she was falling a little bit in love with Josef.

Auntie and I couldn't help but notice that Ma and Josef were calling each other by their first names now. Neither Auntie nor I knew anything about their middle-of-the-night meetings, but we knew something was going on between the two of them. Ma was *nice* to Josef. She even laughed with him. And more than once I'd seen them smile at each other when not a single word had passed between them. I started having wedding thoughts and thinking maybe pretty soon I could be like all the other kids who had a pa.

I was even about to confide to Rosemary that Josef was going to end up my pa when something happened that left me pleasantly confused. Our doorbell rang one evening, and when I answered it, Thomas Diehl stood there with a fistful of golden chrysanthemums from his garden.

"Some of the last of the season," he said. "Won't be long before the frost hits and that'll be it until spring."

"Well, they're real pretty, Mr. Diehl," I said. "Ma's not here, but I'll put them in some water for her."

Mr. Diehl smiled and rocked back on his heels. "Oh, but they're not for your mother, Nova. They're for you."

I could feel the double line forming between my eyebrows. "For me?"

"Yes, I thought I heard you tell your aunt Dortha that you particularly favor mums."

"Oh." I tried to remember. "I guess I did."

"Well, would you like to have these, then?"

I finally realized he'd been holding out the flowers for me to take since I'd opened the door. I took them and touched the blossoms gently. "I never got flowers before," I said, feeling suddenly shy.

"Well." Thomas Diehl laughed quietly. "You'd better get used to it. Pretty girls get lots of pretty flowers."

I couldn't believe it! No one had ever said I was pretty before. Two firsts in a matter of seconds. For a long moment I was too surprised to speak, but I finally managed to thank Mr. Diehl just as he was backing down the porch steps and turning away. He lifted a hand in reply and strode across the street to his own house.

Oh, Mr. Diehl! So kind and a perfect gentleman. Handsome too, though that wasn't as important as the fact that he was a good man, of course. A good man who had read *Sonnets From the Portuguese* almost a dozen times. Even Rosemary's spinster aunt, the librarian, admired him, and that said something coming from a woman who had never found a man good enough to marry.

I sighed. This love business was wonderful but far more complicated than I ever could have imagined even a year ago. How to choose between two men so equally fine as Josef Karski and Thomas Diehl?

Holding the mums to my nose, I sniffed dreamily, savoring a moment with such a marvelous dilemma as one too many people to love.

THE RABBI ON THE HILL

24

"This uncle of yours, this Mr. Biddle, he was not a good man?"

Ma had been expecting Josef's question. Only hours after Aunt Susannah's telegram arrived, everyone in the house knew there had been a death in the family. Everyone knew as well that Auntie was trying to persuade Ma to do the proper thing by going to the funeral. When Ma replied to Josef's question, her voice was quiet, but her face was hard and drawn, her mouth pinched, as though the words left a bitter taste on her tongue. "The Reverend Mr. Haddon Biddle," she said, "was a hypocrite. Oh, he looked virtuous enough by day, but he was a different creature altogether when the clerical collar came off at night."

"Ah," said Josef with a lift of his chin. "I see."

Ma couldn't meet his gaze. "Do you?" she asked hesitantly.

"I believe so, Catherine."

Ma and Josef were no longer surprised to find each other in the kitchen at odd hours of the night. They weren't even surprised when they happened to enter the kitchen at the same time, as though it had all been planned. Called up out of a troubled sleep by dreadful voices and dream-twisted memories, they both, upon awakening, felt called by something benevolent to seek each other out. And there they were, in that dark place between midnight and dawn, talking about Haddon Biddle.

"The day you asked me to leave," Josef ventured gently, "you were afraid for Nova. You were afraid because of your uncle."

Ma tried to look at him but dropped her eyes again. He did understand, only too well.

"I'm sorry, Catherine. If I had known then—"

"How could you have known?" she interrupted. "You knew nothing about me. You still know so little."

"Yes," he agreed. "I know only that your journey has not been easy."

Ma rose and poured them both a cup of coffee from the freshly brewed pot. When she sat again, she sighed. "I have been through nothing, Josef." Now she could look at him, meet his gaze. "Not when I think of what you've been through. The war . . ." She shook her head. "What I've known, any grief I've known—it all becomes nothing next to what you have suffered."

"We are not meant to compare, my dear," he answered. He lifted the coffee cup to his lips, sipped, lowered it again. "Because I lived through the war, does that mean what your uncle did to you was of no consequence? One person's suffering cannot erase that of another. I would never presume to belittle your pain, Catherine."

Ma smiled weakly. "You are very kind, Josef. Do you suppose," she asked, "that's why I trust you?"

Josef pulled back one corner of his mouth, raised a hand palm up to signify that he had no answer.

"Because I do, you know," Ma went on, "even though I swore I would never trust anyone again. I wanted to trust them all—my father, my uncle, my husband. But not one of them could be trusted, and not a day goes by that I don't remember what they did." Her voice trailed off, and her eyes settled on something far away, something far beyond the confines of the shadow-darkened kitchen. Then abruptly she snapped back to the present, looked squarely at Josef, and asked, "Do you think I'm a grieving widow? My only regret is that my husband isn't alive for me to tell him how much I despise him."

She stopped then, shivered slightly. "I'm saying too much, aren't I?" She touched her coffee cup with trembling fingers. "I'm telling you far more than you want to hear."

"I am not thinking of myself right now, Catherine. I am thinking only of you. This concerns me, this hate you feel. If you keep it inside, it will only do you harm."

Ma frowned, shook her head. "But what can I do, Josef? It's far too late to make amends. They're all dead—or at least in my father's case, as good as dead. In the end I loathed them all, and that's where it stays."

"But of what use is your hatred for three dead men? What can it do to them? Nothing. Only you it can hurt."

"I can't help what I feel, Josef. None of us can."

"But don't you see? You contend with these men day after day, and all the while they have the advantage. They are dead. Nothing you can do will hurt them. And yet they go on hurting you because you let them. It is a losing battle, Catherine. . . ."

"If you think I can forget, you're wrong. I'll never forget for as long as I live."

Josef sighed heavily. "Perhaps if you spoke with your aunt Susannah, if you told her what happened—"

"Ha!" Ma's laughter sounded shrill against the quiet night. "Tell my aunt what happened? She knows what happened. She knew while it was happening, and she did nothing to stop it. She didn't lift a finger to help me."

Ma rose from the table and walked to the window over the sink. She stood quietly, collecting herself. When she spoke again, her voice was quieter, more composed. "For the first two years he was kind. He treated me like a daughter, the way a father should treat a daughter, and I loved him. I was almost happy again. You see, I was with them—my aunt and uncle—because my mother died during the influenza epidemic. She and my baby sister both. After that my father gave me to my mother's sister, Aunt Susannah, because he didn't want to raise me alone. I never saw my father again. He said good-bye at the train station, and that was it. Suddenly I had a new mother and father, a whole new family.

"My aunt looked so much like my mother, I sometimes pretended she *was* my mother. It wasn't hard. I eventually began to heal, and I could stop thinking about my own parents without crying. In fact, after a while I didn't think about them much at all. It was just as though I'd always been with the Biddles, as though I was their daughter and their four sons were my brothers instead of my cousins. Life was good, and I guess I was as happy as I've ever been. But then I turned seven. And then he began to come to my room in the night." Ma pulled her quilted robe more tightly around her, crossing her arms against her chest. "The well-respected pastor, the Reverend Haddon Biddle, suddenly had a terrible secret."

She lingered at the window awhile longer, gazing out. Her hair fell in loose waves around her shoulders. She was a colorless cameo there in the dim kitchen light, but I think she must have been beautiful even then, without adornment, in spite of fatigue, in spite of the sadness in her eyes. "It took me three years to work up the courage," she went on, "but I finally went to Susannah one night when my uncle was away from home. He had been called away suddenly after supper to a farm far outside of town where one of his parishioners lay dying. He said not to expect him back until morning.

"I saw it as my chance to confide in Susannah. Up to then I had kept quiet because my uncle had threatened me, said he would deny it, promised to send me to live in an orphanage if I ever breathed a word. I was afraid of the orphanage because of the stories I'd heard, terrible things. But I finally decided life in an orphanage couldn't be any worse than life with Haddon Biddle.

"She was sitting in her room at her vanity table. She had let her hair down for the night, and she was brushing it with her silver-handled hairbrush. She never looked more like my mother than when she was brushing out her long blond hair. Well, I told her what I had come to tell her, and while I talked, she never stopped brushing her hair. She went on looking at herself in the mirror just as though I wasn't there. When I finished, she finally turned to me. When I saw her face at that moment, she didn't look like my mother anymore. Her features were twisted with what might have been rage, or it might have been fear—I don't know. I only know she had become a stranger. 'You must never speak to me of these things again,' she said. And then she turned away and went back to brushing her hair."

Josef squeezed his hands together on the tabletop. After a long moment he asked, "Do you think she believed you?"

"Yes. She must have known. She must have awakened in the night and discovered him gone. She must have known when, hours later, he crawled back into their bed. . . ."

"She must have been afraid of him, as you were."

"Maybe. Or perhaps she was simply afraid to ruin him and to ruin herself as well. She no doubt wanted to avoid a scandal at all costs. Should he lose his church and his position as pastor, what would become of them? She could keep her world intact and running smoothly simply by overlooking certain things."

Josef nodded. "And so it went on?"

"What could I do to stop it? At first I prayed to God to make him stop. I even prayed that God would make him die. But after a while I stopped praying. If God was there, he had decided to be of no more help to me than my aunt."

Josef sat motionless at the table, his eyes narrowed, his jaw working. "Then," he said at length, "I assume you finally escaped Haddon Biddle by marrying your late husband."

"Ironic, isn't it?" Ma agreed. "I was eighteen years old,

and I thought at last everything was going to be different. Life was going to be good."

"But—your husband, he was unfaithful?"

"It's an old story, isn't it, Josef?"

"I am afraid so, yes."

Ma turned from the window then and rejoined Josef at the table. She took a sip of her coffee, then returned the cup to the saucer. "He had a lover," she said evenly, "and he died with her one night when her apartment building caught fire. He might have enjoyed the scandal surrounding his death had he somehow been able to know about it. Royal always did revel in the limelight."

Ma and Josef fell silent then. Even the night was quiet. The room, the whole house, seemed to be floating on a sigh. Ma waited for Josef to respond, but even if he said nothing, it would be all right. Even if they sat there until the morning light rose in the window, the silence would be a circling warmth, the kitchen table a sanctified place of sorts because of the purifying element of confession. Between Ma and Josef there was now a shared knowing. She had told him, and still his face was kind. He understood. She was sure he did.

After several minutes Josef said, "I'm sorry, Catherine. These things should not have happened to you."

Ma looked at Josef, then turned her eyes to the window. "Should such things as you and I have seen," she asked, "should such things as these happen to anyone?"

"They should not, no," Josef replied. "And yet they do. Nothing happens in this world that is not already a very old story."

"Sometimes," Ma said slowly, cautiously, "I wonder how

we all go on living. I wonder why we go on living."

Josef leaned forward over the table. His face softened by shadows and by compassion, he commanded Ma's gaze. Quietly he said, "I believe it is called hope."

Ma looked at Josef a long while. She wanted to lift a hand and reach across the table to touch that face so marked by suffering and compassion. Was it real, she wondered? After what those eyes had seen, how could the mouth still speak of hope? "And do you believe in hope, Josef? After all you have been through . . . surely you can never forget. . . ."

"Catherine—"

"I know you must hate them, the Nazis, every bit as much as I hate . . . them—the people I've known in my life."

"Catherine," he said again, patiently, "I too am only human. I cannot remember the SS in the camp without—" He squeezed his hands together tightly, his fingers pulsing red and white. "Yes, yes, I could kill them all. Surely if I ever saw the men of the Gestapo who murdered my family . . ." He stopped then, shook his head. "You see, Catherine, I understand very well what it is to hate and to be so full of anger you can hardly bear to go on living. I know only too well what all of that can do to a man's soul. That is why I tell you: do not hate. If you can find it in yourself to forgive . . . well . . ." He seemed to want to say more, but he only nodded.

When Ma spoke, her voice was a whisper. "Don't tell me you have forgiven those people, Josef, because I won't believe it."

Josef offered a small, sad smile. "I forgive one day, and the next I must forgive again. Every day I am forgiving them."

Ma looked at him a long while, struggling against doubt. "How can you not be bitter? The first night I saw you here, eating the cold stew, I asked you why you don't curse God."

"Yes." Josef nodded again. "I remember."

"I still don't understand. And now that I know what happened to you in the war, I'm even more confused. Why do you even go on believing in him, much less defending him?"

Her question was met at first with silence while Josef rubbed his brow with both hands. When he finished that task, he sighed deeply. "I have not completely rid myself of the hate that I feel for the Nazis. I struggle with it every day. I will struggle with it every day until I die, of that I'm sure. And sometimes I do want to curse God, just as you say. But I don't because I remember—every day I remember—what a Polish rabbi told me in the camp."

Ma looked at Josef intently, nodded once, a cue for him to go on.

"This rabbi," he continued, "he survived for about a year in the camp, and since he lived in my barrack I could observe him. He spent all his free time praying and reciting long passages of the Torah to anyone who would listen. Sometimes no one listened. Other times a handful of men joined him, mostly on the Jewish holidays. But many mocked him, told him he was mad. Even so, he never lost his faith. Right up to the end he never lost his faith.

"One night as he sat on his bunk muttering his prayers, I asked him, 'Why do you go on in your worship of God? Look at what he has allowed to happen to the Jews.'

"As though I had said nothing, he went on chanting in Hebrew. But when he finished, he looked up at me and invited me to sit beside him on the bunk. I sat down. He was not an old man, I knew, because all the elderly had already been sent to the gas. But his time in Auschwitz had aged him far beyond his years. His skin sagged, and his hair was gray, and his eyes watered like the eyes of a very old man.

"His voice, though, was still young. And when he spoke it was almost as though he were singing, and his words were like a melody. 'You too are here in this place of madness,' he said, 'though you are not a Jew. The suffering of this time is not for the Jews alone.'

" 'Yet it is the Jews who are brought in on the trains and sent to the crematoriums,' I reminded him. 'They have long stopped gassing those of us who aren't Jews. It's your people the Nazis want to destroy.'

" 'Josef,' he said, 'you are my fellow Pole, Jewish or not. You know the Germans would destroy us all, Jew and Gentile alike.'

"Well, I couldn't argue with that. Poland had been very nearly crushed in the first days of the war, and if the Germans were victorious, they would certainly finish the job of destroying Poland altogether.

"The rabbi asked me, 'And you, Josef? Have you turned your back on the God of Abraham?'

"I didn't know how to answer at first. I had been a believing Catholic all my life. But when the war started, God seemed simply to vanish. And so I said, 'Perhaps, Avram, it would be more accurate to say that God has turned his back on me.'

"To that the rabbi shook his head. 'You must never say that, Josef. You must never even allow yourself to think it.'

" 'How can I not, Avram?' I asked. 'We have all been abandoned, those of us who are here. Surely God cannot enter hell itself.'

" 'He can and he does, Josef,' he answered.

" 'No,' I said. 'If God were here, this horror would not be happening. Surely he wouldn't allow it.'

"The rabbi looked at me a long time with his watery eyes. Finally he said, 'Have you never heard the story of the Baal Shem Tov, the rabbi who centuries ago founded the Hasidic movement in our own homeland of Poland?'

"I shook my head. 'Perhaps when I was a little boy in school,' I replied honestly, 'but I don't remember.'

" 'Then let me remind you, Josef. Listen closely. It was a time not unlike this, for there have always been murder and greed in the human heart. On this day centuries ago, the Baal Shem Tov was standing high on a hill with a couple of his students, looking down at the town where his school was. Suddenly a group of Cossacks on horseback attacked the town. As he saw many of his students, along with the men, women, and children of the town being slaughtered, the Baal Shem Tov looked up to heaven and said, "Oh, if only I were God." One of his students said with astonishment, "But, Master, if you were God, what would you do differently?" To which the rabbi replied, "If I were God I would do nothing differently. If I were God, I would understand." ' "

Josef stopped and sat in silence, lost in thought, listening still to the rabbi named Avram in the barrack at Auschwitz. Finally he returned to Ma and focused his eyes on her. "Not long after he told me the story of the Baal Shem Tov, my friend Avram was sent to the wrong side during the selection.

His time had come. But he went peacefully to his death, reciting the Kaddish even as he walked to the showers. 'May the great name of the Lord be exalted and hallowed throughout the world which he hath created according to his will. . . .' "

Horror and wonder, odd bedfellows, met and mingled on Josef's face. Ma could almost see it all played out right there—in his eyes, on his brow, along the corners of his mouth—that day in the camp when the rabbi went to his death praising the God who had allowed it to happen.

"So you see, Catherine"—Josef gave Ma a tentative smile—"I have remembered that rabbi every day since then, his faith and how he died with his face turned toward God. That which gave him the strength to die now gives me the strength to live. There is so much of suffering that I will never even begin to understand. But I am content in believing that I don't have to understand why the story unravels the way it does so long as I know that in the end everything will be all right."

Yes, even as Josef spoke, she saw and heard it all. The finger pointing to the left, the doomed prisoners naked, without hair, without flesh, skin wrapped around bone, shuffling forward, stepping toward the showers. The rabbi quiet, his watery eyes blazing, as though already he could see beyond the carnage, beyond the camp, beyond the moment of dying, repeating over and over, "May the great name of the Lord be exalted and hallowed throughout the world. . . ."

Then Ma realized Josef was gazing at her. "But will it, Josef?" she asked. "Will everything really be all right?"

"Catherine," he replied slowly, "I struggle against a thousand doubts to tell you yes, everything is going to be all right."

TRUMAN DEFEATS DEWEY

Dear Dewey,

I guess you heard by now about Truman winning the elecshun. Did you hear about that paper down in Chicago that said real big in their headline Dewey Defeats Truman? Boy did they mess up but I wish they were right. Anyway, Ma's happy about how it turned out. Aunt Dortha wuldn't tell me who she voted for. She said if Truman won that was fine and if Dewey won that was fine too becose whoever ended up in the white house it wuld be the will of providence. I thought Ma was going to get mad about Auntie talking about providence like she always does but this time she didn't. She just said maybe Auntie was right and then Auntie and I looked at each other with our eyes popping out and our mouths hanging down like we were trying to catch flies or something. Later when Auntie and I were alone I told her Ma's been saying some strange things lately and Auntie put a finger to her lips and said real quiet she thinks Ma's falling in love becose women say funny things when they get smitten and I said is she in love with Josef and Auntie said she didn't know for sure but she hopes so. I told Auntie I thought she wanted Ma to marry Mr. Diehl, and she said they are both good men and Ma can't go wrong in marrying either one. I still like Mr. Diehl too and he gave me flowers and that makes it hard to decide who Ma shuld marry. What do you think, Dewey? When Ma and Josef are with you does Ma say funny things and act like she and Josef are sweethearts? They are calling each other by their first names now, and maybe pretty soon they'll start calling each other honey and dear and all those things sweethearts call each other. Would you be glad if Ma married Josef? Or do you want her to marry Mr. Diehl? Please tell me what you think, Dewey, becose he will be your pa too.

Your loving sister,
Nova Tierney

P.S. Tell Miss Evans to make sure Ma never sees this letter.

———

Dear Tag,

I see you are still trying to get Ma married off. I know you want a pa real bad, but like I told you before, there's nothing you can do about it. Ma's going to have to make up her own mind, not just about who she's going to marry, but even if she wants to get married, which I doubt. I'm not trying to make you feel sad or hurt, really I'm not, but you just have to see how it is.

I know I said once that Josef kind of gives me the

creeps, but I think you will be happy to know I like him now. He's a real good tutor, and it's swell of him to come in and help me. Anyone who can listen to me mangle the French language and still not yell his head off at me for being an idiot, he's all right in my book. So I think he would make a good pa if that happened.

But I don't want you to get your hopes up for nothing. When Ma and Josef are here, they sure don't act like sweethearts. They're nice to each other, but it's not like they're all lovey-dovey or anything like that. Don't go reading anything into it just because they call each other by their first names. I've heard Ma call the butcher by his first name too, but that doesn't mean she's going to run out and start looking for a justice of the peace. Who knows why grown-ups do what they do? Listen, Tag, you'd be better off to stop worrying so much about getting Ma hitched up. Maybe someday we'll have a new pa, but then again, maybe you and I just weren't meant to have one. But that doesn't mean we're not a real family, because we are, you and me and Ma.

Of course I know Truman was elected because you should have heard the Truman fans going crazy around here when the election results were announced. I thought the hospital was going to cave in like the walls of Jericho before the nurses got everyone calmed down. Even some of the nurses and doctors themselves were hooting and hollering. I couldn't care less about who won, but in a way I'm kind of glad Dewey didn't because I wouldn't want to go through the next four years being kidded about my name. Things are hard enough already without that.

The therapist started doing this new trick with me to

try to build up the strength in my lungs. She puts a straw in my mouth with a pea in it, and I have to try to blow that pea up to the ceiling. So far I haven't hit the ceiling, but I'm working on it, and I'm going to do it one of these days too. I'm working my way up to three minutes outside the lung, but it's slow going, and sometimes I think I'll never get out for good. Listen, Tag, never take anything you do for granted. I mean like walking and moving your hands and even breathing. I hope you never have to use a bedpan. I won't even try to tell you how terrible it is.

Lunch trays are coming around. Time for me to put on the bib and be spoon-fed by whatever nurse has feeding duty today. I miss you, but in a way I'm glad you can't see me like this.

I will write again tomorrow.

Love,
Dewey

——————

Dear Dewey,

I wish I could see you and I don't even care what you look like when you're eating, which wasn't such a pritty sight when you were home anyway so I don't know why you think it matters now. Ma still says no when I ask her if I can see you and I don't even know why becose other kids get to go visiting at the hospital. I guess Ma is afraid I'll go in helthy and come out sick and she doesn't want to take any chances.

Did Ma tell you she got her drivers licence? She probably did, she was so excited about it. She even let Mr. Thomas Diehl take her out to supper to celibrate.

They didn't just go to the diner either but they went to that nice place with the green awning over the entrance and the carpeting that looks like grass going up the front steps. I forget the name but you know the place I mean. Mr. Diehl said this was a great acomplishment that called for a grand celibration and the sky was the limit. Ma got all dressed up and put on that perfume I haven't smelled in ever so long. I was sure Josef would be jelous of Mr. Diehl, but when Mr. Diehl came over Josef gave him a big handshake and told him and Ma to have a wonderful time. You know, Josef and Mr. Diehl have become pritty good pals. Sometimes I see them talking out on the front porch for hours and hours, and sometimes Josef goes across to Mr. Diehl's house and looks at his garden and I think they watch the shows on television too. I think they are freinds in spite of Ma and not like the fellas in the movies that are always going after the same lady and always fighting on account of it.

I know what you are thinking, that I shuld stop trying to figure out who Ma will marry but I just can't, Dewey. I try but it is too hard.

Anyway, Ma took me for a drive the day she got her licence and don't tell her I said so but it was scary and also embarissing. Ma drives too fast and then sometimes she puts the brake on real hard when you aren't ready for it. Once I even flew off the seat and ended up on the floor underneath of the dash board. I still have a bruise on my sholder, but I didn't tell Ma. She asked if I was okay and I just tried to laugh but after that I held on pritty tight to the door handle. Then the other bad thing that happened was when we were stopped at a light Eddie Pratt was right there on the sidewalk and he saw me sitting in this old pickup truck with Ma and I could see he was laughing. Mr. Diehl painted it and fixed it up nice but it is still a pickup and I could see Eddie making fun of us to his friends. This made me mad becose only the day before he kidded me at school saying we live in a flophouse. I told him it is not a flophouse but a respectible boardinghouse but he said we take in low-lifes and other trash and I had to turn and run away becose I didn't want him to see me crying. I hate Eddie Pratt and his friends. Rosemary says ignore him but he doesn't tease her like he does me.

I'm glad Ma is happy with the truck but I hope I don't have to ride in it with her too much.

I have spent more than an hour writing this and now I have to do my homework.

Your loving sister,
Nova Tierney

P.S. I almost forgot, did you know it snowed last nite? It was pritty watching the snowflakes coming down but on account of the clouds I couldn't see the moon.

Dear Tag,

I'm real proud of Ma for getting her license, and I told her so. I also told her I'd give just about anything to drive that truck someday, and she said when I get out of the hospital, she'll hand me the keys, and it'll be mine. I said I can't even get my license for a couple more years, and she said it didn't matter, the truck was still mine, and she'd take me out to the country and let me drive it sometimes. I think that's more than swell of her. The first thing I'll do when I get behind the wheel is run down

Eddie Pratt for you. Then you won't have to worry about him anymore, okay? Until then, take Rosemary's advice and ignore him. If he's anything like his older brother Wally, he's not worth stewing about.

I stayed out of the lung for three whole minutes today, and for a while I was really happy. But then I heard someone mention the date, and I wasn't so happy anymore. Did you know today would be Andy Johanson's fourteenth birthday? I keep expecting him to walk down the hall and sit down and tell me a bunch of his corny jokes or something. But he's never going to be telling me any jokes again or anything else for that matter. I don't want to believe he's dead. I keep thinking over and over that it should have been me, not Andy. But that doesn't change anything. His dad has come to see me, but his ma won't. I think she blames me, and maybe Jerry too, for what happened. I don't know if I gave the polio to Andy, but I don't think it really matters who gave it to who or if we all just got it at once from somewhere else. But anyway I wish Mrs. Johanson would come around just so I could tell her I'm sorry, and if I could change it so Andy was still alive and I was dead, I'd do it in a minute.

Love,

Dewey

P.S. I thought I wouldn't say this, but I'm going to say it anyway because I think it's important. Listen, Tag, if I do die because of this polio, you know I've always wanted to be buried up in the trees the way the Indians used to bury their dead. I know people don't do that anymore, but if I do die, would you ask Ma if somehow I can be buried up in the trees? I want to be out in the open where I can see the stars and not underground where it's dark and I can't see anything at all. I can't imagine anything worse than that.

————————

Dear Dewey,

Please don't talk about dying becose I can't stand it. I don't want anybody to die, mostly you. And Ma too. Just yesterday Ma came home from the hospital all shook up because she said the roads were slippery even though there was just a little bit of snow. She said she and Josef almost went off the road when they went around a curve over by the Missisipi River but they didn't go off the road even though they skidded for what seemed like forever. When they got home she was still white as a ghost. She said it was the first time she was afraid of driving the truck becose it seemed like the truck took over and had a mind of its own. It was going to go where it was going to go and it didn't matter what Ma did with the steering wheel. Auntie said it might teach her not to go so fast especially in bad wether, but Josef stood up for Ma and said it culd have happened to anyone no matter how fast they were going. Anyway, they were alright and everyone was glad.

I'm sad Andy Johanson died but I can't lie, Dewey. I'm glad it wasn't you. If you or Ma died I wuldn't want to live anymore. I think I would die of a broken heart, and that is no exageration. So please don't think about it or talk about it. Just think about coming home. I'm praying you will be home for Christmas. If you pray that too maybe it will be true. I think its swell that your out of the lung for three whole minutes now. Just keep trying and I know you can get out for good. You wait and see.

Your loving sister,
Nova Tierney

THANKSGIVING 26

Thanksgiving was the only day of the year the Lassiter sisters stepped into the kitchen with the intention of cooking. Ever since they'd moved into Aunt Dortha's boardinghouse in 1943, they had helped fix the holiday meal for the boarders who had nowhere else to go. Aunt Dortha and Ma were glad for the help, as most often our residents were without close family connections, which meant they stayed and ate with us. Auntie, never one to skimp when it came to her boarders, spent hours—even days—fixing a full-fledged turkey dinner.

The Lassiter sisters prepared the same dishes every year, which as far as I know was the full extent of their culinary capability. They called these dishes Eva Lassiter's Secret Recipe Cornbread and Giblet Stuffing, Ida Lassiter's Secret Recipe Tangerine Sweet Potato Casserole, and Chester Guernsey's Secret Recipe Mincemeat Pie. Chester Guernsey was one of the former husbands of one of the sisters, but I was never sure which one, as neither Eva nor Ida seemed to want to claim him. At any rate, there wasn't anything very secret about the recipe, because the mincemeat came out of a jar.

When I wasn't polishing silverware or setting the table, I hung about the kitchen enjoying the frantic preparations, the womanly camaraderie, and the tantalizing odors of things baking. I loved the atmosphere of high anticipation. A bounty had been gathered, and a feast was in the making!

Every year the celebration unfolded in much the same way. When all was ready, we gathered together and Auntie said a long and heartfelt grace, and then we ate and talked and laughed and ate some more, passing around the bowls and platters of food once and twice and yet again. We ate until we were well beyond full, not even leaving room for dessert but taking a generous helping of dessert anyway and somehow, without much difficulty, getting it down. Afterward the adults lingered at the table sipping coffee and, for a few of them, enjoying a smoke. Even Auntie relaxed and said the dishes could wait until morning. Dewey and I moved into the parlor, where we stretched out on the floor and listened to music on the radio while drifting in and out of a contented sleep. Thanksgiving evening was invariably a time when the house was filled with a certain satisfaction—full stomachs, idle hands, and drowsy minds were the rule.

This year, though, was destined to be different. This year the holiday was, at least for me—and maybe for all of us— doomed from the outset. We had Josef, Henry Udahl, Eva and Ida Lassiter, and Thomas Diehl around our table with us. Otherwise, three people were missing. Betty Singletary and Clyde Munson were eating their Thanksgiving dinners else- where, and that was fine by me. It was the third missing person that made the difference. In fact, Dewey's absence was a sort of presence at our table, more so than in all the weeks past. Today was a holiday, a family day, a day when people came home from near and far to be with one another. If you could. But Dewey couldn't. You didn't travel home and take a seat at the dining room table when you were stuck in an iron lung.

Shortly after Auntie offered grace, Henry Udahl started to say he got another postcard from Henry Jr. down in Texas, but he soon realized no one was comfortable with his tale of the son who wasn't here. Mr. Diehl said something about the preparations for the St. Paul Winter Carnival, but he must have remembered how much Dewey loved that annual event, because one moment he was talking about the ice-sculpting contest and the next he was announcing that his brother-in-law had just been fitted for a new leg. It was an abrupt and unexpected leap from ice sculptures to Philip Townsend's removable leg, but Josef tried to smooth the transition by commenting on how the design of artificial limbs had vastly improved since the war. Now scores of amputee veterans were rising up from their wheelchairs and getting back on their feet, or on brand-new feet, thanks to these better prostheses. While it was a valiant attempt on Josef's part at some positive news, from there the conversation limped off into silence. Wheelchairs spoke of cripples, and cripples spoke of polio, and polio spoke of Dewey. Every avenue of conversation seemed to lead right back around to him, and Dewey was there in the midst of us without his name ever once being mentioned.

We were barely into our first round of helpings, but

already I knew I'd be hard put to finish what was on my plate. The food was tasteless, our residents subdued, and the presence of Dewey's absence was all-consuming. Ma's face was pale as she absently stabbed at the same piece of turkey over and over with her fork. She appeared to want to be anywhere but where she was. I hoped no one would say anything to upset her, and I was especially afraid Auntie might make her annual suggestion of "Let's all name one thing we're thankful for." It was a suggestion that Ma generally greeted with a roll of her eyes, though this year I could well imagine it sending her through the roof. But I needn't have worried. Auntie just kept saying things like "More potatoes, anyone?" and "Eat up. There's plenty more on the stove." She smiled, but her smile looked forced, and I think she was having a hard time feeling thankful herself. Her eyes darted from face to face as though she were looking for someone to pull us up out of our awkwardness.

Finally, thankfully, the Lassiter sisters decided to fill the huge void of our conversation with stories about Thanksgivings on the road. Seasoned narrators, they first took turns telling of the time their vaudeville troupe received a live turkey as a gift from an admiring fan.

"Well, we all dressed up like pilgrims to be in keeping with the holiday, just for a little added fun, and meanwhile this turkey was strutting around the back lot at the motel not knowing what was in store—"

"And we knew *some*body had to kill the poor thing if we were going to *eat* it, of course, but no one was volunteering, so we finally decided to draw numbers from a hat to see who would have the honor of killing that poor Tom."

"And Ida won . . . a-ha-ha-ha. . . ."

"Or you might better say I lost, depending on how you look at it. Well, honestly, what did I know about butchering turkeys? Not the first thing, let me tell you. I mean, I was born and bred in Mil*wau*kee, not on a farm, after all. So I begged Eva to do it, but Eva didn't want to do it either."

"Why, I just felt so *sorry* for the poor bird."

"So we decided to let it go. We borrowed a couple of kitchen knives from the motel owner's wife, and we went out there like we were going to kill the thing, and we started chasing that turkey right down the middle of Main Street. . . . a-ha-ha-ha!"

"Oh my yes, we literally ran that bird out of town! I had no idea turkeys could run so fast. . . ."

"I don't know who was screaming louder—us or the bird—"

"And we didn't stop running until old Tom had crossed the railroad tracks and disappeared beyond the outskirts of town."

"A-ho-ho-ho, and oh my, then of course we had to pretend that it was all a terrible mistake. We had to go back to the motel and tell everyone that their Thanksgiving dinner had just gotten away—"

"And we said, oh my yes, we really had *tried* to kill the turkey, but the old bird was just too fast for us."

"Ha-ha-ha, and we all ended up going to a diner and having corned beef and cabbage—"

"And then when we got back to the motel later, who do you think was strutting around by the back door?"

"A-ha-ha! That old bird was so *stu*pid, he came *back* to the motel just like he'd rented a room there and wasn't *about* to be run out of town before the week was up."

The sisters laughed until mascara-blackened tears ran down their faces. Henry Udahl joined them, screwing up his little mole eyes and hooting until his face turned red. Josef and Mr. Diehl and Auntie laughed too, but I thought it sounded more polite than genuine. Ma didn't laugh at all. Neither did I. I just wasn't in the mood. But the sisters were undeterred. They started another story and kept right on talking all the way up to dessert.

By the time Aunt Dortha brought out the pies, an inch of snow had fallen over the city. No one noticed until Ma glanced at the window and said, "Oh no! I have to get to the hospital, today of all days. I can't let Dewey spend the entire holiday alone."

"Don't worry, Catherine," Mr. Diehl said at once. "I'll drive you."

Ma accepted his offer gratefully. Ever since she had almost slid off the road when she was coming home from the hospital with Josef, she was afraid of driving in the snow.

"If you want to leave now," Aunt Dortha offered, "I'll pack you a basket of food for Dewey."

"Thank you, yes, Dortha," Ma replied, rising from the table. "And if you'll give me just a minute, Tom, I'll get myself ready to go."

Mr. Diehl, halfway through a piece of Chester Guernsey's Secret Recipe Mincemeat Pie, responded with a wave of his fork. "I'll be ready when you are."

I sat on the stairs, my chin in my hands, watching the falling snow pile up on the porch railings and in the yard beyond. We were long past the first frost—there was no more chance I'd catch polio now. *Ollie, Ollie in come free!* No more hiding from or dodging the germ-carrying masses. I'd made it through another polio season, and Ma wouldn't have to worry again until next summer. She had stopped coming around to my bed at night to check for fever, and I missed her hand on my forehead.

Twilight had settled in. Most everyone in the house was snoozing after the big meal, even Aunt Dortha, who'd retreated to her room as soon as she had put away the leftover food. Ma and Mr. Diehl would probably be returning from the hospital any minute. I'd sent a note to Dewey wishing him a happy Thanksgiving, and I was waiting to see if he might send a note back with Ma.

In another moment the stairs creaked behind me, and I turned to see Josef on his way down. I scooted over to let him pass, but instead he sat down beside me, one step up.

He smiled kindly. "What are you doing, Novelka?" he asked.

I shrugged. "Just thinking," I answered dreamily.

"And what are you thinking about, if I may ask?"

"Christmas is one month from today, Josef. Did you know that?"

Josef rubbed his chin. It was darkened by a five o'clock shadow. "So it is," he replied. "And what would you like for Christmas?"

I didn't have to think long. "I'd like Dewey to come home."

"Ah," he said, resorting to his catchall expression. "That, I'm afraid, I cannot give you. But I will hope with you that it will be so."

"Thanks, Josef. Thanksgiving without him was bad enough. I don't want to even *try* to have Christmas without him. Might as well not even *have* Christmas if Dewey can't be here."

Josef nodded knowingly. "Without one's family there are no holidays, are there? No matter what the calendar says."

I chewed the inside of my cheek for a moment while I thought about that. Josef, I realized, must not have any holidays at all—ever. For him, every day was the same, as awkward and empty as my Thanksgiving Day without Dewey. How I wanted to change that for him, to make it right again. If only I could.

"Well, Novelka," Josef went on, "besides having Dewey home, what else do you want for Christmas? Please tell me. I'd like to know what an old man can buy that would make you happy. Some ice skates, perhaps?"

"Oh, Josef," I protested, but only mildly, "you don't have to buy me anything. You sure don't have to get me something expensive like ice skates."

He waved a hand. "Ah," he said again, "they are not so expensive. You see, I know—I have already priced them." He smiled at me and winked.

I did want ice skates, it was true. Ma knew it, and she must have mentioned it to Josef. Josef wasn't much good at keeping it a secret, but his sweetness made me smile.

"All right," I said, "I do want ice skates. Rosemary's had skates for the last two winters, and so have most of the other kids I know. I'm tired of getting on the ice and just sliding around in my boots. It makes me feel stupid."

"I don't blame you, Novelka. Of course you want to be like the other children."

I did, oh, how I did! How I wanted to have a father like Rosemary and most all the other kids I knew. I'd give up the ice skates; I'd give up every birthday and Christmas present for the rest of my childhood if only I could have a father.

My heart pounded rapidly against my ribs, but I was suddenly determined to tell Josef what I really wanted. I leaned toward him a little closer, locked onto his gaze, and said, "But I have to tell you, there's something else I want even more." *Something that would make all of us happy, even you!* I thought.

He cocked his head slightly, raised his brows. "And what would that be, Novelka?"

I whispered conspiratorially, "I want you to be my father." There. It was said. I pulled back and smiled brightly.

To my dismay, though, Josef's smile melted. He shifted uncomfortably and laced his fingers together thoughtfully. His eyes, so bright only a moment ago, clouded over with an unmistakable sadness. "My dear child," he said quietly. "I am honored, but . . . how can I tell you. . . ?" He frowned, pressed his lips together. He seemed to be studying the scars on his hands before he lifted his eyes to me again. "I am so sorry, Novelka, but I cannot be your father."

I didn't want to hear what he'd just said. I wanted to stop the conversation here and now, go backward, rewind it like a tape on Dewey's reel-to-reel tape player, and then erase it. But I couldn't do that, and so, after a moment, I ventured forward. "But why not, Josef? You love Ma, don't you?"

"Yes, of course, but—"

"And she must love you, because she calls you Josef and she's nice to you and she's hardly ever nice to any man I ever saw—"

"But—"

"And it wouldn't be just for me but for Ma and Dewey and you too, Josef. You could have a family again. We'd be a good family for you, Josef. Wouldn't you like that?"

The intangible sadness had gathered and solidified, forming unshed tears that glistened and fluttered with each movement of Josef's eyes. "My dear child . . ." His words were a whisper.

I was close to tears myself. "You do love us, don't you, Josef?"

"Of course I do. You have become very dear to me, Novelka—"

"See—"

He raised a hand. "But let me finish. I love your mother, but you must understand, it's not in that way. It's much more complicated than it seems. How can I explain? Perhaps if things were different, if my heart did not already belong to someone else . . ."

His words trailed off lamely, and I think I actually stopped breathing for a moment. "You mean, you're in love with someone else?" I tried to imagine who it might be. A student in one of his classes? Another teacher at the college? Someone he had met at the cathedral during Mass?

He frowned, as though he couldn't understand why I would ask such a thing. "I . . . well, Novelka, I love my wife."

"But—!" A wave of horror rushed over me, and I shivered. "I thought—"

"Yes. You are right. She died in the war. But I love her anyway. I always will."

My face must have been such a study in consternation that Josef actually laughed. "It is not so hard as all that to believe, is it, that I should still love my wife?"

I found myself unable to utter a word. His wife was gone, buried somewhere in an unimaginable place called Poland, while Ma was here and alive and young and beautiful. Couldn't grown-ups see what was right in front of their noses?

"Child," Josef said quietly. "Think of your own father. Do you love him?"

I thought of Pa. I thought of how he used to hold me on his lap and tickle me and make me laugh. I thought of all the time I spent waiting for him by the window. "Yeah," I admitted. "I do."

"But he is no longer alive?"

I shook my head. It was obvious where Josef was going with this.

"You see, Novelka, in an odd sort of way, some of our strongest relationships are with people who have died. It might be a bad and harmful relationship. . . ." He paused a moment, as though he were thinking of someone in particular. But then he smiled mildly and said, "Or it might be a very good one. We miss the person, we think of them, we wonder what they would want us to do, how they would want us to act. Though they are not here, they still strongly influence our lives. And so we go on loving them, sometimes even more, when they are gone."

We both fell silent. The whole house was silent. So Josef wasn't going to be my pa. All the days of wondering came to an end in one swift moment. I knew there was still Mr. Diehl, and that helped soften the blow, but still, I would have liked to make things right again for Josef.

In spite of my disappointment, I managed to say to Josef, "I'm sorry your wife died in the war."

He acknowledged my comment with a small nod. "As am I, my dear," he said.

Outside, whirling in the light of the streetlamps, falling stars of snow dropped silently to earth.

FAIRY-TALE ENDINGS

Dear Dewey,

I finally know for sure Josef isn't going to marry Ma. It was stupid but I told him I wanted him to be our pa and he said he culdn't marry Ma because he still loves his wife. And you know she is dead. I cried half the night. First I was crying for myself but then I started crying for Josef becose it is all so sad. This morning I wanted to say something to make Josef feel better about missing his wife and all, so I told him Aunt Dortha told me we see our loved ones in heaven and Josef said that was true and that was what gives him hope. It doesn't always make me feel so good becose you know you have to die first before you can see the dead people. I didn't say that to Josef becose I thought maybe he doesn't like that part either. So I just said it must be pretty swell up there in heaven, like a big party where everybody's having a good time and Josef said he didn't know for sure but he thought maybe it was more like being safe at home where nothing bad can ever happen to you again.

Yesterday was the worst Thanksgiving of my whole entire life becose you weren't here and Josef said he can't be our pa. I am still praying every day for you to come home for Christmas. I am just about as sad as I can be but if only you will come home I know I'll be happy no matter what.

> Your loving sister,
> Nova Tierney

———————

Dear Tag,

It really bothers me to think about how sad you are, and I wish I could do something to make you feel better. It wasn't such a swell Thanksgiving here either, though I was glad Ma and Mr. Diehl could get here, even though it was snowing, and bring along some good food from home. It was much better than the turkey the hospital gave us.

I don't want to make things worse for you, but I can't promise I'll be home for Christmas. I'd have to be out of the lung for good, and right now I still can't stay out of it for more than about three minutes at a time. So I think we'll just have to settle for the fact that I'll be here. I'm trying not to feel sorry for myself on account of it. A lot of other kids will be here over the holidays too. I know the nurses will cook up something to try to cheer us up. Maybe you should set your sights on my birthday in March, as far as my getting home. We can have a big party and invite all the kids.

I'm really sorry about Josef not wanting to marry Ma and all that. I'm not surprised, but I know you were really counting on it. I know you really want a pa, but I guess if I've learned anything lately, it's that we don't always get what we want. Ma always said that, but I didn't really know it till now.

But hey, even if we don't get a pa, what about that trip to California? Ma told you about it, didn't she? She started talking about it before Thanksgiving, saying that as soon as I'm up to it, we'll go on out there and visit the Palomar Observatory. Boy oh boy, wouldn't it be swell to see the Hale Telescope? It's the biggest one in the world. I said it'd be expensive to go, but Ma said she'd figure out a way for us to do it, maybe next summer. Josef was here when Ma was talking about it, and she said maybe he would like to come along because he'd see a whole lot of the country from out the train window. Josef said he'd like to go because he'd like to see some more of America. So see, Tag, even if we can't all be a family, maybe we can do stuff together and have fun anyway.

Next time Ma comes will you ask her to bring some of the star charts I was working on in the summer? I was going to ask her myself, but I forgot. They should be on the desk where I left them, unless you're using the desk and put them somewhere else.

Love,
Dewey

Dear Dewey,

I'm having Ma bring your star charts along with this letter. I do my homework at the desk but I haven't touched a singel one of your things. Everything will be just like you left it when you get home. But Ma says maybe by then you can move into Miss Singletary's room and have your own privacy becose she won't be there anymore. She went and had Thanksgiving dinner with Mr. Martin Popp and his folks and you know what that means. We are all pritty sure she's finally going to get married.

Ma didn't tell me about the trip to Californa, but

when I read your letter I asked her and she said yes she is thinking about it. Then I asked Josef if he was coming and he said maybe, if he can. I can hardly believe it! Imagin traveling all that way on a train. Even Rosemary is jelous of me becose she hasn't been all the way to California. I don't know anyone who has been that far. I can hardly wait.

Maybe the trip will be so dreamy and romantical that Ma and Josef will fall in love and get married anyway. Wouldn't that be swell?

Your loving sister,
Nova Tierney

———

Dear Tag,

You never give up, do you? I think you have read Cinderella too many times. But to tell you the truth, I wish you could always be the way you are now, believing in all those happy endings. Sometimes I think one of the hardest things about growing up is finding out that all the fairy tales you were fed as a kid are just a bunch of stuff and nonsense. Real life is about as far from all that as you can get.

But still and all, if Miss Singletary can get herself a beau, I guess anything can happen. So who knows, maybe Ma will get married and maybe it will be Josef. I know that sounds like just the opposite of what I just said about fairy tales, but jiminy cricket, Tag, you're just a kid, and you should go on wishing if you want.

Thanks for sending the star charts. I never got to finish them, but maybe I can do it next summer. Maybe I can work on them in California. Hey, now, that would be a happy ending for you, wouldn't it?

Love,
Dewey

THINGS IN HEAVEN
AND EARTH

On a clear and windless night in early December, as I stood in the snow in the backyard looking up at the sky, I was amazed at how unusually radiant the stars appeared. They seemed so close I felt I was almost floating among them, sailing without a ship amid the glittering lights and the glistening sliver of a moon. If Dewey had been there, he would have reminded me that the night lights shine more brightly at that time of year simply because the winter constellations are made up of the brightest stars. But Dewey wasn't there, and his absence was that presence that rankled me, leaving me vexed and unhappy. I'd been carried through the autumn on the hope that Dewey would be home for Christmas, but now it looked certain he wasn't going to make it. That and Josef's not wanting to be my father brought me down off the wings of hope, crash landing in a field of bitter disappointment.

"The Ram and Bull lead off the line," I recited. "Next

Twins and Crab and Lion shine. . . ." I stopped, trying to recall the next line. But I couldn't find it, not one word. The rhyme that Dewey taught me was supposed to help me remember the names of the constellations, but I couldn't remember the rhyme, much less the groupings of the stars.

I would never know the night sky the way Dewey did. But I could always find some of the easiest constellations if the season was right and they were out. One was Orion—or rather, his belt. I could never quite make out the whole of Orion. Even when Dewey showed me the star formation in one of his astronomy books, I thought it a great stretch of the imagination to say those stars looked like a man hunting with a club. Still, it was easy to spot Orion's three-star belt, and I found it now, shining low in the sky off to the east. I liked to think of those three stars as belonging to me and Ma and Dewey. Mine was the one in the middle, nestled between the other two.

Orion's Belt, Dewey told me, pointed up toward a group of stars called the Pleiades. The cluster was also known as the Seven Sisters, since it was made up of seven stars. I moved my gaze up from Orion's Belt and thought I saw them, but I wasn't completely sure. I wished Dewey were here to tell me.

Turning, I spied the Big Dipper to the north and, higher still, the Little Dipper with Polaris at the tip of its handle. The North Star. "If you ever get lost," Dewey had instructed, "look for the North Star, and at least you'll know what direction you're facing."

I felt a little lost just then, even though I was right there in my own backyard. I felt lost because even as I floated amidst the amazing beauty of the night sky, I didn't have that sense of security the stars usually gave me. The moon was still in its place, and the stars were burning brightly, and the planets were undoubtedly traveling through their spheres, but tonight, while everything was moving like clockwork out there, it just wasn't so down here. Down here where I lived, on Selby Avenue in St. Paul, Minnesota, on planet Earth, everything was out of control, one huge meaningless mess that nothing and no one could tidy up.

Half a year ago I was Tagalong Tierney, shadowing my brother and his friends, living a child's life, happy except for wanting a pa but fairly certain that longing would be fulfilled by the unexpected arrival of Josef in our lives. Now, six months later, Dewey was in an iron lung, and Andy Johanson was dead, and Josef was in love with a ghost instead of Ma, and everything was far worse than I could have begun to imagine the day that I sat on the front porch crying because Dewey had gone swimming without me. I really didn't have anything to cry about then, not the way I did now. It was childish to cry because I'd been left behind. But that's what children do—cry over small things. And I was a child then. But I'd never cry over something like that again.

Everything was different now, changed just since the beginning of the summer when anything had seemed possible. Even I was different. Like Dewey said, kids believe in fairy tales, and now I could see very well the difference between real life and storybooks. I could see life as I'd never seen it before, and with this new vision came a feeling I'd never known before either, something that I couldn't quite pin down, an undefined and maybe indefinable despair, as though I'd suddenly stumbled onto the hidden meaning of the universe and found there was nothing there.

I turned again and watched my breath form clouds in the air, thin wispy clouds that floated upward and disappeared. In the same way, I thought, people come and go, live and die, and in the end it doesn't seem to matter at all. People live through all sorts of terrible things, surviving one awful thing just to move on to another, and then one day those people just aren't there anymore. They suffer alone while they're alive, and after they're gone, no one even remembers them. Not most of them anyway. Not the ordinary people like me. How many people, I wondered, had looked at the same moon I was looking at right now? How many people in the past ten thousand or so years had walked on the earth and looked up at the sky? Too many to count. And I was just one more.

I tried to remember the last time Dewey and I looked through the telescope. I was sad to realize it was that summer night when he started getting sick with polio. That was also the night he told me about the huge cosmic fireball. I couldn't remember everything he said except that scientists were guessing there might have been some sort of gigantic explosion that marked the beginning of the universe. I tried to imagine how loud the explosion must have been, and I decided it must have really been something, to throw out the stars and to hang the moon and to start the planets spinning. Such a spectacular beginning to what had turned out to be such a long, sad story.

I was thinking about the cosmic fireball when I heard the porch door bang shut. In another moment, someone came walking toward me across the snowy yard. I thought at first it must be Ma, but as the figure drew closer, I saw that it wasn't. It was Eva Lassiter. She was bundled up in a heavy woolen coat and big rubber boots, and she had a scarf draped over her head, which she held together with one hand at her throat.

She walked right up to me without saying a word. I wasn't even sure she saw me because she was so intent on looking up at the sky. She stopped before she ran into me, though, and stood there for the longest while just gazing upward. Finally, when she did speak, it was simply to say "Oh my!" over and over again, varying her use of inflection and intonation, but with the same obvious sense of wonder each time. Just when I began to think she'd go on standing there uttering that one phrase for the rest of the night, she said, "You know, Nova, I never looked at the stars very much in my life. To think of what I missed. You're smart to come out here every night the way you do."

I shrugged. "I'm watching the moon for Dewey. Just till he gets home and can do it himself."

She nodded. She finally looked at me. "You're good to your brother, honey. I know you miss him."

"Yeah, something awful."

She sighed sympathetically. "It's hard, I know. But he'll be home soon."

"Not soon enough. He doesn't think he'll be home for Christmas."

"I'm sorry, Nova."

"Yeah, me too."

She turned her face back to the stars. I thought she was going to start saying "Oh my!" again, but she didn't. Instead, she said, "What else is bothering you, child?"

"Everything," I confessed angrily, surprising myself. I

didn't mean to sound angry in front of Miss Eva, but I couldn't help it.

"My goodness," she replied. "That's an awful lot to be upset about. Is there anything specific you can lay a finger on?"

I thought a moment. I'd never talked with either of the Lassiter sisters about anything personal before, but since Miss Eva asked, I figured I'd answer. "I'm mad because Dewey's sick and he's not here, and I'm real mad because Andy Johanson died and I'll never see him again, and I'm pretty mad too because I don't have a pa and I don't think I'm ever gonna get one either."

"Hmm," Miss Eva responded. "Yes, those are big things, aren't they?"

I wasn't finished. "I think everything's pretty rotten, Miss Eva. Every time I think about everything that's happened, my heart gets all twisted up so much I can hardly stand it. I'm afraid of what's going to happen next because I know it's not going to be good."

"Hmm," she said again. "Yes, I can see your problem. Some very bad things have happened recently, haven't they? And I'm sure it isn't easy growing up without a father. But I don't think you should just give up and say nothing good is ever going to happen again."

I frowned so heavily I could see my eyebrows hanging low over my eyelids. "No offense, Miss Eva," I replied, "but you wouldn't know what it's like. Nothing bad ever happened to you."

Eva Lassiter's sudden piercing laughter startled me so much I actually jumped. "Oh, honey!" she cried, her voice shooting up like a firecracker and tumbling back down again like shimmering sparks over the whole of St. Paul. "If only that were true! Oh, my dear, you don't know the half of it!"

I gave her a look that I hoped revealed my skepticism. I'd heard all her stories—time and again—and not one of them was about anything awful. She'd had a glamorous career on the stage, a life of success and applause and travel and parties and friends. It had been a fun and funny life. She could pull up an anecdote from her treasure trove of experience and captivate an audience, sending everyone, including herself, into fits of laughter over something or other that had happened to her along the way. Maybe Aunt Dortha didn't regard the Lassiter sisters as prime examples of human virtue, but all in all, they'd had an enviable time. At least as far as I could see.

Eva Lassiter returned my gaze, and I knew I'd got my unspoken message across. "You don't believe I've seen any trouble in my day?" she said. She spoke quietly now, the laughter gone. She shook her head. "Honey, most of it I can't even tell you. You're too young. But I will tell you I've had my share of tears, some of it my own doing, sure. Some of it no fault of my own. Things just happen, terrible things. There's so much I would change if I could do it all again. But I can't. What's done is done."

Frowning again, this time in thought, I asked, "But like what, Miss Eva? What would you change?"

She continued to look at me. She seemed to want to study me for a long time, as though I were something she'd never really seen, like the night sky. It made me feel funny, her staring at me like that and not saying a word. I wondered what it was she saw and what she was thinking. At last she said, "I think I would have tried to have a child, for one thing."

"Didn't you want children when you were young?" I asked.

"Yes, I did. And I had a son once," she answered. Her voice was unsteady, and I had to strain to hear what she said. "He was stillborn. After that I said never again. I couldn't bear the thought of losing another one. And so there weren't any more. I think now I was wrong not to try again. I gave up too soon."

I could hardly believe it. I'd known Eva Lassiter for more than half my life, but I'd never have guessed there was a dead child in her background. I tried to make my words come out gently when I said, "I'm sure sorry to hear that, Miss Eva."

She smiled at me, a small, barely visible smile. "It's hard to grow old alone, Nova."

"You have your sister," I offered.

"Yes, I do have Ida. But that doesn't quite make up for . . . other things. I should have stayed married, had a real home and a family. But like I said, I can't change all that now. It's too late. You see, you don't know how lucky you are. You haven't made all the mistakes I've made. You haven't run out of time to do what you want to do. You have your whole life ahead of you. Not like me. I've pretty much come down to the end of the show, and I left so much undone. I don't even know where the time went." She paused a moment, then said again, "I just don't know where all the time went."

That's what Aunt Dortha was always saying too. I didn't know how to respond to Miss Eva, because I had no idea why old people had such a problem with time. Time always seemed to speed right past them, like a wild horse kicking up dust across an open plain. I didn't understand it. Time didn't seem to go by so fast as all that. Sometimes it dragged awfully. Just this past summer, for instance. Each and every day seemed as though it would never end.

When I realized she had finished speaking, I said, "I'm really sorry, Miss Eva. I didn't know—about the baby and all."

"How could you know, honey? I don't tell many people about it. Anyway, that was a long time ago."

I took a deep breath of the cold air, let it out. "I didn't mean to make you sad, Miss Eva."

"Oh!" She sounded startled but continued brightly, "I'm not sad, Nova. I'm a little sorry about some things, but I'm not sad. And you shouldn't be either. I know it's hard not to be sometimes, but you've got to remind yourself that good things happen too. You're much too young to give in to despair. Heavens, if anyone should be despairing, it's an old worn-out player like me. But no, I'm not sad."

I looked at her wide-eyed. "But . . ." I didn't quite know how to pose the question, yet she answered me anyway.

"Why, you see, I can't despair. I just can't." She sniffed out a little laugh. "Sometimes I try. It'd be real easy to just throw up my hands and say, 'Enough!' But something doesn't let me."

My eyes stretched even wider. "But . . . what doesn't let you?"

"I don't know," she confessed. "Just a feeling I get . . . a sense of something. It's hard to describe, if you know what I mean."

I didn't know what she meant, but I didn't want to say so. So I didn't say anything. We stood there for a while, both of us looking up at the vast expanse of lights overhead, thinking our own thoughts. Finally she said, " 'There are more things in heaven and earth, Horatio, than are dreamt of in your philosophy.' "

I waited for her to go on, but when she didn't I asked, "What's that?"

"Shakespeare," she replied.

I thought a moment. "Were you in a Shakespeare play once when you were in vaudeville?"

She laughed lightly, shook her head. "Oh no. We didn't do Shakespeare. Nothing important like that."

"Where'd you learn it, then?"

"In school. About a hundred years ago. And later I read Shakespeare when we were on the road, just to pass the time. Sometimes I'd memorize some of the lines and act them out for the other ladies in the dressing room. They'd get a kick out of it. And me—I'd pretend I was a great Broadway actress. Of course I knew I'd never really be on Broadway."

"So what's it mean, Miss Eva? That thing you said?"

"To tell you the truth, honey," she answered quietly, "I don't know."

"You don't know?"

"Well, that is to say, I don't know what it means to the scholars. I only know what it means to me."

"Yeah? What's that?"

Her face looked pensive before she answered. I knew she was thinking about her answer, but I also knew she'd been thinking about it a long while before tonight. After several moments, she said, "That there's more than we can know. That the better part of our lives is a mystery, a wonderful mystery—something good. I think sometimes I catch snatches of it . . . like when I stepped outside tonight and looked up at the stars. Have you ever heard an orchestra play, Nova? Not a record, but a real live orchestra?"

I shook my head no, wondering what an orchestra had to do with anything.

"Before the concert starts, you see, the orchestra spends some time warming up. But it's not something the musicians all do together. They all just kind of practice whatever suits their fancy, so a violin might be playing one thing while a trombone is playing another and a flute is playing something altogether different, and honestly, it makes a terrible racket. You can catch little bits and snatches of a melody but not much. Soon as you think you recognize part of a tune, another instrument comes along and drowns it out. It's just a mess, really. It might be helpful to the musicians, but it's not something you'd want to sit and listen to all night. But then the conductor comes out, and the whole place falls quiet; then after a moment or two the conductor starts to wave his baton, and the next thing you know, all the instruments are playing the same song and it's beautiful."

She paused. She was still looking up at the stars. I was trying to follow where she was going, but she'd lost me somewhere. Quietly, almost reluctantly, I said, "Yeah?"

"Well, you see, Nova. That's it. At least that's how I see it. We're all—I mean, the whole world . . . everything"—she waved an arm as she spoke—"we're all just warming up for something."

I tapped at the snow with the toe of my boot while I thought about what she'd said. I watched my breath on the air again. And then I said, "You mean, things are kind of a mess right now, but someday there's going to be music?"

I watched as Miss Eva's face seemed suddenly to glow. "Yes, that's it precisely, Nova! Someday there's going to be music!" she cried dramatically. But she wasn't acting. I was certain of that. Instead, she sounded to me both excited and satisfied, and relieved that I understood.

I didn't understand fully, but I liked the thought of music anyway. It made me feel hopeful. I slipped my mittened hand into Miss Eva's, and I think she might have been a little bit surprised, but she didn't let on. She just took my hand and squeezed it real hard, and we went on standing there together looking up at the stars.

Funny how even a grain of hope can manage to eclipse a whole world of despair.

STAR IN THE EAST

Thomas Diehl must have noticed that we neglected to put up a Christmas tree right after Thanksgiving, as was our custom, because he came over one evening bearing gifts like the wise men of old. When I heard the doorbell ring, I ran and opened the door to a gust of frigid air and billowing pine branches, and I could scarcely see Mr. Diehl out there on the porch, half hidden as he was by the most beautiful fir tree I'd ever seen.

"Coming through!" he warned, and the next thing I knew he was pushing that tree, trunk first, into the hallway. It was a tight squeeze, and the doorframe stripped dozens of pine needles from the branches, but Mr. Diehl managed to get the tree inside where the branches then sprung open like a ballerina's arms, dropping needles and wet snow on the hardwood floor. Aunt Dortha came hurrying out of the kitchen exclaiming wildly about the tree and, without so much as pausing to take Mr. Diehl's coat, rushed on up to the attic to bring down the ornaments we had tucked away in boxes the previous year. Ma stepped out of the kitchen too, more subdued than Auntie but nonetheless wide-eyed with curiosity.

"What's this?" she asked, as though she couldn't tell.

"Your Christmas tree," Mr. Diehl said easily, as though he had anticipated having to explain.

"Oh, Tom," Ma protested mildly, "you didn't have to do this, you know." But something about her—the tone of her voice, maybe, or a certain look on her face—told me she was secretly pleased.

Mr. Diehl waved off her comment with a sweep of his hand. "I wanted to," he said. "Besides, I'm tired of looking across the street at a house without Christmas decorations. It *is* December, after all."

Ma eyed the tree for what seemed a long time, then said to Mr. Diehl, "Here, let me take your coat. Then we can clear a spot for the tree."

Mr. Diehl balanced the tree up against a wall, took off his fedora, and wiggled his way out of his heavy overcoat. Both were wet with melted snow. Instead of hanging them up, Ma laid them over the radiator there in the hall. Mr. Diehl slipped off his shoes and left them beside the radiator as well. "I have some lights to string up around the porch railing too," he said. "I left them out on the porch and . . ." His voice trailed off as he and Ma went into the parlor to clear some space in the corner where the tree always went.

I stayed in the hall gaping at the tree, feeling breathless with joy. It was a far better tree than Ma and I would have brought home if she'd ever got around to taking me shopping for one. I'd been begging her to take me, but she'd been putting it off with no excuse other than to say, "Not today, Nova." I was almost tempted to go out and cut down a tree myself, if I could find one, because I was determined not to celebrate the holidays without Dewey *and* a Christmas tree both. But Thomas Diehl—good old Thomas Diehl—had saved me the effort and Ma a bit of money too, and he had no doubt spent a pretty penny himself just to make sure we had the best tree ever. *"Dear Dewey,"* I thought, *"you'll never believe what Mr. Diehl went and did. He's the most wonderful man in the whole wide—"*

The stairs creaked loudly behind me, and I thought it might be Auntie on her way back from the attic, but I turned to see that it was Josef. "Look, Josef, look!" I cried. "We have a tree!"

"I see, Novelka." He adjusted his glasses on his nose as though to see even better. "And it's a fine one too."

"It's the most beautiful tree in the world!" I went on. "Now maybe it'll start to feel like Christmas around here!"

I was hopping about and clapping my hands when Ma cut my enthusiasm short by calling to me from the parlor, "Make yourself useful, Nova, and go help Aunt Dortha bring the boxes down from the attic."

I pushed past Josef and hurried up the stairs, eager to help in any way I could. Auntie and I returned to the parlor a few moments later laden with boxes. The room was busy now, as most of our boarders had gathered to find out what all the excitement was about. That is, except for Henry Udahl, who was in bed in his basement room recovering from the flu, and Miss Singletary, who had gone with Martin Popp to view the Christmas lights that had begun springing up all over St. Paul.

"Roll up your sleeves, everyone," Auntie chirped gaily. "It's time to trim the tree!"

Oh, how I looked forward to this moment every year! In our house, trimming the tree was a festive occasion that we shared with whoever happened to be boarding with us when Christmas rolled around. Everyone was welcome. "The more the merrier!" Auntie always said, and certainly everyone was merry for at least an hour as we wrapped garland around the tree's outstretched arms and slipped ornaments on its green needle fingers. Even this year, in spite of everything, my heart thumped with delight as I watched Mr. Diehl and Clyde Munson get the tree settled into the stand. There was joy in the air, as sure as the scent of pine that filled the parlor, now that we had our tree.

Ma stepped briefly into the kitchen to start some spiced apple cider warming on the stove, something she did every year when we decorated the tree. Eva Lassiter, announcing that the moment called for music, sat down at the piano to shower us with Christmas songs. Auntie, Miss Ida, Josef, and I started sifting through the boxes, carefully unwrapping each ornament from the tissue paper that had cradled it for the better part of a year. Many of the ornaments were homemade: plaster of paris angels, clay Santa Claus faces, paper and string snowflakes, Popsicle-stick designs, and even painted eggshells that Dewey and I had made and brought home from school and that had somehow survived the years. Others were pretty store-bought trinkets that Auntie had collected or that boarders had contributed to her medley of Christmas treasures.

Miss Eva sang "O Christmas Tree" as Mr. Diehl wound a string of lights around and through the branches, and then we all crowded around the tree to drape the garland and hang the ornaments.

We'd scarcely begun when, to our surprise, Henry Udahl appeared in the parlor, sniffing and sneezing and saying to no one in particular that he had to do his job. He had heard the commotion overhead and felt inspired to climb up out of his subterranean sickbed to set up the Nativity scene. He had long ago claimed the task as his own, having arranged the crèche every year since he came to the boardinghouse, and he would let no one else do it. Nobody argued. The job was his.

He worked slowly, so it took him just as long to arrange the manger scene as it took the rest of us to decorate the tree. He always cleared the end table by the couch of everything—magazines, ashtrays, coasters—to have a wide-open space on which to work. When the table was empty, he lifted the little wooden stable from its storage box, blew a few quick puffs on it to blow the attic dust away, then placed it reverently on the table, turning it this way and that, moving it a fraction of an inch and back again, until he found exactly the right spot for the Savior's birthplace. He dug about the storage box again until he found the bag of real straw, which he painstakingly scattered about the barn, every piece just so. Then came the little figurines—the animals, the angels, the shepherds, the wise men, the Holy Family. Though they were carved of a sturdy wood, Henry Udahl held each piece as tentatively as if it were a fragment of ancient paper ready to crumble into dust. Carefully, lovingly, he handled those little figurines, eyeing them, pondering their role in the story, studying the scene to decide just where each person, each animal, each angel belonged. Finally he settled them into the scene, one by one, until at long last he held the tiniest figure of all in the palm of his hand, the baby Jesus. He laid the little wooden baby in the manger in a solemn ceremony of his own making, and when he was done, Henry Udahl sighed a deep sigh of satisfaction. He'd sit there then, his hands on his knees, his lower lip protruding slightly, staring at that Nativity scene as though it were the most beautiful piece of art in the world. And maybe to Henry Udahl, it was.

Even though I was busy trimming the tree, I made sure to pause time and again to watch old Henry at his task. Dewey and Ma had never paid any attention, and I thought they were missing something, though the previous year when I tried to explain what it was, I wasn't quite sure myself.

Over at the piano Miss Eva was perspiring in spite of the chill in the room, singing "Santa Claus Is Coming to Town" so loudly that I thought all of Selby Avenue must be feeling forewarned. "You'd better not pout, / you'd better not cry, / you'd better not shout, / I'm telling you why, / *Sannnn*-ta *Claus* is coming to town!"

Even though I didn't believe in Santa Claus any longer, I smiled as I thought about the gifts that would soon appear under the tree. There probably wouldn't be piles of them, but that didn't matter. There never were. But there would be *something*, and that was better than nothing. Maybe Josef would get me those skates he had talked about. And I knew Ma had already hidden some boxes away in her closet. I couldn't afford to buy gifts for anyone, but I'd found a bunch of candles in the dining room buffet and a box of old canning jars in the attic that Auntie said I could have, and I was making candle holders for everyone by decorating the outside of each jar with the wax drippings of the different colored candles. Mr. Diehl had agreed to help me by putting a hole in the lids large enough for a candle to go through. Mr. Diehl didn't know it, but he was getting one of my candle holders for Christmas, along with Ma, Aunt Dortha, Dewey, Josef, and Rosemary.

It wasn't long before the tree was heavy with decorations, gaudy with the mishmash of ornaments but profoundly beautiful to me. I stepped back to admire it, then realized that one thing was missing, the star on top. That was Dewey's job. Every year he settled that big plastic star like a crown on the tip of the evergreen, the act that concluded our trimming of the tree. How he loved that star, the star in the east, the star that led the wise men to the baby Jesus.

The real star, Dewey had once explained, might not have been a star at all. He had read about some scientists who speculated that the bright light that appeared at the time of Christ's birth was actually a grouping of planets, maybe Jupiter, Saturn, and Mars, or Jupiter and Venus. It was called a conjunction or an aligning of the planets, and it was something that had happened before and would probably happen again, so in the overall history of the universe it wasn't really all that unusual. Whatever the planets were, Dewey said, they wouldn't actually be close together, but from Earth, they'd look like they were, and they'd appear as a huge shining star.

Dewey's explanation sent Auntie into something of a theological tizzy. She said she didn't think the star in the east was any sort of planetary thingamabob like that, and she didn't know why scientists felt they always had to find a reasonable explanation for everything, as if there wasn't a God out there capable of doing exactly as he pleased. Since God had made all the stars in the first place, he was perfectly capable of creating a special star for a special occasion, and there was precious little in this world more noteworthy than the birth of Christ, save of course his resurrection from the dead.

Dewey said he agreed that maybe God *had* whipped up a special star because Jesus was born, but that if the star *was* the planets coming together, even that was pretty special, maybe even a miracle, because somehow the planets had fallen together at just the right time.

Dewey and Auntie left it at that, but Dewey confided to me later that whatever had made that star in the east, he was eventually going to find out. It was one of those mysteries he was going to uncover when he became an astronomer, a builder of rocket ships, and the first man on the moon. He said Auntie was wrong to think we shouldn't find the explanations to the mysteries in the universe, because sometimes it wasn't the mysteries so much as the answers that pointed to the hand of God. That's what his science teacher, Mr. Leland, had told him, and ever afterward Dewey was determined to find all the answers.

At any rate, Dewey wasn't there to place the star on the Christmas tree that year, so Ma said she wanted me to do it. Her eyes kind of glistened as she handed me the star, but she managed not to cry. Mr. Diehl hoisted me up on his shoulders, and as I slipped the ornament on the top of the tree, I thought, *Just this once, Dewey, I promise. Next year I'll let you have your old job back.*

When that was done, Mr. Diehl plugged in the string of lights, and the colorful bulbs began to glow. No one said a word. We all simply stood there looking at the tree. I wished Dewey could see it too, since it was the nicest tree ever to grace our parlor at Christmastime.

Miss Eva, ever ready with an appropriate song, struck a chord that broke the silence, and Miss Ida, as though she'd been given a cue from a director, moved to the piano, where she stood clutching a frilly handkerchief in her bony, vein-webbed hands. You could tell those two had been a team for a long time, because they could talk to each other without ever once opening their mouths. From that one chord they slid like skaters right into the first verse of "We Three Kings of Orient Are," Miss Eva pouring heart and soul into the keyboard and Miss Ida warbling out the words with such intensity you'd have thought they were rejoicing with the angels around the throne of God himself. By the time they reached the chorus and Miss Ida was singing about the star with royal beauty bright, her eyes shut as if the light of that star was shining in her face even at that moment, Ma had to leave the room on the pretext of checking the cider, and the rest of us would have surely broken down and cried like babies if Betty Singletary and Martin Popp hadn't burst in through the front door right then. Miss Singletary didn't notice or didn't care that the Lassiter sisters were in the middle of a song. She just waltzed into the parlor as if she weren't Miss Singletary at all but someone with a personality, and waving her left hand in the air for all to see, she announced, "I'm engaged!"

On her ring finger was a diamond that might have easily been mistaken for that star in the east, so huge was it and shiny. From across the room, Auntie raised her hands in a gesture of exclamation and cried, "Land's sakes, Betty, I believe you really are!"

There was a chorus of congratulations all around, and just as though it hadn't been an interruption at all but merely a shift in scenery, the Lassiter sisters swung into a chorus of "Happy Days Are Here Again!" And everyone was laughing so much and shaking Martin Popp's hand and passing around cups of hot cider as if it were champagne, I could almost believe happy days *were* here again and that they'd even settled in for good.

ICE STORM

But it wasn't so, and the very worst day was soon to come. The evening we put up the tree, Dewey started to sneeze. In ordinary circumstances, sneezing doesn't cause any great alarm, but Dewey wasn't living in ordinary circumstances. For someone in an iron lung, every sniffle, every sneeze was suspect, a reason for concern. That simple sneeze might be the prologue to the common cold.

Polios in respirators had their own name for the common cold: the Angel of Terror. Sometimes this Angel of Terror only threatened, stirring up fear and dread in the paralyzed chest of her victim but otherwise doing little real harm. Sometimes she settled in and really got down to business, leaving a person seriously ill. In the weakened body of a polio, the common cold could easily lead to pleurisy or pneumonia, which could in turn lead to death.

With Dewey, the Angel of Terror set up housekeeping.

In only a matter of hours Dewey was coughing and

gagging and fighting to bring up mucus, a nearly impossible task when your chest muscles don't work. Over the next few days, the pressure in Dewey's iron lung was increased to help him cough artificially, but even that wasn't very effective. Sometimes a nurse stood by the lung with her arms in the portholes, pushing on Dewey's diaphragm whenever he needed to cough. He was pumped full of penicillin and dripped full of nose drops, and finally a suctioning apparatus was brought to the room so that when a mucus plug got too bad, they could put a tube down his nostril, sometimes right into the branches of his lungs, to clear it out so he wouldn't choke.

He was moved to isolation as soon as he started sneezing, and Ma, unable to visit him, was beside herself with worry. She tried to stay busy, but mostly she paced about the house, wringing her hands and chewing her lower lip. Once or twice I came upon her talking in low tones with Josef in the parlor, but they always stopped talking when I came in. I can only guess that Josef was trying to comfort Ma, but beyond that I have no way of knowing what was said. I am sure, though, that there were no words in the world that could have comforted Ma during those awful days.

Even Aunt Dortha was unusually quiet and distracted. Her face was pinched, and she didn't sing when she cooked, and she scorched a pot of oatmeal one morning that she'd forgotten on the stove, something I'd never seen her do before. Occasionally while puttering around the kitchen, she'd stop and put a hand over her heart as if she was suffering an attack of angina. Once I asked her if she was all right, and she said yes, she was just sending up some prayers for Dewey. I didn't dare ask her if she thought he would get better, because I didn't want her to start talking about the will of Providence instead of just saying outright that Dewey would be fine. Sometimes thinking about the will of Providence scared me, because I couldn't be certain his will was in line with my own.

One of the hardest times of the day was when we all sat down to the evening meal. Rather than eating alone in the kitchen, I'd been eating in the dining room with everyone else since Dewey went into the hospital. Ma wanted it that way. But once Dewey was shuttled back to isolation, I would have preferred to be alone in my misery. Sitting there with Ma and Auntie and the boarders made everything worse, simply because of the looks on their faces: fear, concern, pity, feigned nonchalance. I couldn't forget for a moment that something was wrong, that Dewey was facing a crisis and the outcome was an open question. At every evening meal we sat under the proverbial ax, just waiting for it to fall, just waiting for that blade to hack both table and diners into a thousand splintered pieces.

It was obvious that everyone feared the worst. We knew what a cold could do because we'd seen it once already. Andy Johanson had died because he'd caught a cold. We'd already seen the shadowy wing of the angel, and we knew just how dark it was. If Andy could die, so could Dewey, in spite of all our hopes and prayers. Our love for him was not enough to keep him anchored to life.

I could barely concentrate in school, and more than once Miss Connor called on me and I didn't respond because I hadn't heard. I was lost somewhere, drifting around in a huge cloud of dread, and Rosemary had to nudge me back to what was happening in class.

At night as I stood outside and watched the moon, I tried to pray that the God who had set the heavens in place would look down now and make Dewey better. And yet even as I prayed, I was burdened with the thought that Dewey had asked me to have him buried up in the trees. I couldn't get rid of the thought, and I wished Dewey hadn't mentioned it because it seemed like a bad omen.

Five, maybe six, days passed in this way, with an unnerving hush in the house, Ma wringing her hands with dread, my heart churning out wordless prayers while my mind wrestled with fearful thoughts. Even the dimes stopped showing up on the windowsill, as though God knew Dewey wasn't going to need them anymore. What would be the use of finding a cure for polio if Dewey was dead?

Then one night I was just about to climb into bed when the call came. Knowing at once that it was bad news, I threw on my bathrobe and was standing right behind Ma by the time she hung up the phone.

"I'm going to the hospital," Ma announced, though she said it with her face turned away, and she wouldn't look at me or Aunt Dortha.

"What'd they say, Catherine?" Auntie's expression was pained, and she was kneading her hands together into a tight ball over her heart.

I trailed Ma like a shifting shadow as she hurried to the hall closet to get her winter wraps.

"He's taken a turn for the worse. They don't think . . ." She stopped. Her jaw trembled as she bit her lower lip.

Auntie moved to the window of the front door while Ma struggled nervously with her coat and hat. An hour earlier a storm had blown in, and now the clouds were spitting hard, angry pellets of freezing rain at the porch roof, the yard, the street.

"You'd be wise to take the streetcar, Catherine," Auntie suggested.

"There isn't time for that, Dortha." Ma stood in front of the hall mirror, tying a scarf around her neck with nervous hands. The dark cloth stood in stark contrast to the pasty white skin of her face. "Besides, I'm not going to walk all the way to University Avenue in this weather."

"Pick it up on Selby."

"I don't want to waste time changing cars."

"Then let me call Tom. He'll drive you. He has more experience in weather like this."

Without waiting for an answer, Aunt Dortha picked up the phone and gave the operator Mr. Diehl's number. She must have let it ring a dozen times or more before she finally gave up and put the receiver reluctantly back in the cradle. "He isn't answering. You don't suppose he's gone out of town again, do you? I don't remember him mentioning anything. . . ."

As Auntie chattered nervously, Ma strode through the hall to the kitchen with me clutching at the tail of her coat. She was on her way out the back door to the garage in the alley, but I wanted to stop her before she left. I wanted to ask her something, wanted to hear her say something that would give me some hope about Dewey, that would let me know he still had a fighting chance. It was all happening too fast. *Stop!* I wanted to yell. *Stop and tell me there's a chance Dewey will be all right.* At the door she turned toward me long enough to pull my hand from her coat. "Go to bed, Nova," she said abruptly. "Don't wait up."

"But, Ma!" Go to bed, just as though this night were as any other night?

She pulled her gaze away from my tear-streaked face and reached for the doorknob. She had her hand on the knob and seemed about to turn it, when suddenly she *did* stop. She stood so still she didn't even appear to be breathing. She was frozen, caught in time, or in a place without time. Auntie and I didn't move either. We all simply stood there waiting for something, some unknown thing. Finally Ma let go her grip on the knob and, turning back, reached out to Auntie, her hand a trembling bird in the air as she gave out a small, pained cry, "Oh, Dortha!" Auntie grabbed Ma's hand with both of her own, but briefly, only a moment, because almost as soon as Auntie touched her, Ma pulled away. As though she knew if she clung to Auntie's hand too long she would break, she would lose completely the strength she needed to walk out the door.

She turned the knob and pushed open the door.

"Call us from the hospital," Auntie urged. Her voice was unnaturally shrill. "Call us the minute you get there and let us know how Dewey is."

Ma nodded. And before I could say anything or even gather my thoughts, she had stepped off the back porch and disappeared into the icy night.

I looked up at Aunt Dortha. She opened her arms, and I fell into them, hugging her tight around the waist. "There, child," she soothed, "we mustn't fret. . . ." But her voice trailed off, and I knew she couldn't say the words because she didn't believe them herself. She trembled. She was weeping.

"Oh, Auntie," I cried, "how will we live without Dewey?"

She took a deep breath. My arms rose with her expanding ribcage. "He isn't dead yet, Nova."

"But what if Ma has an accident?"

"Hush, child. No more thoughts like that." She pulled away slightly and started walking, pulling me along with her. "Come into the parlor. We'll sit awhile and read from the Psalms while we wait for your mother to call."

We walked awkwardly, pressed up against each other, down the hall and into the parlor. Auntie sat on the couch and patted her lap, inviting me to lie down with my head on the cushion of her ample thighs. She covered me with the quilt that rested on the back of the couch, then picked up the Bible she kept on the side table. Henry Udahl had removed it to put up the Nativity scene, but Auntie put it back, saying it belonged there.

She flipped through the pages, paused a moment, then started to read by the light of one dim lamp. Her voice was steady now, quiet but strong. Somehow Auntie had reached into an unseen reservoir of strength and steadied herself. As for me, I couldn't stop my tears. They rolled down the side of my face and made little wet circles on the lap of Auntie's floral-patterned bathrobe. The dread in my chest crowded out everything else, even the air I was trying to breathe. I wiped at my eyes with the sleeve of my robe, shivered as I drew in a deep breath, and tried to listen to Auntie's voice: " 'Bless the Lord, O my soul: and all that is within me, bless his holy name. Bless the Lord, O my soul, and forget not all his benefits: Who forgiveth all thine iniquities; who healeth all thy diseases; Who redeemeth thy life from destruction; who crowneth thee with loving-kindness and tender mercies. . . .' "

As the words rose up off the page, I tried to grab them and squeeze some hope out of them, drops of water from a desert cactus. If God was loving and tender and merciful to the people of the Bible, I reasoned, maybe he would be all those things again tonight.

" 'The Lord is merciful and gracious, slow to anger, and plenteous in mercy. He will not always chide: neither will he keep his anger for ever. He hath not dealt with us after our sins; nor rewarded us according to our iniquities. For as the heaven is high above the earth, so great is his mercy toward them that fear him.' "

"Dortha?" The sound of Josef's voice startled me, and I opened my eyes to find him standing on the threshold between the front hall and the parlor.

Auntie stopped reading. "The hospital called. They asked Catherine to come down."

"The boy?"

"Not well, Josef."

He moved to the window and looked outside. "Catherine drove herself?"

"Yes. She wouldn't wait for the streetcar."

"She shouldn't be out alone, not on a night like this."

He turned and looked at Auntie for an explanation.

"I agree, Josef," Auntie said. "I tried to call Tom, to see if he would drive her, but he wasn't home. Catherine was determined to get to the hospital as soon as possible, of course. I

338

told her to call as soon as she arrives."

Josef nodded, looked out the window, back at us. "May I wait with you?"

"Of course. We were just . . . reading."

"Yes." Another slight movement of his head. "Psalm 103. I know it well."

Auntie took a breath, cleared her throat. " 'As for man, his days are as grass: as a flower of the field, so he flourisheth. For the wind passeth over it, and it is gone; and the place thereof shall know it no more. But the mercy of the Lord is from everlasting to everlasting upon them that fear him . . . The Lord hath prepared his throne in the heavens; and his kingdom ruleth over all. . . .' "

That night I learned there is nothing harder in this life than waiting, especially when you don't know what will meet you in the end but you do know that whatever it is, it probably isn't good. I tried to take comfort from the Bible, but I couldn't rid myself of the awful sense that something terrible was happening, or about to happen, or would surely happen before the night was over.

Auntie read from the Psalms for more than an hour, and then she stopped. And then there was only the ticking of the clock and the pelting of the icy rain upon the windows. Josef got up and paced the room, pausing periodically to look out at the night. Auntie got up and said she would make some coffee, but she didn't get any farther than the phone in the hall. She stood there staring at it, willing it to ring. I lay curled up on the couch, shivering, not so much from cold as from fear.

Auntie walked back into the parlor. "She should have been there by now," she said. Her lips were taut as she spoke, a small thin line, as though she didn't want to say what she was saying.

Josef stopped pacing. "Maybe she is with the boy. Maybe she is too busy or forgot to call."

Auntie shook her head, put a fist to her mouth. She turned toward the phone, hesitated, turned back to Josef. "I'm going to call the hospital and see if they can tell me something."

"Yes, I think you should."

When Aunt Dortha returned to the telephone table, I tried to call out Josef's name. I had to try several times, and even then it came out in a whisper. He looked at me, managed to give me something like a smile. "Yes, Novelka?"

"It's all so terrible—"

I pushed myself up to a sitting position. Josef came and sat beside me. He put an arm around me, and I rested my head on his shoulder. Auntie's voice was a muffled droning in the hall.

In a few moments she came back to the parlor. "They said Dewey is holding his own." In spite of this encouraging news, Auntie's face was pale. She dabbed at her neck and the sides of her mouth with a handkerchief she kept in her robe pocket.

"And Catherine?" Josef asked.

"She hasn't arrived."

The silence that fell over the room was heavy with panic, a tightly controlled fear. I sat rigid, looked at Josef.

He said, "She is making her way very slowly, no doubt. . . ."

Auntie nodded. "They said the roads are very slick. Traffic is crawling, what traffic there is. Not many people want to be out tonight."

"Perhaps we will hear something soon."

"They said if we haven't heard in half an hour to call back."

She went to the kitchen then to start the pot of coffee.

I asked Josef, "Do you think Ma's all right?"

"I'm sure we will hear something soon," he repeated.

"At least Dewey is still . . . okay." I wanted to say "alive," but it was too frightening to think in terms of alive and dead.

"Yes," Josef agreed. "That is good news."

"Maybe by morning he'll be all the way better and Ma can come back home."

"Yes."

The clock went on ticking. The rain went on pelting the windows. Auntie and Josef sipped coffee. I moved to the divan and looked out the front window, waiting. No headlights broke the darkness. No phone call broke the quiet.

After precisely half an hour Auntie stood and announced, "I'm going to call again."

I wrung my hands together while she murmured over the phone lines. When she hung up she didn't have to say anything. We could see it in her face. "I'm going to call Tom."

Josef started to say something, but Auntie didn't stay to listen. She asked the operator to connect her, waited, hung up the phone. "Still not home." She raised a hand to her lips.

"Now I remember—he said something about visiting family in New Ulm."

Josef rose from the couch, started pacing again. "Perhaps we should notify the police."

"Yes, I think you're right, Josef."

She returned to the phone yet again and asked for the police station, but before the connection could go through, the electricity in the house went out, and the phone lines went dead. I heard Auntie replace the phone in its cradle. I sat in the sudden darkness, waiting for my eyes to adjust. I heard Auntie's slippers padding over the hardwood floor toward the kitchen. After a few long moments she returned to the parlor carrying two lighted candles in tin candle holders. She placed one on top of the piano and another on the end table. The light of the candle flickered across the Nativity scene.

"Well," she said, her voice weary, "the phones are down, and the lights are out. What do we do now?"

Just then there was a racket on the stairs, and the Lassiter sisters appeared in their slippers and robes, a flashlight guiding their way. "We were listening to the Tommy Dorsey show on the radio when all the electric went off!" Miss Ida complained.

"Must be some storm out there," Miss Eva added. When she noticed I was there, sitting on the divan, she said, "Nova, what in the world are you doing up at this hour? Watching the storm?"

I shook my head. "Ma was called down to the hospital. . . ."

Josef, who'd been pacing the room again, stopped suddenly, lifted his head, and announced, "I know where she is."

Aunt Dortha frowned skeptically and shook her head. "How could you possibly . . ."

But she hadn't finished her sentence before Josef pushed past her and headed up the stairs.

"What in the world?" Ida Lassiter shined her flashlight on Josef's back, then looked at her sister and shrugged.

"What's going on?" Miss Eva asked Auntie.

"Catherine left for the hospital more than two hours ago, and she hasn't arrived."

"She's out driving in *this?*"

In the next moment Josef was back downstairs. He had on his heavy boots, a knit cap pulled down low over his ears, and he was buttoning up his coat. He didn't have a scarf, but he turned up the coat collar to protect his neck.

"Where are you going?" Auntie cried, her eyes wide with alarm.

"I believe I know where she is." Josef's voice was at once calm and determined.

"But you can't go out in this storm!"

"She might be hurt, Dortha. I must do something."

"But, Josef—"

"Are you crazy?" Miss Eva hollered. She reached for his coat sleeve but missed. He was already headed for the front door.

I ran to him and threw my arms around his waist. "Josef!"

He looked down at me with a tender gaze, put his hand to my cheek. "Don't worry, Novelka," he said. "Everything will be all right."

And then, much as Ma had done two hours earlier, he

pulled away from me, opened the door, and walked out. A gust of frigid air blew into the house and made us shiver. I was still shivering long after the door was closed again and Josef, like Ma, had disappeared into the mean and moonless night.

———

I slept restlessly. I fought against sleep for as long as I could but fell into it finally from sheer exhaustion. The last image I remember is that of Eva Lassiter sitting down at the piano, stroking the keys noiselessly the way a young woman might stroke the face of her beloved, and of Auntie standing immobile beside the piano, her frozen face a backdrop for the dancing shadows of the candlelight. I thought, *I will hear the phone when it rings,* but then remembered that the lines were down and we had no way of knowing what was happening outside in the storm—where Ma was, where Josef was.

For a little while I felt myself lying in a snowdrift. I tried to pull myself up out of the snow, but I had no strength. My arms wouldn't move; my legs had no feeling. I was so cold I couldn't imagine ever being warm again. I wanted to call for help, but no words came. I knew, though, that I couldn't just lie there and let myself freeze. I tried to roll. I wanted to roll myself up out of the snowdrift. But all I could do was rock back and forth, back and forth, a baby in a frozen cradle, until at long last something broke through. Sunlight. I was on the couch in the parlor, and a hint of dawn was shining in through the window. It was morning.

Just then the ringing of the telephone startled me fully awake. I thought, *The storm must be over. The phone is working again.* Auntie, dozing in the wing chair, started up at once and dashed to answer it.

It was the hospital. Ma was there.

But it wasn't Minneapolis General calling. It was Abbott Hospital. Catherine Tierney had been brought in by ambulance a short time earlier. She had suffered a concussion as well as frostbite on her toes, fingers, and ears. An unidentified man who was with her in the pickup truck had been brought in as well. The hospital was sorry to inform us that by the time the road crew found the pickup in the ditch, the man was already dead.

BLAME

She remembered nothing about the accident itself, Ma said. She didn't remember the truck spinning off the road over by the Mississippi River, the same place she and Josef had almost gone off the road a few weeks back. She didn't remember hitting her head on the steering wheel as the truck came to a sudden stop in the snowy ditch. But, oddly, she did remember that Josef was there. She remembered vaguely opening her eyes and seeing him. She didn't know where she was except that it was a dark, cramped place and her head was raging and she was cold, colder than she had ever been. She wanted to ask Josef what had happened, but it hurt too much to open her mouth and ask the question. In the midst of swirling confusion, she saw Josef unbutton his coat and lie across her on the truck seat, and immediately she felt his warmth. "Don't be afraid, Catherine," he said, his voice coming from somewhere far away. "You mustn't be afraid. I will keep you warm until they find us."

"I would be dead, I'm sure," Ma said, her ashen face staring up at us from the hospital bed, "if Josef hadn't found me. I would have frozen to death. Instead, Josef . . ."

She shut her eyes. Tears slid out from under the lids, moved in small ripples down the sides of her face.

"Don't try to talk, Catherine," Auntie whispered.

"But Josef . . ."

He had not frozen to death, the doctor told us. Josef was dead before the cold ever reached him. After walking three miles bent against the freezing rain, he lay down and died when his weakened heart gave out. It happened not long before the road crew found the pickup truck. He was still warm when they pulled him from the cab. He had stayed warm long enough to keep Ma alive.

"Does Dewey know?" Ma opened her eyes again, two blue pools of fear.

Auntie shook her head. "No. All he knows is that you were in an accident and are here at Abbott. He knows nothing about Josef."

"Don't tell him," Ma said. "I'll tell him myself when I get out of here. And when Dewey's stronger."

"All right, Catherine."

"Tell the nurses there not to breathe a word—"

"Don't worry yourself, dear. I've already spoken with the nurses about it."

Ma's face registered pain when she tried to nod. After a moment she asked, "How long will I be here?"

"The doctor said at least a week, maybe more."

Ma lay quietly for a time, looking thoughtful. "That's too long," she said finally, more to herself than to anyone else.

"What's that, dear?" Aunt Dortha bent low over the bed.

"You'll have to tell Dewey for me. If we wait a week or more, word might reach him. He needs to hear it from one of us. About Josef. Will you tell Dewey for me? And tell him I'll see him as soon as I possibly can."

Auntie patted Ma's shoulder. "Don't fret, Catherine. I'll visit Dewey soon, in a couple of days. I'll tell him you're doing well and will see him soon. I'll tell him everything."

Ma didn't respond, but her lips disappeared into a small white line. "Do you really think Dewey will be all right?" she asked.

"As I said," Auntie repeated gently, "there's every indication he'll be fine now. They say he's resting easily. The fever broke, and he started breathing almost normally shortly before dawn. It happened so suddenly, they said they don't know how to explain it. It was almost like a miracle, they said."

"Like a miracle," Ma echoed. She was swathed in bandages around her head, her hands, her feet. The doctor had warned us she might lose some toes to frostbite. But she was alive. That's what mattered. The long night was over, and she was alive and Dewey was alive.

Josef was dead, but that wasn't real to me yet. I knew the words, but they had no place in the realness of the moment. I was numb to it and aware only of my relief and thankfulness that Ma was all right, that I was here in a chair beside her hospital bed, that I could see her and touch her and hear her voice.

I leaned over until my head rested on the pillow next to Ma's. My lips were close to her ear, and I whispered, "Ma."

"Sweetheart," she answered.

"I'm so glad Josef found you."

"I am too, sweetheart."

"I want to thank him somehow."

"Yes." She was quiet a moment, and another tear rolled down from the corner of her eye. "We'll find a way to do that, Nova. Somehow. I promise."

Dear Dewey,

I am sending you a picture I drew of a big heart. Please put it up on your machine where you can see it becose whenever you see it I want you to know how HAPPY HAPPY HAPPY I am that you are better and not sick with that terrible cold anymore. I wish I could give you a big hug in person but anyway here are some hugs and kisses: XOXOXOXOX. Boy Dewey I don't think I was ever as scared as I was when Ma tried to go see you at the hospital and she ended up in a ditch. I didn't know if I would ever see either of you again. But now you are so much better and Ma is getting better too and I am so reliefed. Auntie is about ready to leave to go see you so I have to stop now and give her this letter. I'll tell her it is okay if she reads this to you and not Miss Evans. I will write more soon.

Your loving sister,
Nova Tierney

When Auntie came home grim-faced after visiting Dewey, I knew Josef was dead. Of course I'd already known for three days, but I wasn't willing to face it until that moment. When I heard the front door open, I looked up hoping to see Josef walk in. It was a brief hope, lasting only a fraction of a second, but there it was. And then the door shut, and it was Auntie in the hall, and I knew she had just returned from telling Dewey that Josef was dead.

"Oh, Josef," I whispered, and when I said his name, I felt something falling away from me. I'd been holding on to his image with one hand and clinging to my denial of his death with the other, but in that moment of Auntie's coming into the front hall, I felt both falling away. I had let go of Josef. I accepted in my heart the awful finality of his death.

When Auntie reached into the closet to hang up her coat, I dropped onto the couch in the parlor and wept. In another moment Auntie was beside me, her comforting hand on the back of my head.

"Goodness, child," she said, "what on earth?"

I went on crying for several minutes, Auntie caressing my hair, waiting patiently until I could answer. Finally I lifted my face from the pillows of the couch and confessed, "I've been hoping he'd come back!"

Auntie looked puzzled. "Dewey?" she asked.

"No! Josef!" I sat up and wiped my eyes with the sleeve of my shirt. "I just kept thinking maybe he'd come back."

"Oh." Auntie patted my arm as she tried to smile. "I understand, Nova. It was that way for me when Marvin died. I kept expecting him to walk on through that same door"— she cast her eyes toward the front door—"just like he'd done a thousand times. It took me a good long while to stop thinking it might be him every time I heard the door open."

"Oh, Auntie!" I fell over onto her shoulder, buried my face in her sweater, and cried uncontrollably. She put her arms around me and let me weep.

"There, there, child," she soothed. "I know. Josef was a fine man. And he did a courageous thing, going out in that storm to help your mother. It's not something everyone would have done."

"If he hadn't gone out," I whispered, "Ma would have died."

"It's possible she would have, yes," Auntie said.

I rubbed my eyes, tried to catch my breath. The thought of what Josef had done was so big, I couldn't take it all in. "Did . . . did you tell Dewey?"

Auntie nodded. "I told him."

"What did he say?"

"Well," she answered, "for the longest time, he didn't say anything. Then he said you didn't mention Josef in your letter, and he wondered why."

I shook my head. "I just couldn't, Auntie. I couldn't."

Auntie nodded her understanding. "Then he said he would miss Josef. He'd been a good tutor. Everyone who met Josef at the hospital liked him."

As quickly as I wiped them away, the tears kept coming. "Nothing's ever going to be the same again, Auntie, now that Josef's gone."

"You're right, Nova," Auntie agreed. "Everything changes the minute someone we love dies. But it won't always hurt as much as it does right now. I promise you that. Someday you'll be able to remember Josef fondly, without all the sadness getting in the way."

"How long will that take?" I asked.

"Now, that I can't tell you," Auntie replied. "I only know that one day you'll wake up and realize it doesn't hurt quite so much. Until then you can put yourself in the hands of God—he'll see you through. You can take it from someone who knows, dear. I've found his hands to be an easy place to rest."

Auntie meant to comfort, but her words had the opposite effect on me. All the relief and thankfulness I'd felt about Ma and Dewey disappeared—or at least were overshadowed by anger. I was angry that Josef hadn't been saved too. *Everything will be all right,*" he'd told me just before he left. But everything wasn't all right. Something was terribly wrong.

"I don't know why God couldn't have let Josef live too," I wailed. "He was doing something good. He was trying to save someone else."

"I don't know either, Nova," Auntie said gently. "But then, we can't understand God's ways."

"No, I can't," I agreed angrily.

Auntie was quiet a moment. Then she said, "Nova, you mustn't be bitter toward God. We might have lost your mother and Dewey too. We might have lost all three of them, but we didn't. We should count ourselves fortunate for that."

I didn't know what to say to Auntie. I didn't say anything.

———

Days passed in which I grieved for Josef far more than I had ever grieved for even my own pa. While Ma was still in the hospital, I wrote to Dewey and poured out my sorrow. Auntie delivered my letters for me when she went to visit him, an unwitting conveyor of my angry epistles. I wrote on the envelopes that only Miss Evans could read these letters aloud to Dewey.

Dear Dewey,

I am sadder than I have ever been in my whole life. I am glad you and Ma are alright and I know that is a big thing and that everything would be even much worse if I'd lost one of you too or even both of you. But Dewey I can't help it but I'm crying all the time becose I miss Josef. Not just becose I wanted him to be our pa but becose I just plain loved him, whether he was going to be our pa or not. He was just about the best person I ever knew, next to you and Ma. How could God let him die, Dewey? If God saved you and Ma he could have saved Josef too but he didn't do it and I sure don't understand why. I know he could have if he wanted to. Now I feel like maybe God isn't so good after all. I can't help it, that's what I think. And you know what? Ever since Josef died there hasn't been any more dimes and now I think maybe Josef was leaving them there and not God. Now it is almost Christmas and I don't even want to think about the baby Jesus or anything like that. I can't understand how God could be so mean, and I don't think I will ever be happy again.

Your loving sister,
Nova Tierney

———————

Dear Tag,

I am sad and sorry too and wish I hadn't caught that cold when I did because then none of this would have happened. Ma wouldn't have got in the accident coming to the hospital, and Josef wouldn't have gone out in that storm to try to find her. Everything would be okay again if it hadn't been for me catching cold. I'm real sorry, Tag, and I don't know what to say that will make you feel any better. I don't know whether God had anything to do with it or not. I think it is more my fault than his, so maybe you should be mad at me instead.

Love,
Dewey

Dear Dewey,

I will never be mad at you becose you couldn't help catching cold when you did. Please don't think it is your fault, that wuld be terrible. I know if you were God you wuld have kept Josef from dying. You are still my favorite person and I just want you to get better and come home again.

Ma is doing real good. Auntie and I just got home from visiting her. I don't know why it is okay if I go to that hospital to see her and can't go to your hospital to see you, but Ma told Auntie to bring me so I guess she doesn't think I will get sick in her hospital. That's funny, isn't it? But anyway she looks a whole lot better and says she is feeling better too and she can't wait to get home. Boy oh boy, Dewey I can hardly believe you and Ma both are in the hospital and all I want is for us to be together again. All the kids in school are real excited about Christmas but all I can think is this is the worst and most terrible year of my whole entire life.

Your loving sister,
Nova Tierney

———————

Ma stayed in the hospital for a week, as the doctors had predicted. She suffered no complications from the concussion, and her frostbite turned out to be superficial rather than deep. She didn't lose any toes, but after that, for the rest of her life, she occasionally experienced pain in her hands and feet, especially during the winter months.

On the evening of the day she came home, Thomas Diehl showed up at our door asking to see her. The shoulders of his coat and the top of his fedora were sprinkled with snow. Behind him, the lamps along the street showed a steady, silent shower of whirling flakes. I thought about the last time Mr. Diehl had shown up at our door, with the Christmas tree. It seemed about a thousand years ago. Since that time Dewey had been to the edge of the world and back, and Ma had spun off the road by the river, and Josef had walked out into the night and died. Mr. Diehl looked at me gravely, and I asked him to come in. Neither of us mentioned Josef or Christmas or anything at all, for that matter. I took his coat and hat and laid them over the radiator as I'd seen Ma do, then told him he could wait in the parlor if he wanted while I went and got Ma.

I found her in the front room of our apartment resting in the easy chair with her eyes shut. Thinking she was asleep, I started to turn away quietly so as not to wake her. But she opened her eyes and asked gently, "What is it, Nova?"

"Mr. Diehl's here," I replied. "He says he wants to see you."

I could read nothing at all on Ma's face, neither annoyance nor gladness. Not even surprise. She simply nodded as though she'd been expecting him, then got up and brushed her hair. It wasn't an easy task. Her blistered fingers were still wrapped in gauze bandages. Her feet were bandaged too, and she moved about the room in slippers. She pulled her hair back but kept her ears covered. They too were blistered and red. When she felt she was ready, Ma went out to meet Mr. Diehl.

Of course I wanted to know what they had to say to each other. I walked through our apartment to the kitchen and finally into the dining room, where I could hear the conversation going on in the parlor. I crouched low beside the buffet so as not to be seen.

" . . . came to see how you are," Mr. Diehl was saying. He sounded reserved and not like himself.

"I'm much better, thank you."

"I would have come sooner, of course, but I've been in New Ulm all this time. I should have left a number where I could be reached. It wasn't until late last night when Dortha called that I learned anything about . . . the accident." The last two words dropped heavily from his lips, weighted as they were with the implication of Josef's death. "She said that you . . . well, she told me you were coming home today." He seemed to be fumbling, reaching for words he couldn't quite find.

"Yes," Ma agreed. "I came home this afternoon."

"And you're all right?" He was talking a nervous circle. I could imagine him trying not to look at Ma's bandaged hands, her slippered feet.

"Yes. Much better," Ma repeated.

"You must be tired, you—"

"No, really, I'm much better."

A hush fell over the room, followed by footsteps. Someone pacing, then stopping abruptly. "Catherine, I didn't sleep at all last night. I blame myself for . . . all of this—"

"But, Tom—"

"For Josef . . . my God, to think he's . . ." His words trailed off. He might have said something, but I didn't hear.

Then Ma spoke. "How can you possibly blame yourself for what happened? You weren't even here."

"I gave you the truck."

"But . . ." Ma paused, as though gathering her thoughts. Then she said, "Yes, but I was the one who took it out in an ice storm. If it was anyone's fault, it was mine—"

"No, Catherine, no. You can't think—"

"If I'd taken the streetcar as Dortha suggested—"

"And stood waiting for one to come along in that storm?"

Silence again. Then Ma spoke. "You see, Tom, there are so many factors. I've thought it all through time and again. If one small thing were changed, if one small thing were turned around . . ."

She didn't finish, but after a moment Mr. Diehl finished for her. "You're saying that in the end, it was an accident."

"Yes. An accident. It was no one's fault. We have to believe that, or we will drive ourselves mad."

Even from a distance I could hear Mr. Diehl sigh. Whether a sigh of sorrow or resignation, I don't know. I couldn't tell without seeing his face.

Ma said, "The service is planned for the day after tomorrow at Macalester Presbyterian, if you would like to pay your respects."

"I would, yes. I'll be there."

Another awkward silence, or so it seemed to me. At length Mr. Diehl said, "Catherine, I don't know what to say except I'm sorry—though heaven knows that doesn't seem nearly enough. Josef and I had become friends. But I know that he was . . . important . . . to you." When Ma said nothing, he finished by saying, "Well, I'll go and let you rest." He sounded defeated now and tired, as if he'd just reached the end of a long journey.

Footsteps sounded across the floor, and Mr. Diehl must have been heading to the hall, but Ma called him back. "Tom?"

"Yes, Catherine?"

"Do you have . . . that is, if you don't have plans already, would you care to have Christmas dinner with us?"

I held my breath, unable to believe Ma had invited him for Christmas dinner. I strained to hear his answer but heard nothing. After several long moments passed, I began to think Mr. Diehl had left and I hadn't heard his response. But finally, from some seemingly very faraway place, he replied, "Are you quite sure, Catherine?"

Ma actually let go a little laugh, a small, delighted laugh. "Of course I'm sure, Tom. Unless you have plans . . ."

"Oh no, no, nothing that can't be changed."

"Then won't you say yes?"

"Why, yes, of course. Thank you, Catherine. I'd be delighted."

They exchanged a few words I couldn't hear as Ma walked

Mr. Diehl to the door. Then after the front door opened and closed, I heard Ma walk back into the parlor. She stayed there only briefly before moving across the hall to our apartment.

I came out of my hiding place then and stepped into the parlor. At once I was struck by a sense of wonder. Strangely, Ma had plugged in the Christmas tree lights. It was the second thing she'd done that night that I'd never known her to do before, right up there with asking our neighbor Mr. Thomas Diehl to dinner.

IF I WERE GOD...

32

The next day Ma and Aunt Dortha set about cleaning out Josef's room. I volunteered to help, since I was home for the Christmas holidays. Because Josef had no next of kin, we were the ones left to decide what to do with his few possessions. Shirts, trousers, and jackets we gave to the Salvation Army. Other things—worn-out socks, useless sales receipts, half-used toiletry items—we threw away. But some things we kept and divided up among ourselves, mementos of our time with Josef.

Auntie put his record player and small collection of records in the parlor for everyone to use. We set aside his straight razor and a pair of cuff links for Dewey. Ma claimed Josef's books. He had a dozen or so arranged in piles across the top of his desk. I was about to mention to Ma that she'd never read them because they were mostly in foreign languages, but I decided to keep my mouth shut. It didn't matter,

I knew, if she never read them. It was enough to have them. They had been Josef's.

Among the books on the desk was Josef's Bible. Ma looked at it a minute, then held it out to me, saying she wanted me to have it. I wasn't sure I wanted it. I was angry with God, after all. And yet I did want it, for the very reason Ma wanted a dozen books she'd never read. When I took it and held it in my hands, it seemed as though a little bit of Josef had come back to me.

When we had finished cleaning Josef's room, preparing it for a new boarder, I carried the Bible downstairs to my room and laid it on my bed. I opened it carefully and found Josef's name written on the inside cover page in small, precise handwriting: Josef M. Karski. Josef must have bought it sometime after he came to America, as it was still new. It smelled of leather, and its pages were crisp and clean. The words *American Standard Version* were printed in gold lettering on the spine. I smiled sadly as I pictured the Polish immigrant, the war refugee, reading his American Bible. This, like everything else—his Palmolive shaving cream, his RCA portable record player, his Florsheim shoes—was part of his new beginning in a new world.

But as I turned the pages, I came across a little piece of his old world tucked into the book of John—a picture of Josef with a beautiful woman and two beautiful children, a boy and a girl. Right up until this moment I hadn't known for sure, but now I knew. Josef *had* had a daughter. And a son too. I turned the photo over. Nothing was written on the back. It would be years before I knew their names and their story, but even then, in that moment of finding their likeness, I understood the magnitude of what had been lost.

My heart ached, because Josef had lost them, and we had lost Josef. Dewey was right. I had read too many fairy tales. One begins to wonder where the happy endings are when life is filled with so many losses.

I replaced the photograph in the Bible, carefully tucking the edge back into the center fold. As I did, I noticed a verse Josef had underlined in the same bold black ink in which he had written his name. Later I would realize it was the only verse in the Bible he had marked. It was John 13:7: "Jesus answered and said unto him, What I do thou knowest not now; but thou shalt understand hereafter."

––––––––

The next afternoon we buried Josef M. Karski, three days before Christmas and seven days before his forty-ninth birthday.

His funeral, arranged by the college, was held at the Macalester Presbyterian Church across the street from the school. Ma, Auntie, Thomas Diehl, and I arrived early to claim seats in the front row of pews. Mr. Diehl sat between me and Ma, holding my hand on one side and Ma's on the other. I thought maybe Ma allowed it because these were unusual circumstances.

At the front of the sanctuary was Josef's simple coffin, framed on either end with a huge bouquet of carnations and larkspur. I didn't like to think of Josef being inside that box, and I was glad the coffin wasn't open. I didn't want to see how Josef looked in death. I didn't even want to think of how he'd been in life, with the scramble of scars on his face and the tattoo of numbers on his arm.

What I tried to imagine instead while I sat there waiting for the service to begin was Josef in heaven with his wife and children. I tried to picture them falling into each other's arms and laughing so hard they had tears pouring down their faces, tears that God wouldn't wipe away because they were tears of joy, not sorrow. I wanted to believe that Josef was safe at home now where nothing bad could ever happen to him again.

But I was having some trouble climbing beyond the here and now into more hopeful thoughts of the hereafter because of the funeral music the organist was pumping out. After a while I pulled my hand away from Mr. Diehl's and stuck my fingers in my ears. They made an inadequate muffler, though, and I couldn't block the sound completely. The notes sounded smaller and farther away, but they still made for a mournful accompaniment to the happier thoughts I wanted to have about Josef. But then, I thought, you were meant to be sad at funerals. They were designed to make you sad, even if you wanted to believe the deceased himself was laughing for joy in another place.

When at last the music stopped and the chaplain rose to speak, I let my hands fall to my lap and turned to glance over my shoulder. Our boarders had filled up the row right behind us. There they were: Clyde Munson, looking uncomfortable in a button-down shirt and a tie, a tiny red gash on his jaw where he'd nicked himself shaving; the Lassiter sisters, appropriately somber in black drop-waist dresses and black broad-brimmed hats with little black lace veils that covered their faces; Betty Singletary, sitting shoulder to shoulder with her fiancé, Martin Popp, both stiff and unmoving; and Henry Udahl, red nose dripping—whether because he still had the flu or because he was crying over Josef or maybe just because he was thinking about his lost and wandering son, I didn't know. Maybe all three.

Beyond them the sanctuary overflowed with students, teachers, staff members of the college, and I don't know who all else. All around me people dabbed at tears or cried openly, and for the first time I realized that my family and I weren't the only people who had loved Josef. I had considered him exclusively ours—he did, after all, live in our house, eat at our table—but now I knew that wasn't true. He wasn't ours alone. He never had been.

I turned back toward the chaplain, who had started to speak in a rough and raspy voice. He was an ancient fellow with wispy white tufts of hair combed over the bald dome of his head. He was stooped and slow and colorless and, by all accounts, not very far from the grave himself. He gave a little talk about how Josef was a fine man and how Christ said that if we believe in him, even if we die, we go on living anyway. I thought it was a pretty speech, but it could have been about anyone, and I decided the chaplain had probably said the same thing at a thousand funerals in the thousands of years since he'd been ordained. I wasn't sure he knew who Josef really was, that Josef was someone special, different from anyone I'd ever known.

But then he said whoever wanted to could step up front and say a little something about Josef. His watery old eyes scanned the sanctuary a moment, looking for volunteers. Nobody moved. We all just sat there for what seemed like an embarrassingly long time, though it was probably only a few minutes. Finally Mr. Diehl stood and stepped up to the front. The chaplain offered a relieved smile, nodded at Mr. Diehl, then took a seat in the row across the aisle from where I sat with Ma and Auntie.

Thomas Diehl looked very handsome in his suit and tie, his dark hair slicked back and shiny with some kind of hair tonic. But his face was drawn and serious, and as though he were hot or uncomfortable, he tugged at his shirt collar a couple of times before he began to speak.

"I had the privilege," he said, "of getting to know Josef this past year while he lived across the street from me. But I might have met him some years earlier because we were at the same place at the same time at the end of the war. We were both in Europe, in Germany, but our experience of the war was very different. I was a soldier fighting the Germans. Josef was a prisoner, having been arrested by the Germans in his native Poland, even before the United States was involved in the war. The place we might have met was the camp known as Dachau. I was with the U.S. Seventh Army when we reached the gates of Dachau in April 1945 and liberated the camp. Josef was one of the prisoners there. He'd spent the war in Auschwitz but ended up at Dachau toward the very end of the war.

"Well, what I guess I'm trying to say is that sometimes those of us who were soldiers are called heroes, but I'm here to tell you that the real heroes are people like Josef Karski, who defeated the Nazis simply by still being alive at the end of the war. Some of us soldiers got medals for bravery or purple hearts for being wounded, and I won't belittle our own men because I knew a lot of brave men in the U.S. Army. But I don't think I ever knew anyone braver than my friend Josef. He didn't come out of the camps wearing any medals, and the truth of the matter is I don't think a medal would be near enough to honor a man like him, someone who lived with the Nazis day in and day out for years but still stayed a human being at heart. And even after all he lived through, he still cared more about other people than himself."

Mr. Diehl paused, reached into a side pocket of his jacket, and pulled out an object I didn't recognize. He held it up and eyed it for a moment. "I got this purple heart," he explained, "for being wounded in battle. Even though it's not near enough, I'd like to give it to Josef anyway, to say thanks for trumping the Krauts by staying alive." Then, a little more quietly, he said, "And thanks too for keeping somebody else alive by dying." He turned and stepped to the casket, laid the medal on the closed lid, stood there briefly, as though to say a private farewell, then returned to his seat between me and Ma.

I gazed up at him until he felt the weight of my eyes on his face, and when he looked at me, I smiled. I was glad he gave the medal to Josef. It seemed the right thing to do.

Before I turned my gaze from Mr. Diehl, Aunt Dortha had risen from the pew. She was standing primly now in front of Josef's casket, her gloved hands clasped over her heart. She cleared her throat before she spoke. "Josef Karski," she announced, "was one of the finest men I've ever had the privilege of knowing. Providence was kind to us when he brought Mr. Karski to my door looking for a room. He won't soon be forgotten. May God rest his soul."

When Auntie sat, a young man walked to the front. He was one of Josef's students. He told of how just a few weeks ago he'd flunked a test in Mr. Karski's class, but Mr. Karski said if he came for tutoring every afternoon for a week, he'd let him take the same test over. "That's what he did," the young man said. "Professor Karski spent about eight hours of his own time just going over all the material with me, and then he let me take the test again, and I passed it. He gave me a second chance."

Then a white-haired woman got up and said she'd been working at the college as a secretary for thirty years, and while everyone there was a joy to work with, Mr. Karski was the only person she knew who came in every day and asked her how her children and her grandchildren were and who remembered all their names, which was no small task as she had five of the former and twelve of the latter. "It was just like he'd known them all their lives," she marveled, "and he seemed to genuinely care about them. He even offered to tutor my granddaughter, who was having trouble with Latin."

Another student, a pretty young woman who looked like she'd stepped off a Coca-Cola billboard, confessed that she hadn't had enough money to buy the book for Mr. Karski's class. She'd been having to borrow the book from other students, but it wasn't working out so well because she couldn't always borrow a copy in time to get the assignments done. When Mr. Karski found out what her trouble was, he bought a book for her out of his own pocket, saying she could pay him back by studying hard and getting an A in the class. At least I think that's what the young woman said. By the time she finished, she was crying so hard that it was difficult to understand her.

A constant stream of people moved forward over the next hour or more, one walking up the aisle even before the last had sat down. It seemed that after an initial hesitation, everyone was eager to say something about Josef. I thought about getting up myself—surely I had more to say about Josef than anyone there—but I was too shy, and I knew I couldn't say anything without breaking down into tears anyway. I might get a few words out, but then I'd just have to sit back down again without really getting anything said, and there wasn't any use in doing that. So I sat and listened and cried quietly.

Finally after the president of the college offered his piece about Josef, I figured the chaplain would get up and pray, and then we'd move on to the cemetery, where one of the priests from St. Paul's Cathedral would be officiating at the burial. Sometimes in Minnesota when someone dies in the winter, you have to wait until spring to bury them, when the ground is no longer frozen. But this year the earth was kind, and a hole was ready to receive Josef's coffin.

I was waiting for the chaplain to get up and dismiss us when one more person stood to speak, and that was Ma. I could hardly believe it. She didn't like to talk in front of crowds. Once during the war she'd been invited to address a group of ladies at a Red Cross meeting, and she'd turned it down because she said she'd be so nervous she wouldn't be able even to breathe, much less get any words out.

But she stood now and pushed past me and Mr. Diehl and Auntie to get out to the center aisle. She walked up to the front of the church and looked out over all the faces in the place as if she was looking for someone in particular but couldn't find him. She wrung her black-gloved hands a moment and took a deep breath, and I could almost see the front of her dress quiver with the beating of her heart. My palms began to sweat just looking at her.

She looked down at the floor, then up again. She dropped her hands and threw back her shoulders slightly. When she spoke, her voice was quiet but steady. "We've heard a lot of good things this afternoon about Josef Karski," she began, "and I guess that's no surprise, since Josef Karski was a good man." She swallowed hard, looked about the sanctuary, tried to smile. "Of everyone here, it might be that . . . well, I just might know better than anyone just how good a man Josef was because I'm the one whose life he saved on the night he died."

She pursed her lips then, and I thought maybe she was going to cave in and start sobbing, but she didn't. After another deep breath she went on. "I guess I've asked myself about a thousand times since the accident why a good man like Josef Karski had to die. I don't understand it. None of us understands it. I mean, the world is full of awful people who we could just as soon do without, but then someone like Josef has to be the one who goes and dies—"

She stopped abruptly, as though she had headed down a road she didn't want to go down. A startled hush fell over the church. No one coughed; no one whispered; no one moved. Even Henry Udahl stopped blowing his nose. We all sat waiting for Ma to go on.

She glanced at Tom. He nodded for her to continue. She looked back over the room, moistened her lips with her tongue, wrung her hands again. "What I want to tell you is something Josef—Mr. Karski—told me. He was in Auschwitz during the war." She stopped and smiled. "Well, Mr. Diehl already told you about that. Mr. Karski saw a lot of awful things, things most of us can't even imagine. He spent six years in the most horrible place I suppose the world has ever seen. While he was there, his whole family was killed by the Nazis. Somehow he survived, and after the war he left Poland and came over here to America, and that's how we all were able to know him, even if only for a little while.

"Well, I asked him how he could go on living after all that loss, and not just go on living but go on believing in God the way he did. And he said he didn't want to turn away from God because if he did, there wouldn't be anything to turn to. And besides, he said, every day he remembered a story that a rabbi had told him in the camp. I'm not sure I can remember it word for word, but the story went something like this.

"There was a rabbi who lived in Poland a long time ago. I think hundreds of years ago. And one day he was out with his students having a picnic or something up on a big hill that overlooked the town. While they were there, a bunch of people came riding into the town—people who hated the Jews—and started killing everyone, even the women and children. And here was the rabbi and his students looking down from the hill and seeing it all happen. Well, of course they were horrified. And the rabbi said, 'If only I were God.' And one of his students said, 'If you were God, what would you do differently?' And the rabbi said, 'If I were God, I wouldn't do anything differently. If I were God, I would understand.' "

Ma stopped, touched her hair nervously, shifted her

weight from one foot to the other while her eyes roamed the room like two beacons still searching for that lost someone. At last she concluded, "I guess that's all I wanted to say."

She gave a slight nod, glanced at the chaplain, then came back to our row and sat down again on the other side of Mr. Diehl. Her fingers trembled as she slipped her hand into his. He gently squeezed her hand a moment, and she offered him a small, uncertain smile.

That was the first time I had heard the story of the rabbi on the hill. Ma would make sure it wasn't the last.

———

I lay in bed that night with sleep creeping over me like a harbor fog, and somewhere in the brown consciousness before dream images take over, I decided that Josef would want me to give God the benefit of the doubt. If both he and that rabbi on the hill could keep their faces turned toward God after all they'd seen and been through, then I could too.

When I awoke in the morning, I went to the window in the parlor to pray and tell God I wasn't going to be angry with him anymore. But I hadn't so much as said a word when my eye was caught by the glint of a shiny new 1948 dime sitting regally among the dust and paint chips on the weathered sill.

MA REACHES FOR THE STARS

The landscape outside the train window rolled by in a collage of freshly unfurled leaves and undulating hills and the perfect furrows of recently plowed fields. The winter was past, and I felt as alive and cheerful as the newly resurrected world. Dewey had steadily improved over the past few months to the point he was almost ready to stay out of the lung for good. Plans were he would soon be moved to a rehabilitation center not far from us in St. Paul, and Ma said once he was settled there, I could visit him. As if that weren't enough to make a person happy, Thomas Diehl had officially begun courting Ma. She even seemed as happy about it as I was. I had every hope that I'd be getting a pa very soon.

At the moment, though, Ma and I were on our way to Chippewa Falls, Wisconsin. Some days ago I'd heard Ma telling Aunt Dortha she had some unfinished business to attend to. Ma arranged for me to be out of school for a couple of days, and the next thing I knew, Tom was driving us to Union

Station and putting us on the train to Chippewa Falls. I didn't know for certain why we were going to Wisconsin, but I was excited to be going anyway, as I'd taken precious few trips in my life.

We were met at the other end by a solemn little woman Ma introduced to me as Aunt Susannah. She was bent with age and burdened with a load I couldn't see, and the minute I saw her, I felt sorry for her. Ma gave her aunt a brief and awkward hug, kissing the air rather than the old woman's cheek, then stood back stiffly and nodded for me to do the same. I put my arms around this stranger—she was no taller than I, and she felt like a sack of bones, and her skin smelled old and powdery. She accepted my embrace, then held on to my hand a moment and said, "You look just like your mother when she was a little girl." When she said it, her eyes clouded over as if she had just told me the saddest thing in the world. It almost put a damper on my spirits, but I shook it off and reminded myself that sometimes old people do strange things.

We walked to a car where a man named Cousin Will sat behind the wheel waiting for us. He said hello to Ma and called her Kate but otherwise acted as though he'd never seen her before. On the way to wherever we were going, Ma and her aunt and Cousin Will seemed to be traveling in different spheres and talking at each other from a great distance.

I knew that Aunt Susannah was the wife of Haddon Biddle, whose death my mother had greeted as good news. And I knew that Haddon Biddle and Aunt Susannah had raised Ma and that this fellow who was driving was a cousin Ma had grown up with. But I still didn't know why Ma didn't like Haddon Biddle and why we were here with his widow when

I had the feeling Ma didn't like the widow any better than she had liked the man himself.

We had no sooner reached Aunt Susannah's house and dropped our one suitcase off than Ma said, "Well, let's go," and we were back in the car, making our way through the streets of Chippewa Falls. Riding in the backseat with Ma, I kept my face to the window, taking in what was at once both strange and familiar, like a place I'd visited in a dream. I recognized the Rivoli Theatre and the Federal Building where the post office was, but my recollection of other landmarks was vague.

I was hungry, and I didn't know where we were going, but I hoped we were going somewhere to eat. I tried to remember some of the places we might have eaten when we lived in Chippewa Falls, but before I could call up any specific locales, Cousin Will was turning off State Street and into Forest Hill Cemetery, a turn that dashed my hopes for a hot meal.

We rolled wordlessly through the maze of cemetery roads and stopped at what seemed to be nowhere in particular. I didn't know what to expect nor why we had come all the way from St. Paul to visit a graveyard with a couple of people Ma didn't appear very fond of. But I decided I'd go along with it all without complaint, as I knew that however unknown to me, Ma had her reasons.

We got out of the car and stepped into the warm spring sun. After a morning of traveling, it felt amazingly good to stand and stretch. Our surroundings, cemetery or no, were lovely, green, and lush with plantings of tulips and daffodils. Birdsong filled the gaping hole of silence surrounding the four of us. I might have stood there awhile just enjoying the world in bloom, but Ma took my hand, and we followed Aunt Susannah through a winding route of headstones. Cousin Will stayed behind at the car, leaning up against the hood with arms crossed, a cigarette dangling from his lips.

We hiked across the green and finally stopped at a rather large headstone. Aunt Susannah stepped aside then, seemingly to leave Ma and me alone. I was surprised to see my own name on the headstone, not the Nova part, but the Tierney part. I'd never seen our family name carved in granite. Royal Tierney, the stone read. I had to read it twice, then three times, to make sure I was seeing it right.

"Pa?" I asked, looking up at Ma.

She nodded. "I never gave you the chance to say good-bye."

I turned my gaze back to the stone, trying to reconcile the name, the stone, the grassy soil beneath my feet with the few remaining memories I had of Royal Tierney. I had waited at the window, watching for him for months while he had been here all along.

I looked to Ma for guidance, for a hint as to what it was I ought to do. She said nothing.

Finally I asked, "Why didn't we come before, Ma?"

She took a deep breath, let it out. "Someday I'll tell you. For now, I just want you to know that he loved you."

Ma's mouth was a small flat line. Her face looked pained. It almost hurt to look at her.

"He loved you too, Ma." I was an innocent child. I wanted to ease her pain.

She didn't answer for a long while. She seemed almost to disappear, as though she were reaching inside herself, searching for a place in the past. When she found it, she said, "There was a time when he did." She tried to smile.

"I wish," I said, "he could have gone on being with us." It seemed the right thing to say under the circumstances. Though I wasn't sure at all that I really meant it. He was part of another life, a life I wasn't living anymore.

Ma nodded, one small tilt of her head. "We have to forgive him for going away."

Forgive him? Does a person need to be forgiven for dying? I didn't understand, but I said, "It's all right, Ma. I forgive him."

"You stay here," Ma said. "Just for a minute. Then we'll go."

She turned and looked at Aunt Susannah. The older woman started walking, and again Ma followed. I stayed and stared at Royal Tierney's grave, feeling only an odd curiosity at the fact that I really didn't feel anything at all. The memory of Josef in my heart and the presence of Thomas Diehl in my life were much more real to me, and much more precious, than the memory of the man whose name I bore. I found it easy to say good-bye.

I looked about the cemetery, noting the flowers given by the living for the dead who couldn't see them. I listened to the birds, watched a fly buzzing about my freshly polished shoes, and squinted against the needles of sunlight coming through the leaves of a red oak tree. I wondered how long we would be there, and when we might get some lunch, and whose grave it was Ma and Aunt Susannah stood beside, their arms around each other as if they had only just this minute discovered that the other one was there.

Even from a distance I could tell they were crying. Over at the car, Cousin Will went on smoking a cigarette, his face tilted up toward the sun, his fedora down over his eyes, as though to catch a catnap while the women went about the business of weeping. I myself was intensely curious, wanting to know what was going on, what this trip was all about, whom the two women were mourning. But I stayed where I was, fidgeting, turning, tapping at the ground with the toe of my shoe.

Hours seemed to pass before Ma finally waved me over, not to the grave but to the car. I deliberately went out of my way to pass close enough to the headstone where Ma and Aunt Susannah had stood to see who was buried there. Ah, of course. I should have known. Haddon Biddle.

That night I slept fitfully, and every time I awoke I heard low voices coming from the next room. Ma's and Aunt Susannah's. Not until sometime early in the morning did I realize the murmuring had stopped and Ma was asleep beside me in the bed, and I thought, *They must have had an awful lot of catching up to do.*

The next day Aunt Susannah seemed to me a little less old and a little less bent, and when she said good-bye to us at the train station, she hugged me as if I were her own child and she feared she'd never see me again. But she smiled through her tears, and she held Ma close for the longest time and asked Ma to please come back again before long. Ma kissed Aunt Susannah's cheek—really did kiss it this time—and promised her we'd come back as soon as we could.

We got on the train, and the "All aboard!" sounded and the whistle blew, and even before I could be sure what the trip was all about, we were headed west again, back home. Ma sat placidly, hands in her lap, gazing out at the green Wisconsin dairy land. Even though she had been up most of the night, she looked rested. She even looked beautiful. She was quiet, but it wasn't a sorrowful quiet. It was a peaceful quiet.

I thought of our trip along this same route some six years before—more than half my lifetime ago. I had had so many questions then but was given no answers. This time I had questions too, and I thought since I was older Ma might be more inclined to give me some answers. Still, it took me a long time to work up the courage to ask. We were far beyond the outskirts of Chippewa Falls—we may have already reached the next county—before I finally touched Ma's hand and said timidly, "Ma?"

She smiled, a small upturn at the corners of her mouth. "Yes, Nova?"

"What were you doing at that guy's grave? Not Pa's. The other guy's."

Ma didn't answer for a time. She gazed thoughtfully out the window at the rolling hills, the leafy trees, the vast stretches of dairy farms passing by. Finally she smiled again. "I was saying thank you to Josef," she said.

When she saw the look on my face, she actually laughed. I can well imagine that my features were twisted with bewilderment, because I felt as if I'd been handed a riddle on a silver platter. What did Josef have to do with Haddon Biddle? And besides, how do you say thank you to someone who is dead?

When Ma said, "Someday I'll explain it all to you," I knew I wasn't going to get much more out of her right then.

But I went on thinking about it and puzzling over it the rest of the way to St. Paul, and somewhere in all that mulling, I turned up the memory of my head on Ma's pillow at the hospital and whispering into her ear, "I want to thank him somehow." I wanted to thank Josef for saving her life, and Ma said we'd find a way. I had nearly forgotten all about that, but evidently Ma had remembered.

Uncovered too was the image of Josef sitting with me on the staircase Thanksgiving Day, talking about his wife. *"You see, Novelka,"* he had said, *"in an odd sort of way some of our strongest relationships are with people who have died. We miss them, we think of them, we wonder what they would want us to do, how they would want us to act. Though they are not here, they still so strongly influence our lives."*

Funny how the dead go right on playing an active part in our lives. But it was true, and Josef was right. Sometimes you might even find yourself on a train to Chippewa Falls, Wisconsin, because a dead person pointed you in that direction and said "Go."

By the time Mr. Diehl met us at the station and drove us home, I was satisfied I had some idea what Ma meant. She had to make her peace with Haddon Biddle, and after all these years she finally did it. She did it because Josef had saved her life and given her a second chance. Now she could thank Josef by trying to do what was right.

Wasn't that what I kind of decided for myself on the night of Josef's funeral? That I'd try to give God the benefit of the doubt because Josef would say that was the right thing to do?

Ma and I didn't usually think along the same lines, but it

seems then that we did. I think we both discovered the same way to say thank you to Josef.

———————

The defining moment of Ma's new life—at least it seemed so to me—was an August morning, very early, when she and I were on the front porch waiting for Tom to pick us up. It was polio season again, but in spite of that, Tom was going to drive us up to Duluth, where we could picnic and walk the shore of Lake Superior together. I hadn't gone to the lake cabin with Rosemary for the summer because I actually preferred to be at home with Ma and Tom.

I was beside myself with excitement, and I paced the porch waiting for a glimpse of Tom's car in the alley across the street. But something Ma said stopped me like a hand on my shoulder. "Oh, look, Nova. Look!" She was pointing toward the vines twining themselves around the porch railing, their blue blossoms spread out like open hands to catch the sun. "How lovely that we have morning glories blooming on the railing this year."

That was when I knew that somehow, between last summer and this, all of the sadness had fallen out of Ma's eyes, and like the blind man given the gift of sight, she was finally able to see what she had never seen before, like the morning glories that had been blooming along the porch every year for as long as I could remember.

About that time I started having a dream about Ma that I've had many times since. In the dream I see Josef walking in an open field at night with a child sitting high on his shoulders. The moon is round and full, so bright it casts moon shadows across the sleeping grass. The open sky is a vast expanse of twinkling lights.

As I watch Josef step across the field, I begin to recognize the child. Though it's night, I can see her faintly in the moonlight. There is the familiar shape of the face, the narrow nose, the soft blond hair. She is my mother.

The child is Catherine, age three, before the influenza epidemic, before the house of her uncle the minister, before marriage and widowhood, before polio. She's a child again, untouched by time, riding on Josef's shoulders across a field on a startlingly clear night.

I hear laughter, a few words, and then Ma raises her hand. She reaches up toward the sky, her body lifting, her fingers stretching. Upward, upward she reaches until at last she touches a star! The light spills out over her fingertips, and she smiles, her face bright with joy.

DEWEY REACHES THE MOON

As I said in the beginning, the story of my mother and Josef is a love story, but not the happily-ever-after kind where the two people end up getting married and living out the rest of their lives together. It wasn't that kind of ending because Josef died. And it wasn't that kind of love either, because I'm certain that even if Josef had lived, he and Ma would never have married. But there was love between them all the same because they shared a bond of trust and understanding. They were joined in their tears and their anger and their hope. And in the end, Josef laid down his life for his friend, and there is no greater love than that.

More than fifty years have passed since we buried Josef. In those years my family and I have lived simple lives, and yet, I believe the course our path took is different from what it might have been had Josef never befriended us. He came to us seemingly out of nowhere and then just as suddenly disappeared, but because he had been with us even briefly, so much was turned around for good.

So how *did* Josef wind up living at our boardinghouse, coming all the way from Poland to land in such an unlikely place? Auntie had no doubt got it right when she said Providence brought him to our door. God knew we needed him. God foresaw the day that Josef's life and death and unquenchable hope would change us all, and so he brought Josef our way.

On September 10, 1949, Ma married Thomas Diehl in a simple ceremony in the parlor of the boardinghouse. Our pastor from the Methodist church officiated. All our boarders were there, along with the newlyweds Martin and Betty Popp. Auntie beamed through the whole ceremony as though she was the mother of the bride. Miss Eva played the wedding march on the piano, while Miss Ida, fortified with several lace-trimmed hankies, acted as official crier. They both did a good job. I was something of a bridesmaid, and while I stood beside Ma listening to her and Tom exchanging vows, I found myself feeling thankful to Josef for making it happen. I didn't know how he did it, but I was sure that without Josef, Ma never would have figured out that Thomas Diehl was in love with her and that she could love him back. I could only imagine it had something to do with the sadness falling out of her eyes so that she could see things for the first time or maybe see them in a different way.

When Ma and my new pa got married, Pa sold his house and, with little effort, persuaded Aunt Dortha to sell her house as well. The couple who bought it continued to run it as a boardinghouse, so none of our tenants had to leave, though eventually we did get word that Clyde Munson finally married his long-suffering sweetheart and moved into an apartment in North St. Paul.

With the profit made on Pa's and Aunt Dortha's houses, we moved into a two-story Victorian over on Laurel Avenue. Now the only people who lived in our house were family. Auntie could retire and live out her final years volunteering at church, puttering in her garden, and reading all the books she'd never before had the chance to read.

The same month Ma and Pa got married, Dewey was transferred to the rehabilitation center in St. Paul. Ma took me to see him shortly afterward. By that time I hadn't seen him in more than a year.

I remember the day very well. Excitement made sleep difficult the night before, but I jumped out of bed in the morning full of the energy of anticipation. I put on my best Sunday dress and my patent leather shoes and even tied a couple of ribbons in my hair, though Ma said I didn't have to dress up for the occasion. But I wanted to. What occasion could be more special than this? I was going to see Dewey!

We still had the truck, which had been only slightly damaged in the accident, but Ma didn't drive it very often. She said she'd just as soon get rid of it except that she'd promised Dewey it would be his someday, and as long as the truck was running, she didn't want to go back on her promise. Generally Pa drove us where we needed to go, and he might have driven us to see Dewey if he hadn't had to go to work at the appliance store as usual that Saturday morning. Ma and I took the streetcar.

It was an unusually hot September day, and all the windows on the streetcar were open. Ma tied a scarf around her head so her hair wouldn't get all blown apart, and the woman behind us kept grumbling to her seatmate about how the humidity had ruined a perfectly good permanent. The sidewalks and store windows sent off sharp stabs of sunlight, and I sat there half blinded and sweating, my dress sticking to the seat, but happy, so happy to be going to see Dewey. I was tempted to yell out the window, "I'm going to see Dewey!" except that Ma would have objected, and a scolding would have put a damper on the morning. Finally we reached our stop, and though I didn't know where we were going, I ran on ahead of Ma until she had to lasso me in and steer me in the right direction.

We came to a low brick building that looked like it had been there since the city was called Pig's Eye about a hundred years before. The moment we stepped through the double glass doors into the front lobby, everything changed. With a shiver, I felt a certain dread come over me. It started in my chest and spread like poison gas to every limb, so that even my hands and feet tingled with it. At once it started to nibble away at my joy. The lobby was Spartan, drab and dreary, and smelled of sickness and of something old. There and everywhere, down the long halls, in the soulless rooms, scores of patients—children, most of them—sat in wheelchairs or walked with crutches, dragging useless limbs made heavy with braces. I didn't want to look. I should have followed Ma with my eyes downcast, but like a spectator at a circus freak show, I was drawn in. "Come and see!" the hawker cries. "The bearded lady, the man with three eyes, the werewolf boy! One thin dime will get you in to see Nature's misfits!" I had to look at these children, polio's misfits, the ones who had been caught under the wheels of the Crippler on its annual migration around the globe. I met briefly the eyes of some, and in them I saw the long weariness, the lost childhood, and maybe too a certain envy that I could walk by on my own two feet, straight up and tall, untouched by what had touched them. *I was just like you once,* they seemed to say with their eyes. *I was just like you.*

Ma had kept me distanced not only from the disease itself but also from the full effects of it. Now, though, here it was: this is what polio did. My mind called up the photo I'd seen in *Life* magazine when Dewey was first diagnosed: the little crippled boy sitting on a bridge in braces from hip to heel, soliciting money for the March of Dimes. I was afraid then, looking at that picture. I was terrified now, surrounded by the walking wounded. And now I couldn't shut it all out by simply closing the magazine. I had to move forward and see Dewey in this place.

Ma led me to a sort of dayroom, a large room all the way at the end of the hall. The windows were thrown open, and ceiling fans whirled overhead, but the room was hot and stuffy anyway, and the potted geraniums beneath the windows were red patches of wilting blossoms. Several clusters of people added to the closeness. Patients and visitors mingled in isolated groups, sharing food among themselves, laughing occasionally, attempting to bring a snatch of normalcy into a place that had nothing at all to do with normal life. Not my normal life anyway.

And then I saw him. He sat beside an open window looking out. Only I didn't really recognize him as Dewey at first. He was someone small and gaunt, and his legs were so thin they made me think of the legs on a praying mantis. His long, angular arms rested on the arms of his wheelchair. I thought, *If that's Dewey, it would have been better to see him in the lung, where I couldn't really see him at all.*

He turned his head and saw us. He smiled. He managed to maneuver the chair around so that he faced us. He tried to roll himself across the room, but his arms were so weak he couldn't get very far. Ma took my hand, and together we walked to Dewey.

"Hello, sweetheart," Ma said cheerfully as she bent to kiss him.

"Hi, Ma. Hi, Tag. Holy smokes, look at you! You're all grown up!"

He sat there looking at me with that same smile on his face, and I was trying for all the world to find in that face the Dewey I'd always known. As I stood there dumbly searching for the person that seemed to be gone forever, what was left of my excitement crumbled into a little ash pile of misery in my throat. I couldn't get a single word around that barricade to even greet my brother. I leaned over and gave him an awkward hug, and when I drew back he gave me a look that said he understood and that he was sorry he couldn't be the same Dewey that he'd been before the polio. I didn't want to cry, but I did anyway, not hard, just two big tears coursing down either cheek.

"Don't worry, Tag," Dewey said gently. "I'm getting better every day. I'm going to walk out of here. You'll see."

I put a hand to my mouth. "Oh, Dewey," I whispered.

He did get better and he did walk out of there—with crutches, but he was walking. He was at the rehabilitation center for almost a year, and in that time I'd occasionally wake up and find a dime on my bedside table, the place God had chosen to leave the dimes in our new house. While Dewey struggled through rehab, those dimes gave me continued hope for his recovery, and they gave him hope too, I think. I visited him a couple times a month until he came home, and while I got to the point that I could go to the center without crying, I never really got used to the place.

At long last Pa and Ma brought Dewey home on a warm July day in 1950, two years after he had come down with polio. Auntie and I were waiting for them on the front porch of our new house, and when Pa pulled the car up to the curb and Dewey got out of the front seat by himself, pulling himself up on his crutches until he was standing, Auntie whispered, "Praise be to God," and I had tears in my eyes all over again. This time I ran and threw my arms around my brother, nearly knocking us both off balance. We wobbled a moment but stayed upright in an awkward dance of an embrace, and the next thing we knew, Ma was there with her arms around us too, and Pa was there, smiling and patting Dewey on the back. "Welcome home, son," Pa said, and I don't know about Dewey, but I thought those words were about the prettiest thing I'd ever heard in my life.

———

Ma and Pa didn't take their honeymoon until that August of 1950, after Dewey came home. Then, just as Ma had promised, we all traveled together out to California to visit the Palomar Observatory. The long trip by train wore Dewey out physically, but all in all I think seeing that observatory strengthened Dewey's resolve to hold on to the part of his dream he could still hold on to.

The following spring, Ma had a baby girl, whom she named Amanda after her sister who had died in infancy. Pa was about as proud as a humble man can be, and I don't think there was a customer, man or woman alike, who left the appliance store without a cigar on the day Amanda was born. From the time she came home from the hospital, Pa made a habit of pushing Amanda around the neighborhood in a baby carriage to show her off to all the neighbors. I myself was somewhat in awe of the child, never having dreamed I'd get a baby sister as part of the deal of getting a pa. Many were the times I'd sit by her cradle while she napped, just staring down at her and marveling that life could be even better than you'd hoped.

When Amanda was about two, Dewey and I started taking her outside at night to show her the moon and the stars. I could see the starlight reflected in her big brown eyes—Pa's eyes—as she gazed up at the heavens in wonder.

"See the moon?" Dewey asked the first time we took her out.

Amanda nodded.

"Someday," Dewey said, "someone's gonna go there. Someday someone's gonna walk on the moon."

"Oohh!" our little sister said, her small mouth puckered in amazement. "I wanna walk on the moon!"

I looked at Dewey. He was looking up at the sky. I wanted to tell him he'd be the first person to walk on the surface of that shiny orb, but I knew it wouldn't be so. It was difficult enough for him to walk on earth. My heart dropped down to my stomach, and I felt a terrible sadness for my brother.

He must have felt my gaze, because he turned to look at me. He smiled. "I'll do my best to get you there, Amanda."

In every life there's a certain letting go. But as I said, Dewey found the corner of his dream that he could still hold on to. He was, I knew, going to sail among the stars, one way or another.

———————

Dewey continued to improve over the years, though he never got completely well. He exchanged the crutches for a cane, but he never did walk unaided again. For years he was able to breathe on his own until in late middle age he needed a chest respirator to help him breathe at night. But he was alive, and he went on to college, and he even got married and had children.

Once Dewey got out of the rehab center, I felt like I didn't need to ask for dimes anymore, and right about that same time they stopped showing up. For a long time I wondered about those dimes. The older I got, the more I decided it must have been Ma who left them for me. Eventually I more or less forgot about them, but when Ma was dying and telling me her stories, she mentioned something about Josef leaving the dimes. I reminded her that they kept on appearing long after Josef was gone. "For some reason when I was a kid," I said, "you wanted me to believe Josef was leaving those dimes. At least you told me he was. But I know it must have been you, Ma, and I'm thankful to you for doing it."

But Ma shook her head. Josef had started leaving the

dimes, she said, but she had carried on for him after he died.

When I asked her why she did that, she smiled impishly. "You were so certain God was leaving those coins," she replied. "I didn't want you to lose your faith if you went on praying and they didn't show up anymore."

"But Ma!" I wanted to protest. *"You had no faith yourself!"* I wanted to say that, but I didn't.

I decided that sometimes what's been lost can also be found again. I decided too that faith must be the strongest thing in the world because an ounce of it can change the course of an entire life.

———

If there was one story Ma made sure was passed down in our family, it was the story Josef told her, the story of the rabbi on the hill. She told it many times over to Dewey and Amanda and me and later to her many grandchildren. And finally she told it to the first of her great-grandchildren shortly before she died. I think she thought of that story every day. I think she thought of Josef every day.

"Remember Josef," she told me. Yet how could I forget? Even if those had not been among her final words and her last request of me, I would never forget Josef. He has been the unseen but beloved guest in our household since 1948. As Dewey continued to struggle with the effects of his illness, when Auntie was diagnosed with cancer, when teenaged Amanda spent weeks recuperating from a car accident, when I lost my first baby to a miscarriage, Josef was right there to remind us that even though we can't always know why such things happen, there is One who does know and who understands all.

———————

Dewey never built the Nova Machine, so we've never heard the music of the spheres—if there is such a thing. I think there is, but of course I can't be sure. Some things just have to remain a mystery until that time when there are no more mysteries.

In 1965 a couple of scientists named Penzias and Wilson actually detected the cosmic fireball that Dewey told me about that fateful night in 1948. It seems these two men had been listening on their special equipment for faint radio whispers that travel through the universe. What they at first thought was a bunch of static turned out to be the radiation left over from the fireball that filled the universe at the beginning of time.

Dewey was ecstatic at the news of the Big Bang Theory. He told me that if you take the Big Bang Theory on the one hand, and you look at the second law of thermodynamics on the other—that is, the second law of thermodynamics as applied to the cosmos, which indicates the universe is winding down like a clock—you have a clear beginning and a clear end. I don't pretend to understand all the science involved. I'm a homemaker with six children and fourteen grandchildren, and I never took the time to study the cosmos the way Dewey did. But I know what he was trying to tell me. There's a story unfolding with a definite beginning and an eventual end, and even though we can't begin to imagine what the whole plot is, and we can hardly even see beyond the present moment, someday we're going to see and understand all of it. For now, we trust. Later, we'll know. The rabbi on the hill will have his answer.

Dewey entered college on an academic scholarship and came out an aerospace engineer. He never sailed the ships that traveled among the stars, but he did help build them. He was with NASA, in Mission Control, at the time of the moon landing on July 20, 1969.

We were all crowded around our black-and-white Zenith console that night, Ma and Pa and Amanda, my husband, Bill, and me. We were tense with excitement, breathlessly watching the images on the screen, hoping like mad that nothing would prevent Buzz Aldrin and Neil Armstrong from landing the lunar module somewhere in the dusty craters of the Sea of Tranquility.

At an altitude of five hundred feet above the surface of the moon, the two astronauts discovered that the smooth landing site they were hoping for was actually littered with boulders. One of those boulders could easily tip the lunar module over if the astronauts landed on it. They had to find a more suitable spot. As they searched the moon's surface, a flashing red warning light signaled that they'd used up ninety-five percent of the landing fuel. If they didn't land within exactly ninety-four seconds, they would have to abort the landing.

The seconds ticked away. The astronauts searched. A voice from Mission Control, tense but firm, told them they had thirty seconds left. I held my breath, clenched my fists.

And then, after several more agonizing seconds passed, Armstrong radioed Mission Control, telling all of us back on Earth what Dewey and I had waited decades to hear, "Houston, Tranquility Base here. The *Eagle* has landed." We had made it to the moon!

Mission Control cheered. America cheered. The world cheered. And in a house on Laurel Avenue in St. Paul, Minnesota, five people jumped up from their seats and danced about the room and screamed their hearts out with joy. And then, on the television screen, there it was: the dusty, barren, colorless, beautiful moon as Armstrong and Aldrin, walking on its surface, beamed pictures back to Earth.

Bill grabbed my hand, and together we ran out into the night, drinking in moonlight as we lifted our faces to the sky. Dewey's someday was today, and the moon was ours.

Discussion Questions

1. Nova, narrating the story, calls it a "love story" but not a "romance" and insists there is a difference. What is the difference? Which would you rather read? Which would you rather have in your own life?

2. The Tierney family eventually takes to heart a Jewish parable about a rabbi on a hill who, upon seeing tragedy, wishes to be God, not so he can change the events, but so he can understand them. How does this parable come to comfort the Tierneys? Are there events in your own life that seem beyond anything but celestial comprehension?

3. With which character's faith did you most relate? Which do you desire?

    Nova's innocent pondering?
    Aunt Dortha's steadfast belief in Providence?
    Catherine's anger and frustration?
    Dewey's rational exploration of God through creation?
    Josef's deep and mature faith?

4. Dewey sees God in the cosmos. Where do you find wonder in God's presence? How did Dewey's love of the stars and the moon rub off on his younger sister?

5. Throughout the book Nova is constantly on the lookout for a father. How does her family, as it is, shape her young life? In the end she has a chance to add closure to the loss of her birth father. Do you think she would have been on such a search if closure had happened earlier? How does her search for a father mirror her trying to understand God's place in the world?

6. Much of the heart of *I'll Watch the Moon* is about the different ways in which people deal with true pain, suffering, and loss in

their lives. If you feel comfortable, think about or discuss a situation in your own life. What approach did you take? What are other options besides Catherine's anger and Josef's solemn acceptance? How can you offer hope to others who may be struggling with deep grief?

7. Viktor E. Frankl, a Holocaust survivor and esteemed Jewish psychiatrist, said this in his bestselling book *Man's Search for Meaning:* "There is nothing in the world, I venture to say, that would so effectively help one to survive even the worst conditions as the knowledge that there is a meaning in one's life." How does this inform Josef Karski's life? Do you agree with the statement? Are there things too great for even hope to overcome?

8. Nova remembers the night her brother got sick and says that even small moments can divide your life into "before and after." Can you think of a dividing moment—good or bad—in your own life? How clear and memorable is that moment? Why do those moments stay with us for so long?

9. Epidemics like polio and Spanish flu also play a large part in the book. What is so terrifying about an epidemic? How do we live now in the face of potentially deadly epidemics—spread either by nature or by man?

10. Discuss the character of Mr. Diehl. What is his defining characteristic? What does he have in common with the 1937 Chevrolet pickup truck he gives to Catherine?

11. The miracle of the dimes is Nova's first interaction, personally, with God. What is the miracle? What do you think of Josef's statement: "Providence prefers small blessings to large miracles"? Do you think that is true? Have you experienced either one? Why does it seem that large miracles occurred much more frequently in biblical times than they do now?

12. The name "Providence" is substituted for God on numerous occasions by both Aunt Dortha and Josef. Do you think of God as "providential?" What does it mean, or how does it change your

life, to believe in a God who always knows what is about to happen?

13. In the descriptions of Josef's time in the prison camps he talks
about the *muselman*—the walking dead. Are there people in your
life who fit that description now? How do we not live life like
muselmen, but instead live with hope and purpose?

14. Talk about Catherine's turn from anger. Who is most influential
in that change? When she speaks at Josef's funeral about his saving
her, she means both literally and figuratively. What do you think
he sacrificed, even before he died in the snowstorm, by reliving his
tragic life in his late-night talks with her?

15. Josef's death hearkens to the ending of the classic Leo Tolstoy story
Master and Man. If you have time, read that story (available for
free online) and discuss the similarities and differences between
Josef and Tolstoy's "master", Vasili Andreevich.